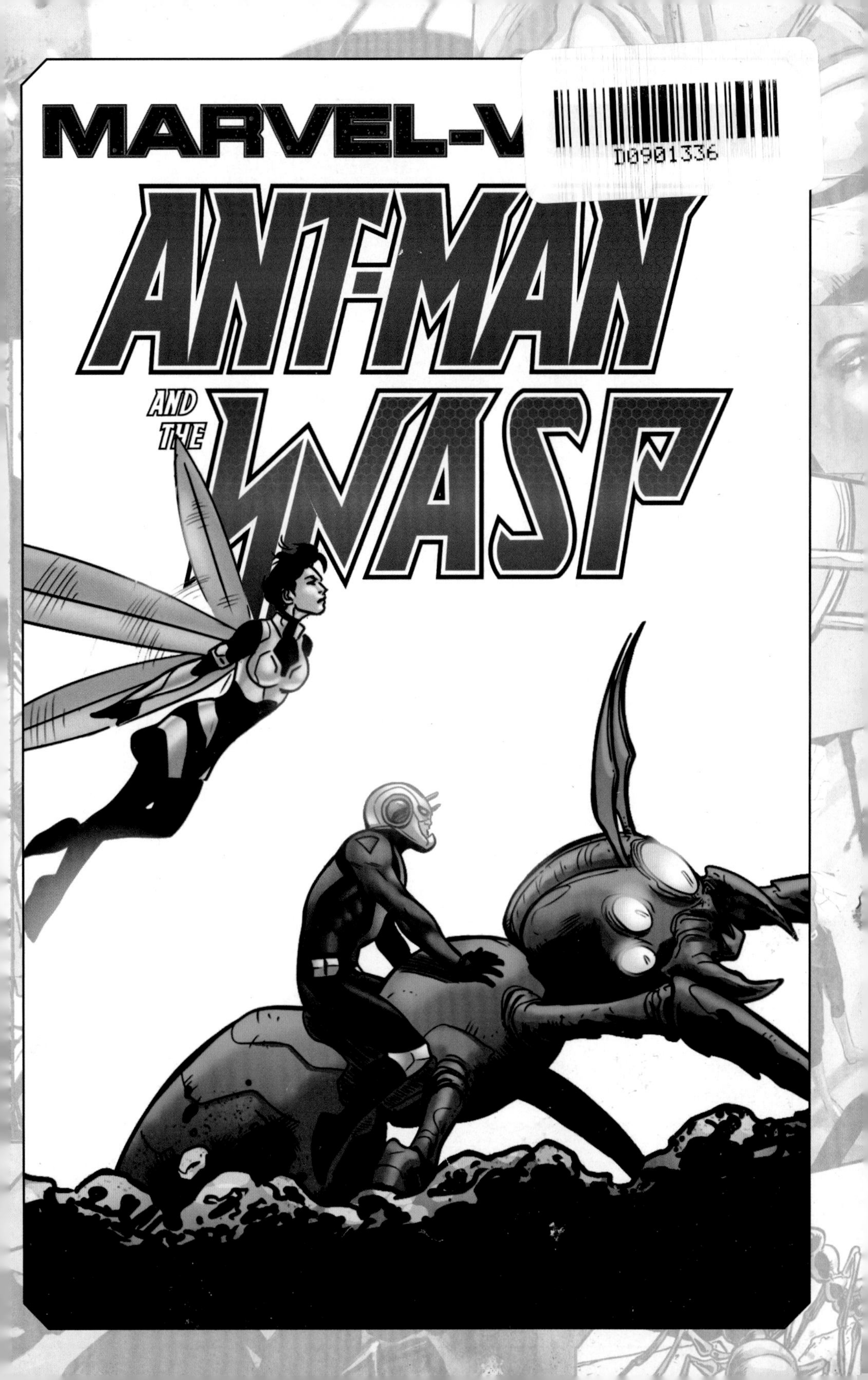
MARVEL-V
ANT-MAN
AND THE
WASP

MARVEL-VERSE

ANT-MAN AND THE WASP

ANT-MAN: LARGER THAN LIFE

WRITER: **WILL CORONA PILGRIM**
ARTIST: **ANDREA DI VITO**
COLOR ARTIST: **VERONICA GANDINI**
LETTERER: **VC's CLAYTON COWLES**
COVER ART: **JUNG-SIK AHN**
EDITORS: **MARK BASSO & EMILY SHAW**

AVENGERS ORIGINS: ANT-MAN & THE WASP

WRITER: **ROBERTO AGUIRRE-SACASA**
ARTIST: **STEPHANIE HANS**
LETTERER: **DAVE LANPHEAR**
COVER ART: **MARKO DJURDJEVIĆ**
ASSISTANT EDITOR: **JOHN DENNING**
EDITOR: **LAUREN SANKOVITCH**
EXECUTIVE EDITOR: **TOM BREVOORT**

MARVEL-VERSE: ANT-MAN & THE WASP. Contains material originally published in magazine form as AVENGERS ORIGINS: ANT-MAN & THE WASP (2011) #1, ANT-MAN: LARGER THAN LIFE (2015) #1, MARVEL PREMIERE (1972) #47-48 and ANT-MAN & THE WASP: LIVING LEGENDS (2018) #1. First printing 2022. ISBN 978-1-302-95066-8. Published by MARVEL WORLDWIDE, INC., a subsidiary of MARVEL ENTERTAINMENT, LLC. OFFICE OF PUBLICATION: 1290 Avenue of the Americas, New York, NY 10104. © 2022 MARVEL No similarity between any of the names, characters, persons, and/or institutions in this book with those of any living or dead person or institution is intended, and any such similarity which may exist is purely coincidental. **Printed in Canada.** KEVIN FEIGE, Chief Creative Officer; DAN BUCKLEY, President, Marvel Entertainment; DAVID BOGART, Associate Publisher & SVP of Talent Affairs; TOM BREVOORT, VP, Executive Editor; NICK LOWE, Executive Editor, VP of Content, Digital Publishing; DAVID GABRIEL, VP of Print & Digital Publishing; SVEN LARSEN, VP of Licensed Publishing; MARK ANNUNZIATO, VP of Planning & Forecasting; JEFF YOUNGQUIST, VP of Production & Special Projects; ALEX MORALES, Director of Publishing Operations; DAN EDINGTON, Director of Editorial Operations; RICKEY PURDIN, Director of Talent Relations; JENNIFER GRÜNWALD, Director of Production & Special Projects; SUSAN CRESPI, Production Manager; STAN LEE, Chairman Emeritus. For information regarding advertising in Marvel Comics or on Marvel.com, please contact Vit DeBellis, Custom Solutions & Integrated Advertising Manager, at vdebellis@marvel.com. For Marvel subscription inquiries, please call 888-511-5480. **Manufactured between 11/4/2022 and 12/6/2022 by SOLISCO PRINTERS, SCOTT, QC, CANADA.**

10 9 8 7 6 5 4 3 2 1

ANT-MAN & THE WASP: LIVING LEGENDS

WRITER: **RALPH MACCHIO**

ARTIST: **ANDREA DI VITO**

COLOR ARTIST: **LAURA VILLARI**

LETTERER: **VC's TRAVIS LANHAM**

COVER ART: **ANDREA DI VITO & LAURA VILLARI**

EDITOR: **MARK BASSO**

MARVEL PREMIERE #47-48

WRITER: **DAVID MICHELINIE**

PENCILER: **JOHN BYRNE**

INKER: **BOB LAYTON**

COLOR ARTISTS: **BOB SHAREN & MARIO SEN**

LETTERERS: **TOM ORZECHOWSKI & DIANA ALBERS**

ASSISTANT EDITOR: **JIM SALICRUP**

EDITOR: **ROGER STERN**

ANT-MAN CREATED BY **STAN LEE, LARRY LIEBER** & **JACK KIRBY**
WASP CREATED BY **STAN LEE, ERNIE HART** & **JACK KIRBY**

COLLECTION EDITOR: **JENNIFER GRÜNWALD** ASSISTANT EDITOR: **DANIEL KIRCHHOFFER**
ASSISTANT MANAGING EDITOR: **MAIA LOY** ASSOCIATE MANAGER, TALENT RELATIONS: **LISA MONTALBANO**
ASSOCIATE MANAGER, DIGITAL ASSETS: **JOE HOCHSTEIN** MASTERWORKS EDITOR: **CORY SEDLMEIER**
VP PRODUCTION & SPECIAL PROJECTS: **JEFF YOUNGQUIST** RESEARCH: **JESS HARROLD**
BOOK DESIGNER: **SARAH SPADACCINI** SENIOR DESIGNER: **JAY BOWEN**
SVP PRINT, SALES & MARKETING: **DAVID GABRIEL** EDITOR IN CHIEF: **C.B. CEBULSKI**

AVENGERS ORIGINS:
ANT-MAN&
THE WASP

AVENGERS ORIGINS: ANT-MAN & THE WASP

IT'S INSECT LOVE, MARVEL-STYLE, AS WE REVISIT THE
UNLIKELY ORIGIN (AND COURTSHIP) OF THE ASTONISHING
ANT-MAN AND THE WINSOME WASP!

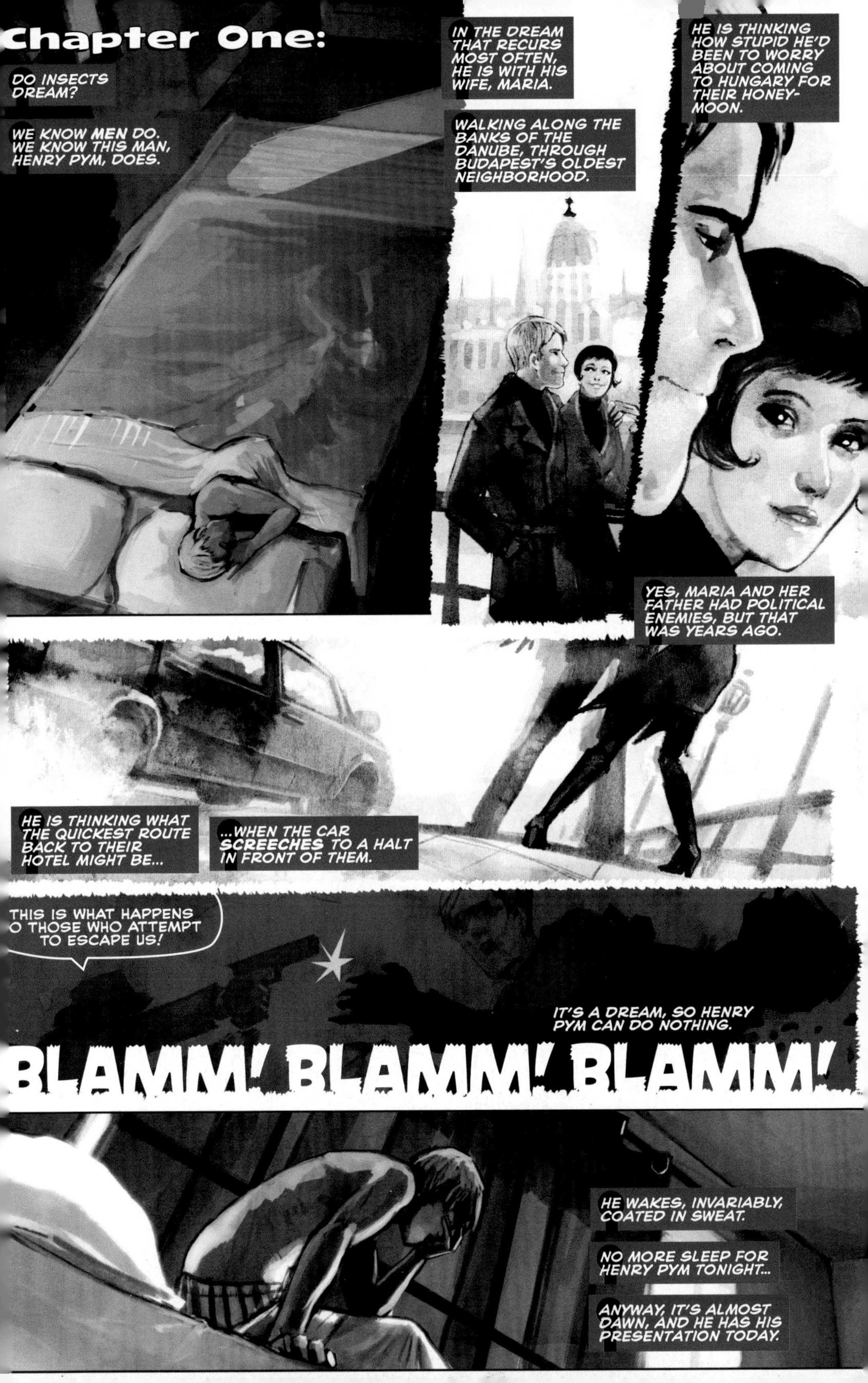
Chapter One:
DO INSECTS DREAM?
WE KNOW MEN DO. WE KNOW THIS MAN, HENRY PYM, DOES.
IN THE DREAM THAT RECURS MOST OFTEN, HE IS WITH HIS WIFE, MARIA.
WALKING ALONG THE BANKS OF THE DANUBE, THROUGH BUDAPEST'S OLDEST NEIGHBORHOOD.
HE IS THINKING HOW STUPID HE'D BEEN TO WORRY ABOUT COMING TO HUNGARY FOR THEIR HONEY-MOON.
YES, MARIA AND HER FATHER HAD POLITICAL ENEMIES, BUT THAT WAS YEARS AGO.
HE IS THINKING WHAT THE QUICKEST ROUTE BACK TO THEIR HOTEL MIGHT BE...
...WHEN THE CAR SCREECHES TO A HALT IN FRONT OF THEM.
THIS IS WHAT HAPPENS O THOSE WHO ATTEMPT TO ESCAPE US!
IT'S A DREAM, SO HENRY PYM CAN DO NOTHING.
BLAMM! BLAMM! BLAMM!
HE WAKES, INVARIABLY, COATED IN SWEAT.
NO MORE SLEEP FOR HENRY PYM TONIGHT...
ANYWAY, IT'S ALMOST DAWN, AND HE HAS HIS PRESENTATION TODAY.

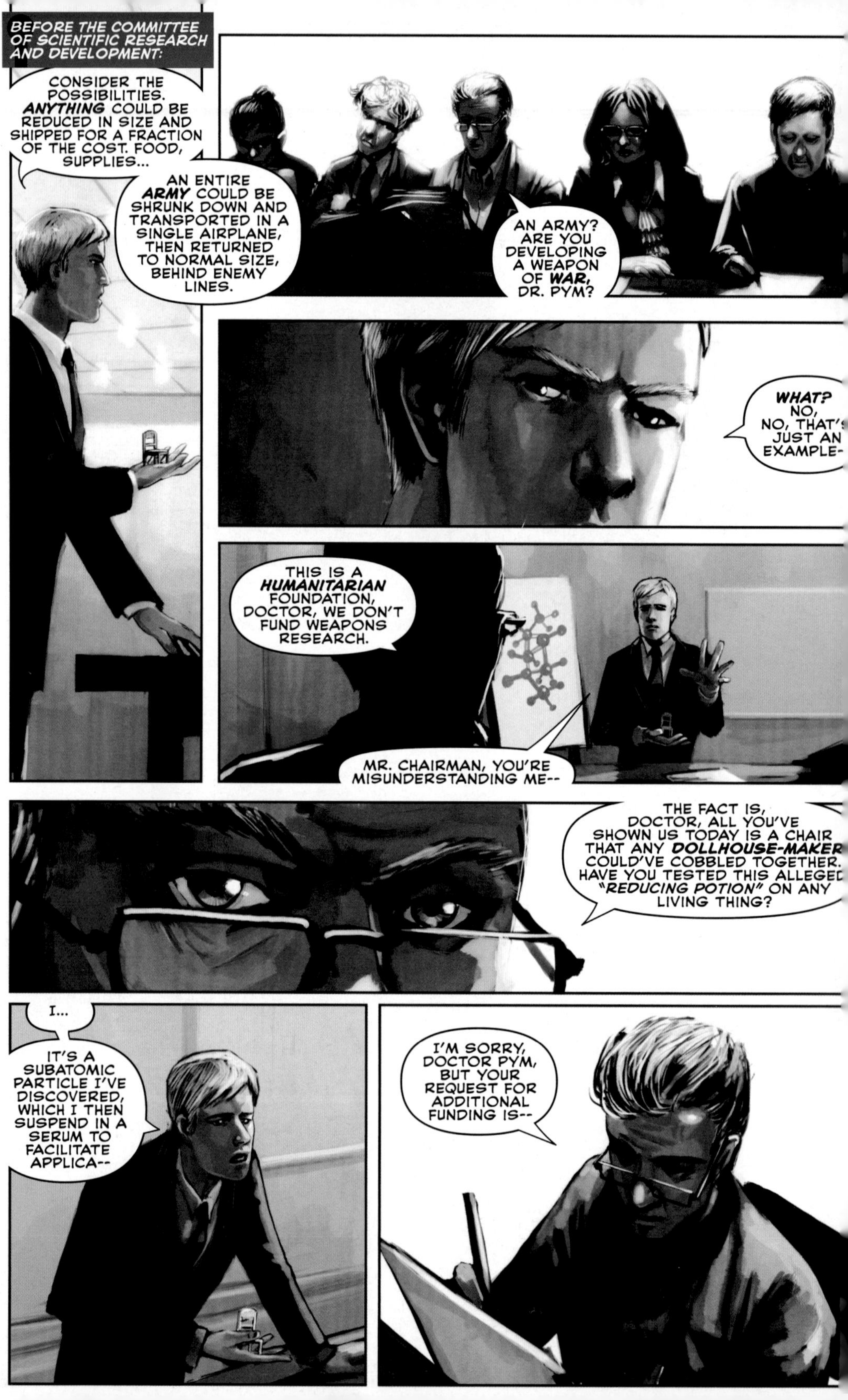
BEFORE THE COMMITTEE OF SCIENTIFIC RESEARCH AND DEVELOPMENT:
CONSIDER THE POSSIBILITIES. ANYTHING COULD BE REDUCED IN SIZE AND SHIPPED FOR A FRACTION OF THE COST. FOOD, SUPPLIES...
AN ENTIRE ARMY COULD BE SHRUNK DOWN AND TRANSPORTED IN A SINGLE AIRPLANE, THEN RETURNED TO NORMAL SIZE, BEHIND ENEMY LINES.
AN ARMY? ARE YOU DEVELOPING A WEAPON OF WAR, DR. PYM?
WHAT? NO, NO, THAT'S JUST AN EXAMPLE-
THIS IS A HUMANITARIAN FOUNDATION, DOCTOR, WE DON'T FUND WEAPONS RESEARCH.
MR. CHAIRMAN, YOU'RE MISUNDERSTANDING ME--
THE FACT IS, DOCTOR, ALL YOU'VE SHOWN US TODAY IS A CHAIR THAT ANY DOLLHOUSE-MAKER COULD'VE COBBLED TOGETHER. HAVE YOU TESTED THIS ALLEGED "REDUCING POTION" ON ANY LIVING THING?
I...
IT'S A SUBATOMIC PARTICLE I'VE DISCOVERED, WHICH I THEN SUSPEND IN A SERUM TO FACILITATE APPLICA--
I'M SORRY, DOCTOR PYM, BUT YOUR REQUEST FOR ADDITIONAL FUNDING IS--

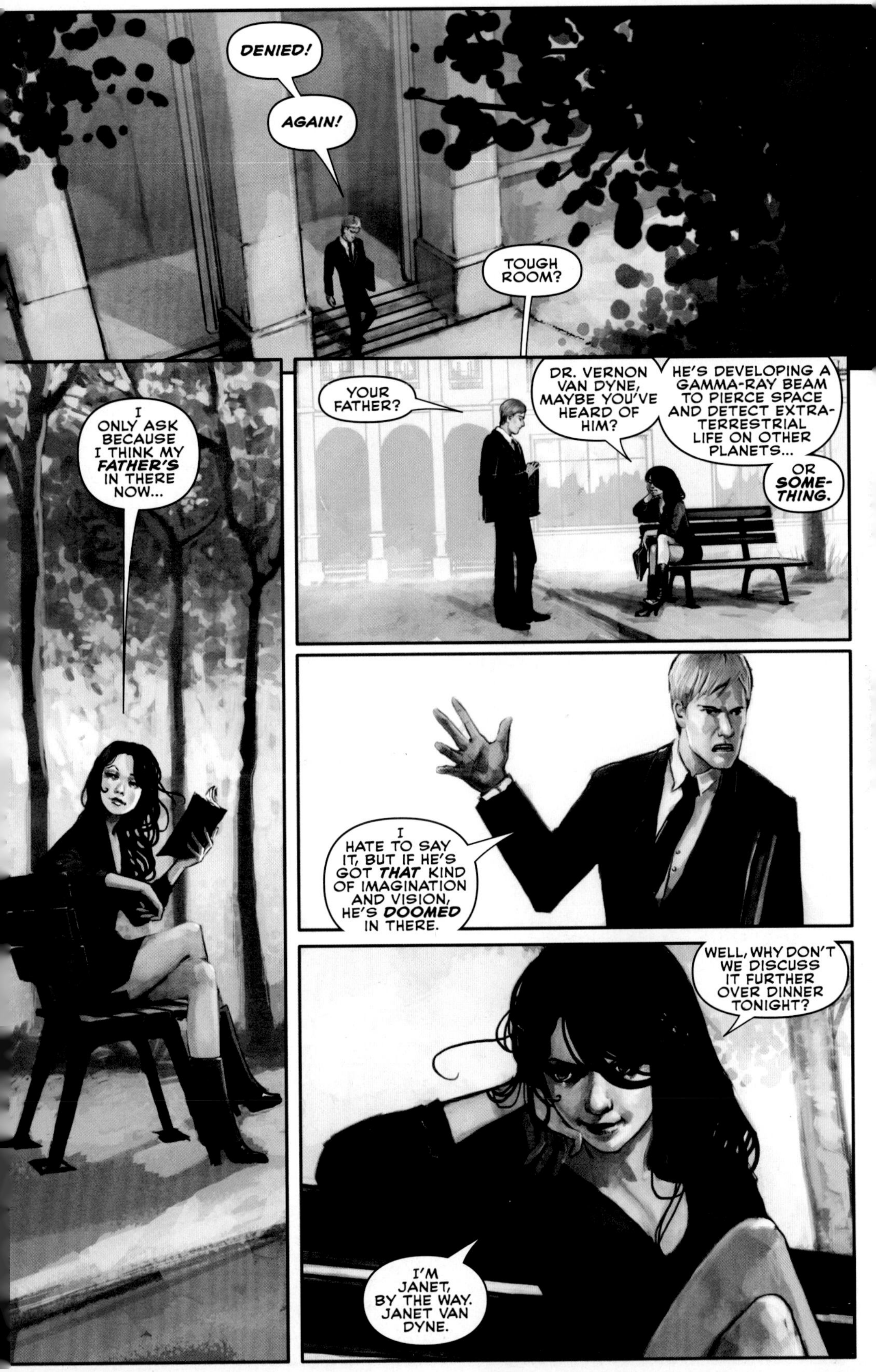
DENIED!
AGAIN!
TOUGH ROOM?
I ONLY ASK BECAUSE I THINK MY FATHER'S IN THERE NOW...
YOUR FATHER?
DR. VERNON VAN DYNE, MAYBE YOU'VE HEARD OF HIM?
HE'S DEVELOPING A GAMMA-RAY BEAM TO PIERCE SPACE AND DETECT EXTRA-TERRESTRIAL LIFE ON OTHER PLANETS...
OR SOME-THING.
I HATE TO SAY IT, BUT IF HE'S GOT THAT KIND OF IMAGINATION AND VISION, HE'S DOOMED IN THERE.
WELL, WHY DON'T WE DISCUSS IT FURTHER OVER DINNER TONIGHT?
I'M JANET, BY THE WAY. JANET VAN DYNE.

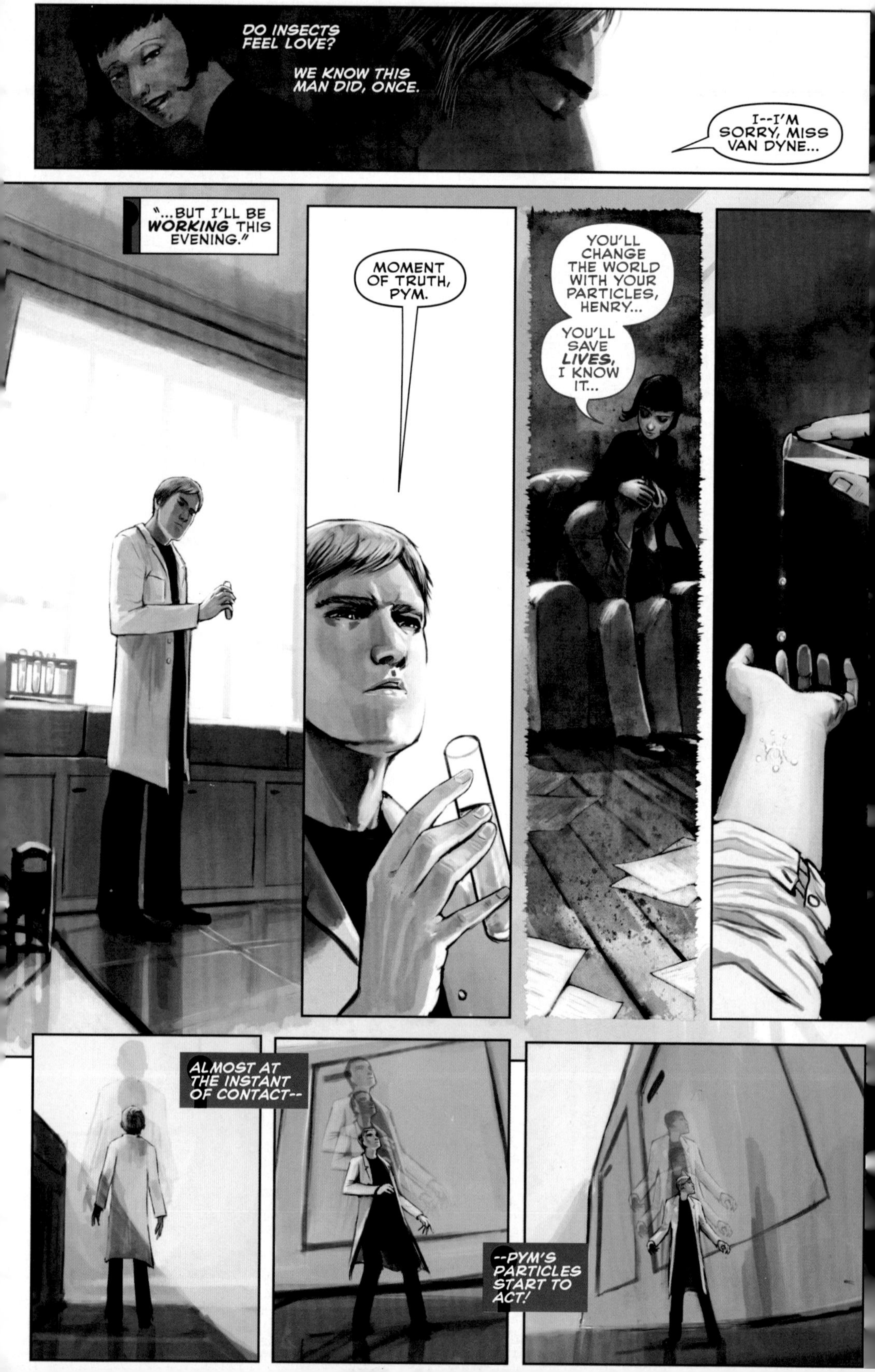
DO INSECTS FEEL LOVE?
WE KNOW THIS MAN DID, ONCE.
I--I'M SORRY, MISS VAN DYNE...
"...BUT I'LL BE WORKING THIS EVENING."
MOMENT OF TRUTH, PYM.
YOU'LL CHANGE THE WORLD WITH YOUR PARTICLES, HENRY...
YOU'LL SAVE LIVES, I KNOW IT...
ALMOST AT THE INSTANT OF CONTACT--
--PYM'S PARTICLES START TO ACT!

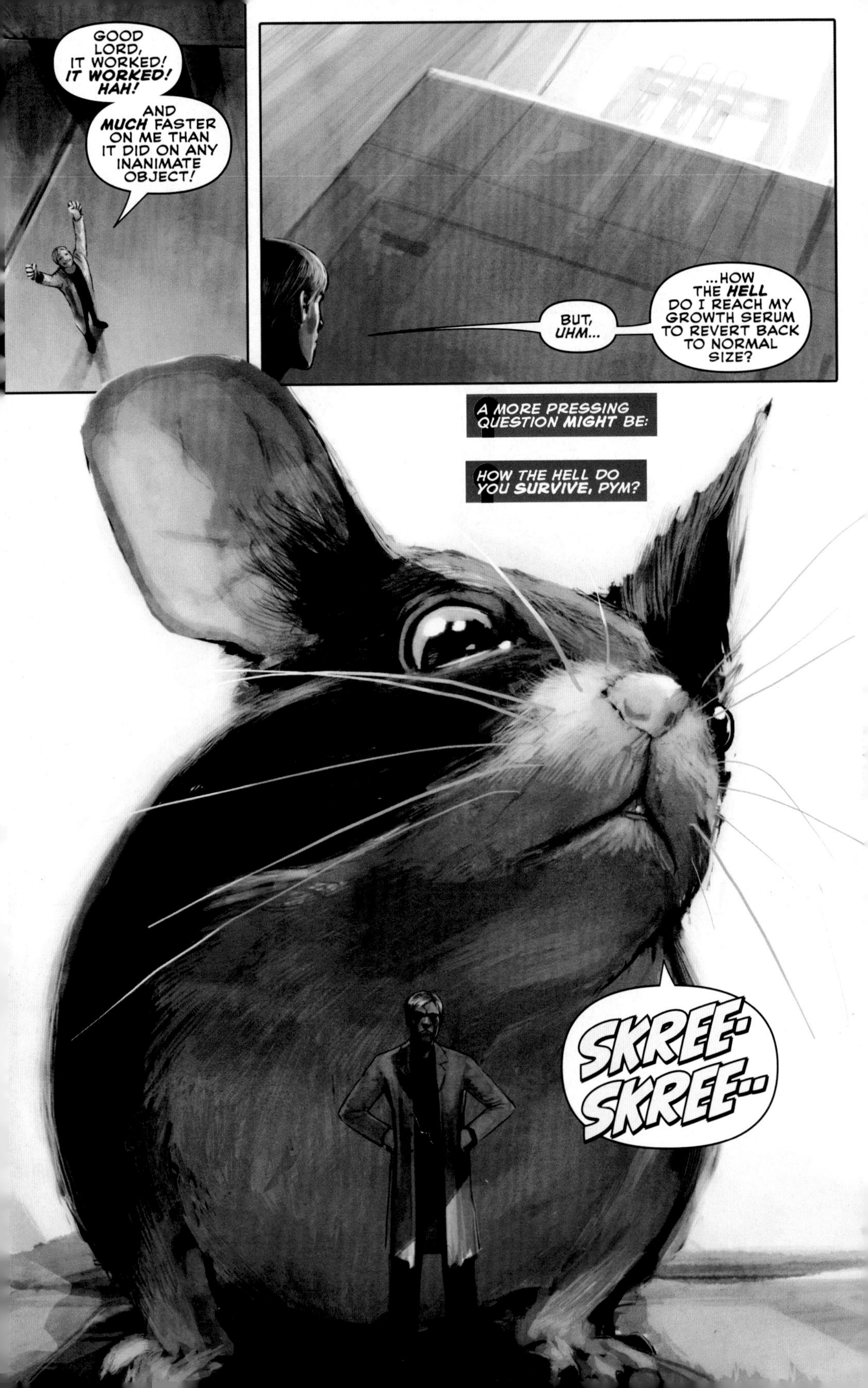
GOOD LORD, IT WORKED! IT WORKED! HAH!
AND MUCH FASTER ON ME THAN IT DID ON ANY INANIMATE OBJECT!
BUT, UHM...
...HOW THE HELL DO I REACH MY GROWTH SERUM TO REVERT BACK TO NORMAL SIZE?
A MORE PRESSING QUESTION MIGHT BE:
HOW THE HELL DO YOU SURVIVE, PYM?
SKREE-SKREE..

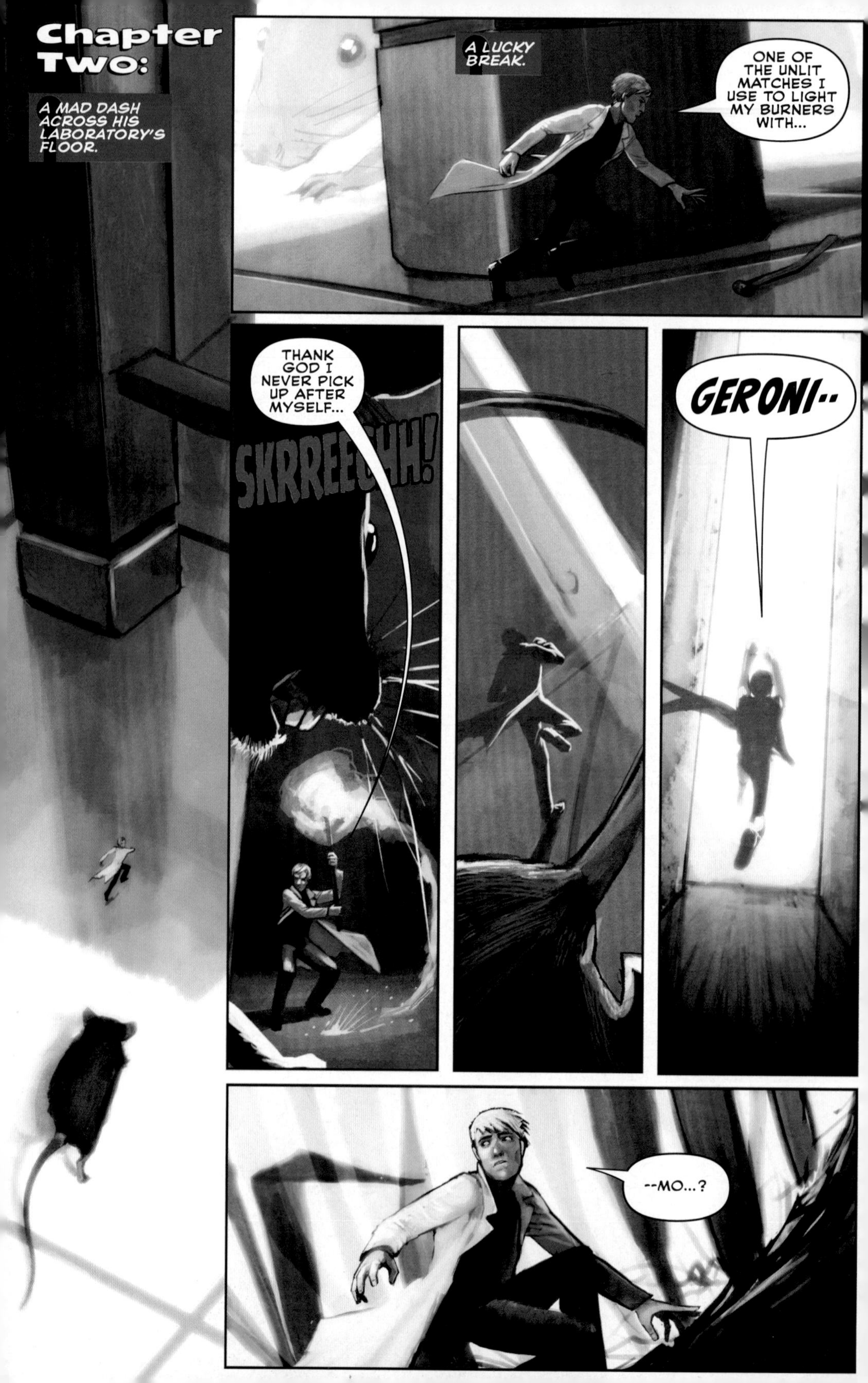
Chapter Two:
A MAD DASH ACROSS HIS LABORATORY'S FLOOR.
A LUCKY BREAK.
ONE OF THE UNLIT MATCHES I USE TO LIGHT MY BURNERS WITH...
THANK GOD I NEVER PICK UP AFTER MYSELF...
SKRREECHH!
GERONI--
--MO...?

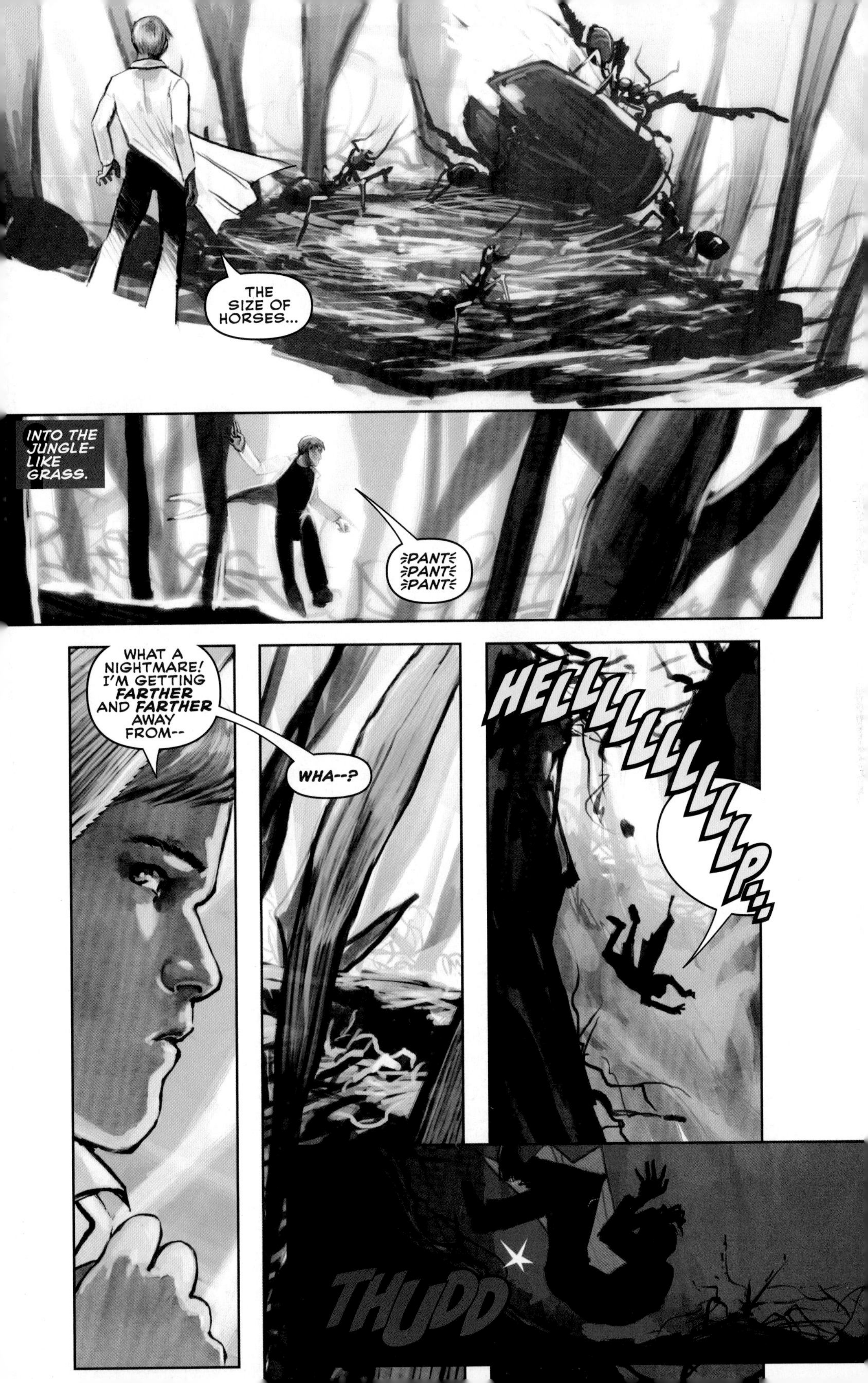
THE SIZE OF HORSES...
INTO THE JUNGLE-LIKE GRASS.
PANT PANT PANT
WHAT A NIGHTMARE! I'M GETTING FARTHER AND FARTHER AWAY FROM--
WHA--?
HELLLLLLLLLP...
THUDD

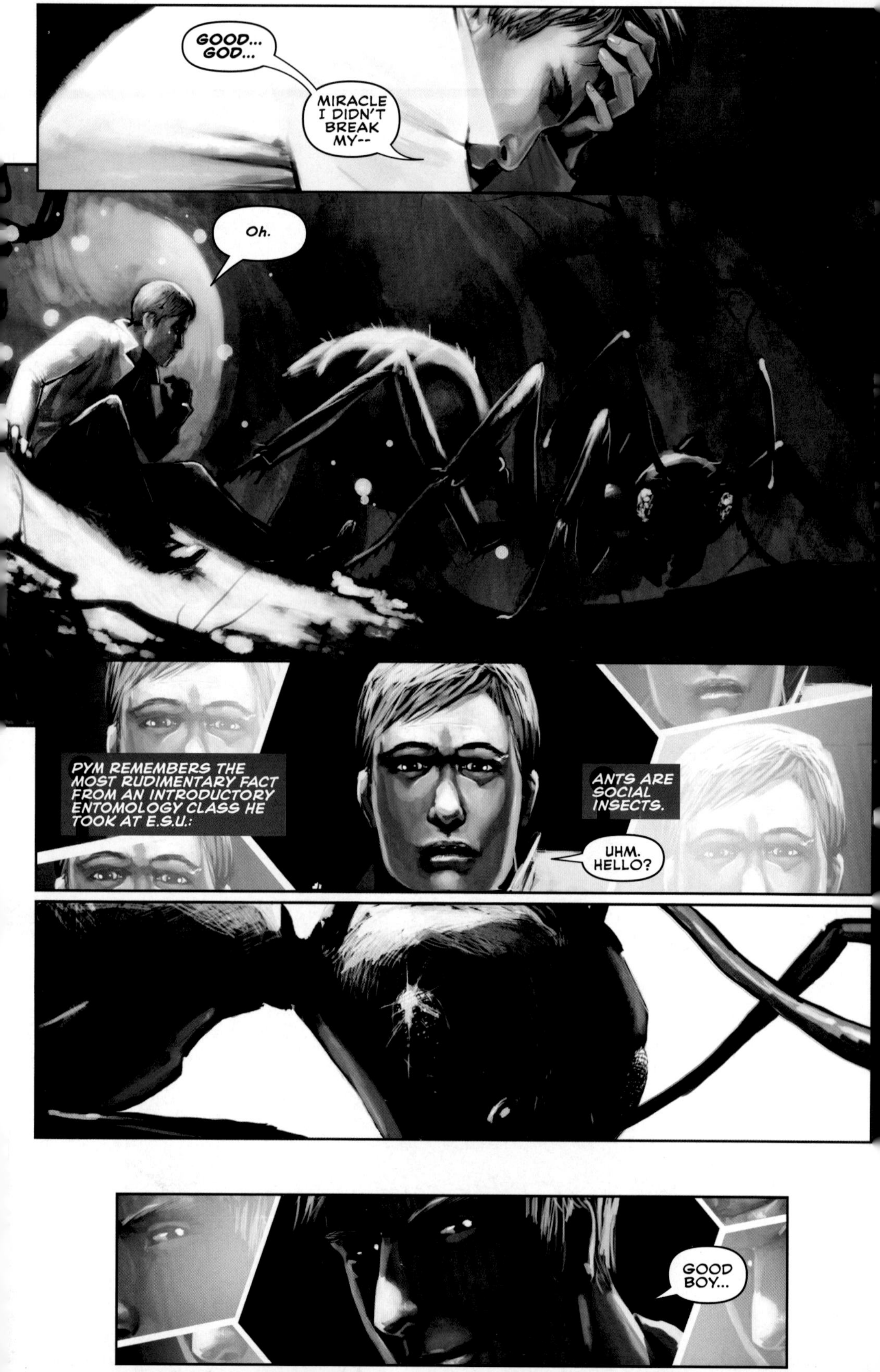
GOOD... GOD...
MIRACLE I DIDN'T BREAK MY--
Oh.
PYM REMEMBERS THE MOST RUDIMENTARY FACT FROM AN INTRODUCTORY ENTOMOLOGY CLASS HE TOOK AT E.S.U.:
ANTS ARE SOCIAL INSECTS.
UHM. HELLO?
GOOD BOY...

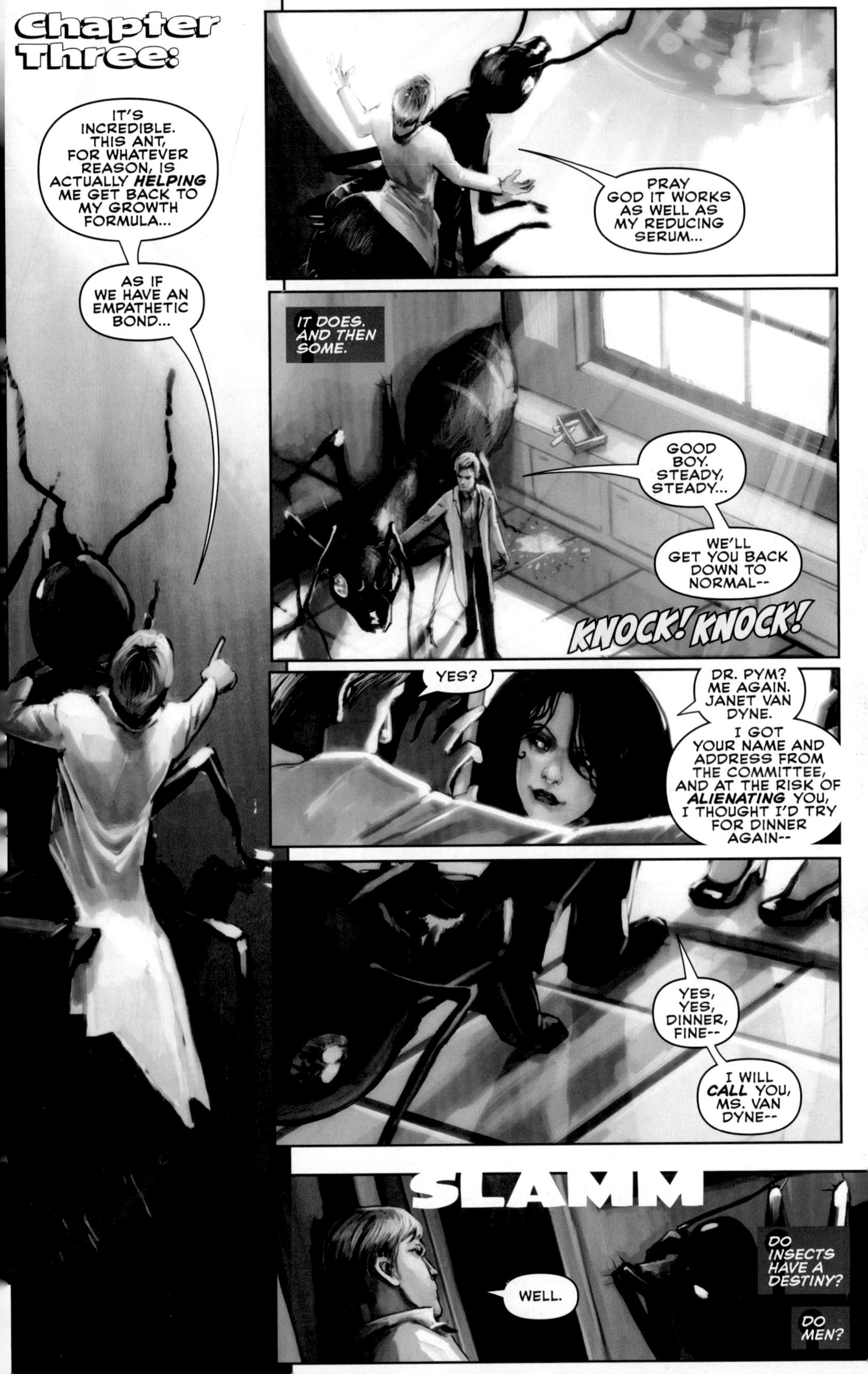
Chapter Three:
IT'S INCREDIBLE. THIS ANT, FOR WHATEVER REASON, IS ACTUALLY HELPING ME GET BACK TO MY GROWTH FORMULA...
AS IF WE HAVE AN EMPATHETIC BOND...
PRAY GOD IT WORKS AS WELL AS MY REDUCING SERUM...
IT DOES. AND THEN SOME.
GOOD BOY. STEADY, STEADY...
WE'LL GET YOU BACK DOWN TO NORMAL--
KNOCK! KNOCK!
YES?
DR. PYM? ME AGAIN. JANET VAN DYNE.
I GOT YOUR NAME AND ADDRESS FROM THE COMMITTEE, AND AT THE RISK OF ALIENATING YOU, I THOUGHT I'D TRY FOR DINNER AGAIN--
YES, YES, DINNER, FINE--
I WILL CALL YOU, MS. VAN DYNE--
SLAMM
WELL.
DO INSECTS HAVE A DESTINY?
DO MEN?

Chapter Four:

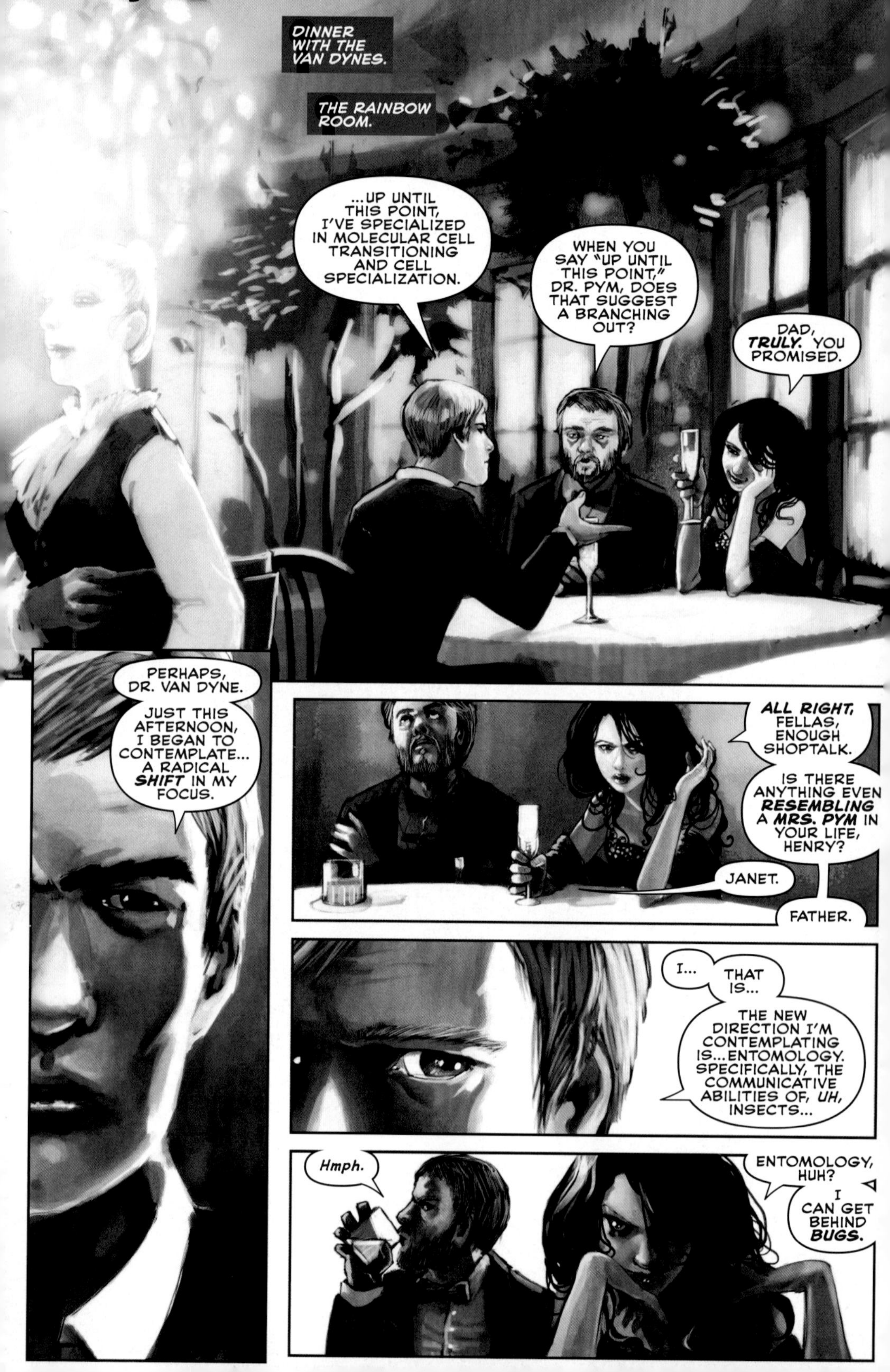
DINNER WITH THE VAN DYNES.
THE RAINBOW ROOM.
...UP UNTIL THIS POINT, I'VE SPECIALIZED IN MOLECULAR CELL TRANSITIONING AND CELL SPECIALIZATION.
WHEN YOU SAY "UP UNTIL THIS POINT," DR. PYM, DOES THAT SUGGEST A BRANCHING OUT?
DAD, TRULY. YOU PROMISED.
PERHAPS, DR. VAN DYNE.
JUST THIS AFTERNOON, I BEGAN TO CONTEMPLATE... A RADICAL SHIFT IN MY FOCUS.
ALL RIGHT, FELLAS, ENOUGH SHOPTALK.
IS THERE ANYTHING EVEN RESEMBLING A MRS. PYM IN YOUR LIFE, HENRY?
JANET.
FATHER.
I...
THAT IS...
THE NEW DIRECTION I'M CONTEMPLATING IS...ENTOMOLOGY. SPECIFICALLY, THE COMMUNICATIVE ABILITIES OF, UH, INSECTS...
Hmph.
ENTOMOLOGY, HUH?
I CAN GET BEHIND BUGS.

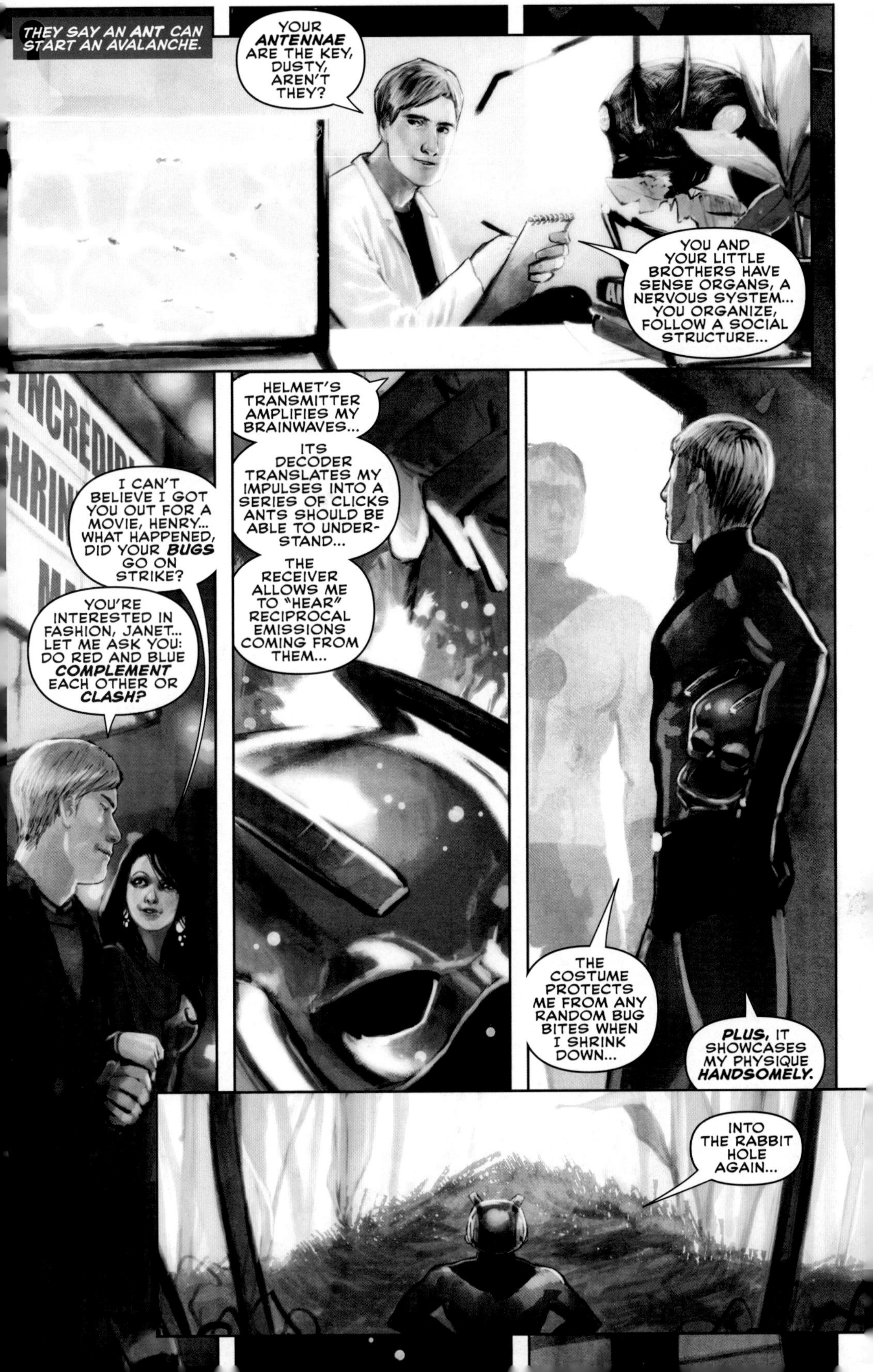
THEY SAY AN ANT CAN START AN AVALANCHE.
YOUR ANTENNAE ARE THE KEY, DUSTY, AREN'T THEY?
YOU AND YOUR LITTLE BROTHERS HAVE SENSE ORGANS, A NERVOUS SYSTEM... YOU ORGANIZE, FOLLOW A SOCIAL STRUCTURE...
INCREDIBL SHRIN
I CAN'T BELIEVE I GOT YOU OUT FOR A MOVIE, HENRY... WHAT HAPPENED, DID YOUR BUGS GO ON STRIKE?
YOU'RE INTERESTED IN FASHION, JANET... LET ME ASK YOU: DO RED AND BLUE COMPLEMENT EACH OTHER OR CLASH?
HELMET'S TRANSMITTER AMPLIFIES MY BRAINWAVES...
ITS DECODER TRANSLATES MY IMPULSES INTO A SERIES OF CLICKS ANTS SHOULD BE ABLE TO UNDERSTAND...
THE RECEIVER ALLOWS ME TO "HEAR" RECIPROCAL EMISSIONS COMING FROM THEM...
THE COSTUME PROTECTS ME FROM ANY RANDOM BUG BITES WHEN I SHRINK DOWN...
PLUS, IT SHOWCASES MY PHYSIQUE HANDSOMELY.
INTO THE RABBIT HOLE AGAIN...

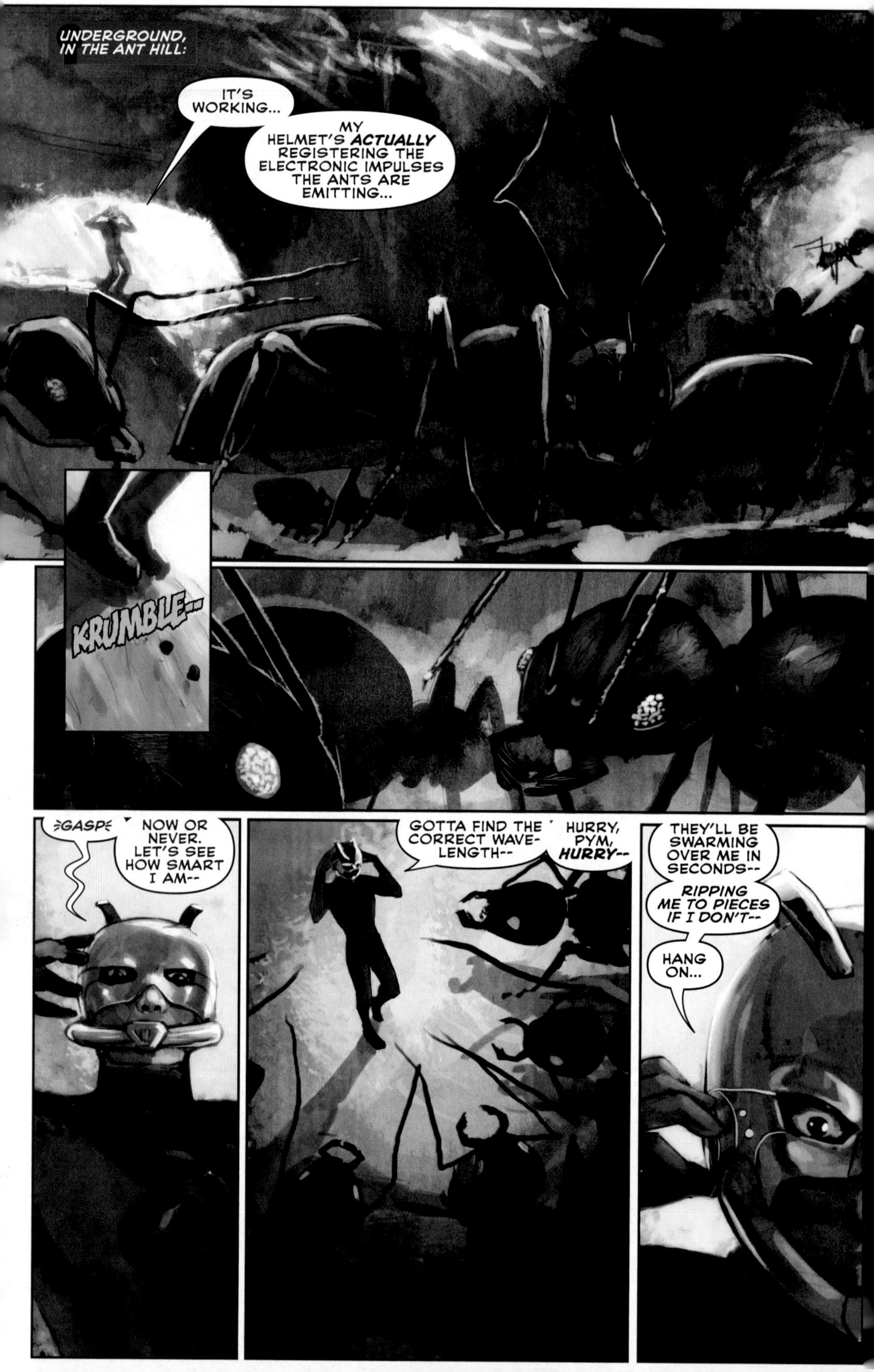
UNDERGROUND, IN THE ANT HILL:
IT'S WORKING...
MY HELMET'S ACTUALLY REGISTERING THE ELECTRONIC IMPULSES THE ANTS ARE EMITTING...
KRUMBLE--
GASP
NOW OR NEVER. LET'S SEE HOW SMART I AM--
GOTTA FIND THE CORRECT WAVE-LENGTH--
HURRY, PYM, HURRY--
THEY'LL BE SWARMING OVER ME IN SECONDS--
RIPPING ME TO PIECES IF I DON'T--
HANG ON...

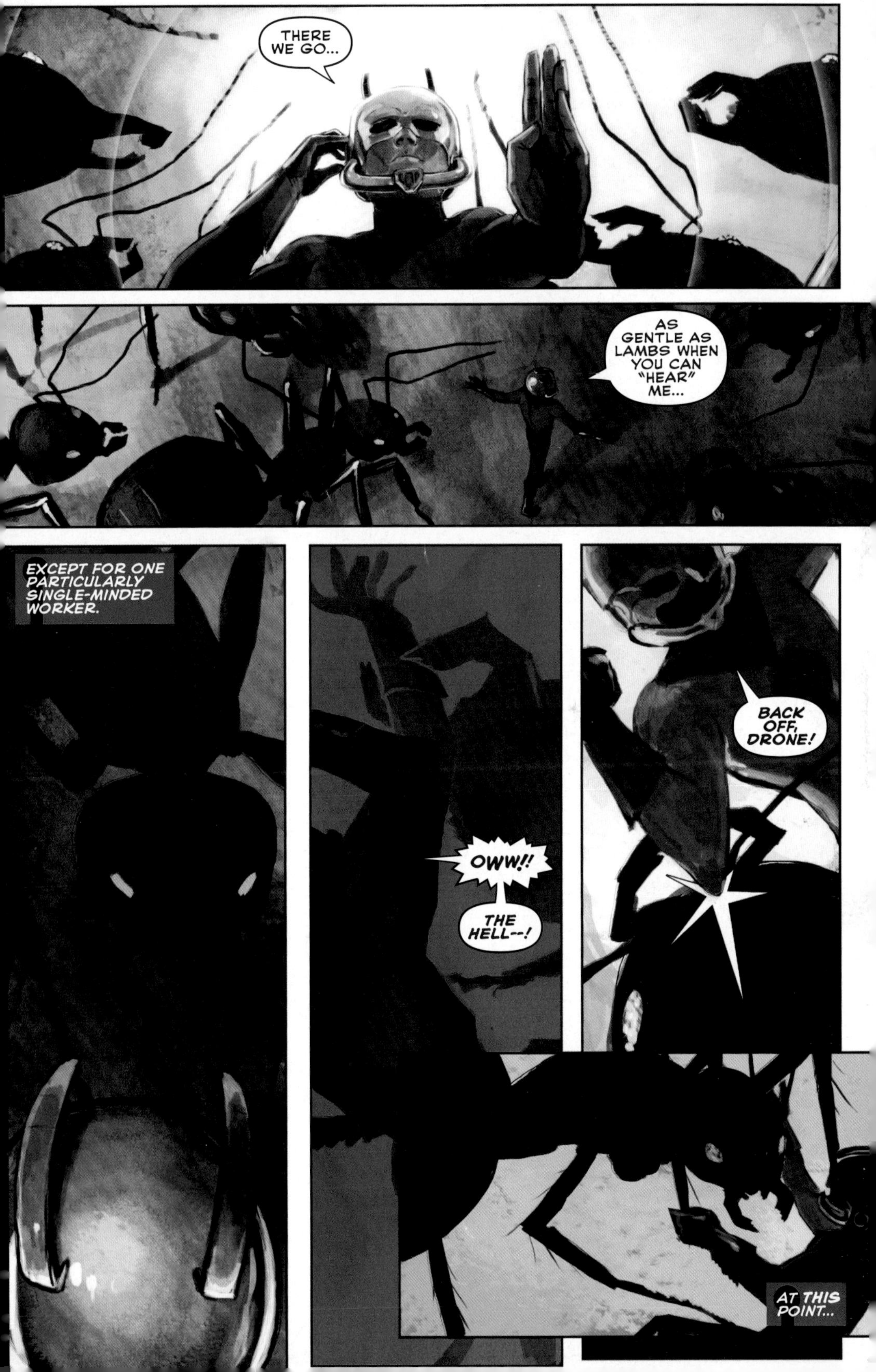
THERE WE GO...
AS GENTLE AS LAMBS WHEN YOU CAN "HEAR" ME...
EXCEPT FOR ONE PARTICULARLY SINGLE-MINDED WORKER.
OWW!!
THE HELL--!
BACK OFF, DRONE!
AT THIS POINT...

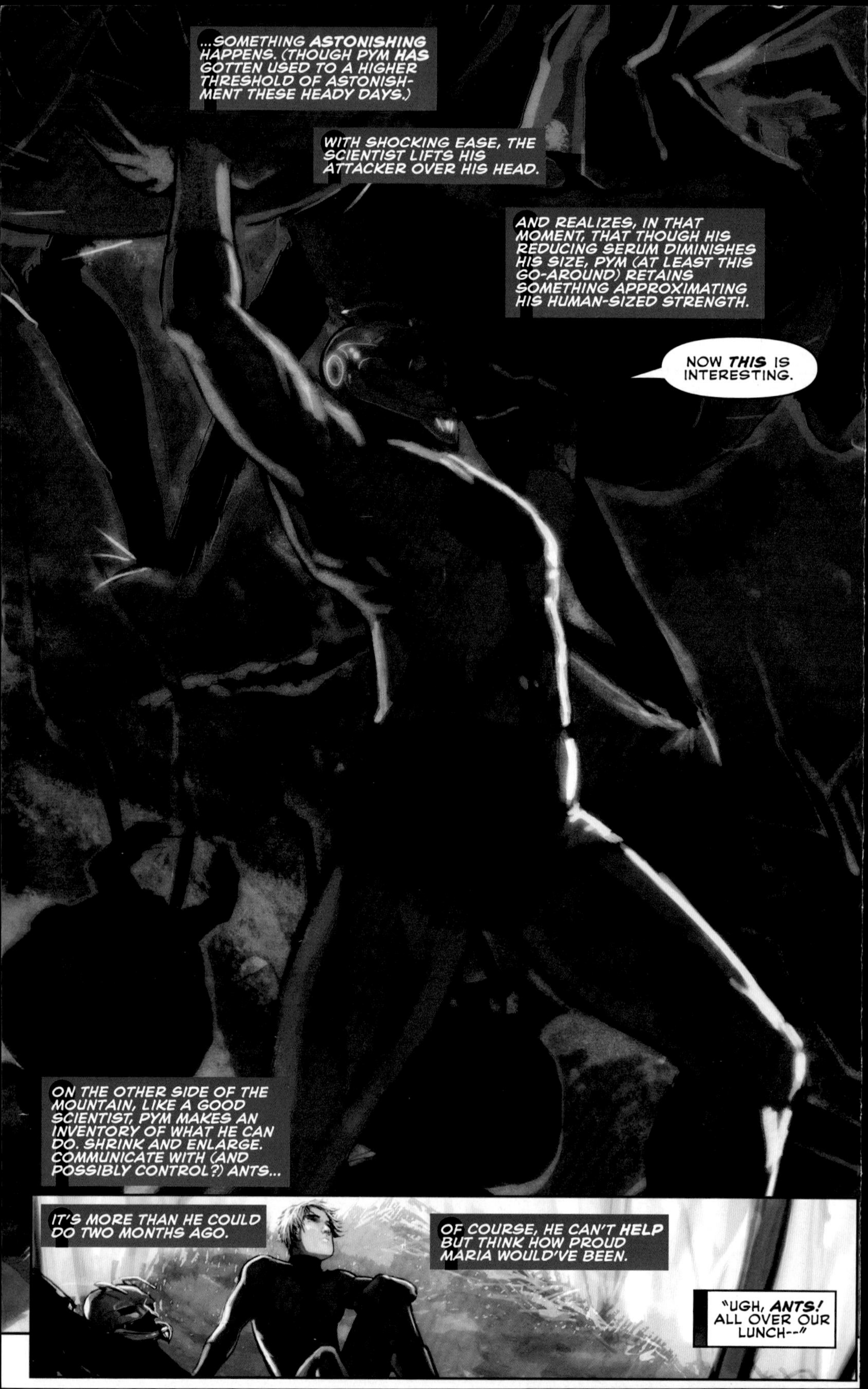
...SOMETHING ASTONISHING HAPPENS. (THOUGH PYM HAS GOTTEN USED TO A HIGHER THRESHOLD OF ASTONISHMENT THESE HEADY DAYS.)
WITH SHOCKING EASE, THE SCIENTIST LIFTS HIS ATTACKER OVER HIS HEAD.
AND REALIZES, IN THAT MOMENT, THAT THOUGH HIS REDUCING SERUM DIMINISHES HIS SIZE, PYM (AT LEAST THIS GO-AROUND) RETAINS SOMETHING APPROXIMATING HIS HUMAN-SIZED STRENGTH.
NOW THIS IS INTERESTING.
ON THE OTHER SIDE OF THE MOUNTAIN, LIKE A GOOD SCIENTIST, PYM MAKES AN INVENTORY OF WHAT HE CAN DO. SHRINK AND ENLARGE. COMMUNICATE WITH (AND POSSIBLY CONTROL?) ANTS...
IT'S MORE THAN HE COULD DO TWO MONTHS AGO.
OF COURSE, HE CAN'T HELP BUT THINK HOW PROUD MARIA WOULD'VE BEEN.
"UGH, ANTS! ALL OVER OUR LUNCH--"

Chapter Five:

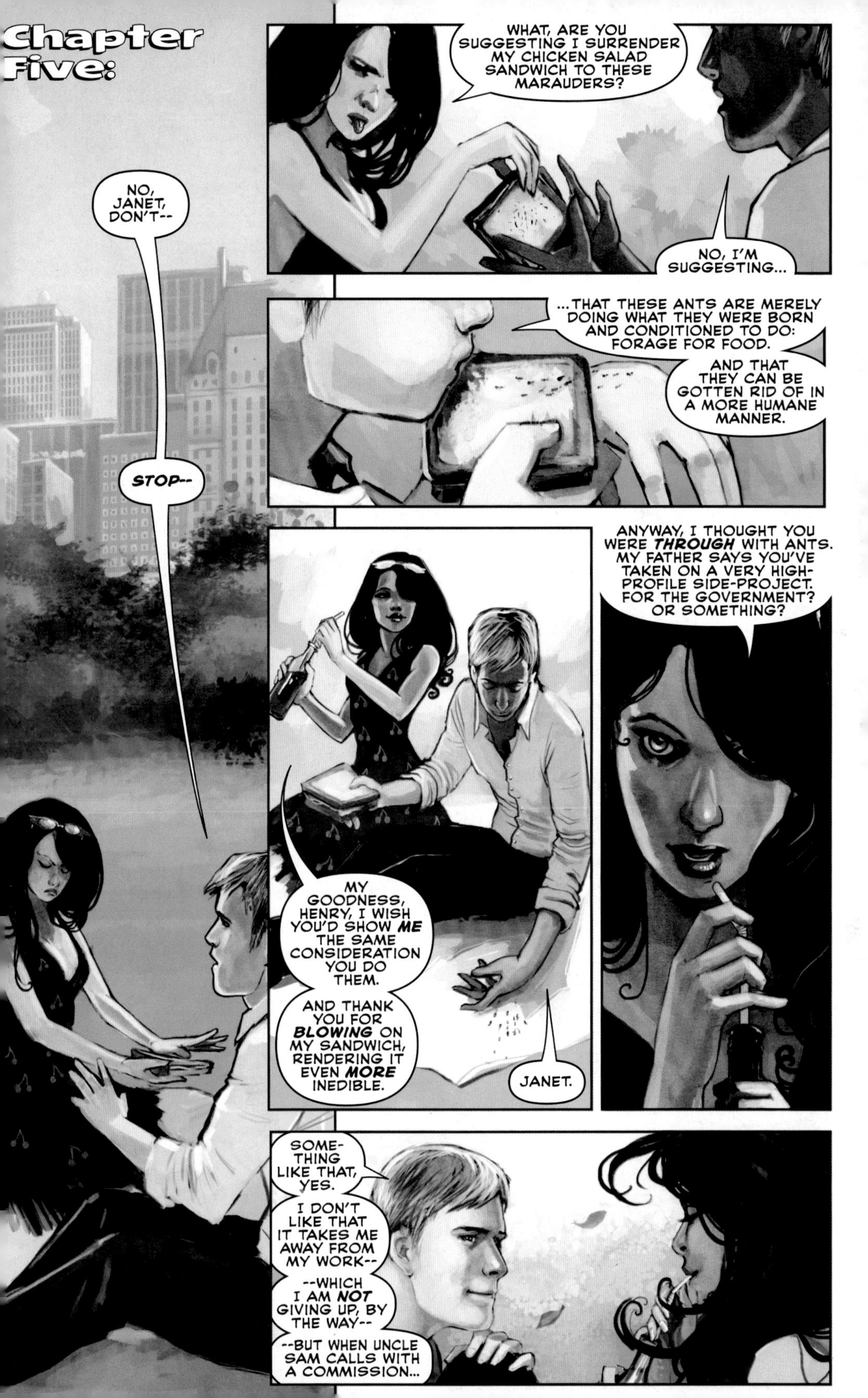

WHAT, ARE YOU SUGGESTING I SURRENDER MY CHICKEN SALAD SANDWICH TO THESE MARAUDERS?
NO, I'M SUGGESTING...
...THAT THESE ANTS ARE MERELY DOING WHAT THEY WERE BORN AND CONDITIONED TO DO: FORAGE FOR FOOD.
AND THAT THEY CAN BE GOTTEN RID OF IN A MORE HUMANE MANNER.
NO, JANET, DON'T--
STOP--
MY GOODNESS, HENRY, I WISH YOU'D SHOW ME THE SAME CONSIDERATION YOU DO THEM.
AND THANK YOU FOR BLOWING ON MY SANDWICH, RENDERING IT EVEN MORE INEDIBLE.
JANET.
ANYWAY, I THOUGHT YOU WERE THROUGH WITH ANTS. MY FATHER SAYS YOU'VE TAKEN ON A VERY HIGH-PROFILE SIDE-PROJECT. FOR THE GOVERNMENT? OR SOMETHING?
SOME-THING LIKE THAT, YES.
I DON'T LIKE THAT IT TAKES ME AWAY FROM MY WORK--
--WHICH I AM NOT GIVING UP, BY THE WAY--
--BUT WHEN UNCLE SAM CALLS WITH A COMMISSION...

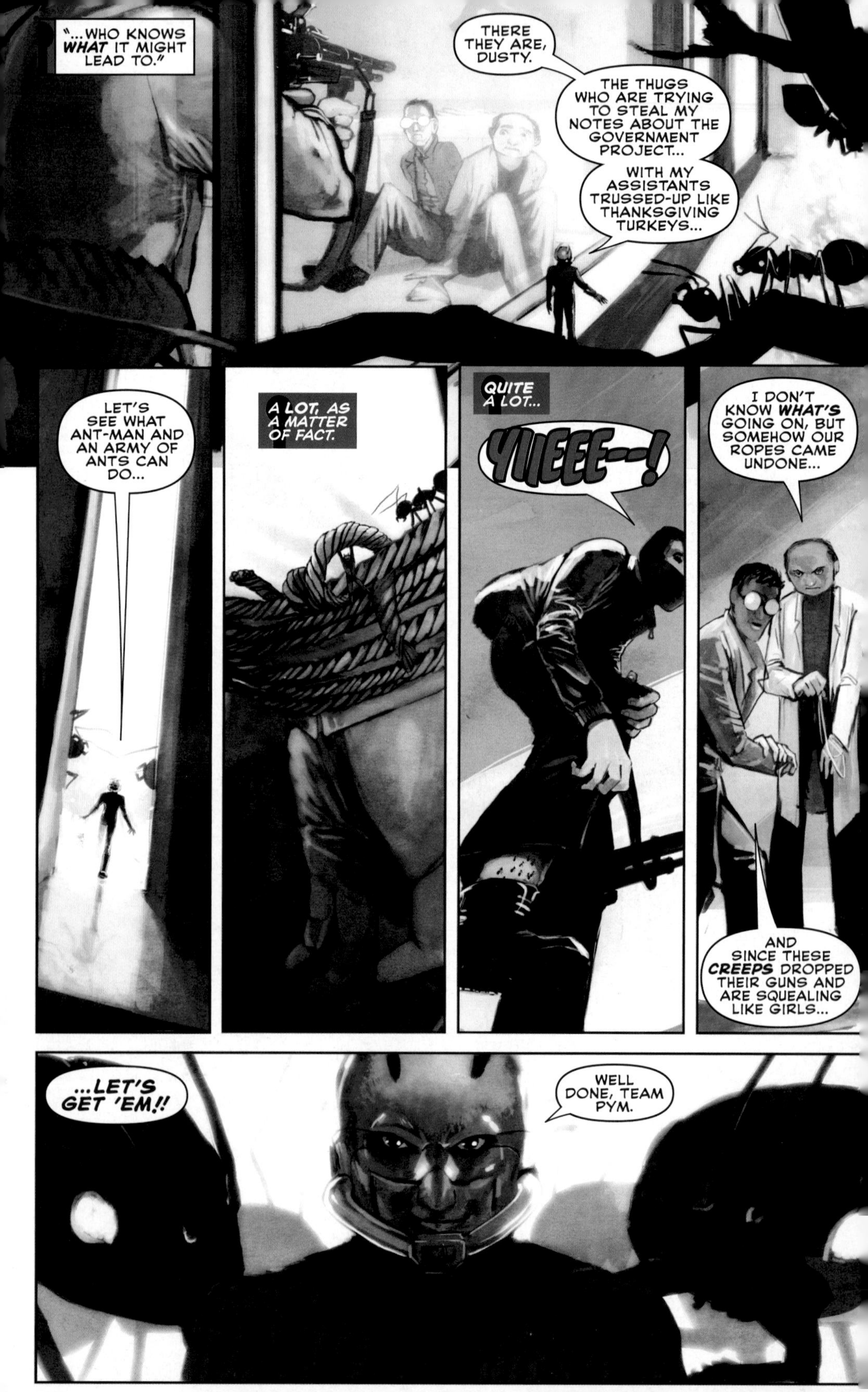
"...WHO KNOWS *WHAT* IT MIGHT LEAD TO."
THERE THEY ARE, DUSTY.
THE THUGS WHO ARE TRYING TO STEAL MY NOTES ABOUT THE GOVERNMENT PROJECT...
WITH MY ASSISTANTS TRUSSED-UP LIKE THANKSGIVING TURKEYS...
LET'S SEE WHAT ANT-MAN AND AN ARMY OF ANTS CAN DO...
A LOT, AS A MATTER OF FACT.
QUITE A LOT...
YIIEEE--!
I DON'T KNOW *WHAT'S* GOING ON, BUT SOMEHOW OUR ROPES CAME UNDONE...
AND SINCE THESE *CREEPS* DROPPED THEIR GUNS AND ARE SQUEALING LIKE GIRLS...
...*LET'S GET 'EM!!*
WELL DONE, TEAM PYM.

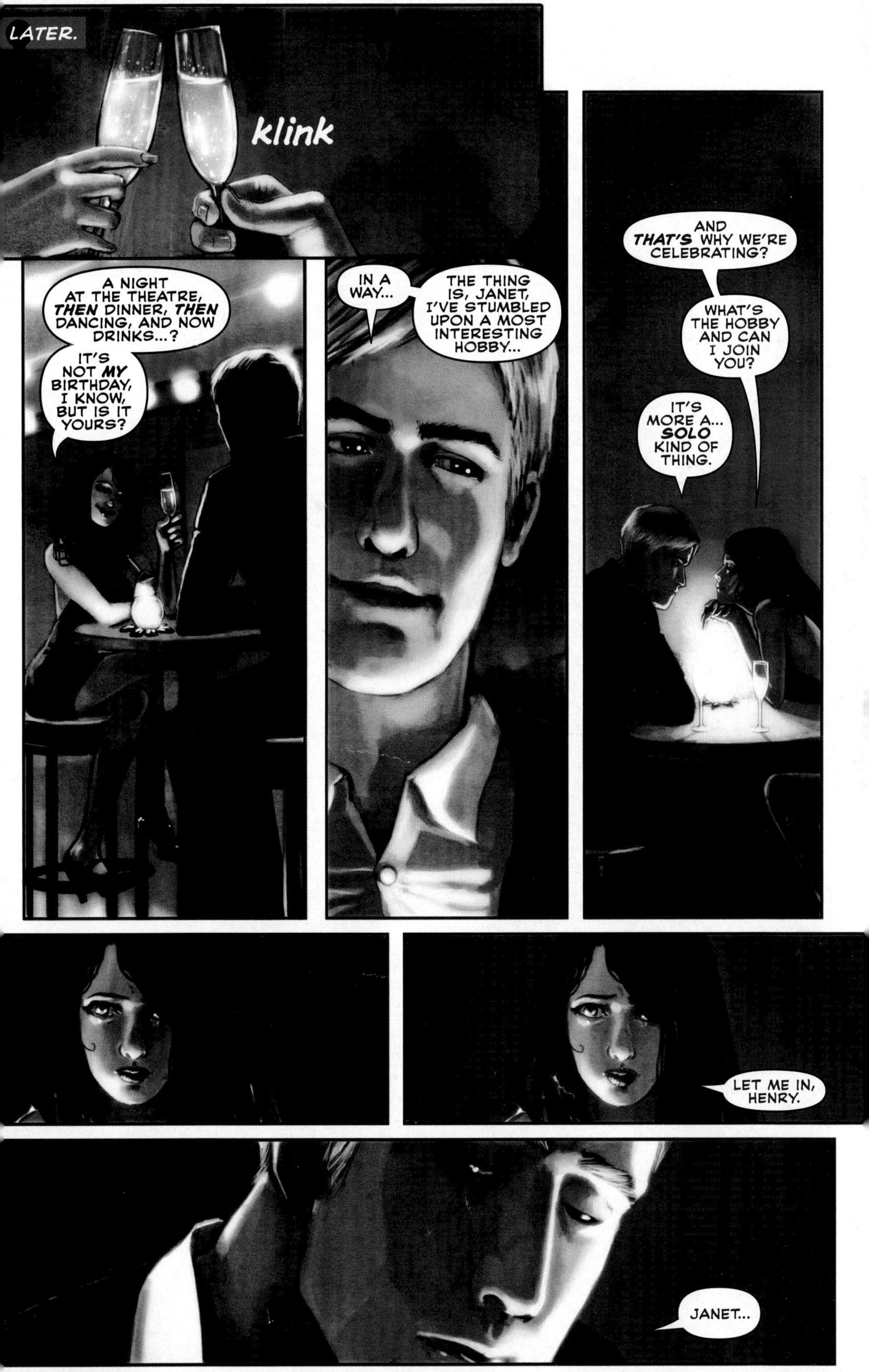
LATER.
klink
A NIGHT AT THE THEATRE, THEN DINNER, THEN DANCING, AND NOW DRINKS...?
IT'S NOT MY BIRTHDAY, I KNOW, BUT IS IT YOURS?
IN A WAY...
THE THING IS, JANET, I'VE STUMBLED UPON A MOST INTERESTING HOBBY...
AND THAT'S WHY WE'RE CELEBRATING?
WHAT'S THE HOBBY AND CAN I JOIN YOU?
IT'S MORE A... SOLO KIND OF THING.
LET ME IN, HENRY.
JANET...

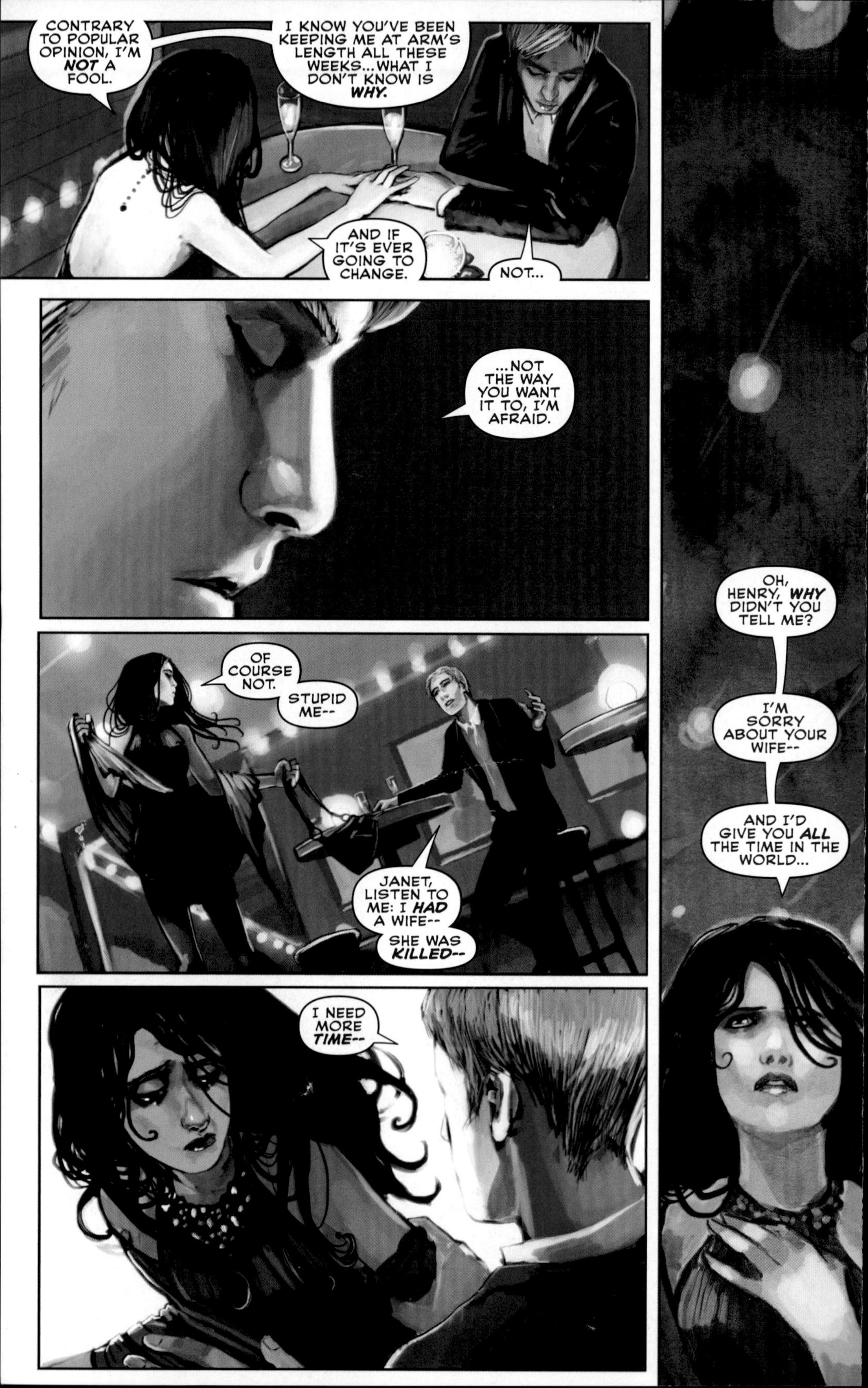
CONTRARY TO POPULAR OPINION, I'M NOT A FOOL.
I KNOW YOU'VE BEEN KEEPING ME AT ARM'S LENGTH ALL THESE WEEKS...WHAT I DON'T KNOW IS WHY.
AND IF IT'S EVER GOING TO CHANGE.
NOT...
...NOT THE WAY YOU WANT IT TO, I'M AFRAID.
OF COURSE NOT.
STUPID ME--
JANET, LISTEN TO ME: I HAD A WIFE--
SHE WAS KILLED--
I NEED MORE TIME--
OH, HENRY, WHY DIDN'T YOU TELL ME?
I'M SORRY ABOUT YOUR WIFE--
AND I'D GIVE YOU ALL THE TIME IN THE WORLD...

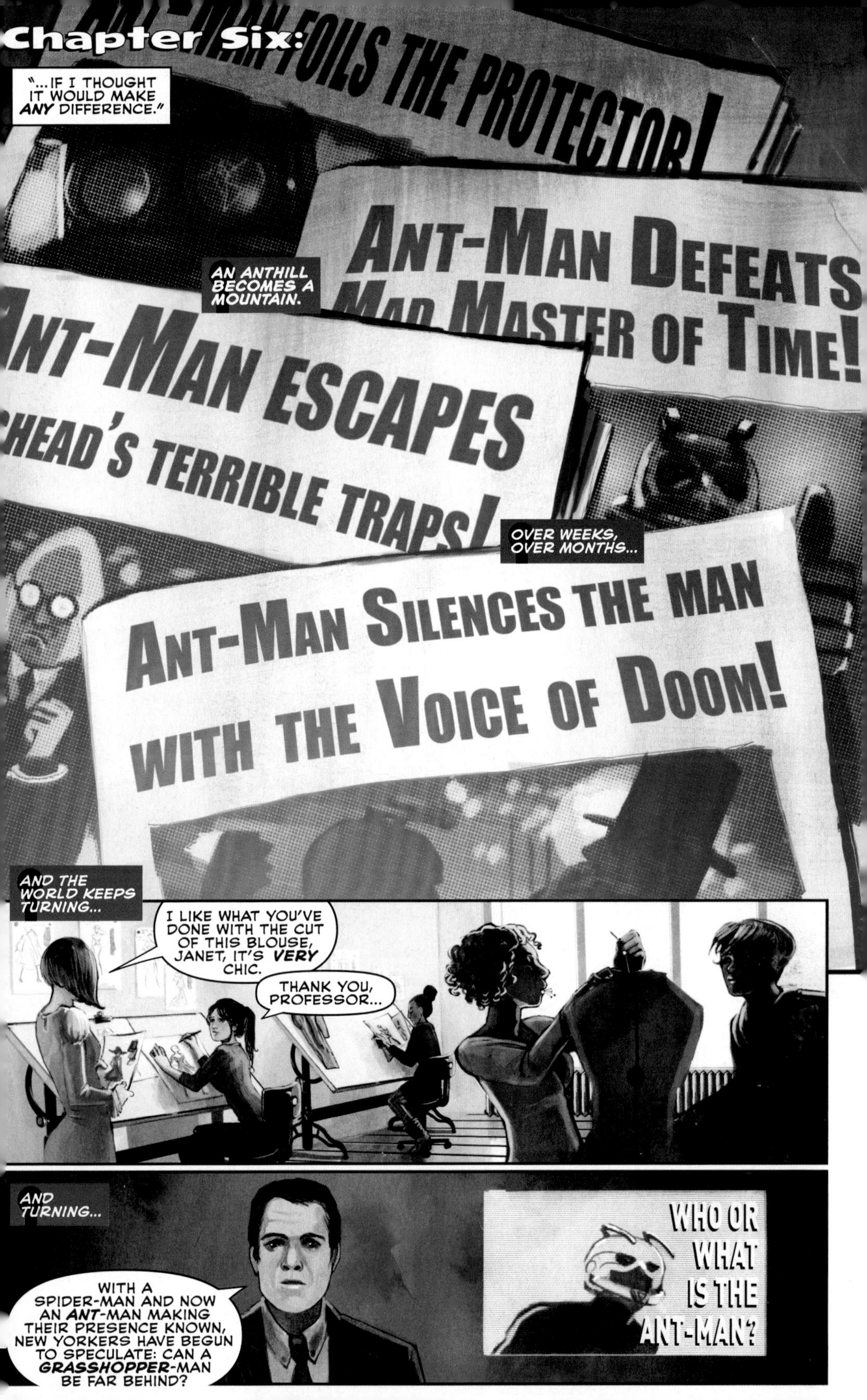
Chapter Six:
"...IF I THOUGHT IT WOULD MAKE ANY DIFFERENCE."
FOILS THE PROTECTOR!
ANT-MAN DEFEATS
MASTER OF TIME!
AN ANTHILL BECOMES A MOUNTAIN.
ESCAPES
'S TERRIBLE TRAPS!
OVER WEEKS, OVER MONTHS...
ANT-MAN SILENCES THE MAN WITH THE VOICE OF DOOM!
AND THE WORLD KEEPS TURNING...
I LIKE WHAT YOU'VE DONE WITH THE CUT OF THIS BLOUSE, JANET, IT'S VERY CHIC.
THANK YOU, PROFESSOR...
AND TURNING...
WITH A SPIDER-MAN AND NOW AN ANT-MAN MAKING THEIR PRESENCE KNOWN, NEW YORKERS HAVE BEGUN TO SPECULATE: CAN A GRASSHOPPER-MAN BE FAR BEHIND?
WHO OR WHAT IS THE ANT-MAN?

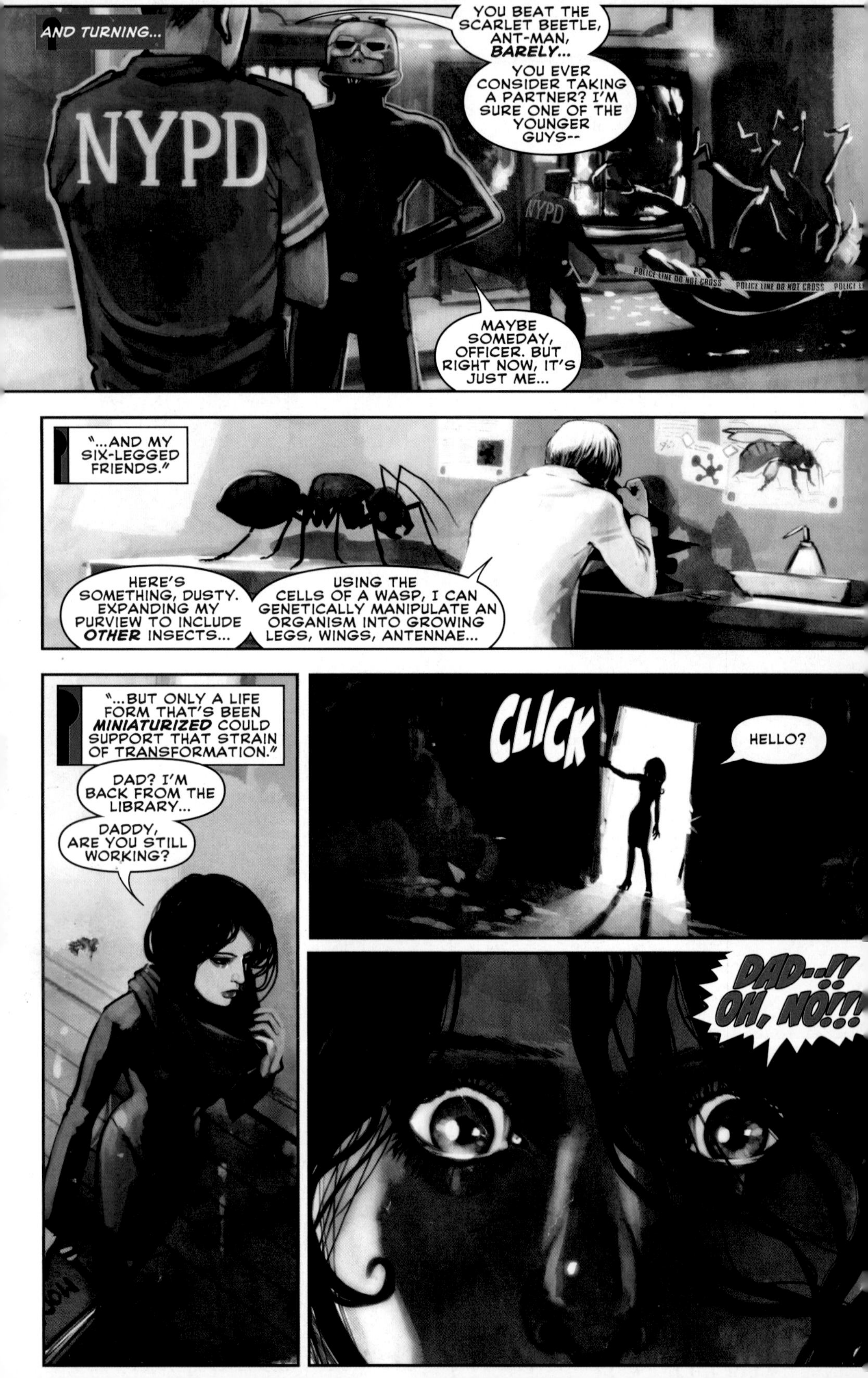
AND TURNING...
YOU BEAT THE SCARLET BEETLE, ANT-MAN, BARELY...
YOU EVER CONSIDER TAKING A PARTNER? I'M SURE ONE OF THE YOUNGER GUYS--
NYPD
NYPD
POLICE LINE DO NOT CROSS
MAYBE SOMEDAY, OFFICER. BUT RIGHT NOW, IT'S JUST ME...
"...AND MY SIX-LEGGED FRIENDS."
HERE'S SOMETHING, DUSTY. EXPANDING MY PURVIEW TO INCLUDE OTHER INSECTS...
USING THE CELLS OF A WASP, I CAN GENETICALLY MANIPULATE AN ORGANISM INTO GROWING LEGS, WINGS, ANTENNAE...
"...BUT ONLY A LIFE FORM THAT'S BEEN MINIATURIZED COULD SUPPORT THAT STRAIN OF TRANSFORMATION."
DAD? I'M BACK FROM THE LIBRARY...
DADDY, ARE YOU STILL WORKING?
CLICK
HELLO?
DAD..!? OH, NO!?!

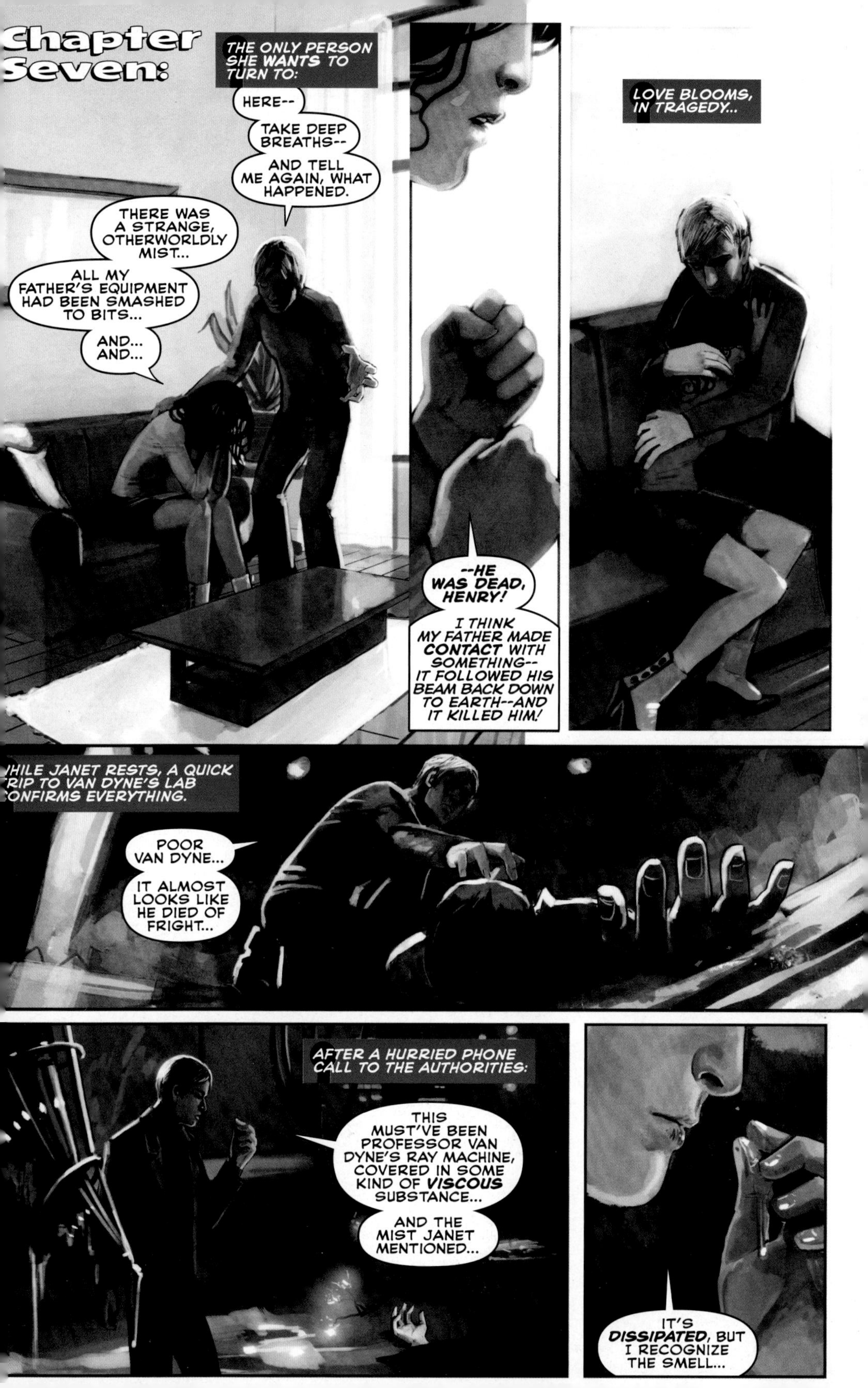
Chapter Seven:
THE ONLY PERSON SHE WANTS TO TURN TO:
HERE--
TAKE DEEP BREATHS--
AND TELL ME AGAIN, WHAT HAPPENED.
THERE WAS A STRANGE, OTHERWORLDLY MIST...
ALL MY FATHER'S EQUIPMENT HAD BEEN SMASHED TO BITS...
AND... AND...
--HE WAS DEAD, HENRY!
I THINK MY FATHER MADE CONTACT WITH SOMETHING-- IT FOLLOWED HIS BEAM BACK DOWN TO EARTH--AND IT KILLED HIM!
LOVE BLOOMS, IN TRAGEDY...
HILE JANET RESTS, A QUICK RIP TO VAN DYNE'S LAB ONFIRMS EVERYTHING.
POOR VAN DYNE...
IT ALMOST LOOKS LIKE HE DIED OF FRIGHT...
AFTER A HURRIED PHONE CALL TO THE AUTHORITIES:
THIS MUST'VE BEEN PROFESSOR VAN DYNE'S RAY MACHINE, COVERED IN SOME KIND OF VISCOUS SUBSTANCE...
AND THE MIST JANET MENTIONED...
IT'S DISSIPATED, BUT I RECOGNIZE THE SMELL...

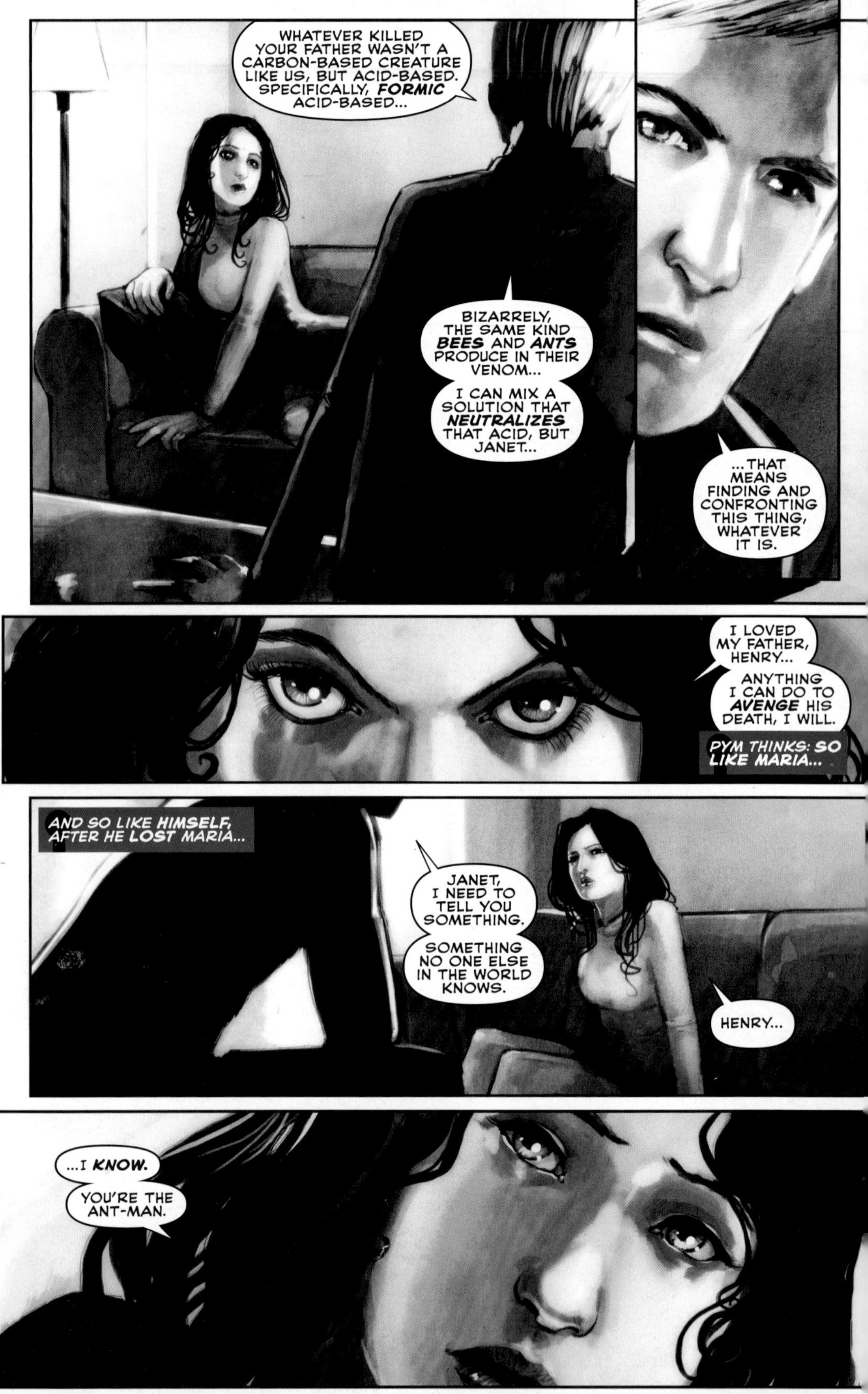
WHATEVER KILLED YOUR FATHER WASN'T A CARBON-BASED CREATURE LIKE US, BUT ACID-BASED. SPECIFICALLY, FORMIC ACID-BASED...
BIZARRELY, THE SAME KIND BEES AND ANTS PRODUCE IN THEIR VENOM...
I CAN MIX A SOLUTION THAT NEUTRALIZES THAT ACID, BUT JANET...
...THAT MEANS FINDING AND CONFRONTING THIS THING, WHATEVER IT IS.
I LOVED MY FATHER, HENRY...
ANYTHING I CAN DO TO AVENGE HIS DEATH, I WILL.
PYM THINKS: SO LIKE MARIA...
AND SO LIKE HIMSELF, AFTER HE LOST MARIA...
JANET, I NEED TO TELL YOU SOMETHING.
SOMETHING NO ONE ELSE IN THE WORLD KNOWS.
HENRY...
...I KNOW.
YOU'RE THE ANT-MAN.

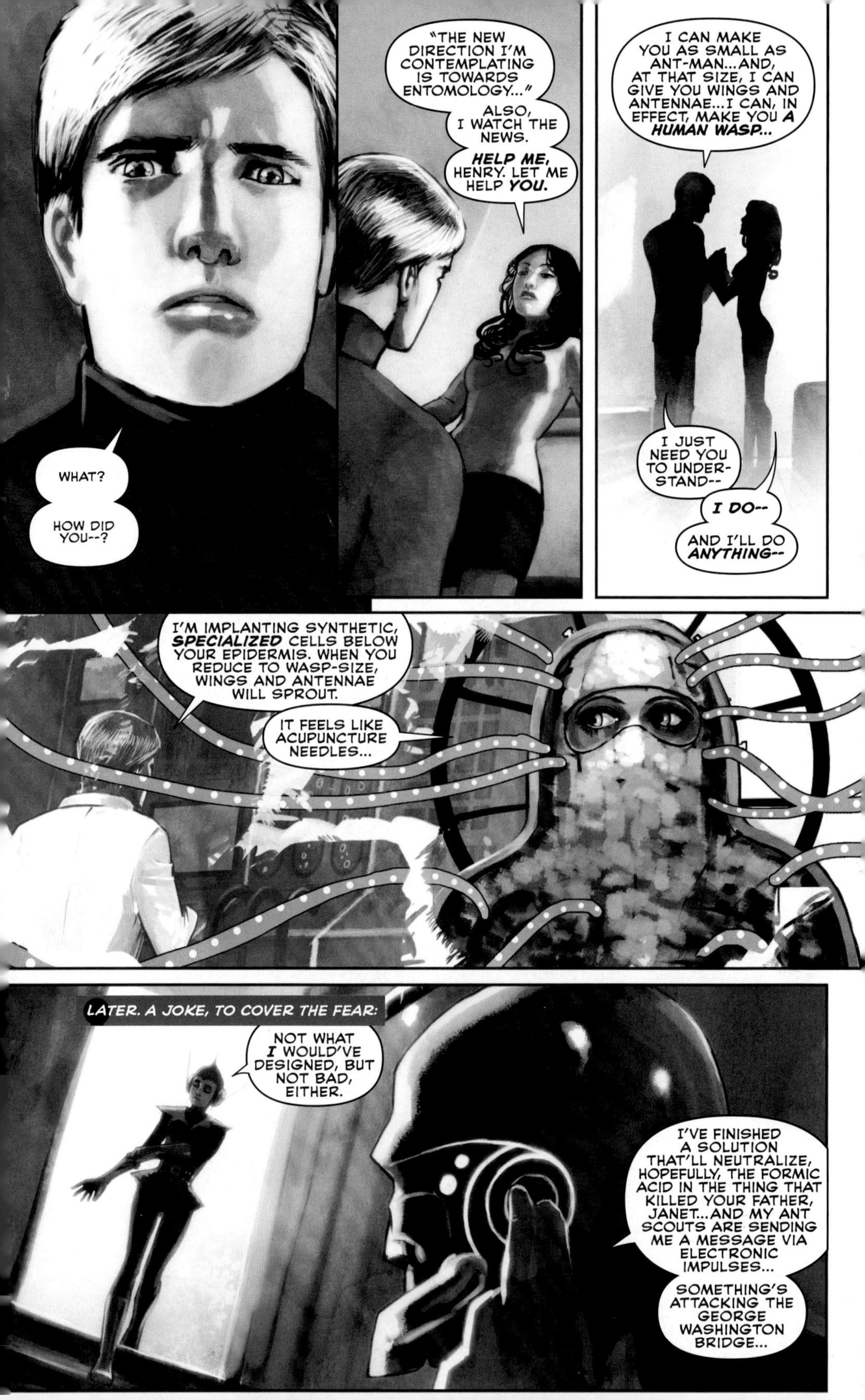
WHAT?
HOW DID YOU--?
"THE NEW DIRECTION I'M CONTEMPLATING IS TOWARDS ENTOMOLOGY..."
ALSO, I WATCH THE NEWS.
HELP ME, HENRY. LET ME HELP YOU.
I CAN MAKE YOU AS SMALL AS ANT-MAN...AND, AT THAT SIZE, I CAN GIVE YOU WINGS AND ANTENNAE...I CAN, IN EFFECT, MAKE YOU A HUMAN WASP...
I JUST NEED YOU TO UNDER-STAND--
I DO--
AND I'LL DO ANYTHING--
I'M IMPLANTING SYNTHETIC, SPECIALIZED CELLS BELOW YOUR EPIDERMIS. WHEN YOU REDUCE TO WASP-SIZE, WINGS AND ANTENNAE WILL SPROUT.
IT FEELS LIKE ACUPUNCTURE NEEDLES...
LATER. A JOKE, TO COVER THE FEAR:
NOT WHAT I WOULD'VE DESIGNED, BUT NOT BAD, EITHER.
I'VE FINISHED A SOLUTION THAT'LL NEUTRALIZE, HOPEFULLY, THE FORMIC ACID IN THE THING THAT KILLED YOUR FATHER, JANET...AND MY ANT SCOUTS ARE SENDING ME A MESSAGE VIA ELECTRONIC IMPULSES...
SOMETHING'S ATTACKING THE GEORGE WASHINGTON BRIDGE...

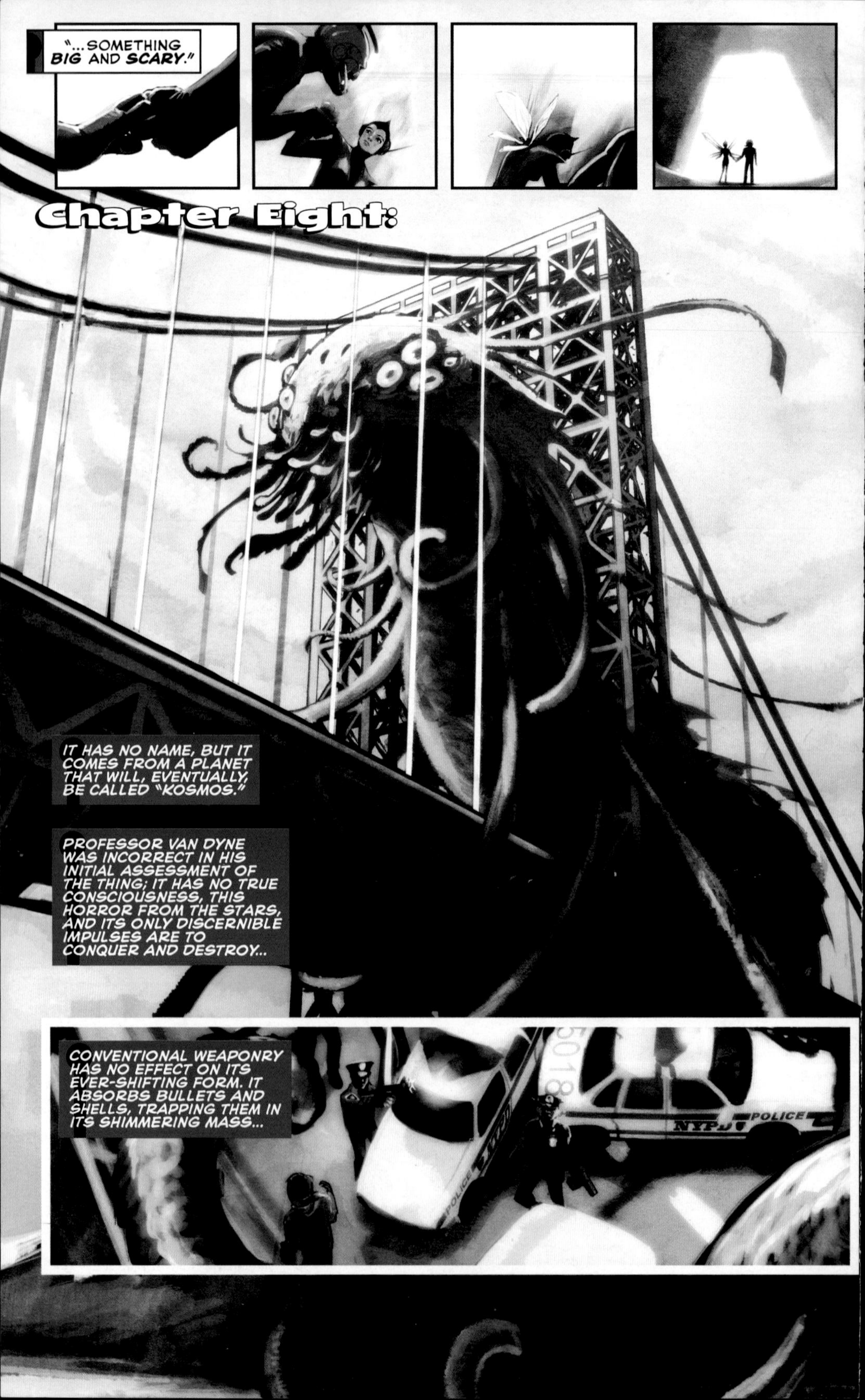
"...SOMETHING BIG AND SCARY."
Chapter Eight:
IT HAS NO NAME, BUT IT COMES FROM A PLANET THAT WILL, EVENTUALLY, BE CALLED "KOSMOS."
PROFESSOR VAN DYNE WAS INCORRECT IN HIS INITIAL ASSESSMENT OF THE THING; IT HAS NO TRUE CONSCIOUSNESS, THIS HORROR FROM THE STARS, AND ITS ONLY DISCERNIBLE IMPULSES ARE TO CONQUER AND DESTROY...
CONVENTIONAL WEAPONRY HAS NO EFFECT ON ITS EVER-SHIFTING FORM. IT ABSORBS BULLETS AND SHELLS, TRAPPING THEM IN ITS SHIMMERING MASS...
5018
NYPD
POLICE

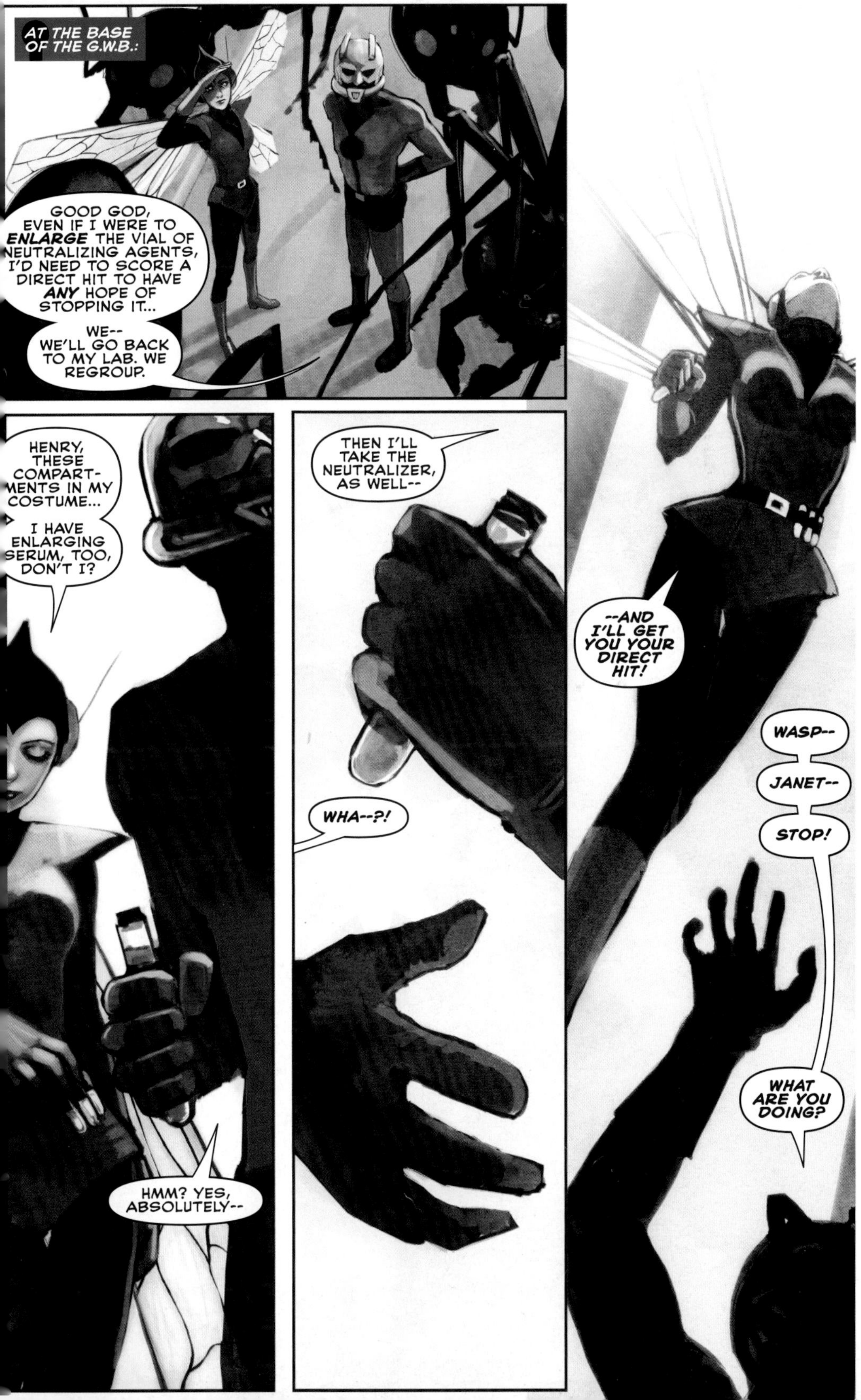
AT THE BASE OF THE G.W.B.:
GOOD GOD, EVEN IF I WERE TO ENLARGE THE VIAL OF NEUTRALIZING AGENTS, I'D NEED TO SCORE A DIRECT HIT TO HAVE ANY HOPE OF STOPPING IT...
WE-- WE'LL GO BACK TO MY LAB. WE REGROUP.
HENRY, THESE COMPART-MENTS IN MY COSTUME...
I HAVE ENLARGING SERUM, TOO, DON'T I?
HMM? YES, ABSOLUTELY--
THEN I'LL TAKE THE NEUTRALIZER, AS WELL--
WHA--?!
--AND I'LL GET YOU YOUR DIRECT HIT!
WASP--
JANET--
STOP!
WHAT ARE YOU DOING?

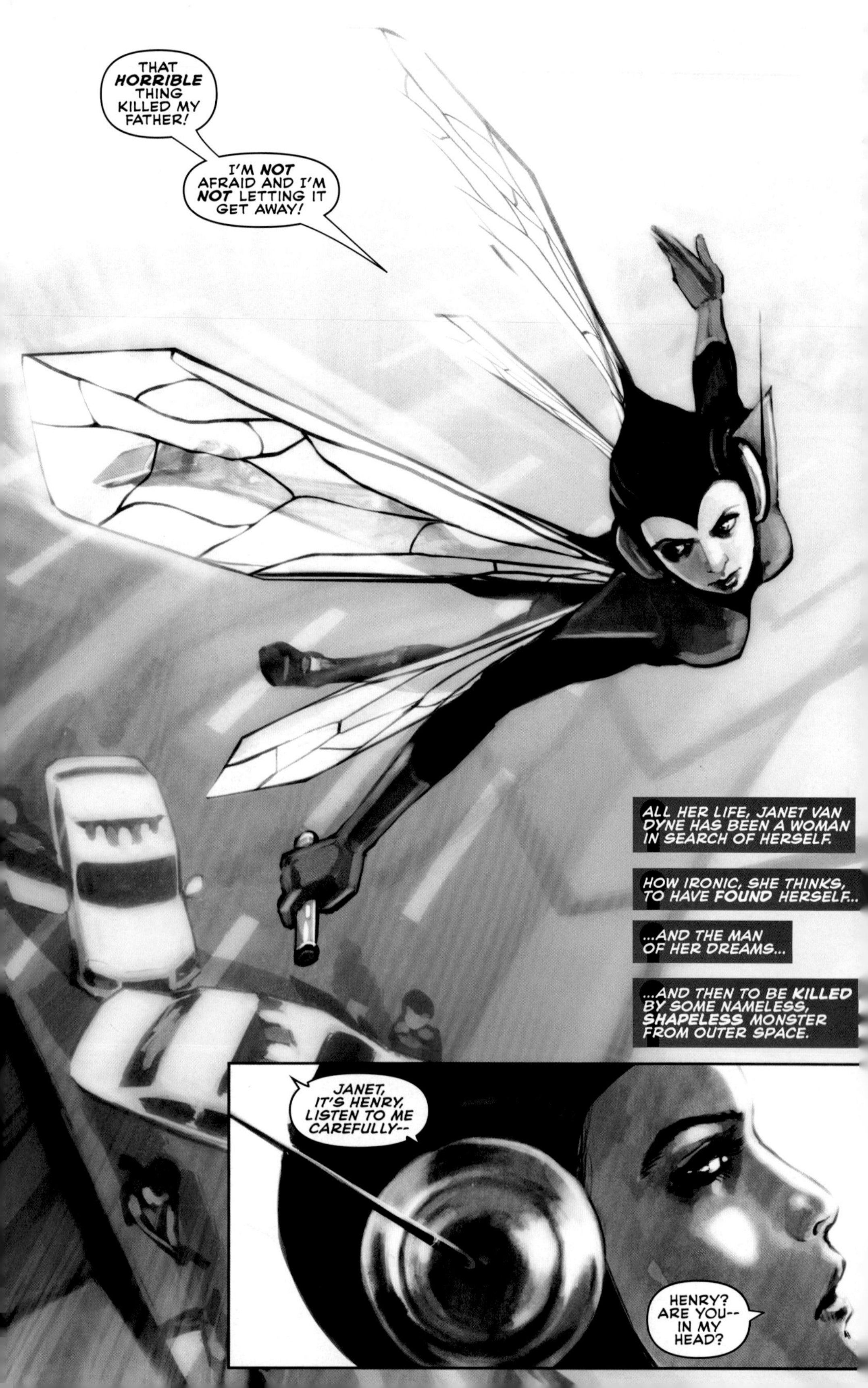
THAT HORRIBLE THING KILLED MY FATHER!
I'M NOT AFRAID AND I'M NOT LETTING IT GET AWAY!
ALL HER LIFE, JANET VAN DYNE HAS BEEN A WOMAN IN SEARCH OF HERSELF.
HOW IRONIC, SHE THINKS, TO HAVE FOUND HERSELF...
...AND THE MAN OF HER DREAMS...
...AND THEN TO BE KILLED BY SOME NAMELESS, SHAPELESS MONSTER FROM OUTER SPACE.
JANET, IT'S HENRY, LISTEN TO ME CAREFULLY--
HENRY? ARE YOU-- IN MY HEAD?

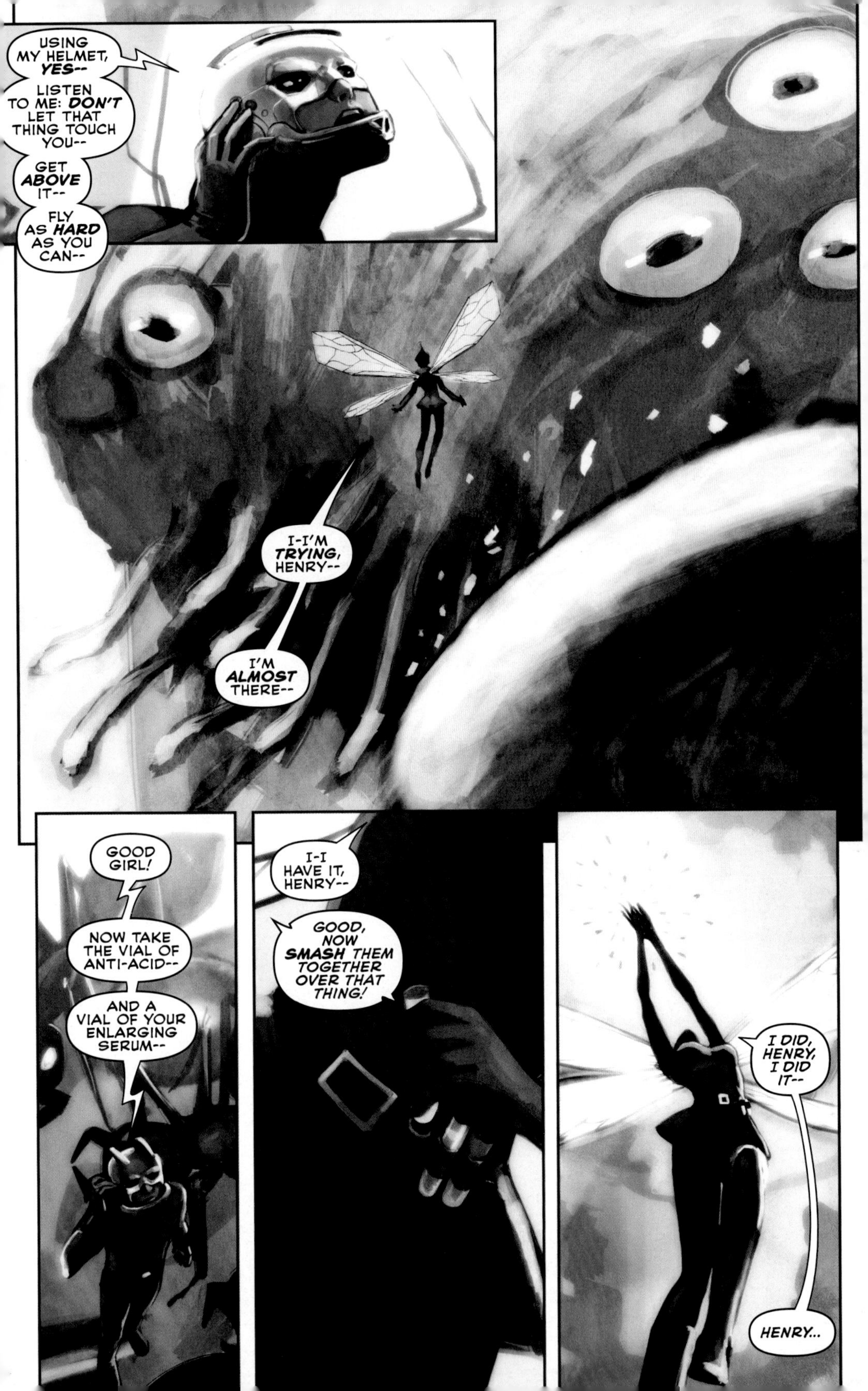
USING MY HELMET, YES--
LISTEN TO ME: DON'T LET THAT THING TOUCH YOU--
GET ABOVE IT--
FLY AS HARD AS YOU CAN--
I-I'M TRYING, HENRY--
I'M ALMOST THERE--
GOOD GIRL!
NOW TAKE THE VIAL OF ANTI-ACID--
AND A VIAL OF YOUR ENLARGING SERUM--
I-I HAVE IT, HENRY--
GOOD, NOW SMASH THEM TOGETHER OVER THAT THING!
I DID, HENRY, I DID IT--
HENRY...

...I LOVE YOU.

IGNORE IT, THINKS PYM, SHE *DIDN'T* JUST SAY THAT.

IGNORE IT AND PRAY THIS LUNACY PAYS OFF...

BY SOME MIRACLE, IT DOES.

...SO THAT THE LIQUID COMES DOWN ON THE THING LIKE A CANOPY OF RAIN...

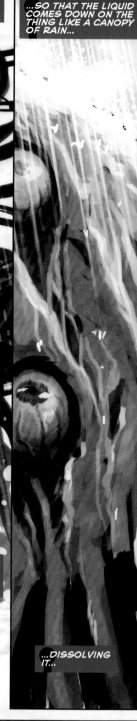

THE ENLARGING SERUM MIXES WITH THE ANTI-ACID, EXPANDING IT...

...DISSOLVING IT...

AS EASY, JANET THINKS GRIMLY, AS POURING SALT ON A GARDEN SLUG...

...AND HER FATHER IS AVENGED.

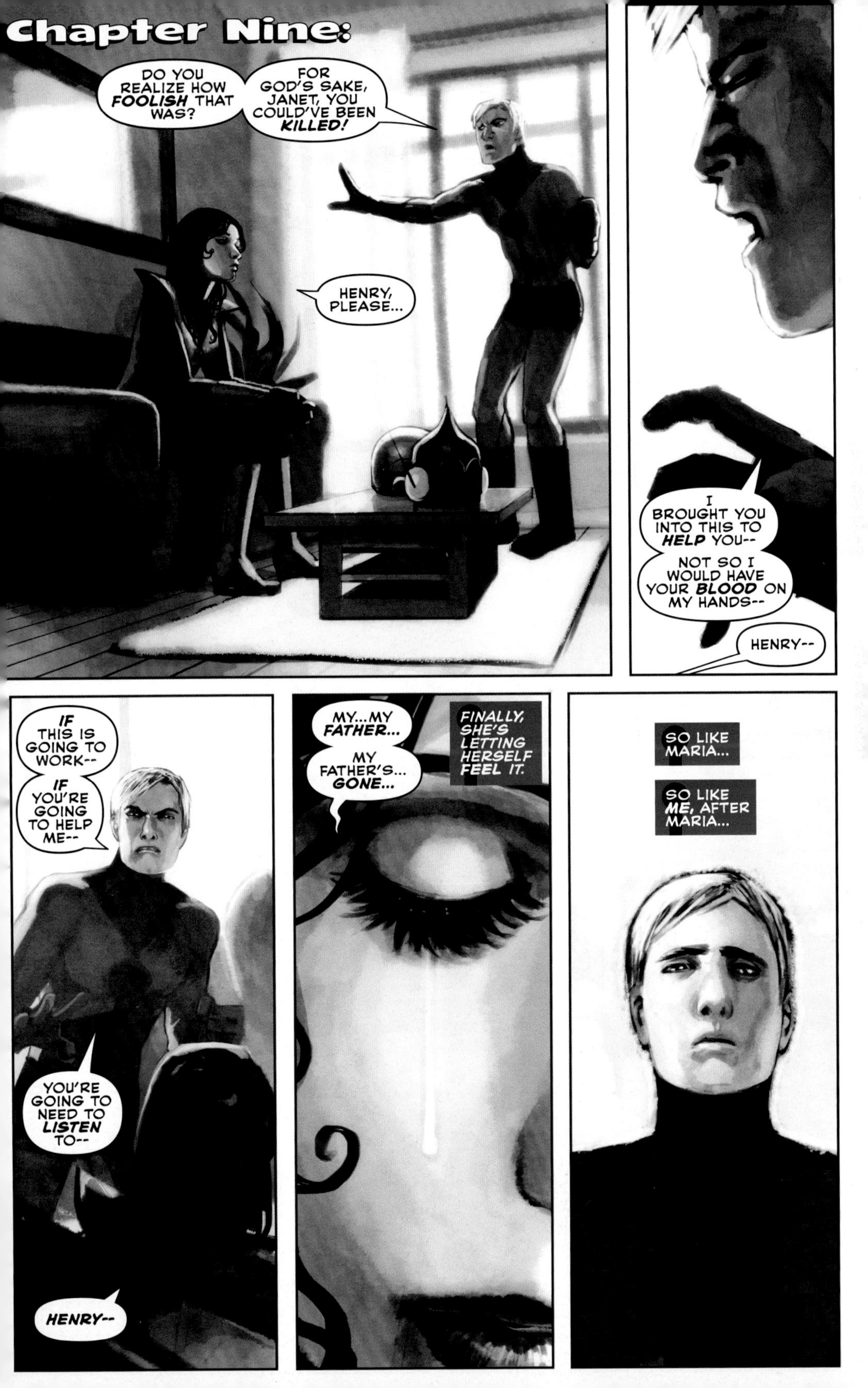
Chapter Nine:
DO YOU REALIZE HOW FOOLISH THAT WAS?
FOR GOD'S SAKE, JANET, YOU COULD'VE BEEN KILLED!
HENRY, PLEASE...
I BROUGHT YOU INTO THIS TO HELP YOU--
NOT SO I WOULD HAVE YOUR BLOOD ON MY HANDS--
HENRY--
IF THIS IS GOING TO WORK--
IF YOU'RE GOING TO HELP ME--
YOU'RE GOING TO NEED TO LISTEN TO--
HENRY--
MY...MY FATHER...
MY FATHER'S... GONE...
FINALLY, SHE'S LETTING HERSELF FEEL IT.
SO LIKE MARIA...
SO LIKE ME, AFTER MARIA...

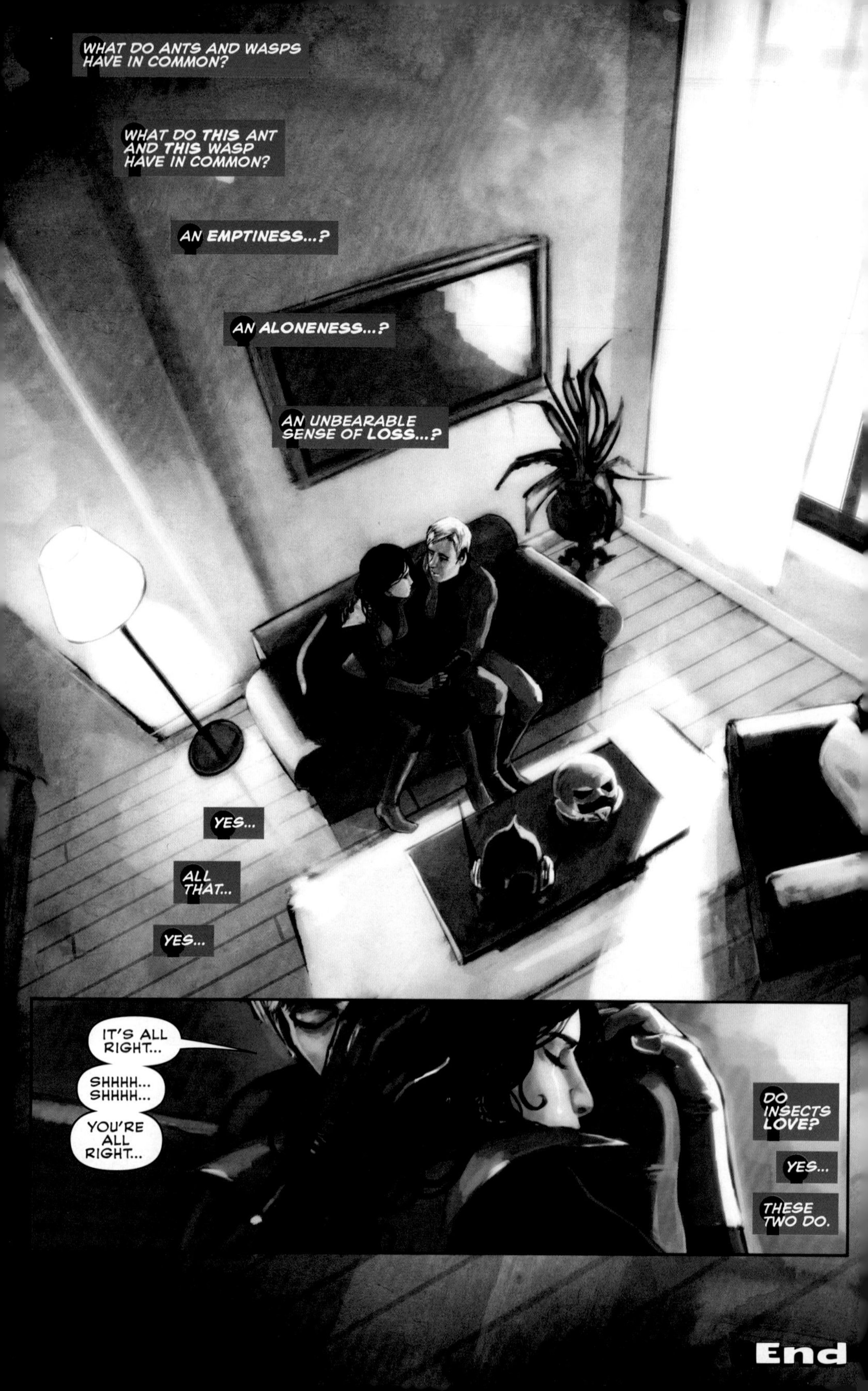
WHAT DO ANTS AND WASPS HAVE IN COMMON?
WHAT DO THIS ANT AND THIS WASP HAVE IN COMMON?
AN EMPTINESS...?
AN ALONENESS...?
AN UNBEARABLE SENSE OF LOSS...?
YES...
ALL THAT...
YES...
IT'S ALL RIGHT...
SHHHH... SHHHH...
YOU'RE ALL RIGHT...
DO INSECTS LOVE?
YES...
THESE TWO DO.
End

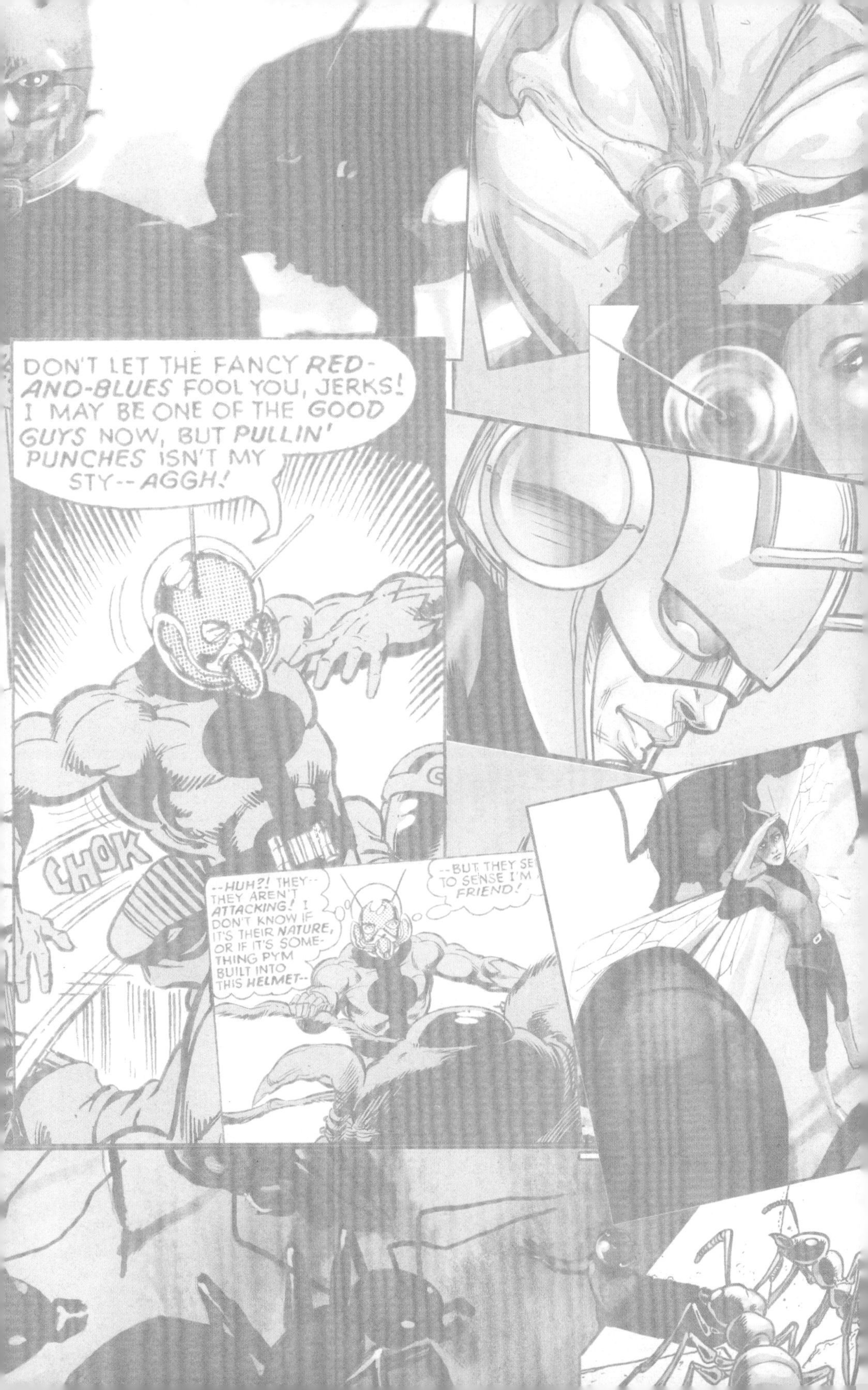

DON'T LET THE FANCY *RED-AND-BLUES* FOOL YOU, JERKS! I MAY BE ONE OF THE *GOOD GUYS* NOW, BUT *PULLIN' PUNCHES* ISN'T MY STY-- *AGGH!*
CHOK
--*HUH?!* THEY-- THEY AREN'T *ATTACKING!* I DON'T KNOW IF IT'S THEIR *NATURE,* OR IF IT'S SOME-THING PYM BUILT INTO THIS *HELMET*--
--BUT THEY SE TO SENSE I'M *FRIEND!*

ANT-MAN: LARGER THAN LIFE

JOIN HANK PYM AS HE LEARNS THAT A LITTLE
EXPERIMENT CAN LEAD TO SOME BIG TROUBLE!

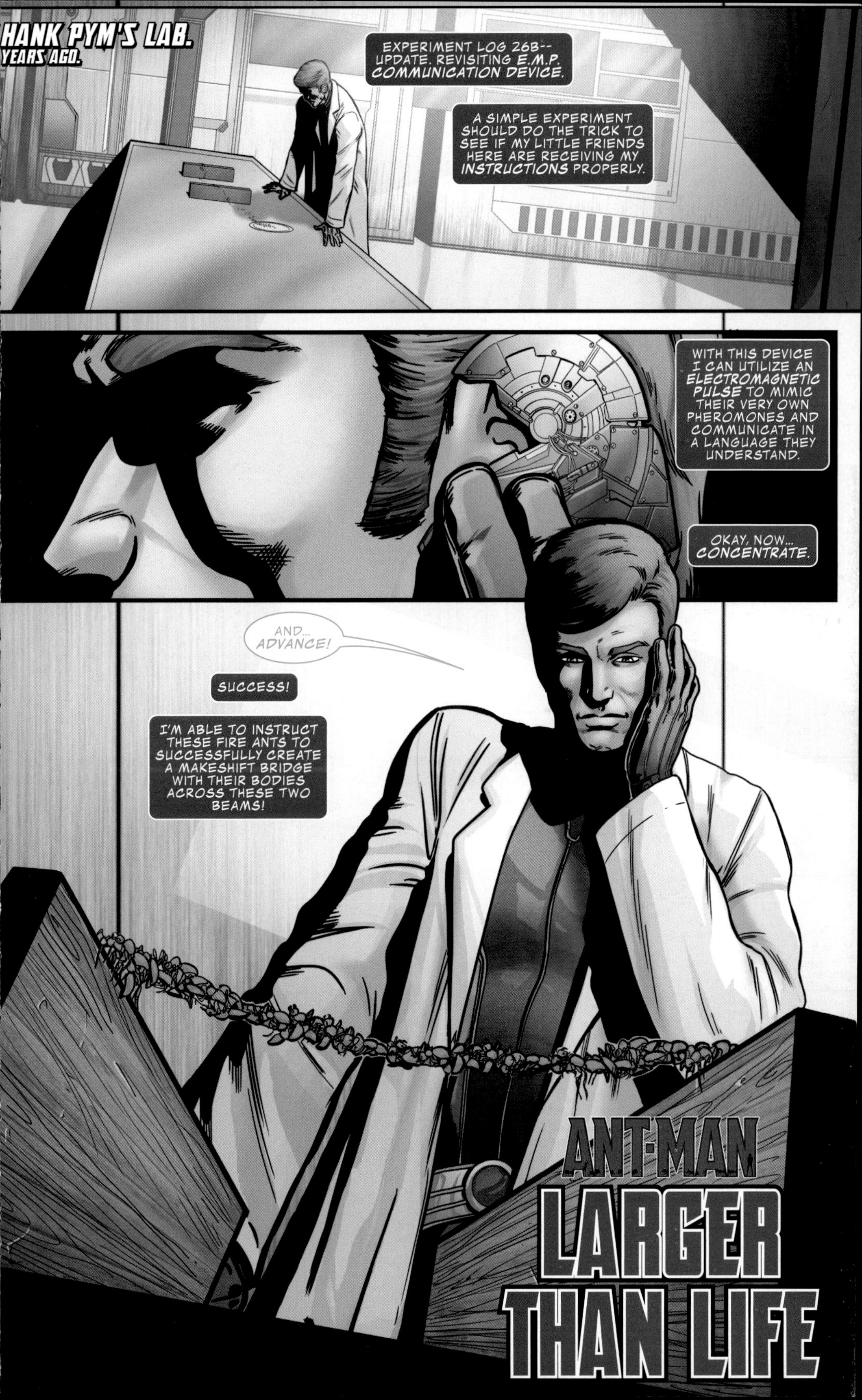

HANK PYM'S LAB. YEARS AGO.
EXPERIMENT LOG 26B-- UPDATE. REVISITING E.M.P. COMMUNICATION DEVICE.
A SIMPLE EXPERIMENT SHOULD DO THE TRICK TO SEE IF MY LITTLE FRIENDS HERE ARE RECEIVING MY INSTRUCTIONS PROPERLY.
WITH THIS DEVICE I CAN UTILIZE AN ELECTROMAGNETIC PULSE TO MIMIC THEIR VERY OWN PHEROMONES AND COMMUNICATE IN A LANGUAGE THEY UNDERSTAND.
OKAY, NOW... CONCENTRATE.
AND... ADVANCE!
SUCCESS!
I'M ABLE TO INSTRUCT THESE FIRE ANTS TO SUCCESSFULLY CREATE A MAKESHIFT BRIDGE WITH THEIR BODIES ACROSS THESE TWO BEAMS!
ANT-MAN
LARGER THAN LIFE

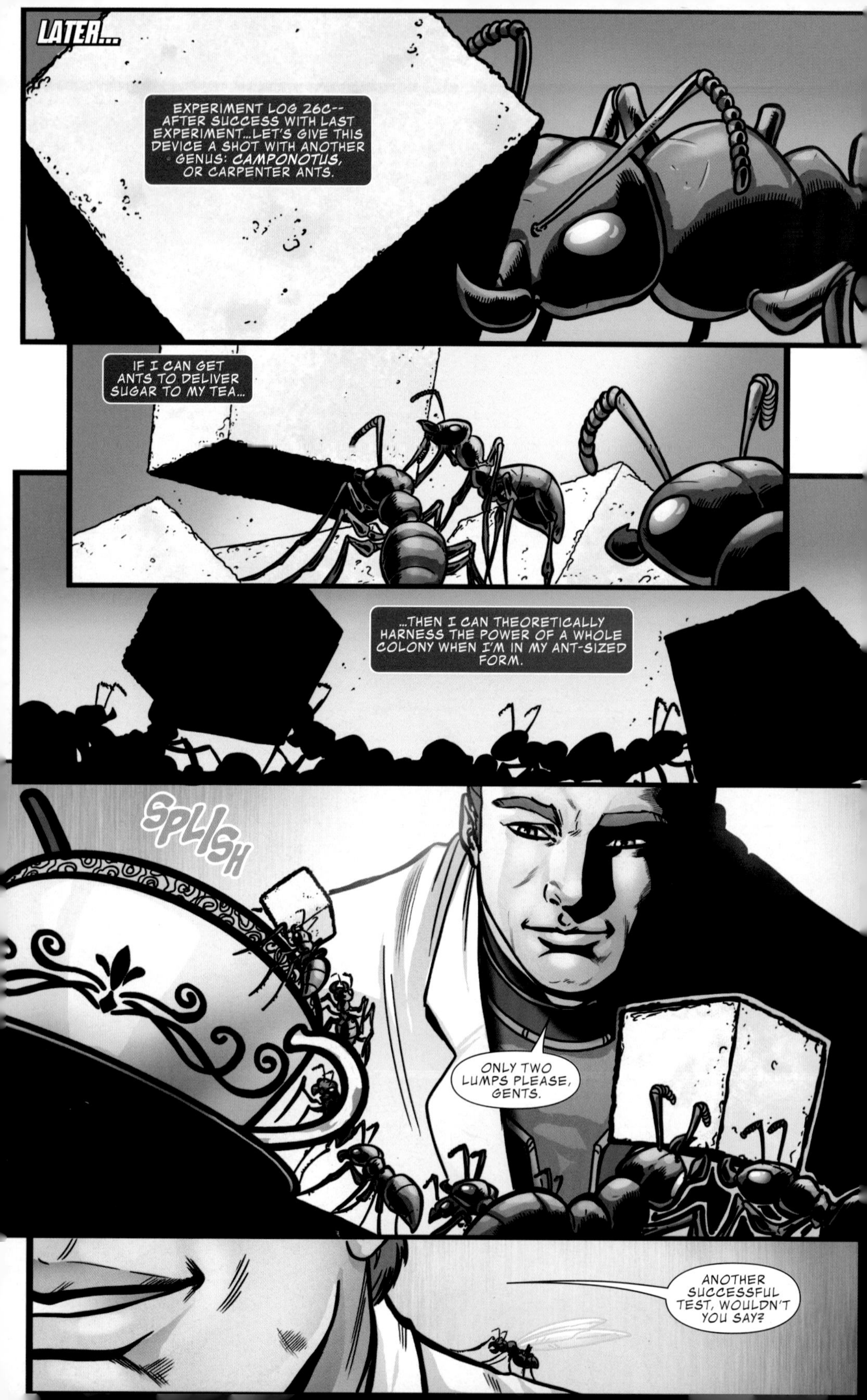
LATER...
EXPERIMENT LOG 26C-- AFTER SUCCESS WITH LAST EXPERIMENT...LET'S GIVE THIS DEVICE A SHOT WITH ANOTHER GENUS: CAMPONOTUS, OR CARPENTER ANTS.
IF I CAN GET ANTS TO DELIVER SUGAR TO MY TEA...
...THEN I CAN THEORETICALLY HARNESS THE POWER OF A WHOLE COLONY WHEN I'M IN MY ANT-SIZED FORM.
SPLISH
ONLY TWO LUMPS PLEASE, GENTS.
ANOTHER SUCCESSFUL TEST, WOULDN'T YOU SAY?

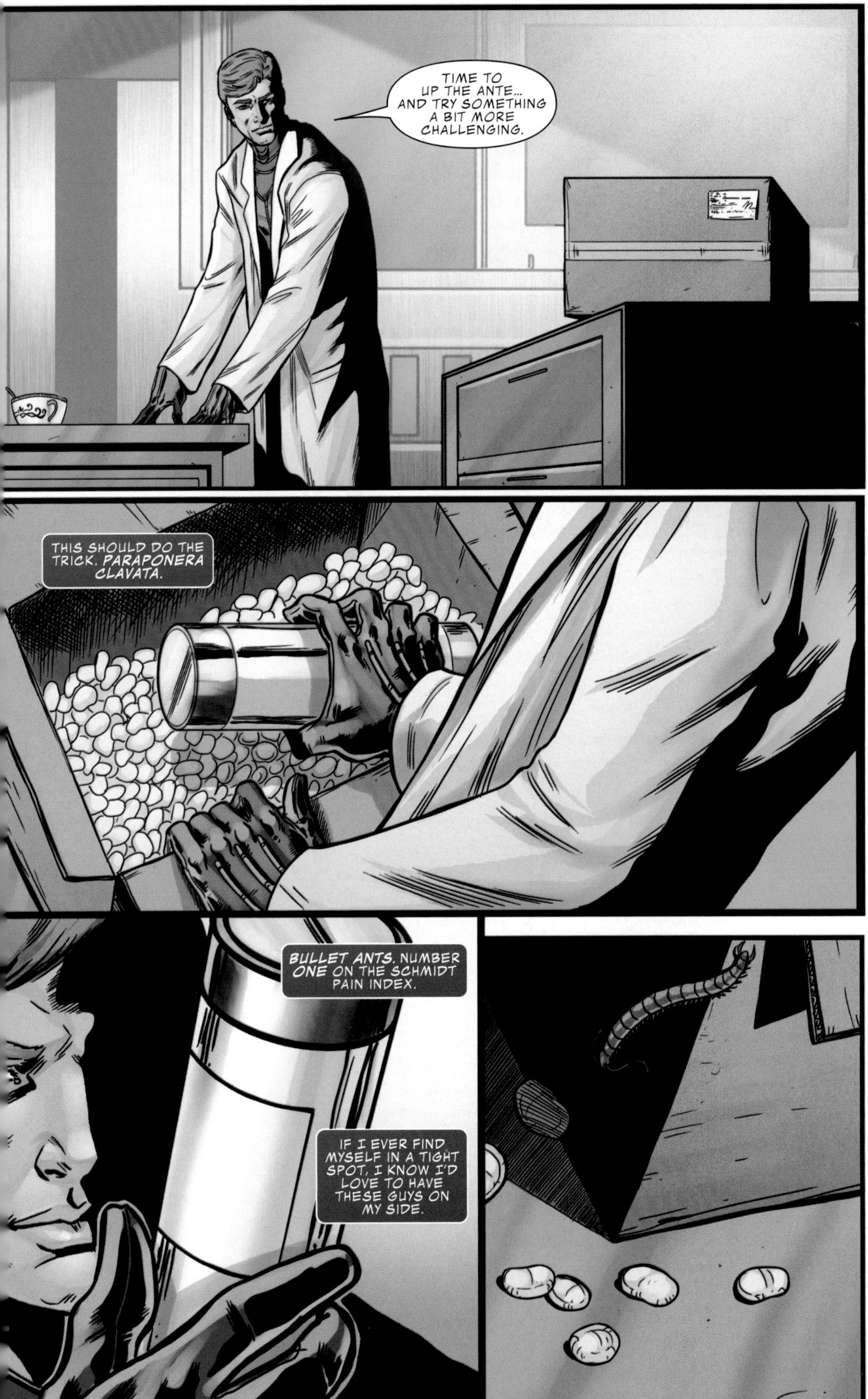
TIME TO UP THE ANTE... AND TRY SOMETHING A BIT MORE CHALLENGING.
THIS SHOULD DO THE TRICK. *PARAPONERA CLAVATA.*
BULLET ANTS. NUMBER *ONE* ON THE SCHMIDT PAIN INDEX.
IF I EVER FIND MYSELF IN A TIGHT SPOT, I KNOW I'D LOVE TO HAVE THESE GUYS ON MY SIDE.

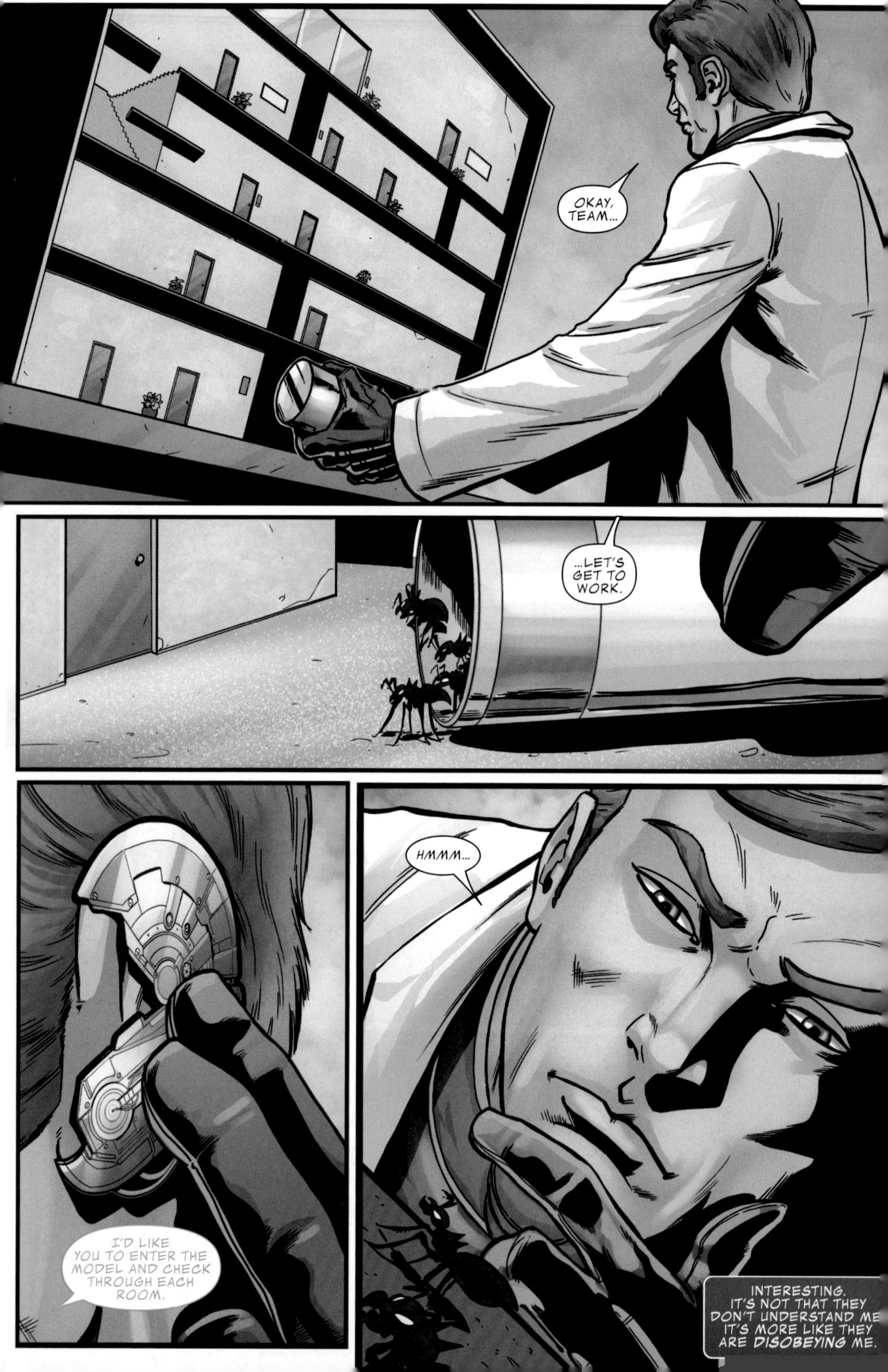
OKAY, TEAM...
...LET'S GET TO WORK.
I'D LIKE YOU TO ENTER THE MODEL AND CHECK THROUGH EACH ROOM.
HMMM...
INTERESTING. IT'S NOT THAT THEY DON'T UNDERSTAND ME. IT'S MORE LIKE THEY ARE DISOBEYING ME.

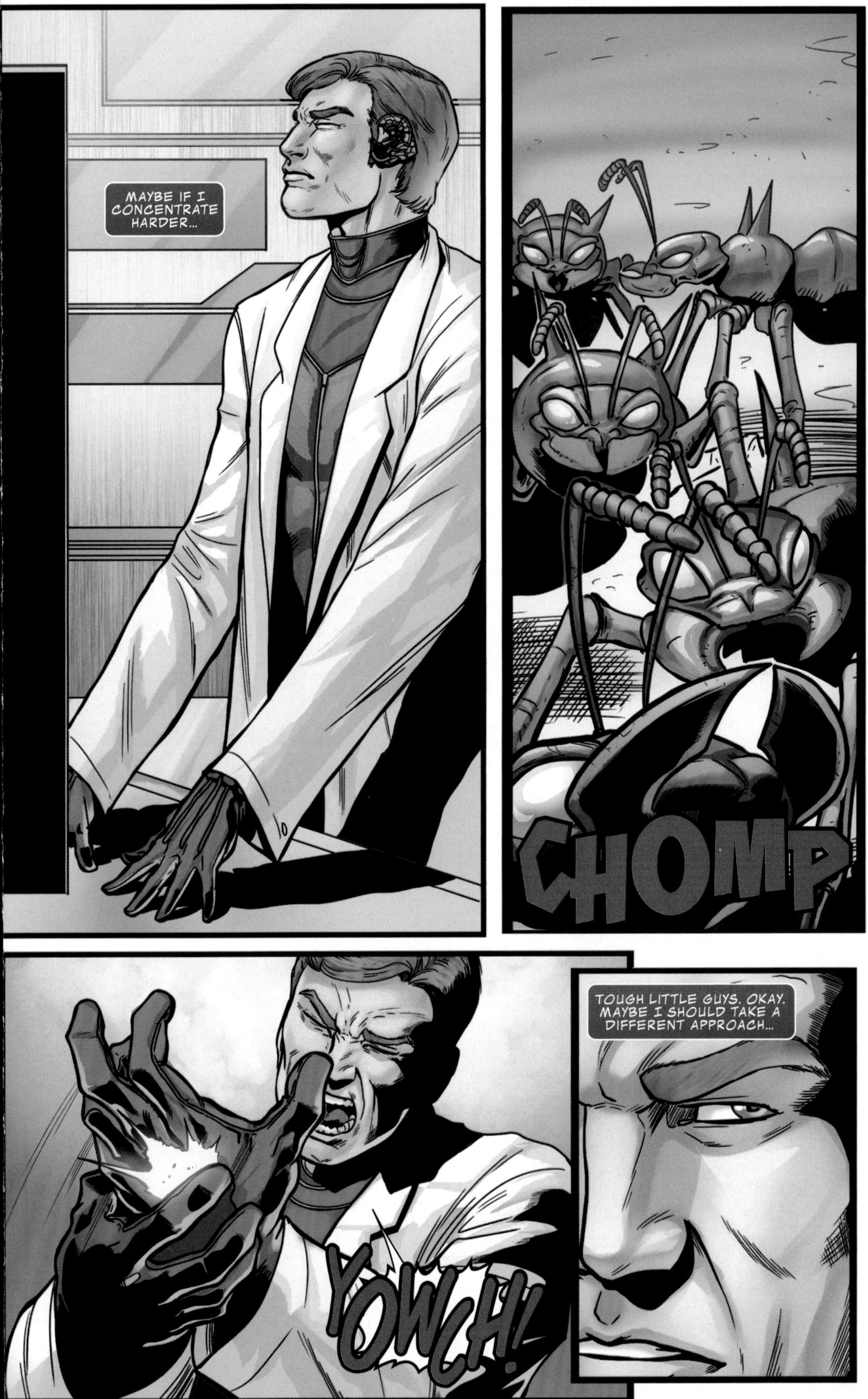
MAYBE IF I CONCENTRATE HARDER...
CHOMP
YOWCH!
TOUGH LITTLE GUYS. OKAY. MAYBE I SHOULD TAKE A DIFFERENT APPROACH...

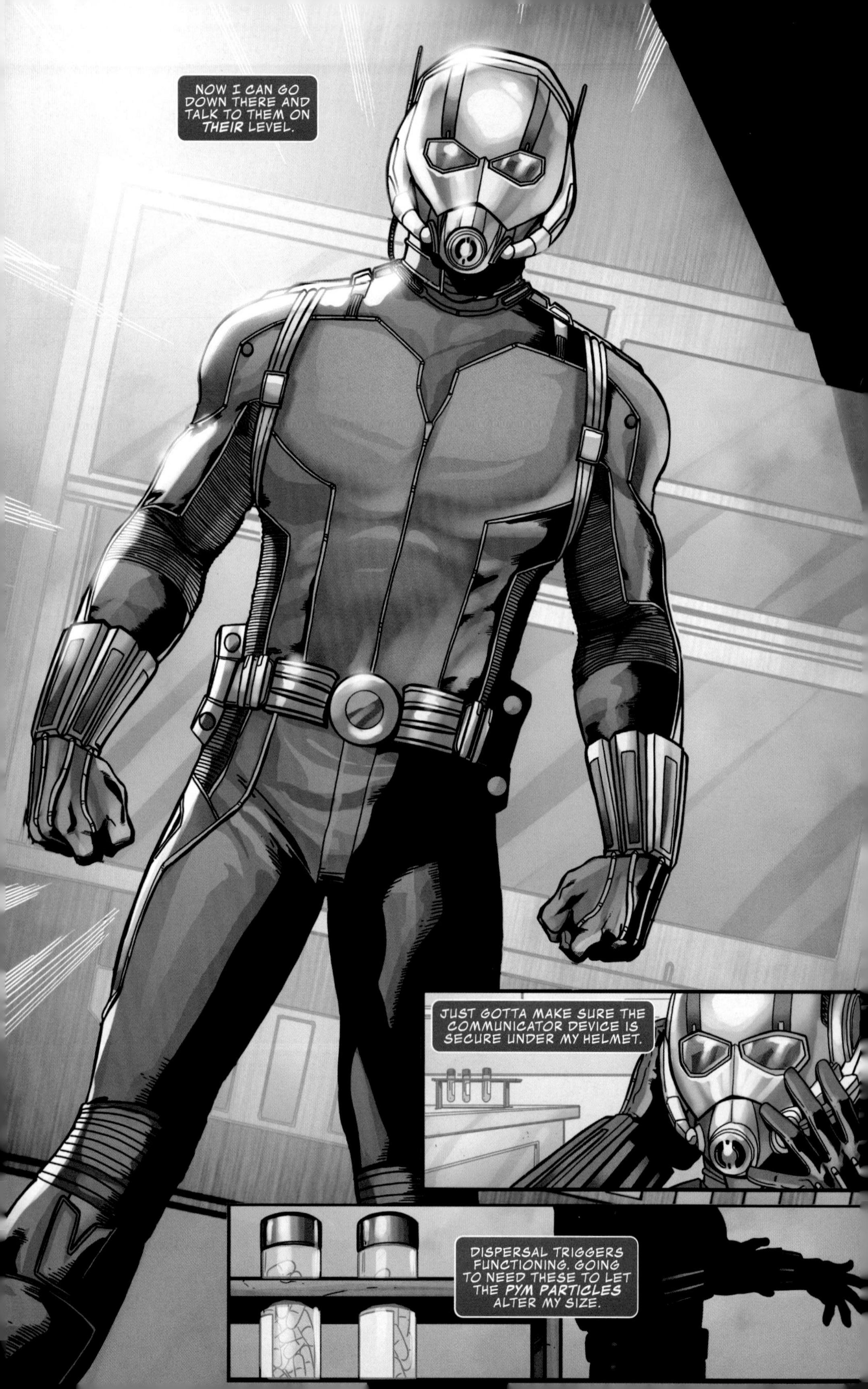
NOW I CAN GO DOWN THERE AND TALK TO THEM ON *THEIR* LEVEL.
JUST GOTTA MAKE SURE THE COMMUNICATOR DEVICE IS SECURE UNDER MY HELMET.
DISPERSAL TRIGGERS FUNCTIONING. GOING TO NEED THESE TO LET THE *PYM PARTICLES* ALTER MY SIZE.

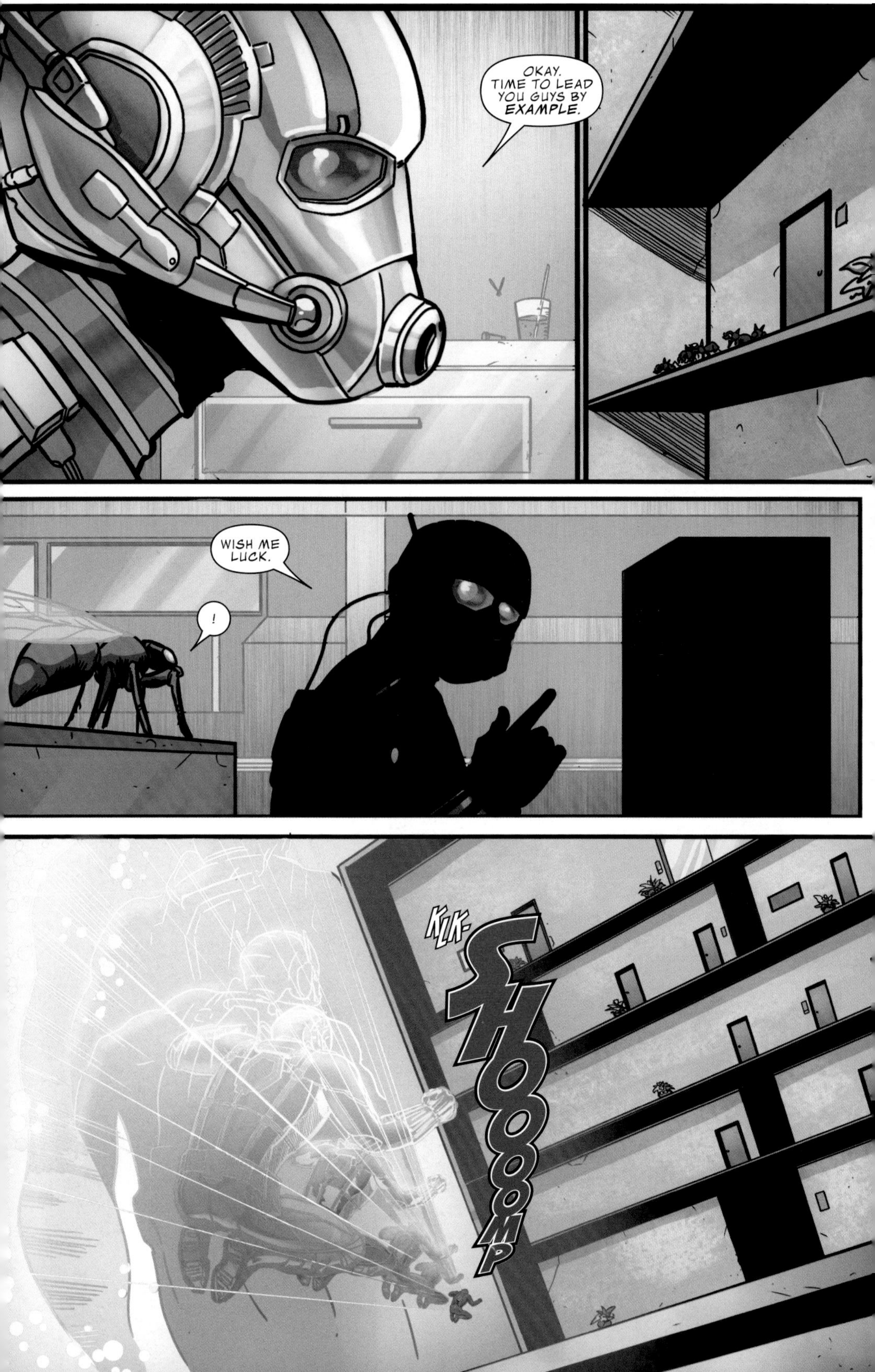
OKAY. TIME TO LEAD YOU GUYS BY EXAMPLE.
WISH ME LUCK.
!
KLK-
SHOOOOOMP

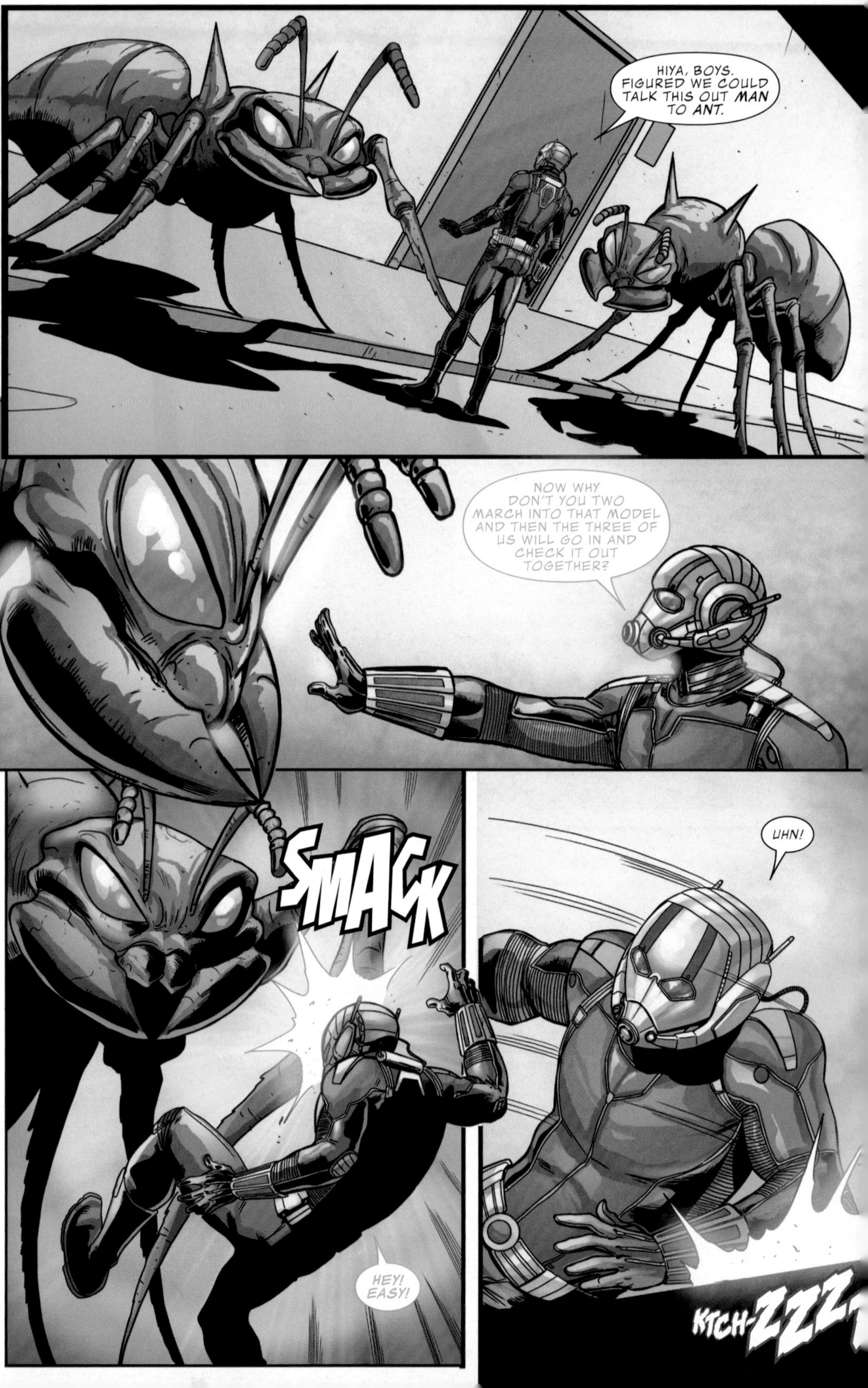
HIYA, BOYS. FIGURED WE COULD TALK THIS OUT MAN TO ANT.
NOW WHY DON'T YOU TWO MARCH INTO THAT MODEL AND THEN THE THREE OF US WILL GO IN AND CHECK IT OUT TOGETHER?
SMACK
HEY! EASY!
UHN!
KTCH-ZZZ

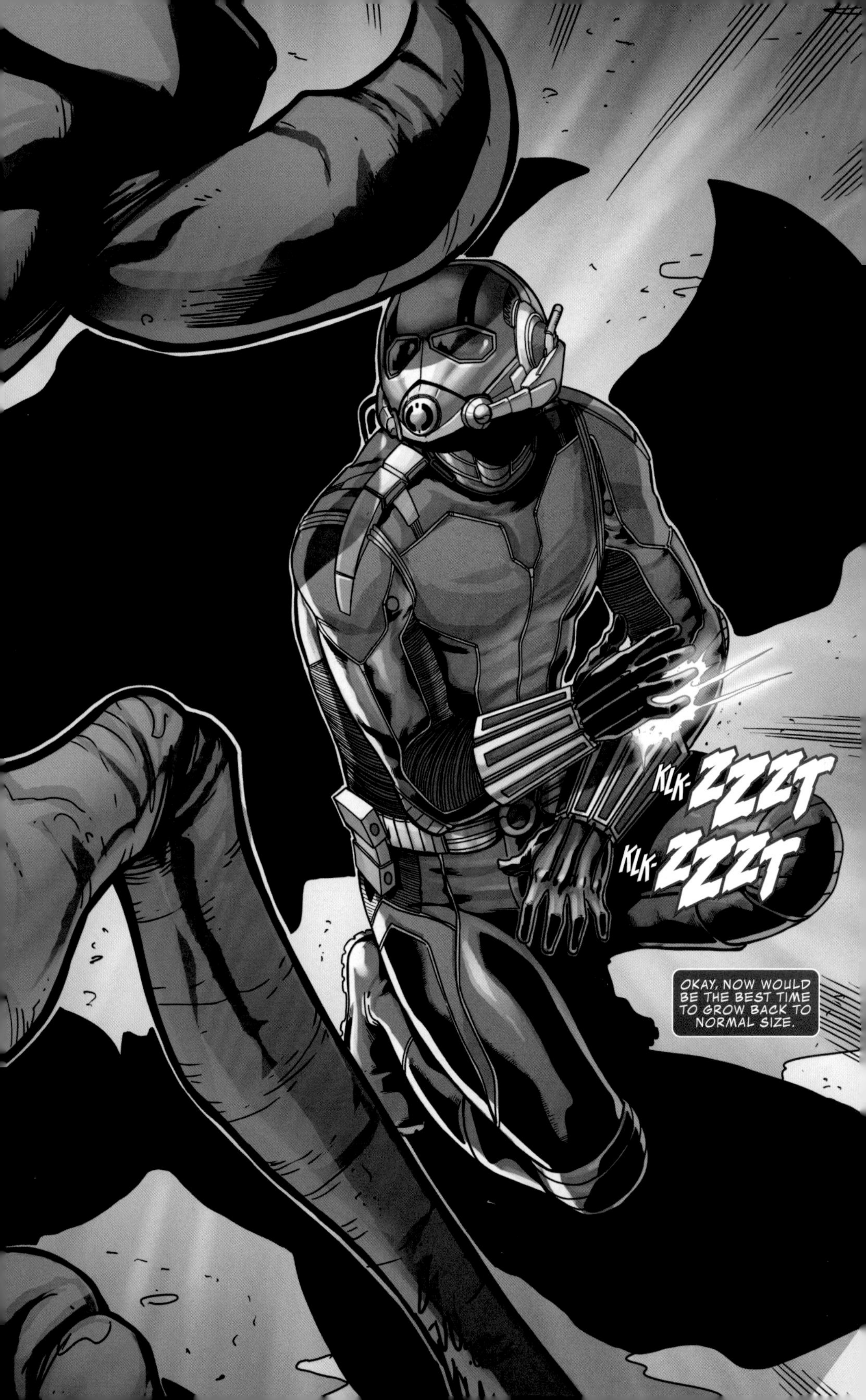
KLK-ZZZT
KLK-ZZZT
OKAY, NOW WOULD BE THE BEST TIME TO GROW BACK TO NORMAL SIZE.

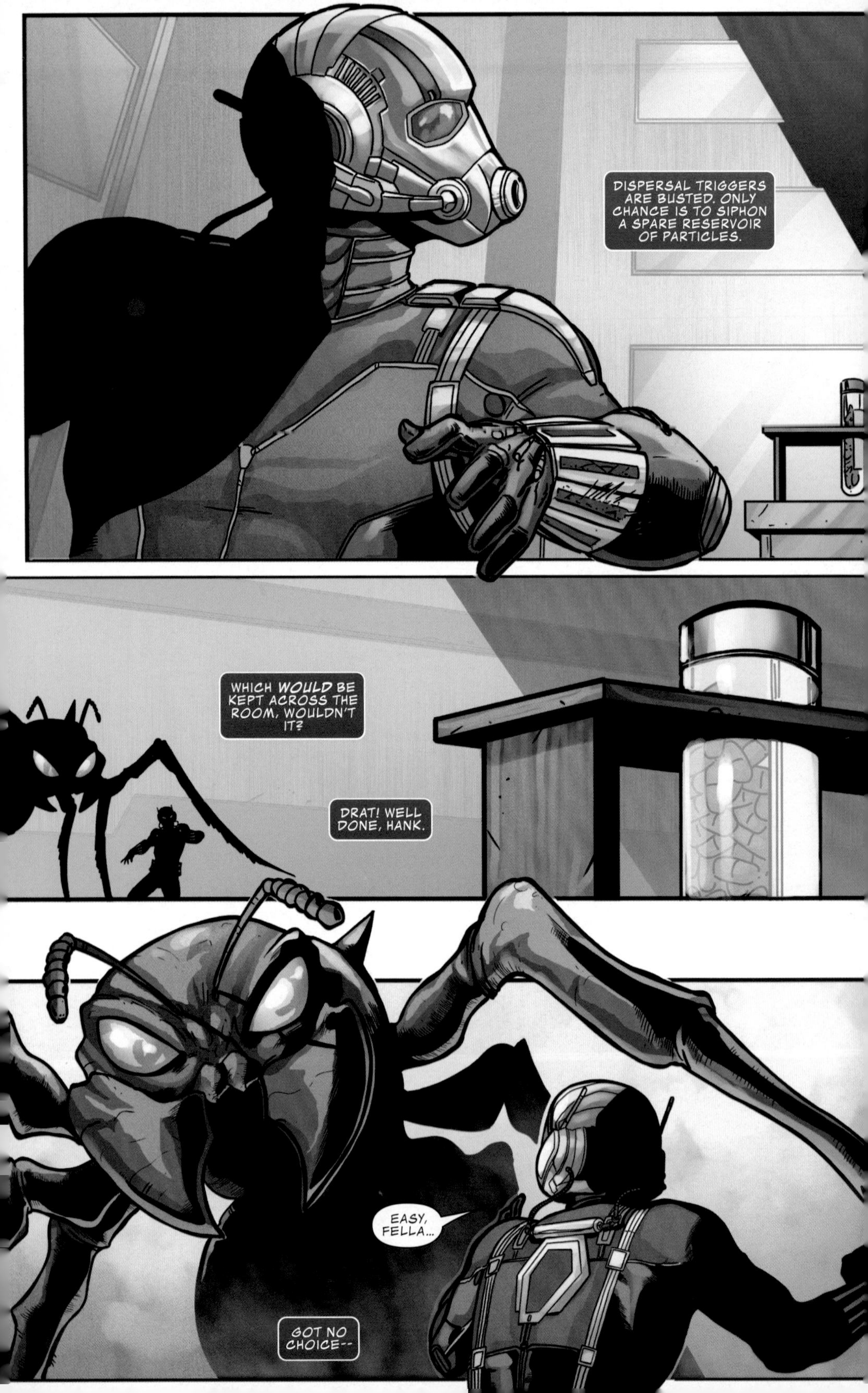
DISPERSAL TRIGGERS ARE BUSTED. ONLY CHANCE IS TO SIPHON A SPARE RESERVOIR OF PARTICLES.
WHICH *WOULD* BE KEPT ACROSS THE ROOM, WOULDN'T IT?
DRAT! WELL DONE, HANK.
EASY, FELLA...
GOT NO CHOICE--

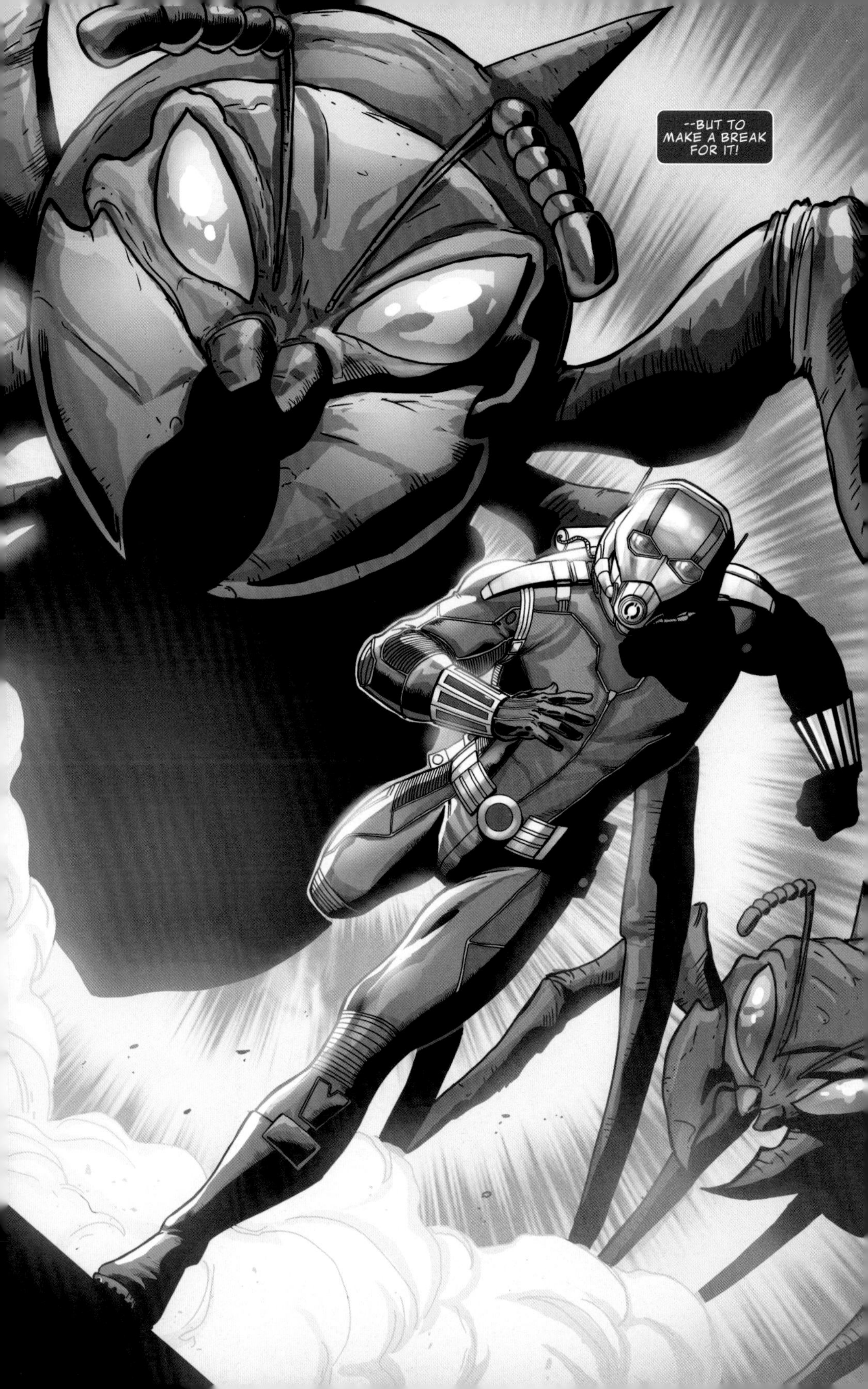
--BUT TO MAKE A BREAK FOR IT!

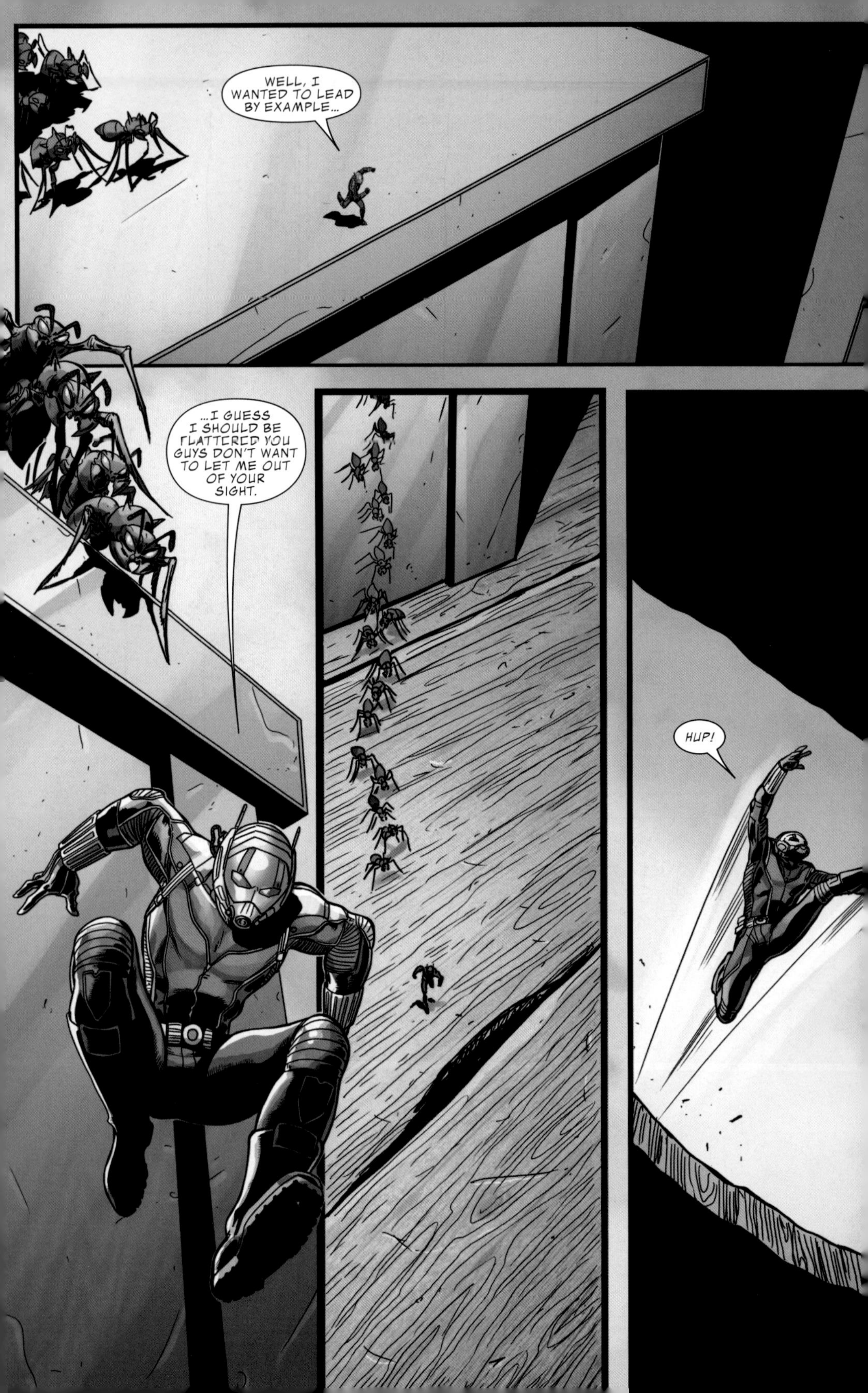
WELL, I WANTED TO LEAD BY EXAMPLE...
...I GUESS I SHOULD BE FLATTERED YOU GUYS DON'T WANT TO LET ME OUT OF YOUR SIGHT.
HUP!

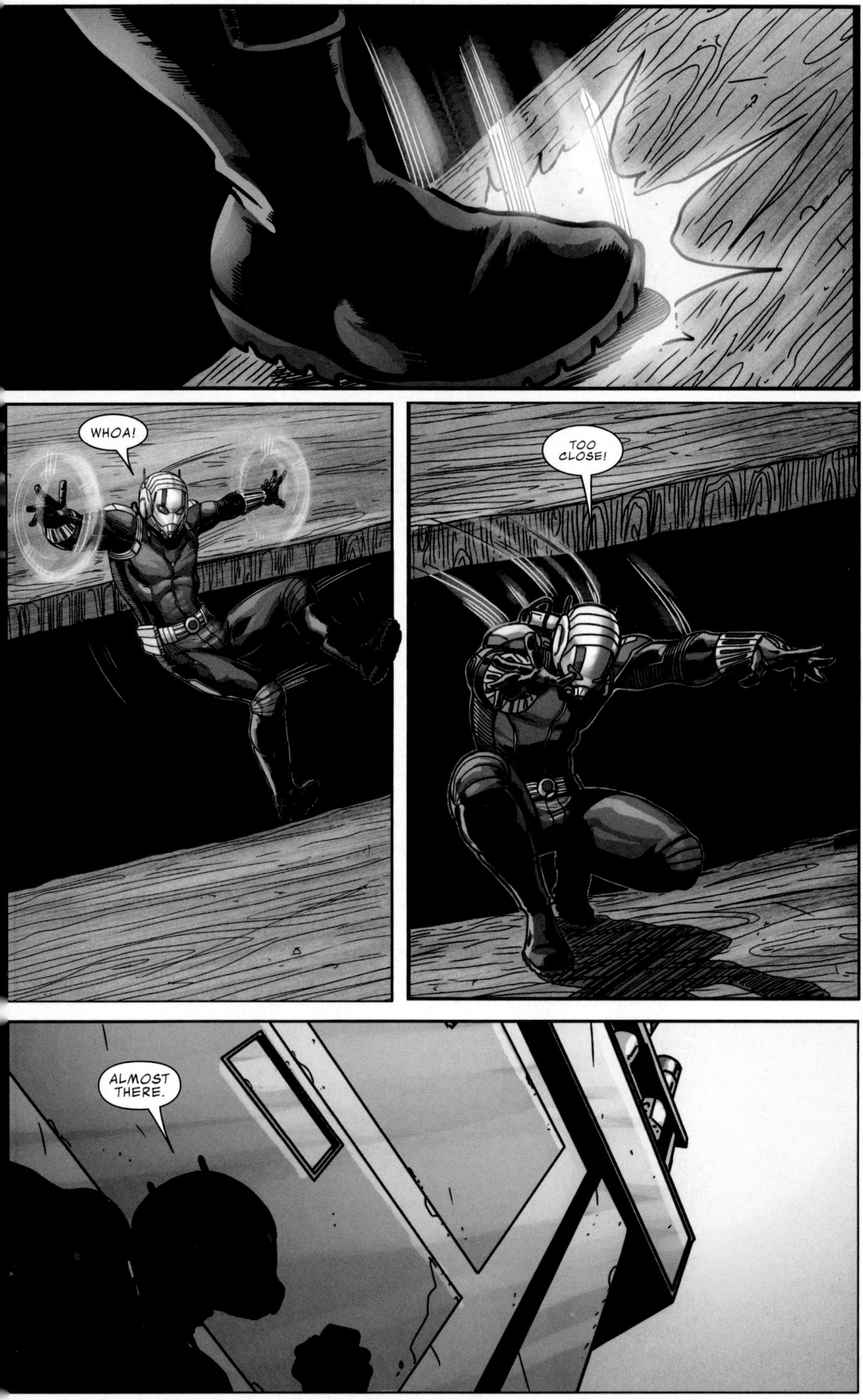
WHOA!
TOO CLOSE!
ALMOST THERE.

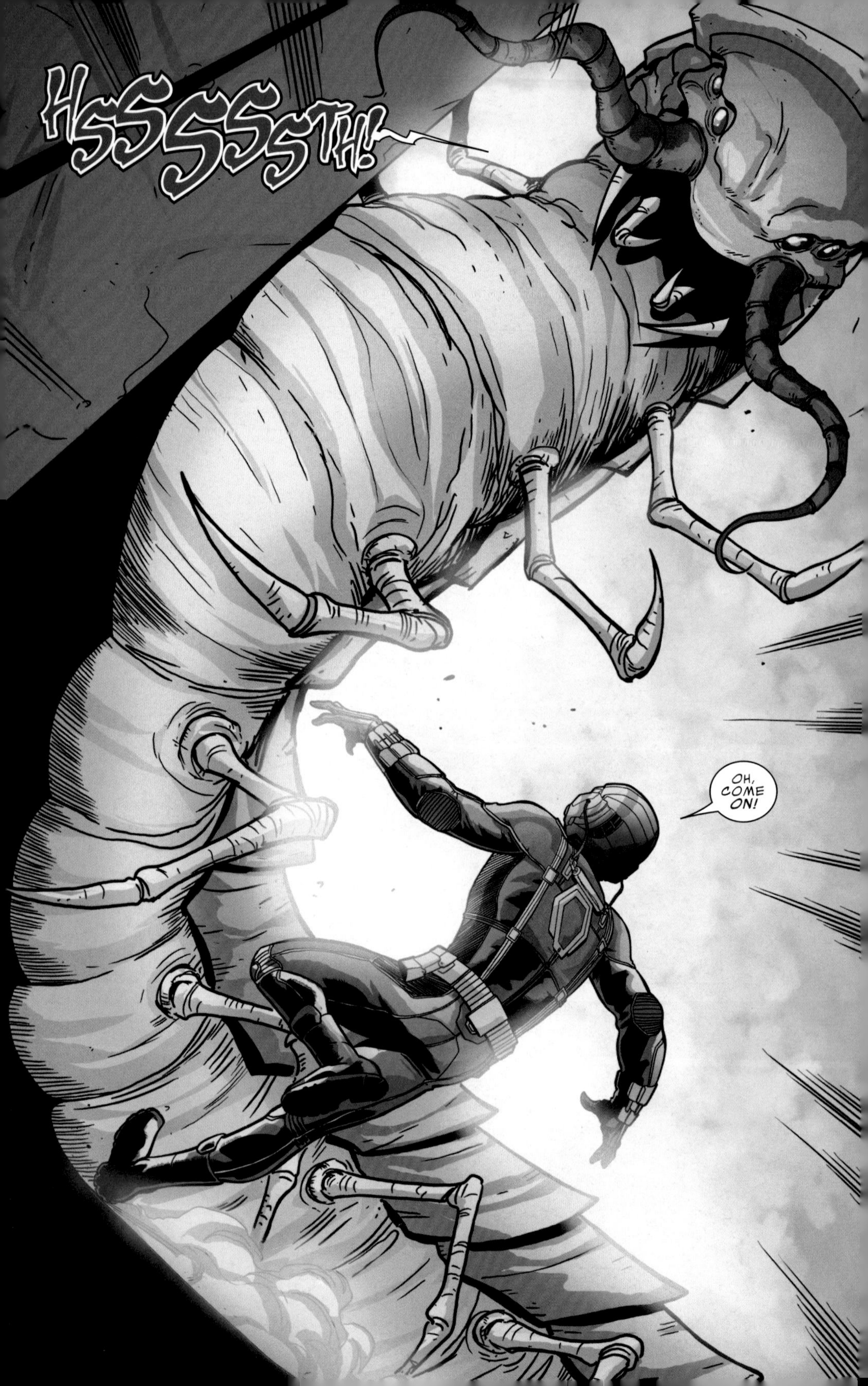
HSSSSSTH!
OH, COME ON!

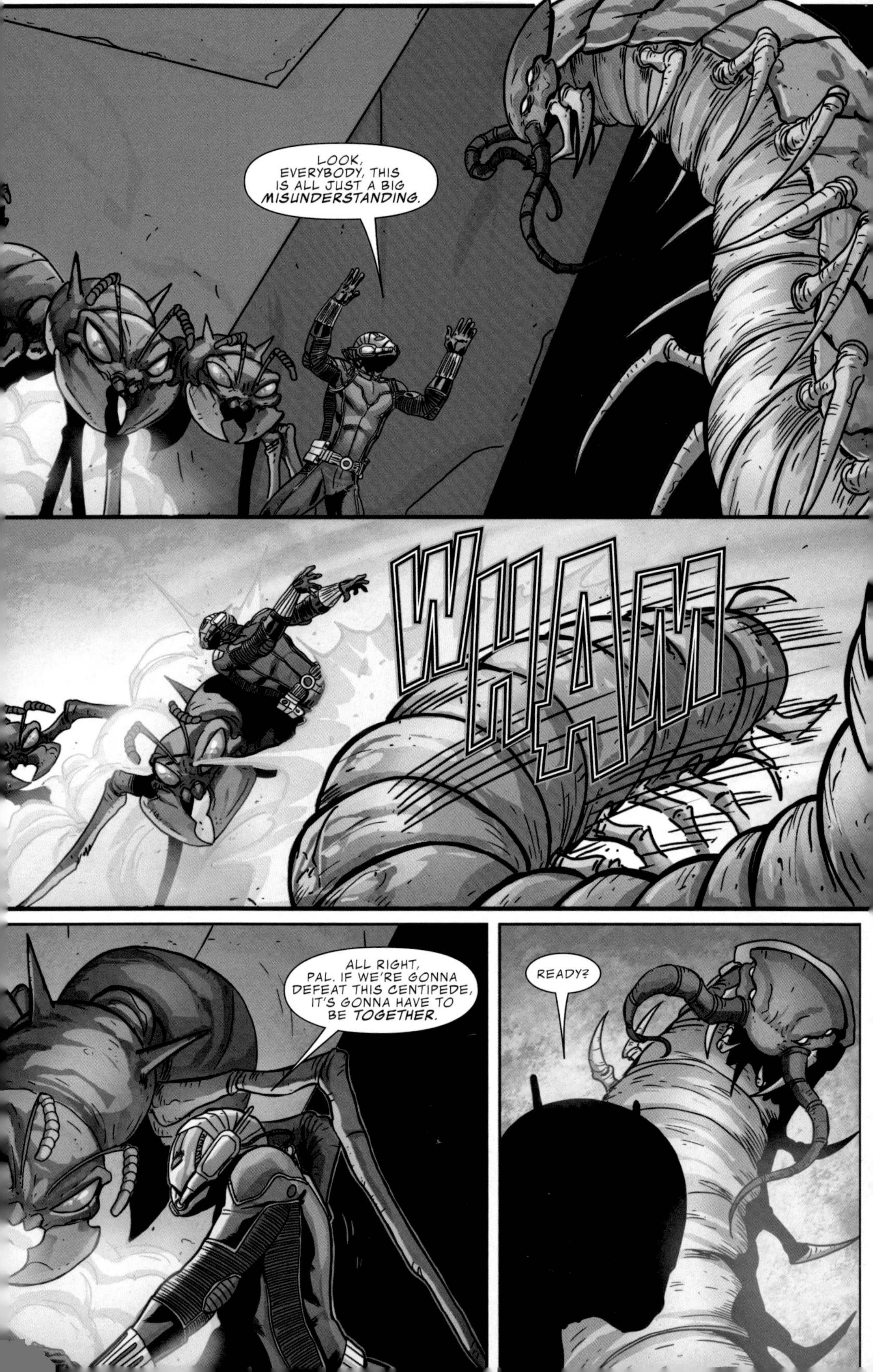
LOOK, EVERYBODY, THIS IS ALL JUST A BIG *MISUNDERSTANDING*.
WHAM
ALL RIGHT, PAL. IF WE'RE GONNA DEFEAT THIS CENTIPEDE, IT'S GONNA HAVE TO BE *TOGETHER*.
READY?

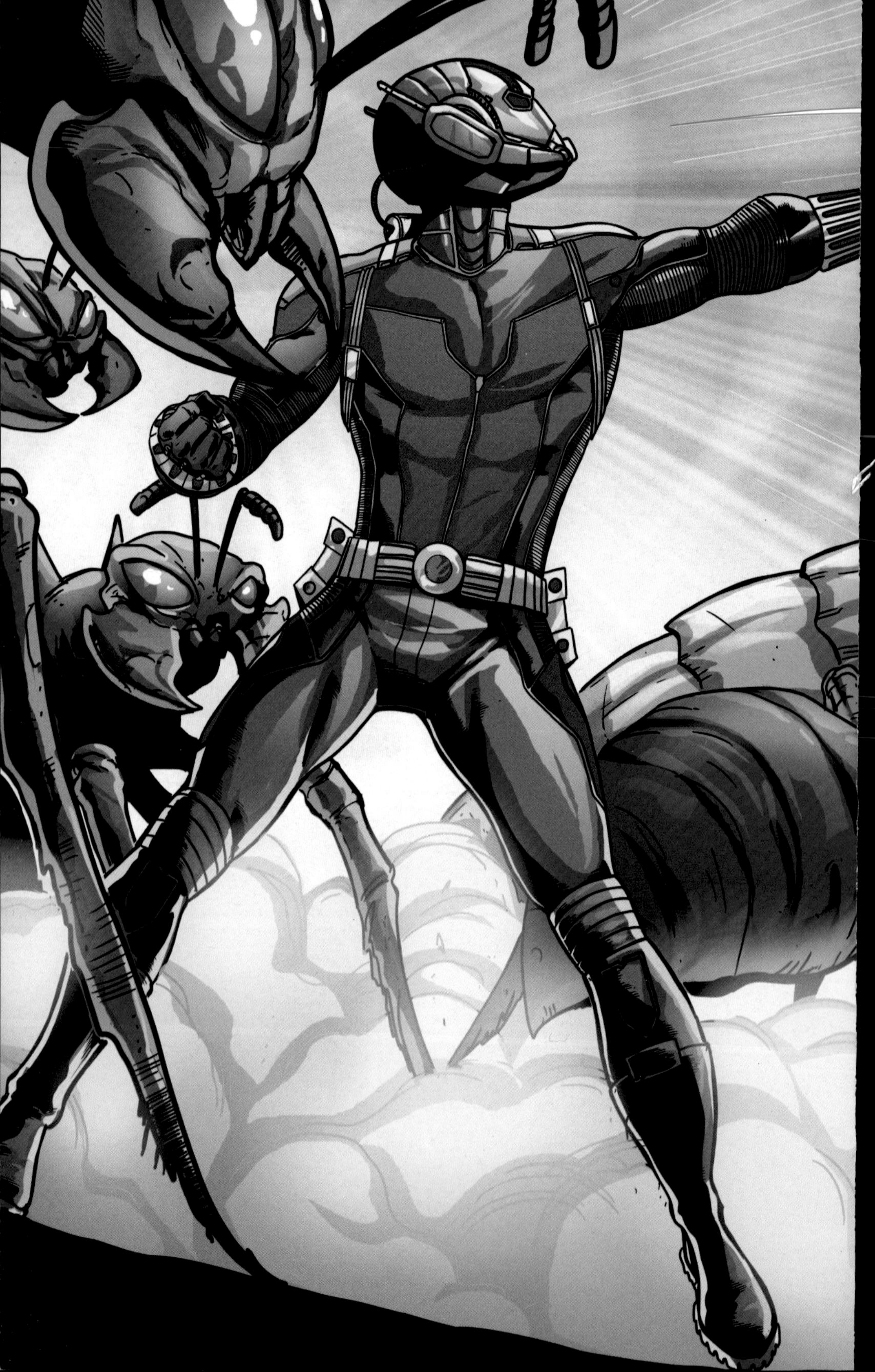

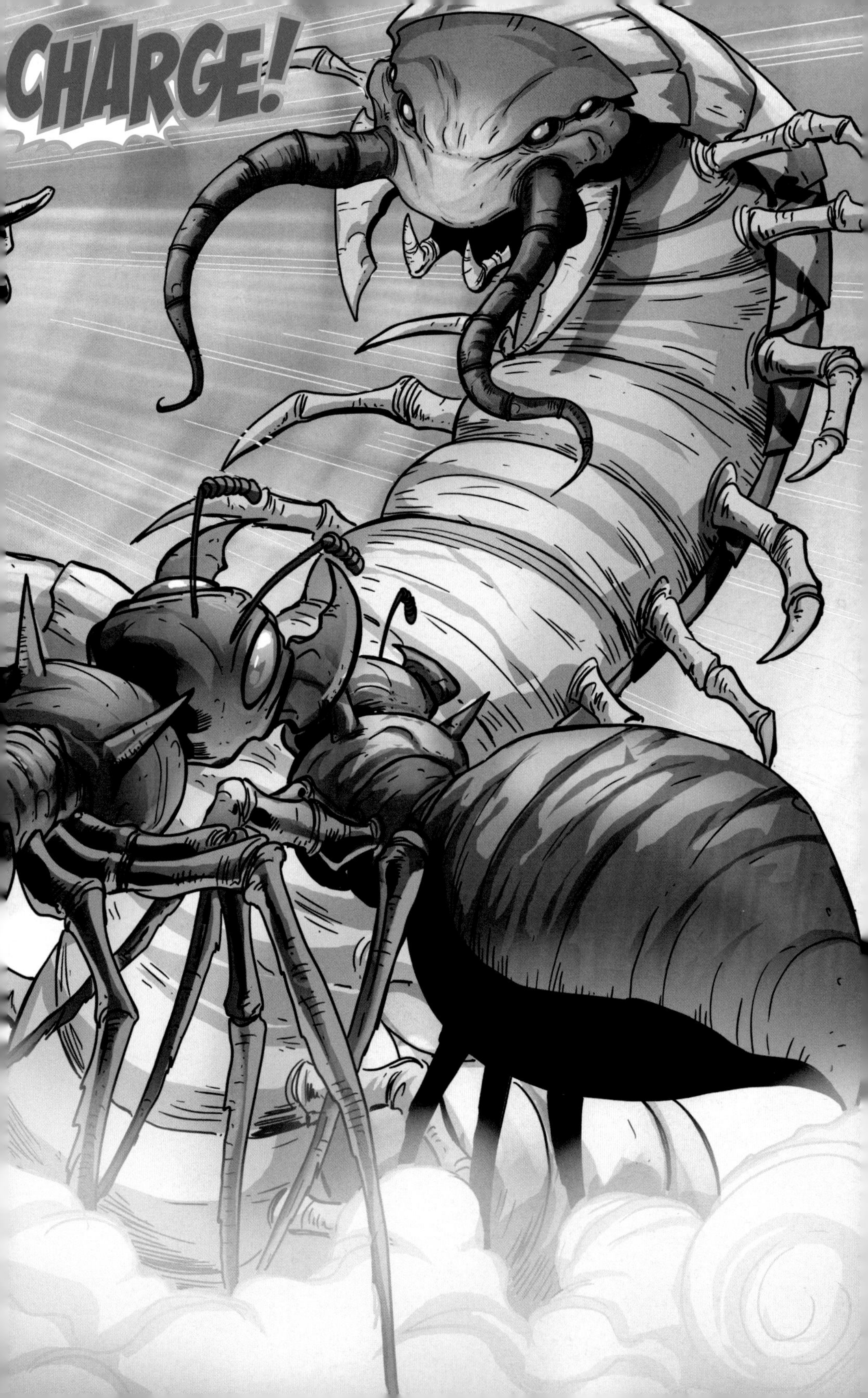
CHARGE!

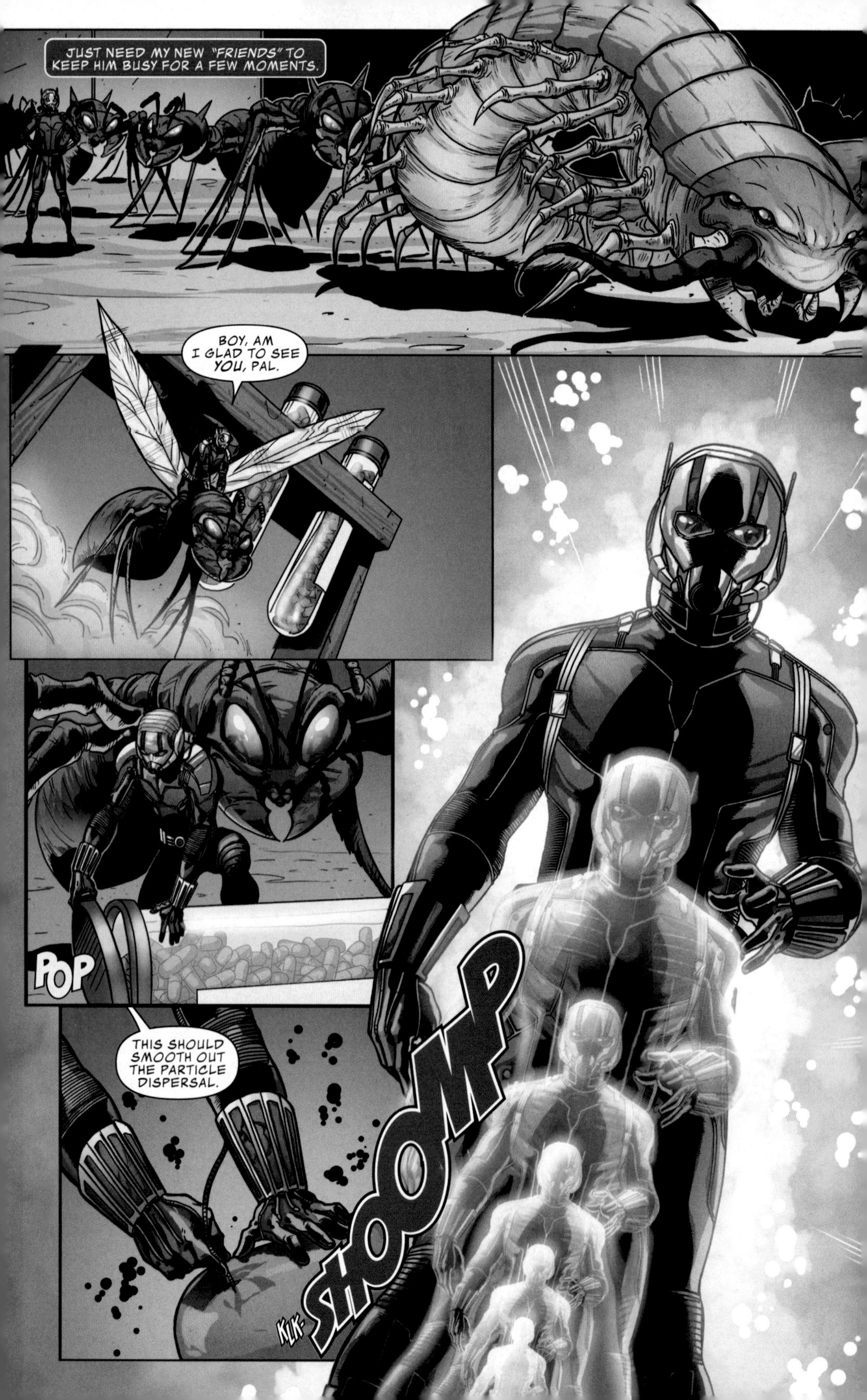
JUST NEED MY NEW "FRIENDS" TO KEEP HIM BUSY FOR A FEW MOMENTS.
BOY, AM I GLAD TO SEE YOU, PAL.
POP
THIS SHOULD SMOOTH OUT THE PARTICLE DISPERSAL.
KLIK-
SHOOMP

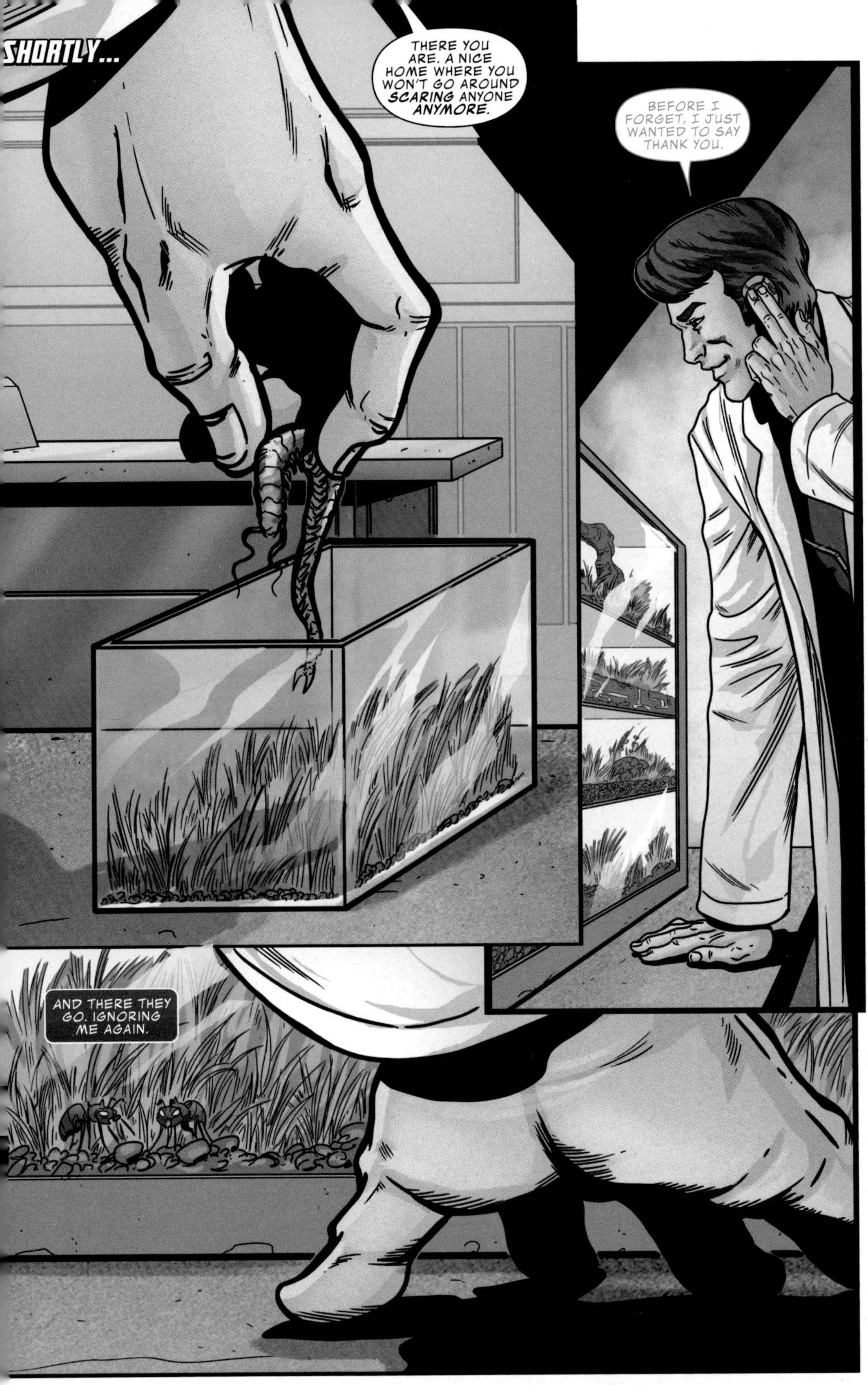
SHORTLY...
THERE YOU ARE. A NICE HOME WHERE YOU WON'T GO AROUND SCARING ANYONE ANYMORE.
BEFORE I FORGET, I JUST WANTED TO SAY THANK YOU.
AND THERE THEY GO. IGNORING ME AGAIN.

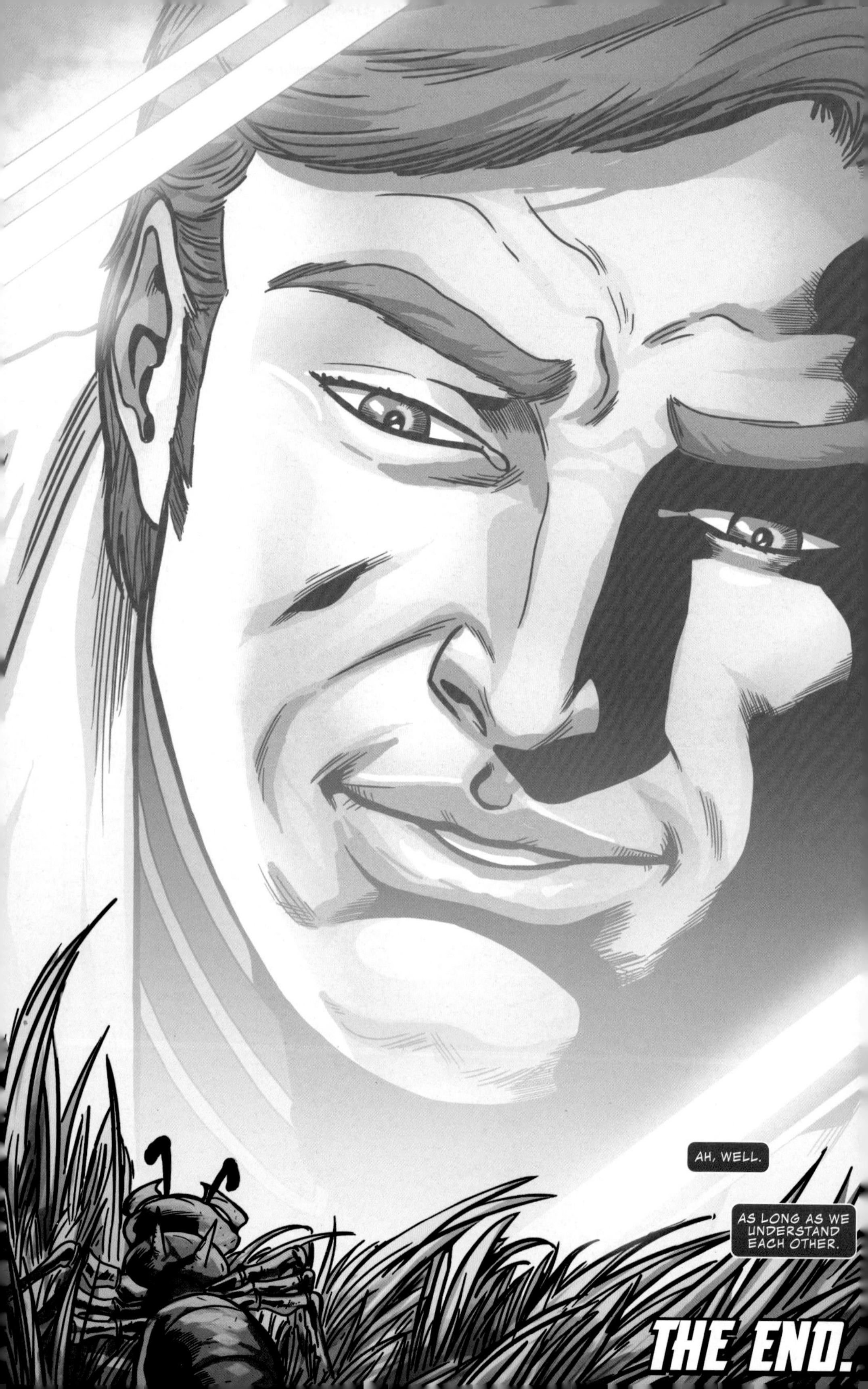
AH, WELL.
AS LONG AS WE UNDERSTAND EACH OTHER.
THE END.

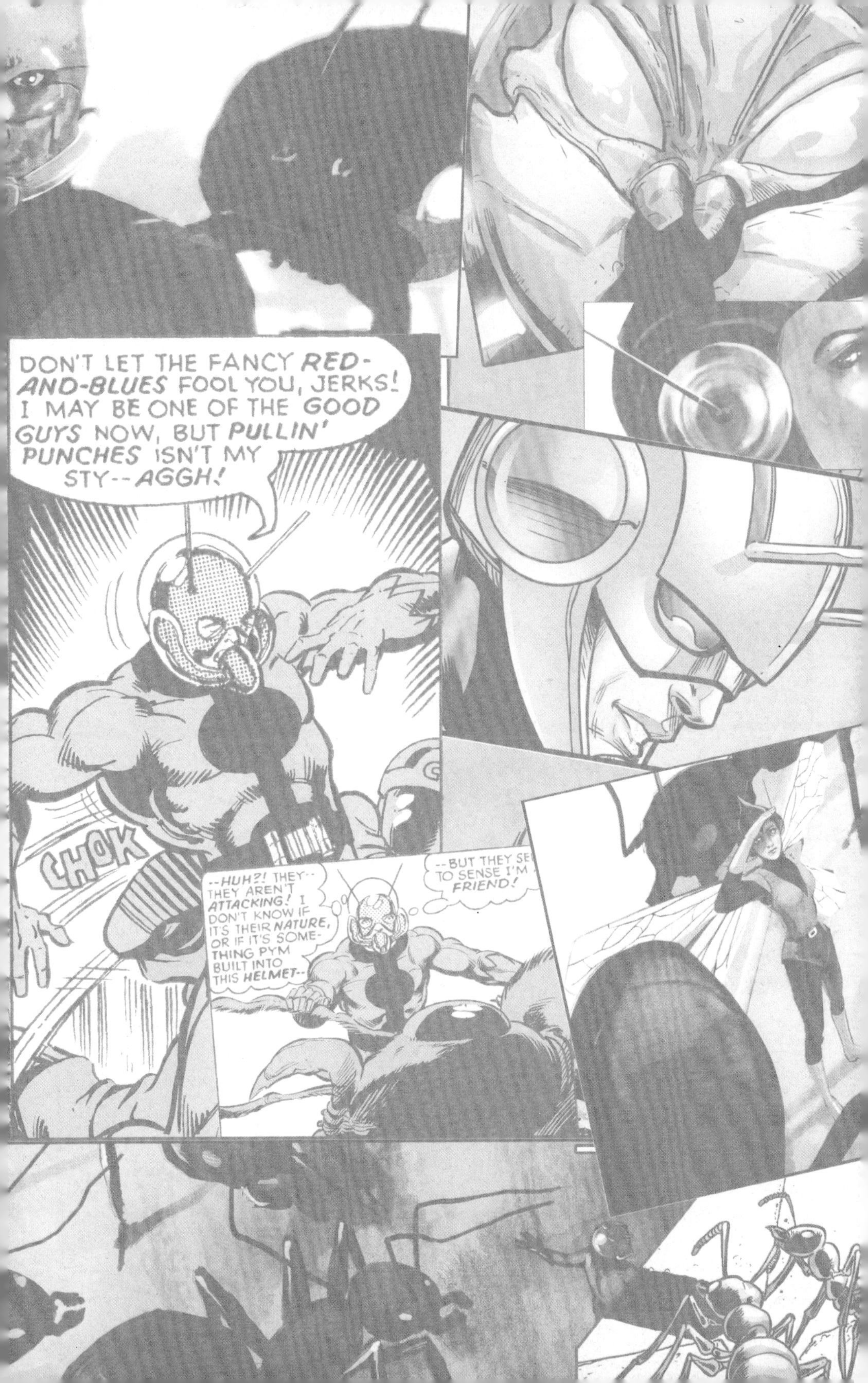
DON'T LET THE FANCY RED-AND-BLUES FOOL YOU, JERKS! I MAY BE ONE OF THE GOOD GUYS NOW, BUT PULLIN' PUNCHES ISN'T MY STY--AGGH!
CHOK
--HUH?! THEY--THEY AREN'T ATTACKING! I DON'T KNOW IF IT'S THEIR NATURE, OR IF IT'S SOME-THING PYM BUILT INTO THIS HELMET--
--BUT THEY SE
TO SENSE I'M
FRIEND!

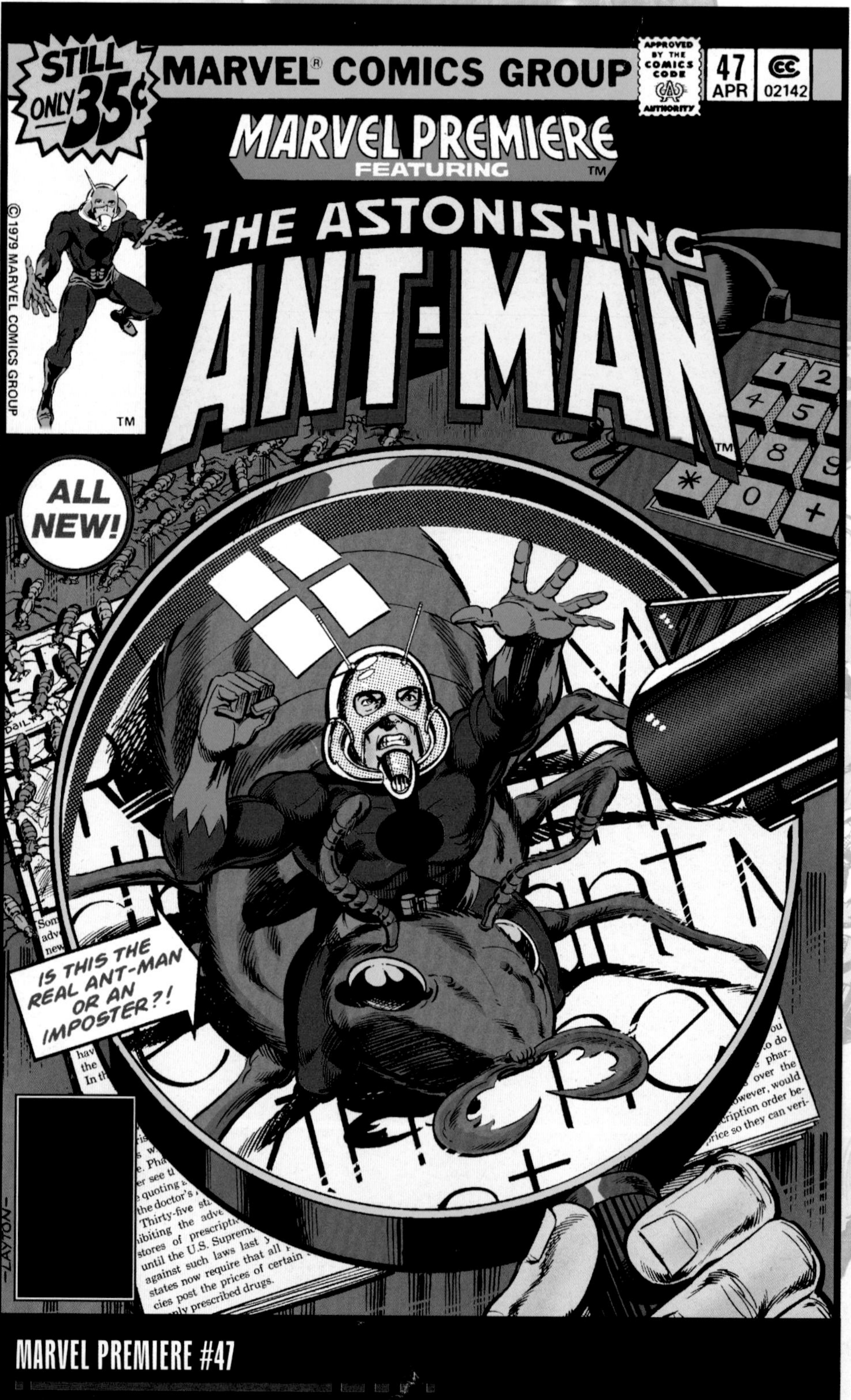
STILL ONLY 35¢
MARVEL® COMICS GROUP
APPROVED BY THE COMICS CODE AUTHORITY
47 APR
CC 02142
MARVEL PREMIERE FEATURING ™
THE ASTONISHING ANT-MAN ™
© 1979 MARVEL COMICS GROUP
™
ALL NEW!
IS THIS THE REAL ANT-MAN OR AN IMPOSTER?!
-LAYTON-

MARVEL PREMIERE #47

SCOTT LANG SHRINKS ONTO THE SCENE AS THE NEW ANT-MAN IN HIS FIRST ADVENTURE, PITTING HIM AGAINST DARREN CROSS!

Stan Lee Presents: **THE ALL-NEW ANT-MAN** ™

DAVID MICHELINIE, *writer* •• JOHN BYRNE & BOB LAYTON, *artists*
TOM ORZECHOWSKI, *letterer* • BOB SHAREN, *colorist* • ROGER STERN, *editor* • JIM SHOOTER, *editor-in-chief*

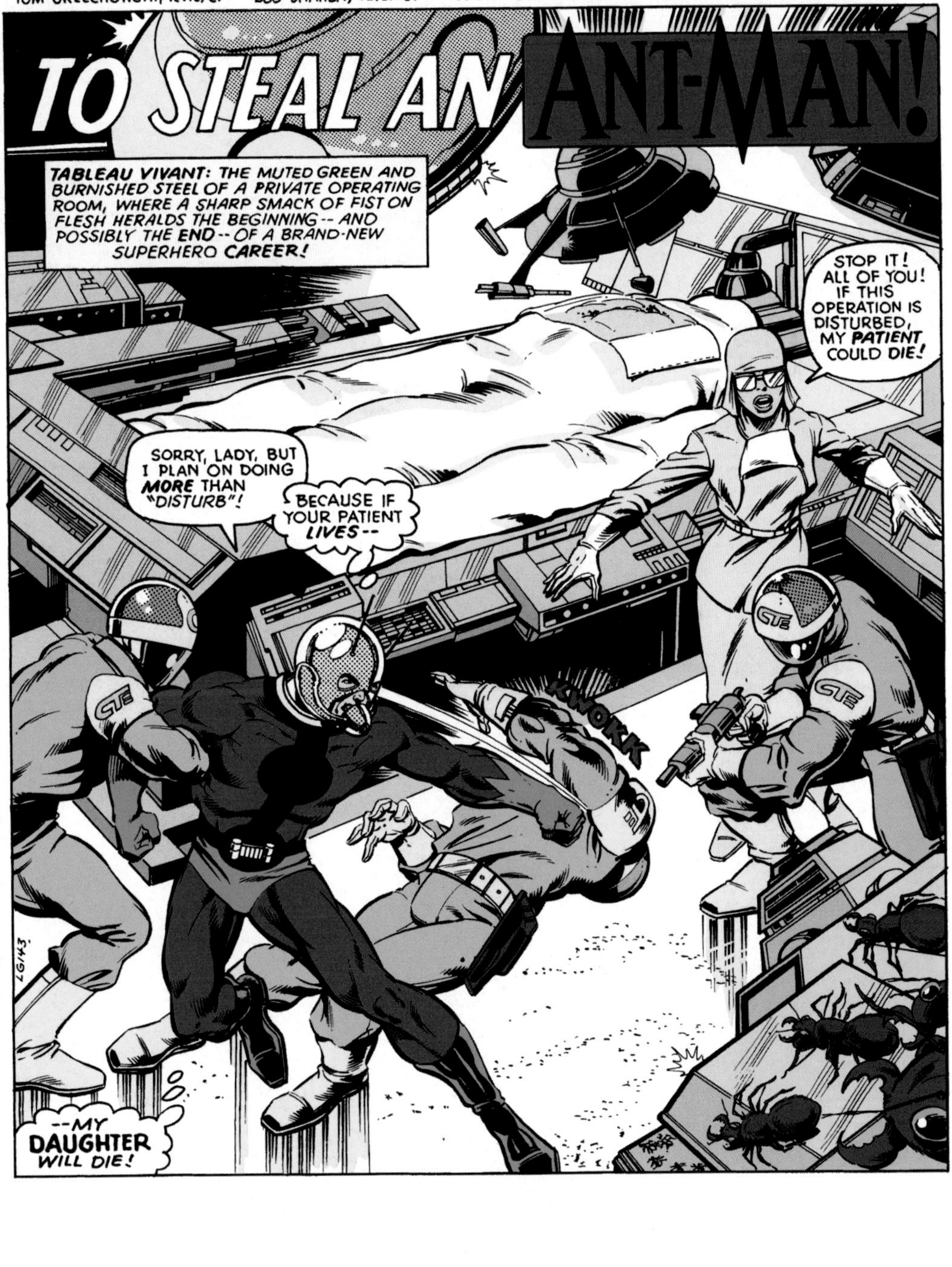
TO STEAL AN ANT-MAN!
TABLEAU VIVANT: THE MUTED GREEN AND BURNISHED STEEL OF A PRIVATE OPERATING ROOM, WHERE A SHARP SMACK OF FIST ON FLESH HERALDS THE BEGINNING -- AND POSSIBLY THE END -- OF A BRAND-NEW SUPERHERO CAREER!
STOP IT! ALL OF YOU! IF THIS OPERATION IS DISTURBED, MY PATIENT COULD DIE!
SORRY, LADY, BUT I PLAN ON DOING MORE THAN "DISTURB"!
BECAUSE IF YOUR PATIENT LIVES --
--MY DAUGHTER WILL DIE!
KWOKK

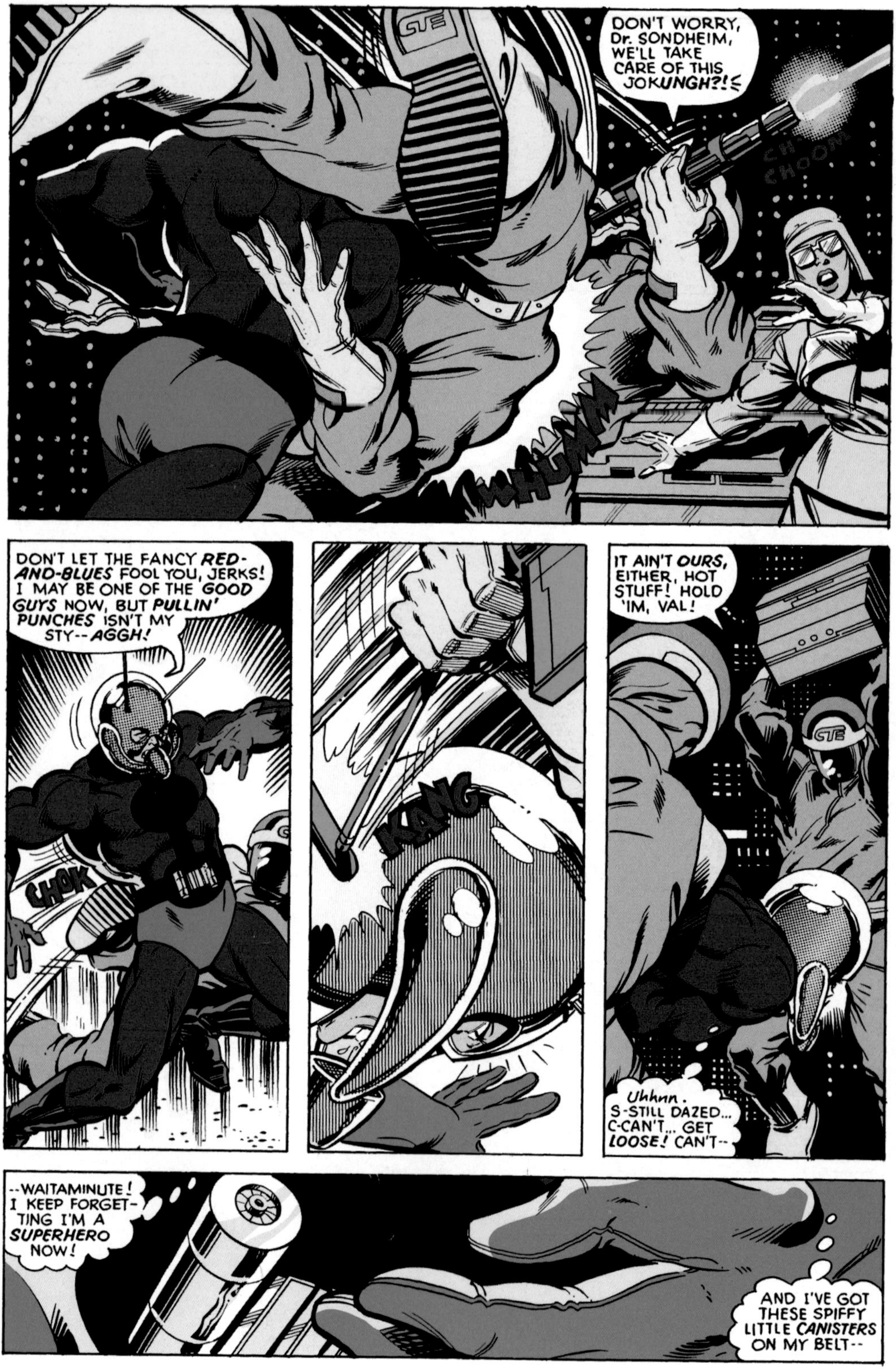
DON'T WORRY, Dr. SONDHEIM, WE'LL TAKE CARE OF THIS JOKUNGH?!
CH-CHOOM
WHUMM
DON'T LET THE FANCY RED-AND-BLUES FOOL YOU, JERKS! I MAY BE ONE OF THE GOOD GUYS NOW, BUT PULLIN' PUNCHES ISN'T MY STY--AGGH!
CHOK
KANG
IT AIN'T OURS, EITHER, HOT STUFF! HOLD 'IM, VAL!
Uhhnn. S-STILL DAZED... C-CAN'T... GET LOOSE! CAN'T--
--WAITAMINUTE! I KEEP FORGETTING I'M A SUPERHERO NOW!
AND I'VE GOT THESE SPIFFY LITTLE CANISTERS ON MY BELT--

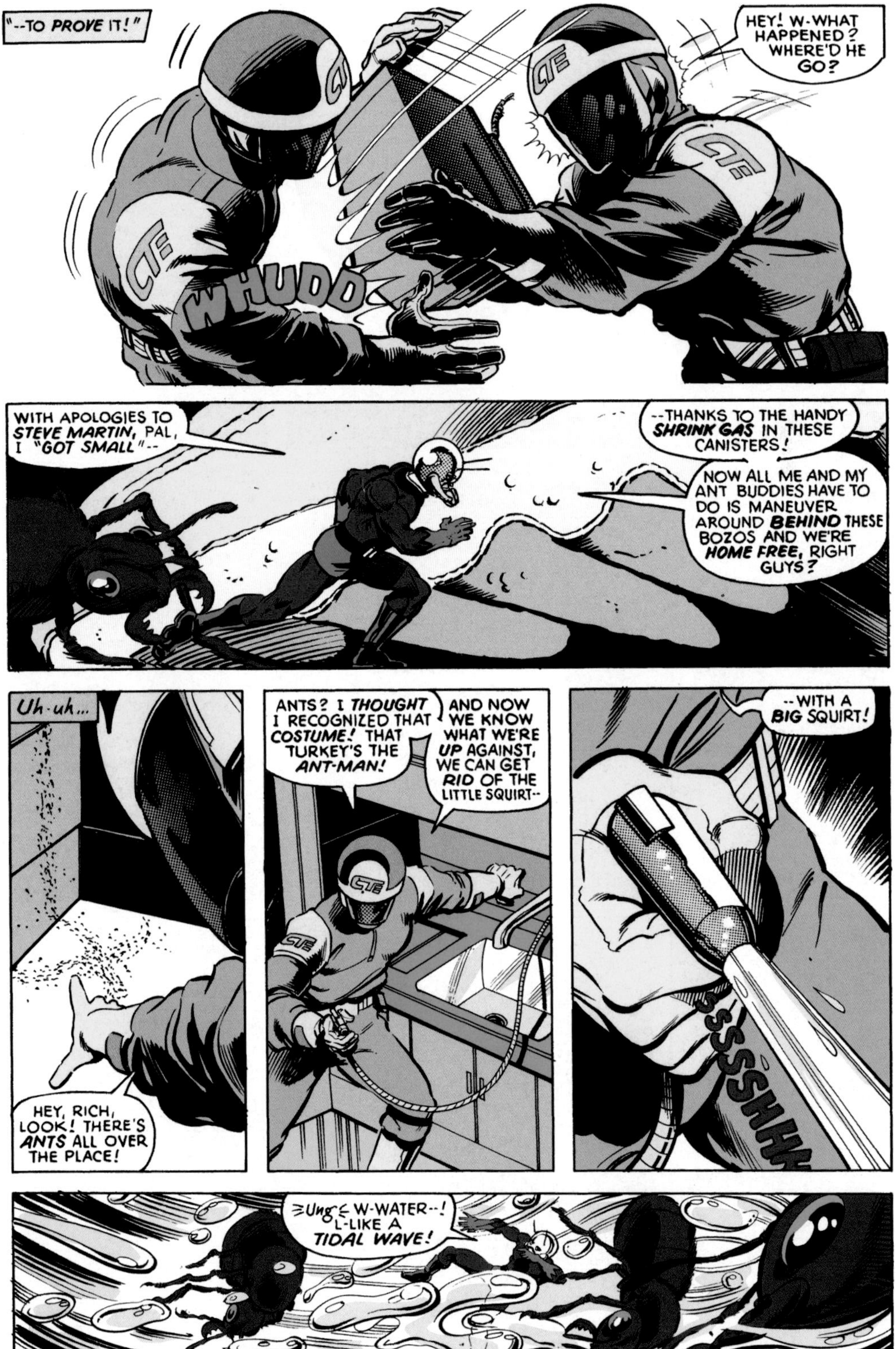
"--TO PROVE IT!"
HEY! W-WHAT HAPPENED? WHERE'D HE GO?
WHUDD
WITH APOLOGIES TO STEVE MARTIN, PAL, I "GOT SMALL"--
--THANKS TO THE HANDY SHRINK GAS IN THESE CANISTERS!
NOW ALL ME AND MY ANT BUDDIES HAVE TO DO IS MANEUVER AROUND BEHIND THESE BOZOS AND WE'RE HOME FREE, RIGHT GUYS?
Uh-uh...
HEY, RICH, LOOK! THERE'S ANTS ALL OVER THE PLACE!
ANTS? I THOUGHT I RECOGNIZED THAT COSTUME! THAT TURKEY'S THE ANT-MAN!
AND NOW WE KNOW WHAT WE'RE UP AGAINST, WE CAN GET RID OF THE LITTLE SQUIRT--
--WITH A BIG SQUIRT!
SSSSSHHH
Ung! W-WATER--! L-LIKE A TIDAL WAVE!

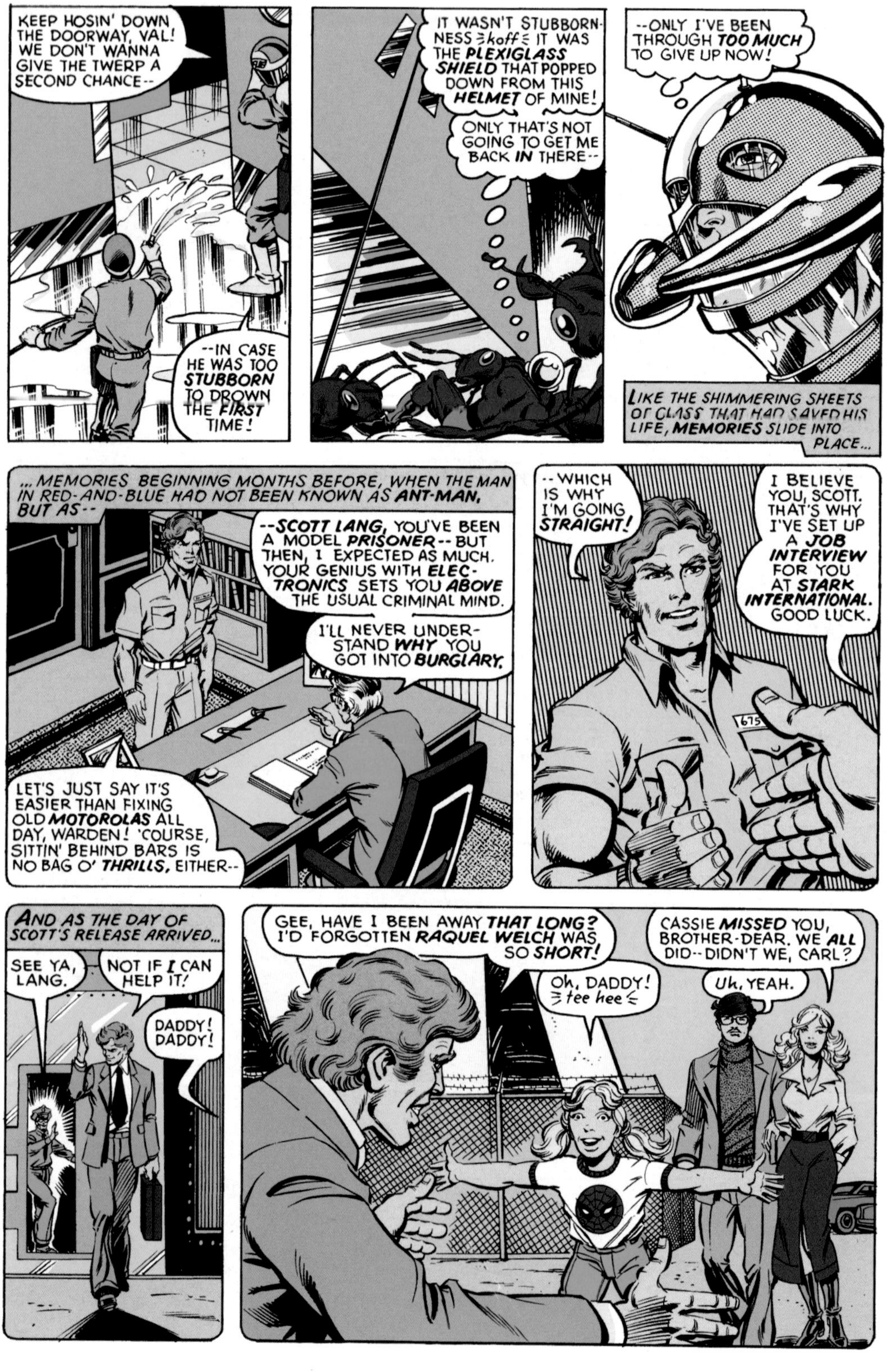
KEEP HOSIN' DOWN THE DOORWAY, VAL! WE DON'T WANNA GIVE THE TWERP A SECOND CHANCE--
--IN CASE HE WAS TOO STUBBORN TO DROWN THE FIRST TIME!
IT WASN'T STUBBORNNESS ≶koff≷ IT WAS THE PLEXIGLASS SHIELD THAT POPPED DOWN FROM THIS HELMET OF MINE!
ONLY THAT'S NOT GOING TO GET ME BACK IN THERE--
--ONLY I'VE BEEN THROUGH TOO MUCH TO GIVE UP NOW!
LIKE THE SHIMMERING SHEETS OF GLASS THAT HAD SAVED HIS LIFE, MEMORIES SLIDE INTO PLACE...
...MEMORIES BEGINNING MONTHS BEFORE, WHEN THE MAN IN RED-AND-BLUE HAD NOT BEEN KNOWN AS ANT-MAN, BUT AS--
--SCOTT LANG, YOU'VE BEEN A MODEL PRISONER--BUT THEN, I EXPECTED AS MUCH. YOUR GENIUS WITH ELECTRONICS SETS YOU ABOVE THE USUAL CRIMINAL MIND.
I'LL NEVER UNDERSTAND WHY YOU GOT INTO BURGLARY.
LET'S JUST SAY IT'S EASIER THAN FIXING OLD MOTOROLAS ALL DAY, WARDEN! 'COURSE, SITTIN' BEHIND BARS IS NO BAG O' THRILLS, EITHER--
--WHICH IS WHY I'M GOING STRAIGHT!
I BELIEVE YOU, SCOTT. THAT'S WHY I'VE SET UP A JOB INTERVIEW FOR YOU AT STARK INTERNATIONAL. GOOD LUCK.
AND AS THE DAY OF SCOTT'S RELEASE ARRIVED...
SEE YA, LANG.
NOT IF I CAN HELP IT!
DADDY! DADDY!
GEE, HAVE I BEEN AWAY THAT LONG? I'D FORGOTTEN RAQUEL WELCH WAS SO SHORT!
Oh, DADDY! ≶tee hee≷
CASSIE MISSED YOU, BROTHER-DEAR. WE ALL DID--DIDN'T WE, CARL?
Uh, YEAH.

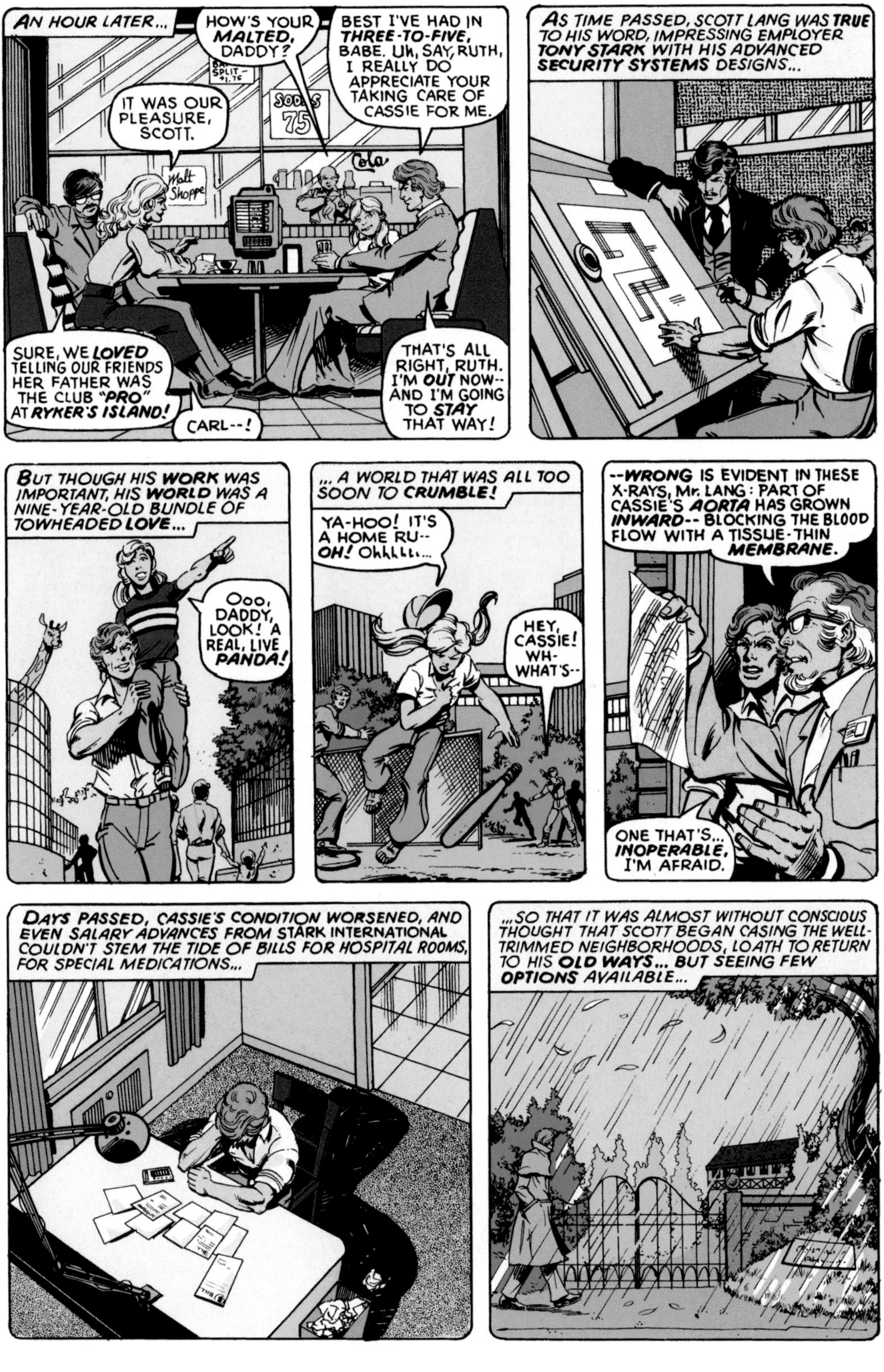
AN HOUR LATER...
HOW'S YOUR MALTED, DADDY?
BEST I'VE HAD IN THREE-TO-FIVE, BABE. Uh, SAY, RUTH, I REALLY DO APPRECIATE YOUR TAKING CARE OF CASSIE FOR ME.
IT WAS OUR PLEASURE, SCOTT.
SODAS 75
Malt Shoppe
Cola
SURE, WE LOVED TELLING OUR FRIENDS HER FATHER WAS THE CLUB "PRO" AT RYKER'S ISLAND!
CARL--!
THAT'S ALL RIGHT, RUTH. I'M OUT NOW-- AND I'M GOING TO STAY THAT WAY!
AS TIME PASSED, SCOTT LANG WAS TRUE TO HIS WORD, IMPRESSING EMPLOYER TONY STARK WITH HIS ADVANCED SECURITY SYSTEMS DESIGNS...
BUT THOUGH HIS WORK WAS IMPORTANT, HIS WORLD WAS A NINE-YEAR-OLD BUNDLE OF TOWHEADED LOVE...
Ooo, DADDY, LOOK! A REAL, LIVE PANDA!
...A WORLD THAT WAS ALL TOO SOON TO CRUMBLE!
YA-HOO! IT'S A HOME RU-- OH! Ohhhhh...
HEY, CASSIE! WH-WHAT'S--
--WRONG IS EVIDENT IN THESE X-RAYS, Mr. LANG: PART OF CASSIE'S AORTA HAS GROWN INWARD-- BLOCKING THE BLOOD FLOW WITH A TISSUE-THIN MEMBRANE.
ONE THAT'S... INOPERABLE, I'M AFRAID.
DAYS PASSED, CASSIE'S CONDITION WORSENED, AND EVEN SALARY ADVANCES FROM STARK INTERNATIONAL COULDN'T STEM THE TIDE OF BILLS FOR HOSPITAL ROOMS, FOR SPECIAL MEDICATIONS...
BILL
...SO THAT IT WAS ALMOST WITHOUT CONSCIOUS THOUGHT THAT SCOTT BEGAN CASING THE WELL-TRIMMED NEIGHBORHOODS, LOATH TO RETURN TO HIS OLD WAYS... BUT SEEING FEW OPTIONS AVAILABLE...

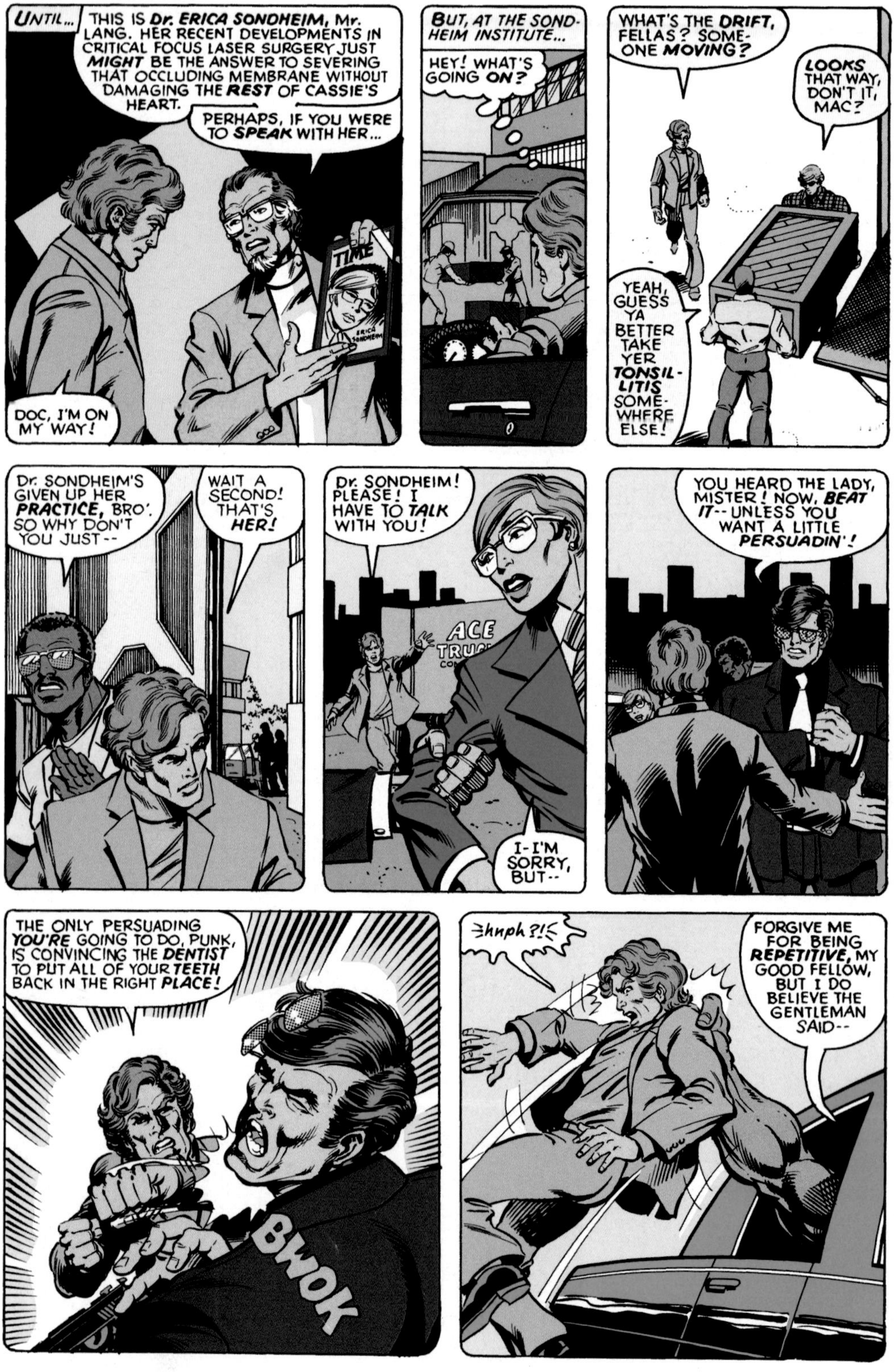

UNTIL...
THIS IS Dr. ERICA SONDHEIM, Mr. LANG. HER RECENT DEVELOPMENTS IN CRITICAL FOCUS LASER SURGERY JUST MIGHT BE THE ANSWER TO SEVERING THAT OCCLUDING MEMBRANE WITHOUT DAMAGING THE REST OF CASSIE'S HEART.
PERHAPS, IF YOU WERE TO SPEAK WITH HER...
TIME
ERICA SONDHEIM
DOC, I'M ON MY WAY!
BUT, AT THE SONDHEIM INSTITUTE...
HEY! WHAT'S GOING ON?
WHAT'S THE DRIFT, FELLAS? SOMEONE MOVING?
LOOKS THAT WAY, DON'T IT, MAC?
YEAH, GUESS YA BETTER TAKE YER TONSIL-LITIS SOME-WHERE ELSE!
Dr. SONDHEIM'S GIVEN UP HER PRACTICE, BRO'. SO WHY DON'T YOU JUST--
WAIT A SECOND! THAT'S HER!
Dr. SONDHEIM! PLEASE! I HAVE TO TALK WITH YOU!
ACE
I-I'M SORRY, BUT--
YOU HEARD THE LADY, MISTER! NOW, BEAT IT--UNLESS YOU WANT A LITTLE PERSUADIN'!
THE ONLY PERSUADING YOU'RE GOING TO DO, PUNK, IS CONVINCING THE DENTIST TO PUT ALL OF YOUR TEETH BACK IN THE RIGHT PLACE!
BWOK
hnph?!
FORGIVE ME FOR BEING REPETITIVE, MY GOOD FELLOW, BUT I DO BELIEVE THE GENTLEMAN SAID--

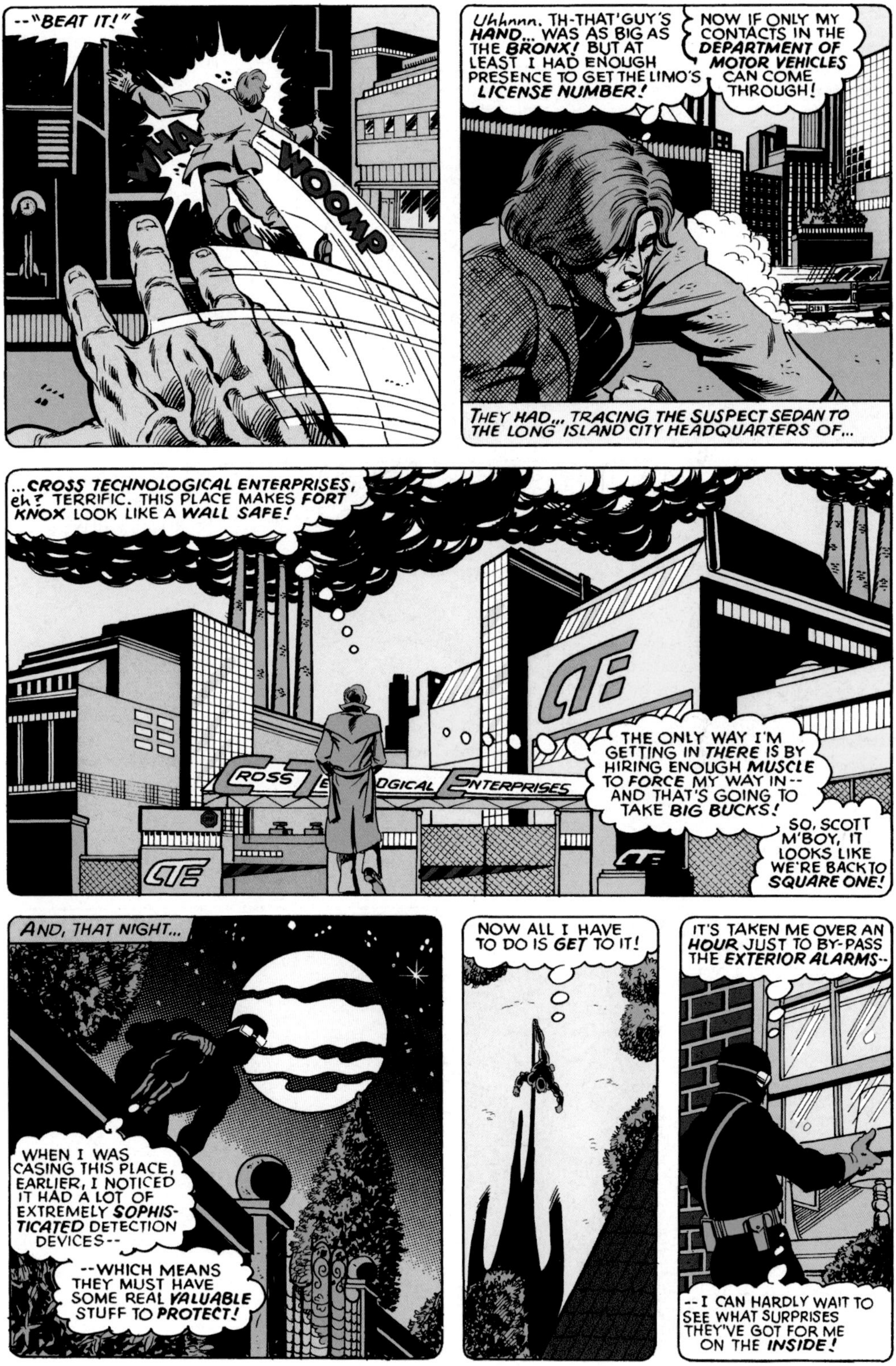
--"BEAT IT!"
WHA
WOOMP
Uhhnnn. TH-THAT GUY'S HAND... WAS AS BIG AS THE BRÖNX! BUT AT LEAST I HAD ENOUGH PRESENCE TO GET THE LIMO'S LICENSE NUMBER!
NOW IF ONLY MY CONTACTS IN THE DEPARTMENT OF MOTOR VEHICLES CAN COME THROUGH!
THEY HAD... TRACING THE SUSPECT SEDAN TO THE LONG ISLAND CITY HEADQUARTERS OF...
...CROSS TECHNOLOGICAL ENTERPRISES, eh? TERRIFIC. THIS PLACE MAKES FORT KNOX LOOK LIKE A WALL SAFE!
CTE
CROSS TE OGICAL ENTERPRISES
THE ONLY WAY I'M GETTING IN THERE IS BY HIRING ENOUGH MUSCLE TO FORCE MY WAY IN-- AND THAT'S GOING TO TAKE BIG BUCKS!
SO, SCOTT M'BOY, IT LOOKS LIKE WE'RE BACK TO SQUARE ONE!
AND, THAT NIGHT...
WHEN I WAS CASING THIS PLACE, EARLIER, I NOTICED IT HAD A LOT OF EXTREMELY SOPHISTICATED DETECTION DEVICES--
--WHICH MEANS THEY MUST HAVE SOME REAL VALUABLE STUFF TO PROTECT!
NOW ALL I HAVE TO DO IS GET TO IT!
IT'S TAKEN ME OVER AN HOUR JUST TO BY-PASS THE EXTERIOR ALARMS--
--I CAN HARDLY WAIT TO SEE WHAT SURPRISES THEY'VE GOT FOR ME ON THE INSIDE!

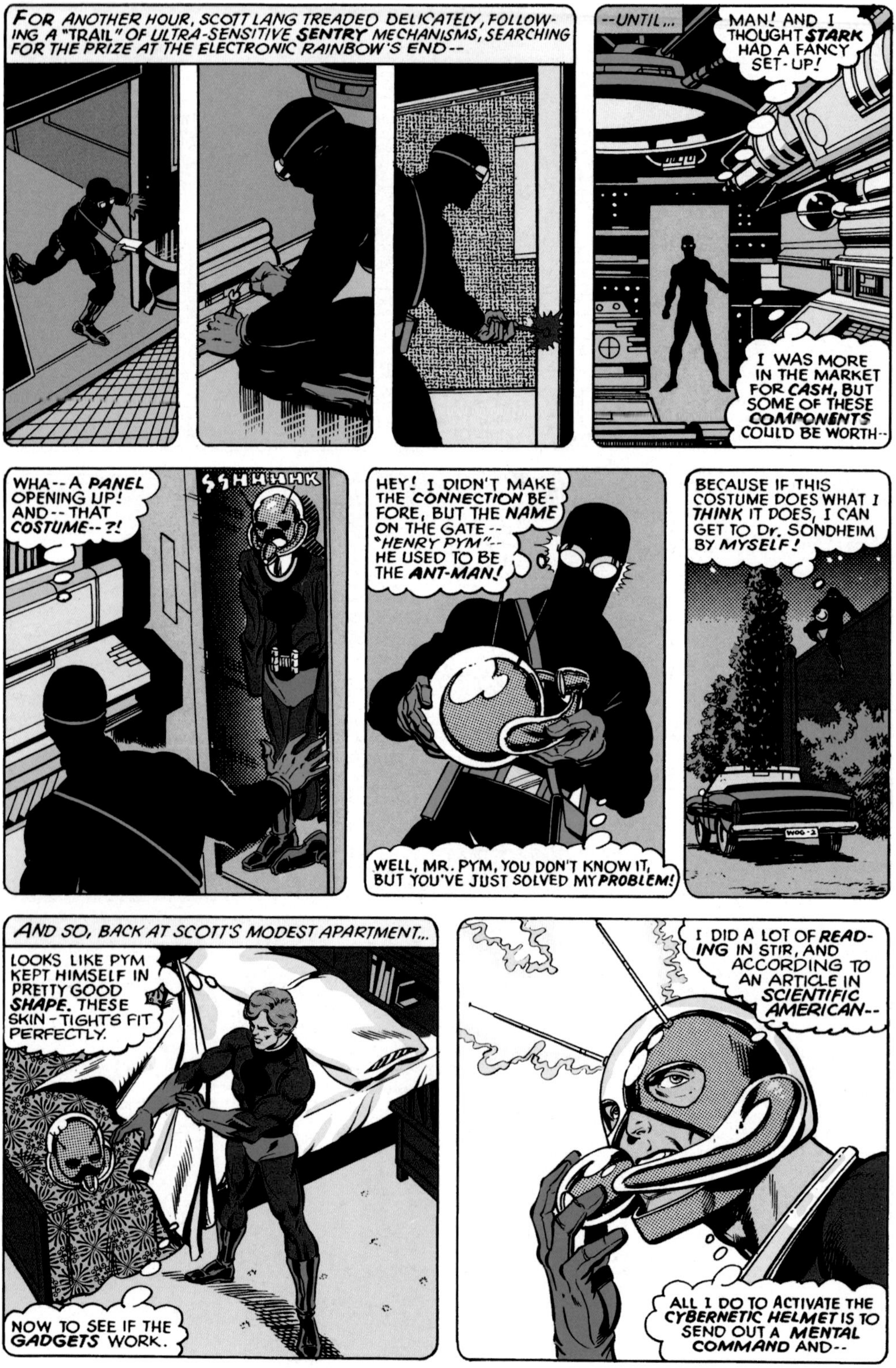
FOR ANOTHER HOUR, SCOTT LANG TREADED DELICATELY, FOLLOWING A "TRAIL" OF ULTRA-SENSITIVE SENTRY MECHANISMS, SEARCHING FOR THE PRIZE AT THE ELECTRONIC RAINBOW'S END--
--UNTIL...
MAN! AND I THOUGHT STARK HAD A FANCY SET-UP!
I WAS MORE IN THE MARKET FOR CASH, BUT SOME OF THESE COMPONENTS COULD BE WORTH--
WHA--A PANEL OPENING UP! AND--THAT COSTUME--?!
SSHHHHHK
HEY! I DIDN'T MAKE THE CONNECTION BEFORE, BUT THE NAME ON THE GATE--"HENRY PYM"--HE USED TO BE THE ANT-MAN!
WELL, MR. PYM, YOU DON'T KNOW IT, BUT YOU'VE JUST SOLVED MY PROBLEM!
BECAUSE IF THIS COSTUME DOES WHAT I THINK IT DOES, I CAN GET TO Dr. SONDHEIM BY MYSELF!
WOG-2
AND SO, BACK AT SCOTT'S MODEST APARTMENT...
LOOKS LIKE PYM KEPT HIMSELF IN PRETTY GOOD SHAPE. THESE SKIN-TIGHTS FIT PERFECTLY.
NOW TO SEE IF THE GADGETS WORK.
I DID A LOT OF READING IN STIR, AND ACCORDING TO AN ARTICLE IN SCIENTIFIC AMERICAN--
ALL I DO TO ACTIVATE THE CYBERNETIC HELMET IS TO SEND OUT A MENTAL COMMAND AND--

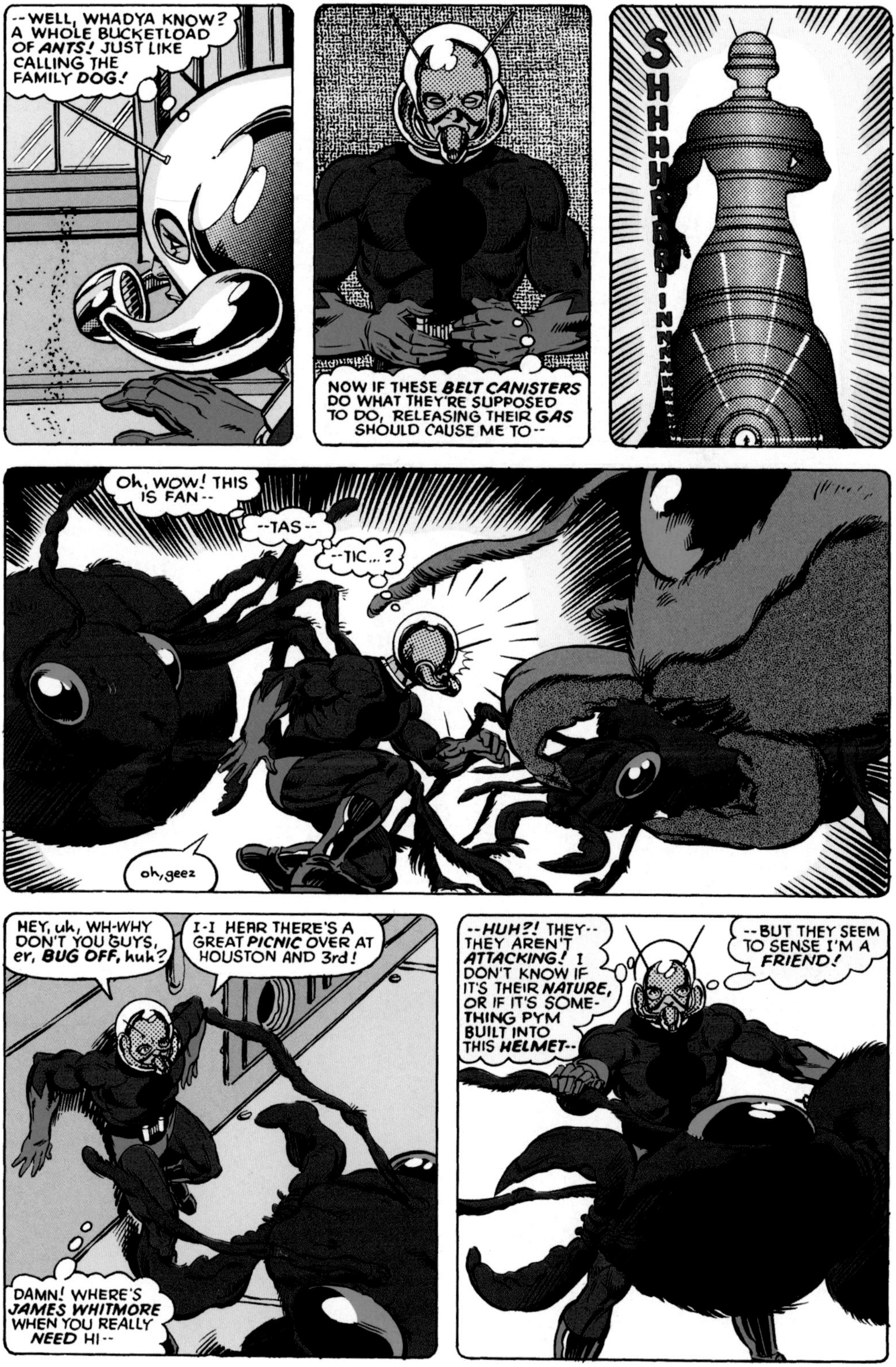

--WELL, WHADYA KNOW? A WHOLE BUCKETLOAD OF ANTS! JUST LIKE CALLING THE FAMILY DOG!
NOW IF THESE BELT CANISTERS DO WHAT THEY'RE SUPPOSED TO DO, RELEASING THEIR GAS SHOULD CAUSE ME TO--
SHHHHRRRT-INNN
Oh, WOW! THIS IS FAN--
--TAS--
--TIC...?
oh, geez
HEY, uh, WH-WHY DON'T YOU GUYS, er, BUG OFF, huh?
I-I HEAR THERE'S A GREAT PICNIC OVER AT HOUSTON AND 3rd!
DAMN! WHERE'S JAMES WHITMORE WHEN YOU REALLY NEED HI--
--HUH?! THEY--THEY AREN'T ATTACKING! I DON'T KNOW IF IT'S THEIR NATURE, OR IF IT'S SOMETHING PYM BUILT INTO THIS HELMET--
--BUT THEY SEEM TO SENSE I'M A FRIEND!

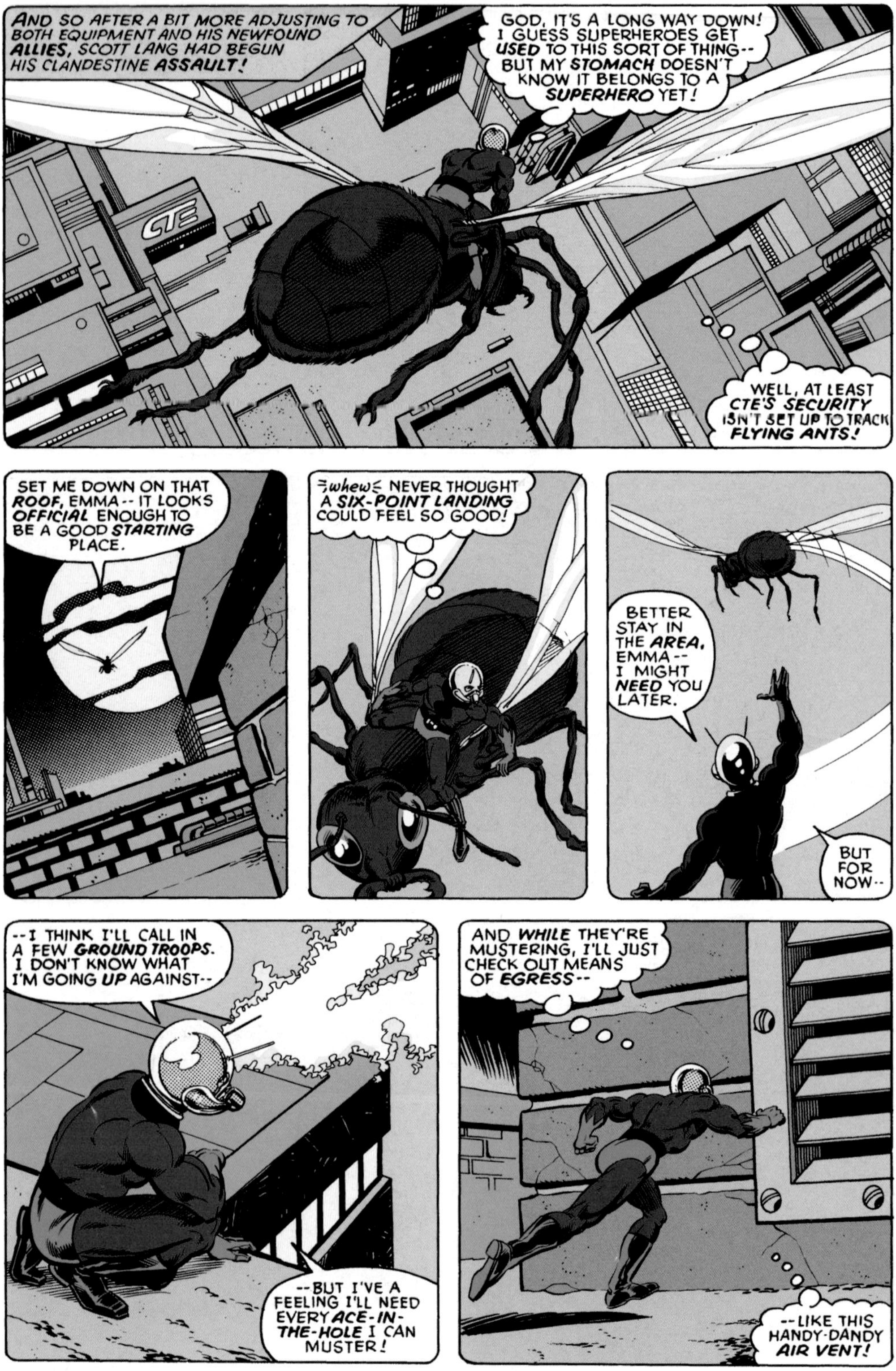
AND SO AFTER A BIT MORE ADJUSTING TO BOTH EQUIPMENT AND HIS NEWFOUND ALLIES, SCOTT LANG HAD BEGUN HIS CLANDESTINE ASSAULT!
GOD, IT'S A LONG WAY DOWN! I GUESS SUPERHEROES GET USED TO THIS SORT OF THING-- BUT MY STOMACH DOESN'T KNOW IT BELONGS TO A SUPERHERO YET!
CTE
WELL, AT LEAST CTE'S SECURITY ISN'T SET UP TO TRACK FLYING ANTS!
SET ME DOWN ON THAT ROOF, EMMA-- IT LOOKS OFFICIAL ENOUGH TO BE A GOOD STARTING PLACE.
=whew= NEVER THOUGHT A SIX-POINT LANDING COULD FEEL SO GOOD!
BETTER STAY IN THE AREA, EMMA-- I MIGHT NEED YOU LATER.
BUT FOR NOW--
--I THINK I'LL CALL IN A FEW GROUND TROOPS. I DON'T KNOW WHAT I'M GOING UP AGAINST--
--BUT I'VE A FEELING I'LL NEED EVERY ACE-IN-THE-HOLE I CAN MUSTER!
AND WHILE THEY'RE MUSTERING, I'LL JUST CHECK OUT MEANS OF EGRESS--
--LIKE THIS HANDY-DANDY AIR VENT!

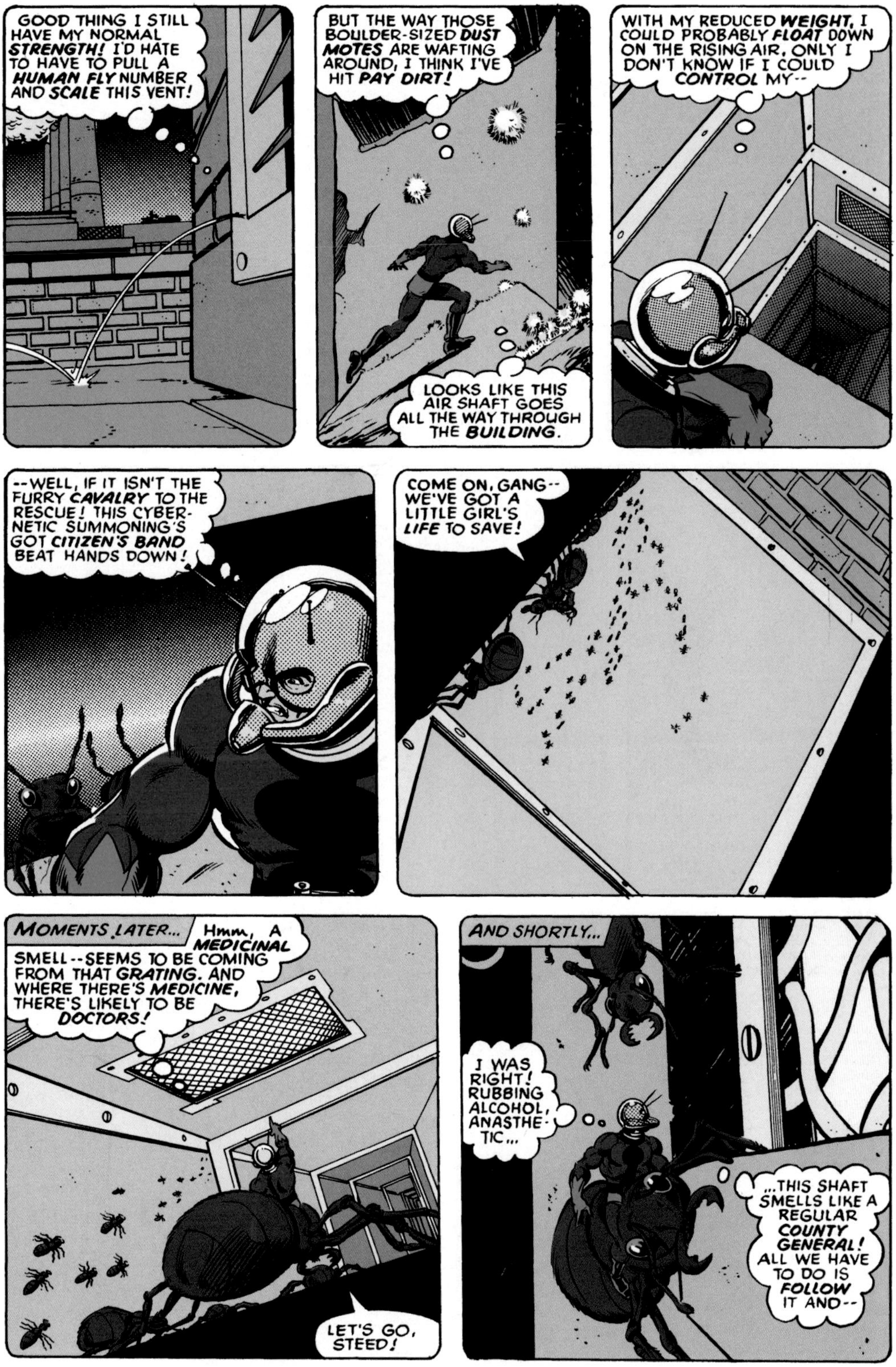
GOOD THING I STILL HAVE MY NORMAL STRENGTH! I'D HATE TO HAVE TO PULL A HUMAN FLY NUMBER AND SCALE THIS VENT!
BUT THE WAY THOSE BOULDER-SIZED DUST MOTES ARE WAFTING AROUND, I THINK I'VE HIT PAY DIRT!
LOOKS LIKE THIS AIR SHAFT GOES ALL THE WAY THROUGH THE BUILDING.
WITH MY REDUCED WEIGHT, I COULD PROBABLY FLOAT DOWN ON THE RISING AIR, ONLY I DON'T KNOW IF I COULD CONTROL MY--
--WELL, IF IT ISN'T THE FURRY CAVALRY TO THE RESCUE! THIS CYBER-NETIC SUMMONING'S GOT CITIZEN'S BAND BEAT HANDS DOWN!
COME ON, GANG-- WE'VE GOT A LITTLE GIRL'S LIFE TO SAVE!
MOMENTS LATER...
Hmm, A MEDICINAL SMELL--SEEMS TO BE COMING FROM THAT GRATING. AND WHERE THERE'S MEDICINE, THERE'S LIKELY TO BE DOCTORS!
LET'S GO, STEED!
AND SHORTLY...
I WAS RIGHT! RUBBING ALCOHOL, ANASTHE-TIC...
...THIS SHAFT SMELLS LIKE A REGULAR COUNTY GENERAL! ALL WE HAVE TO DO IS FOLLOW IT AND--

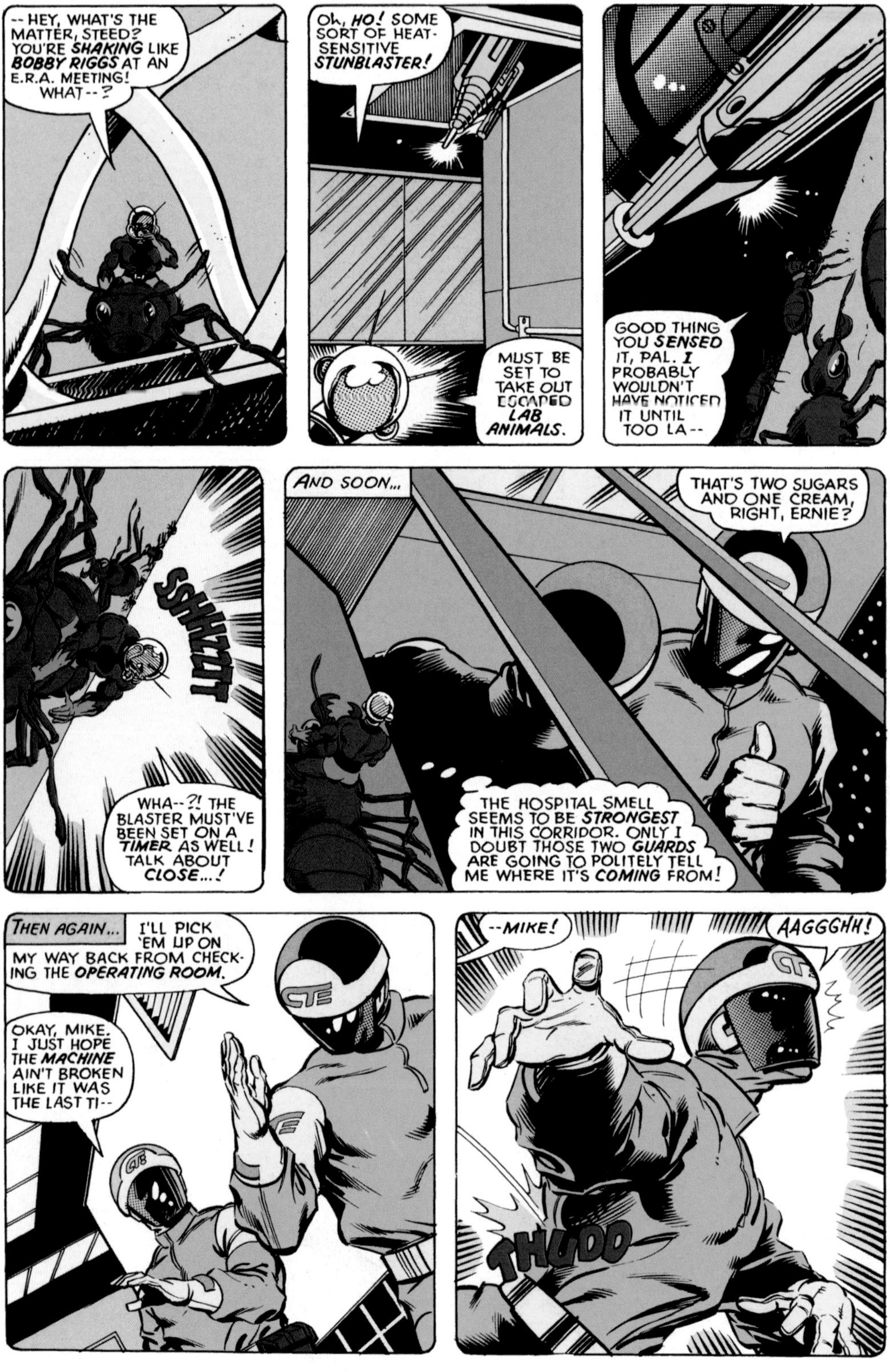
-- HEY, WHAT'S THE MATTER, STEED? YOU'RE SHAKING LIKE BOBBY RIGGS AT AN E.R.A. MEETING! WHAT--?
Oh, HO! SOME SORT OF HEAT-SENSITIVE STUNBLASTER!
MUST BE SET TO TAKE OUT ESCAPED LAB ANIMALS.
GOOD THING YOU SENSED IT, PAL. I PROBABLY WOULDN'T HAVE NOTICED IT UNTIL TOO LA--
SSHHZZZTT
WHA--?! THE BLASTER MUST'VE BEEN SET ON A TIMER AS WELL! TALK ABOUT CLOSE...!
AND SOON...
THAT'S TWO SUGARS AND ONE CREAM, RIGHT, ERNIE?
THE HOSPITAL SMELL SEEMS TO BE STRONGEST IN THIS CORRIDOR. ONLY I DOUBT THOSE TWO GUARDS ARE GOING TO POLITELY TELL ME WHERE IT'S COMING FROM!
THEN AGAIN...
I'LL PICK 'EM UP ON MY WAY BACK FROM CHECKING THE OPERATING ROOM.
OKAY, MIKE. I JUST HOPE THE MACHINE AIN'T BROKEN LIKE IT WAS THE LAST TI--
--MIKE!
AAGGGHH!
THUDD

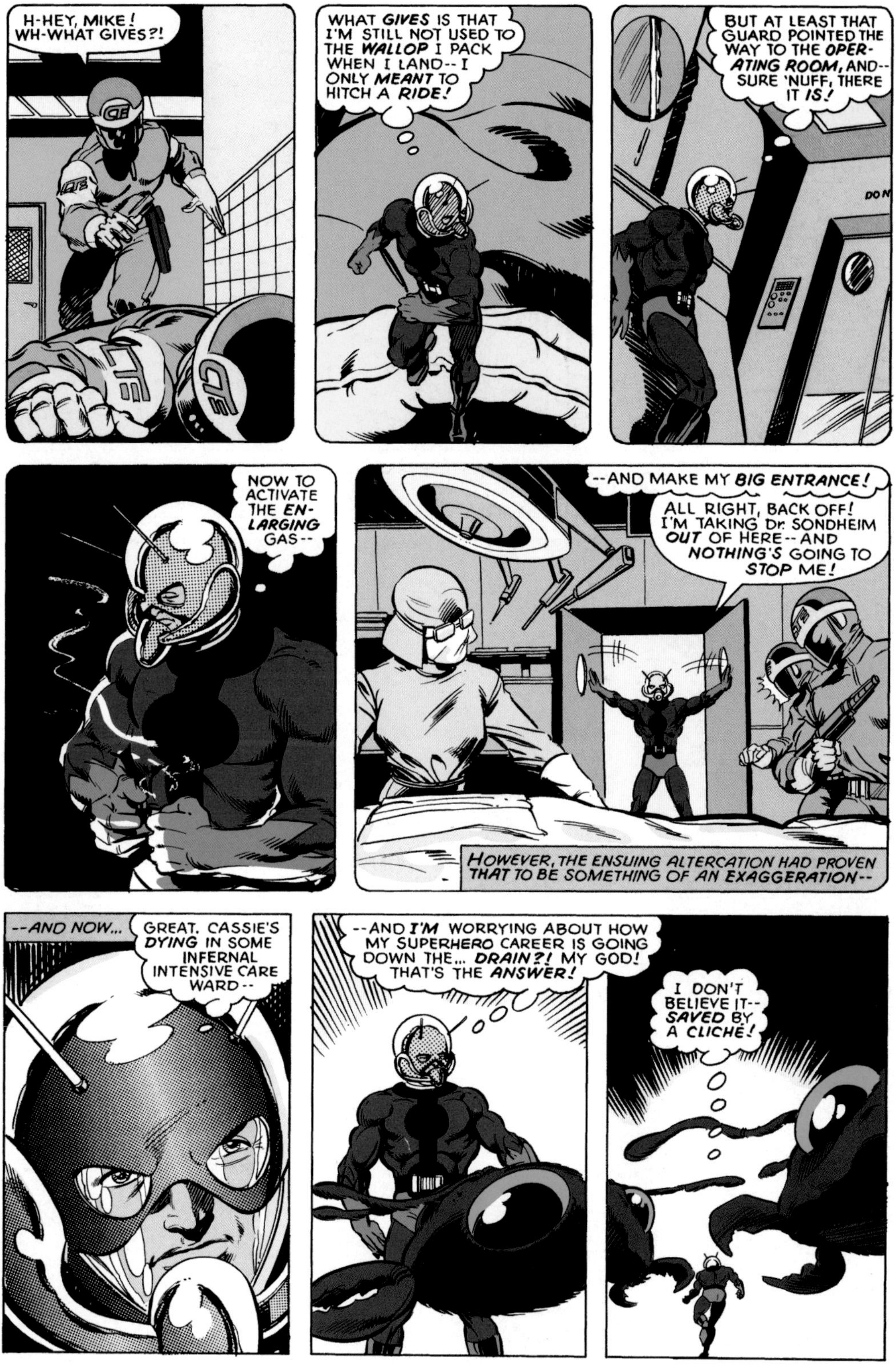
H-HEY, MIKE! WH-WHAT GIVES?!
WHAT GIVES IS THAT I'M STILL NOT USED TO THE WALLOP I PACK WHEN I LAND-- I ONLY MEANT TO HITCH A RIDE!
BUT AT LEAST THAT GUARD POINTED THE WAY TO THE OPERATING ROOM, AND-- SURE 'NUFF, THERE IT IS!
NOW TO ACTIVATE THE ENLARGING GAS--
--AND MAKE MY BIG ENTRANCE!
ALL RIGHT, BACK OFF! I'M TAKING Dr. SONDHEIM OUT OF HERE--AND NOTHING'S GOING TO STOP ME!
HOWEVER, THE ENSUING ALTERCATION HAD PROVEN THAT TO BE SOMETHING OF AN EXAGGERATION--
--AND NOW...
GREAT. CASSIE'S DYING IN SOME INFERNAL INTENSIVE CARE WARD--
--AND I'M WORRYING ABOUT HOW MY SUPERHERO CAREER IS GOING DOWN THE... DRAIN?! MY GOD! THAT'S THE ANSWER!
I DON'T BELIEVE IT-- SAVED BY A CLICHÉ!

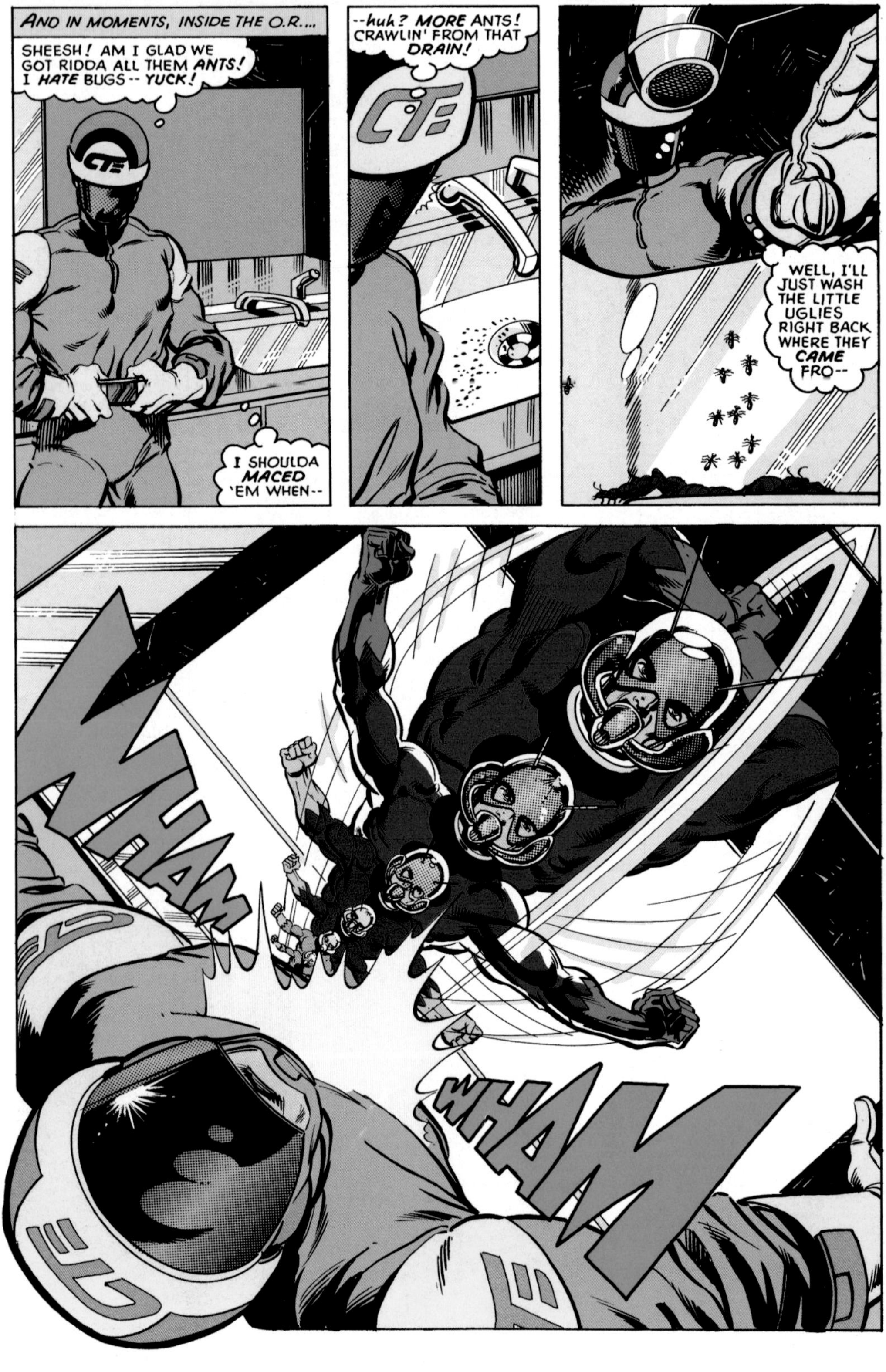
AND IN MOMENTS, INSIDE THE O.R....
SHEESH! AM I GLAD WE GOT RIDDA ALL THEM ANTS! I HATE BUGS -- YUCK!
I SHOULDA MACED 'EM WHEN--
--huh? MORE ANTS! CRAWLIN' FROM THAT DRAIN!
WELL, I'LL JUST WASH THE LITTLE UGLIES RIGHT BACK WHERE THEY CAME FRO--
WHAM
WHAM

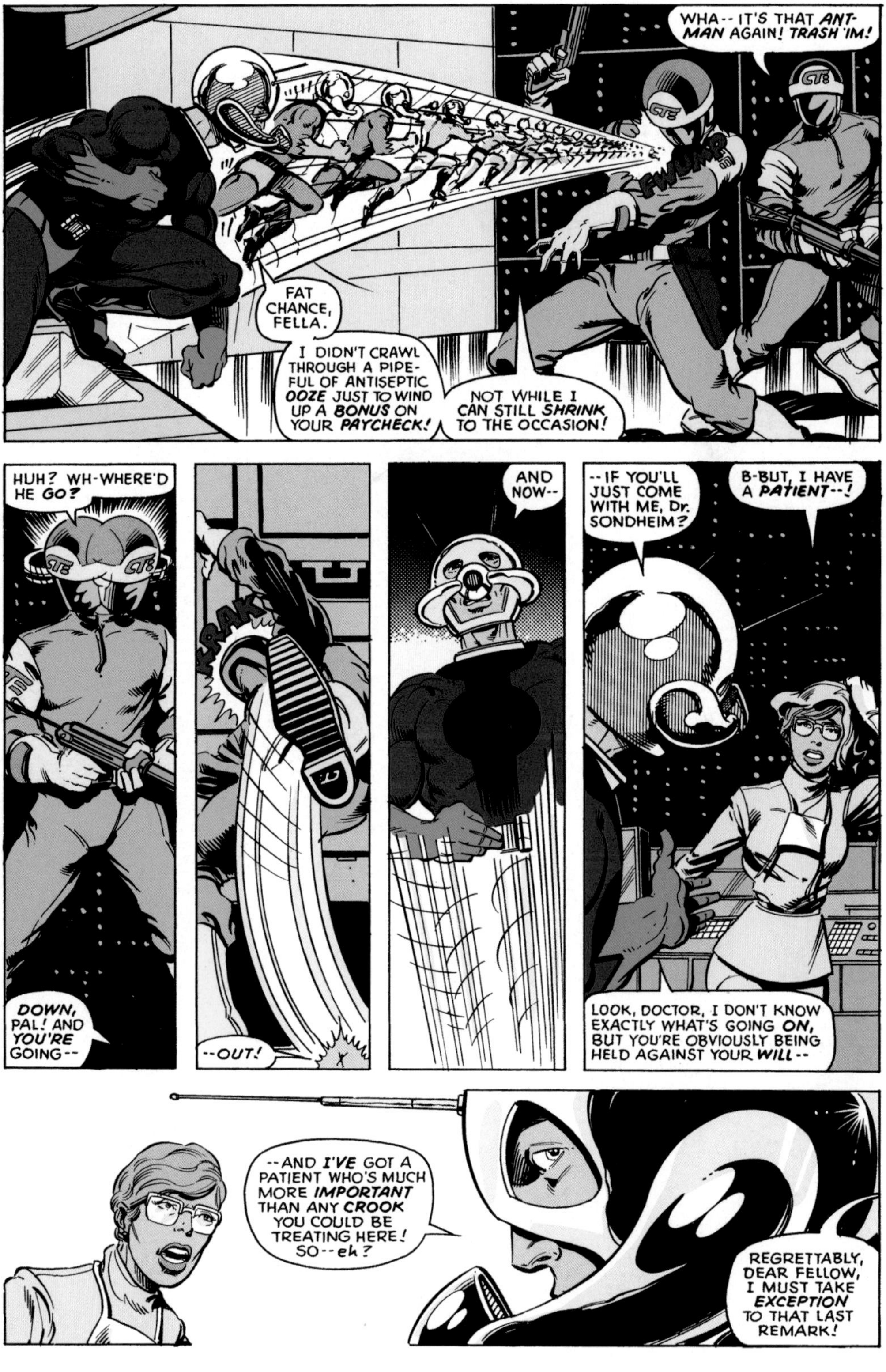

WHA-- IT'S THAT ANT-MAN AGAIN! TRASH 'IM!
FWUMP
FAT CHANCE, FELLA.
I DIDN'T CRAWL THROUGH A PIPE-FUL OF ANTISEPTIC OOZE JUST TO WIND UP A BONUS ON YOUR PAYCHECK!
NOT WHILE I CAN STILL SHRINK TO THE OCCASION!
HUH? WH-WHERE'D HE GO?
DOWN, PAL! AND YOU'RE GOING--
KRAK
--OUT!
AND NOW--
--IF YOU'LL JUST COME WITH ME, Dr. SONDHEIM?
B-BUT, I HAVE A PATIENT--!
LOOK, DOCTOR, I DON'T KNOW EXACTLY WHAT'S GOING ON, BUT YOU'RE OBVIOUSLY BEING HELD AGAINST YOUR WILL--
--AND I'VE GOT A PATIENT WHO'S MUCH MORE IMPORTANT THAN ANY CROOK YOU COULD BE TREATING HERE! SO--eh?
REGRETTABLY, DEAR FELLOW, I MUST TAKE EXCEPTION TO THAT LAST REMARK!

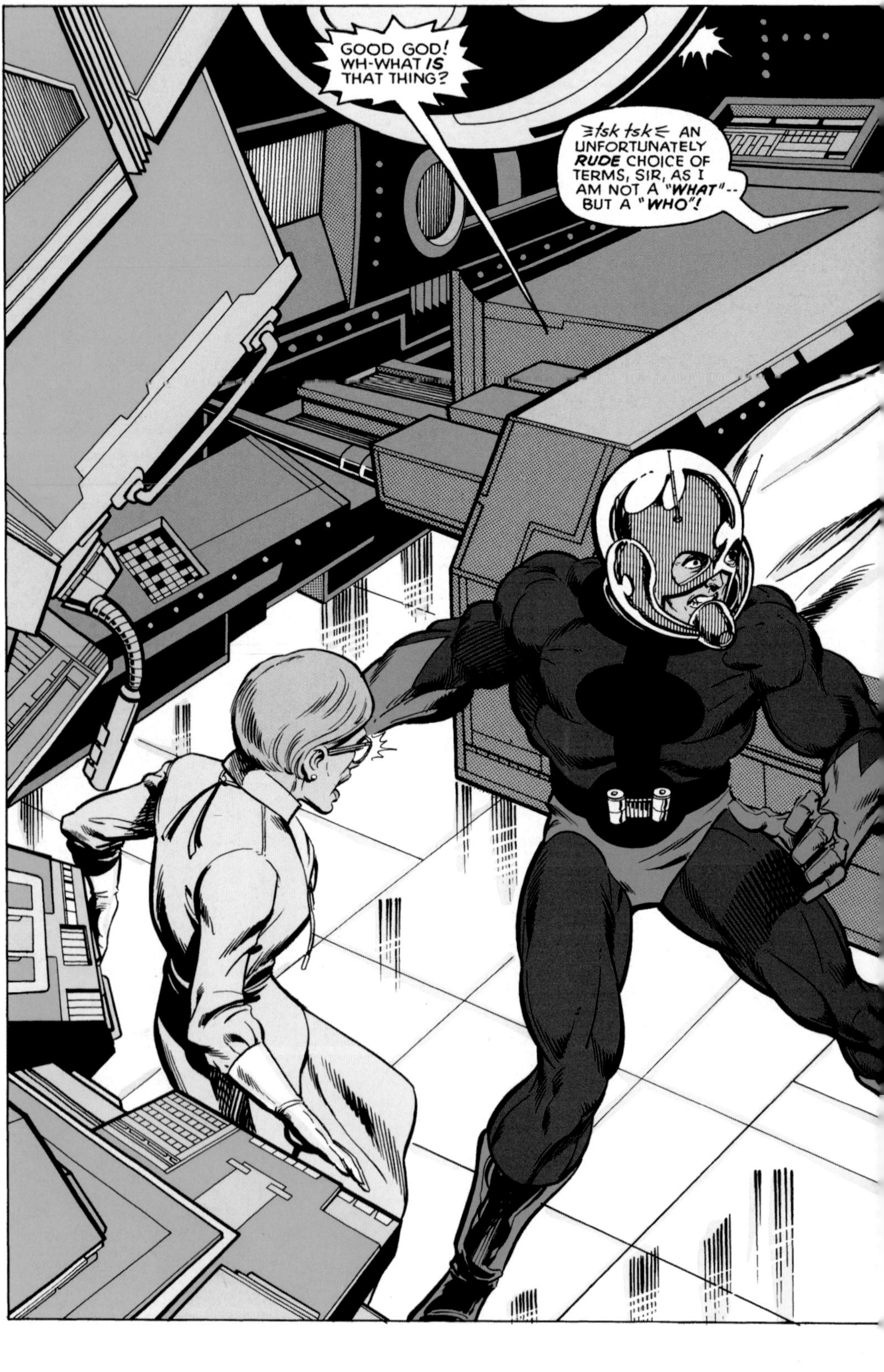
GOOD GOD! WH-WHAT IS THAT THING?
≡tsk tsk≡ AN UNFORTUNATELY RUDE CHOICE OF TERMS, SIR, AS I AM NOT A "WHAT"-- BUT A "WHO"!

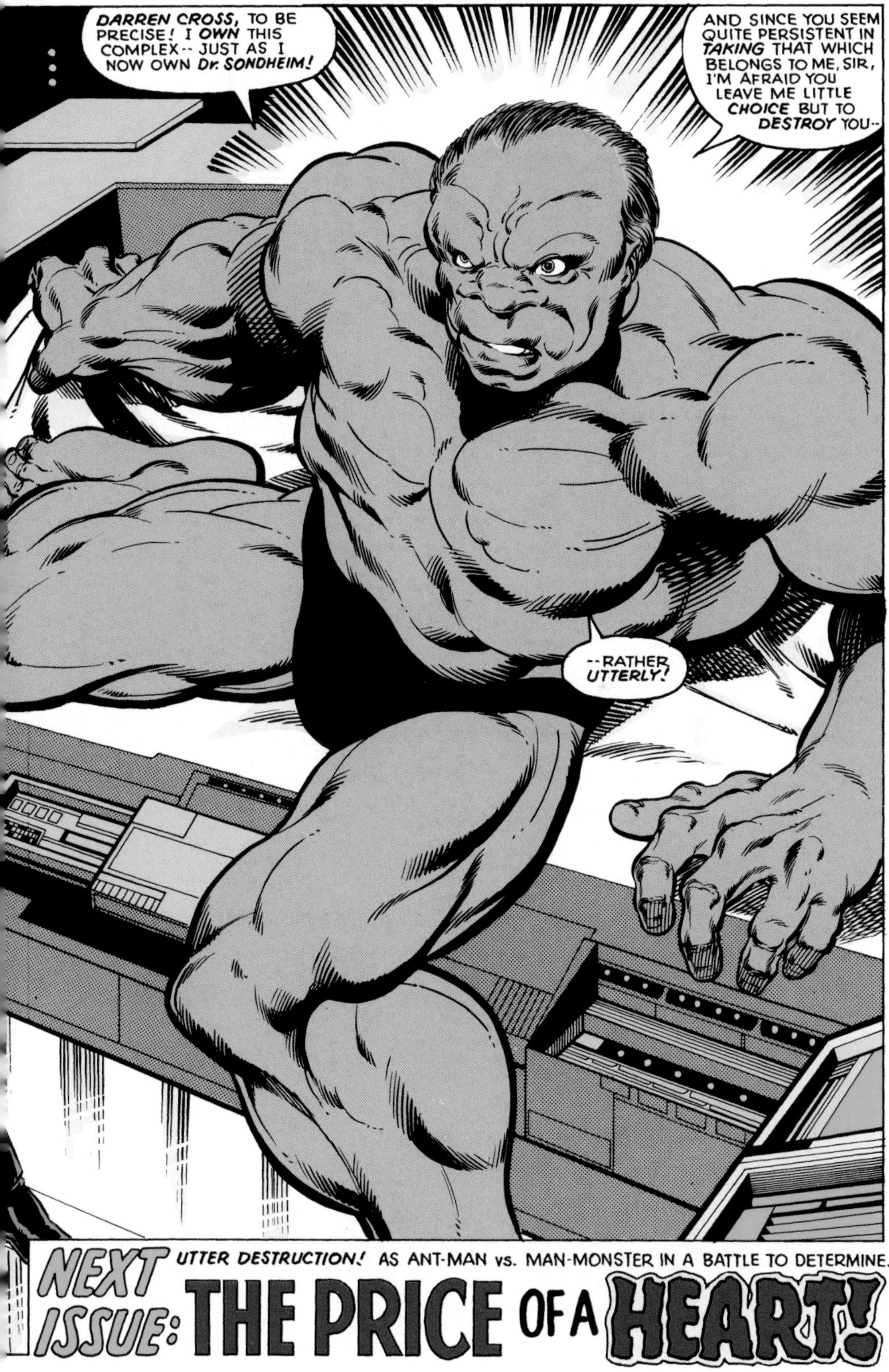
DARREN CROSS, TO BE PRECISE! I OWN THIS COMPLEX -- JUST AS I NOW OWN Dr. SONDHEIM!
AND SINCE YOU SEEM QUITE PERSISTENT IN TAKING THAT WHICH BELONGS TO ME, SIR, I'M AFRAID YOU LEAVE ME LITTLE CHOICE BUT TO DESTROY YOU--
--RATHER UTTERLY!

NEXT ISSUE: UTTER DESTRUCTION! AS ANT-MAN vs. MAN-MONSTER IN A BATTLE TO DETERMINE...

THE PRICE OF A HEART!

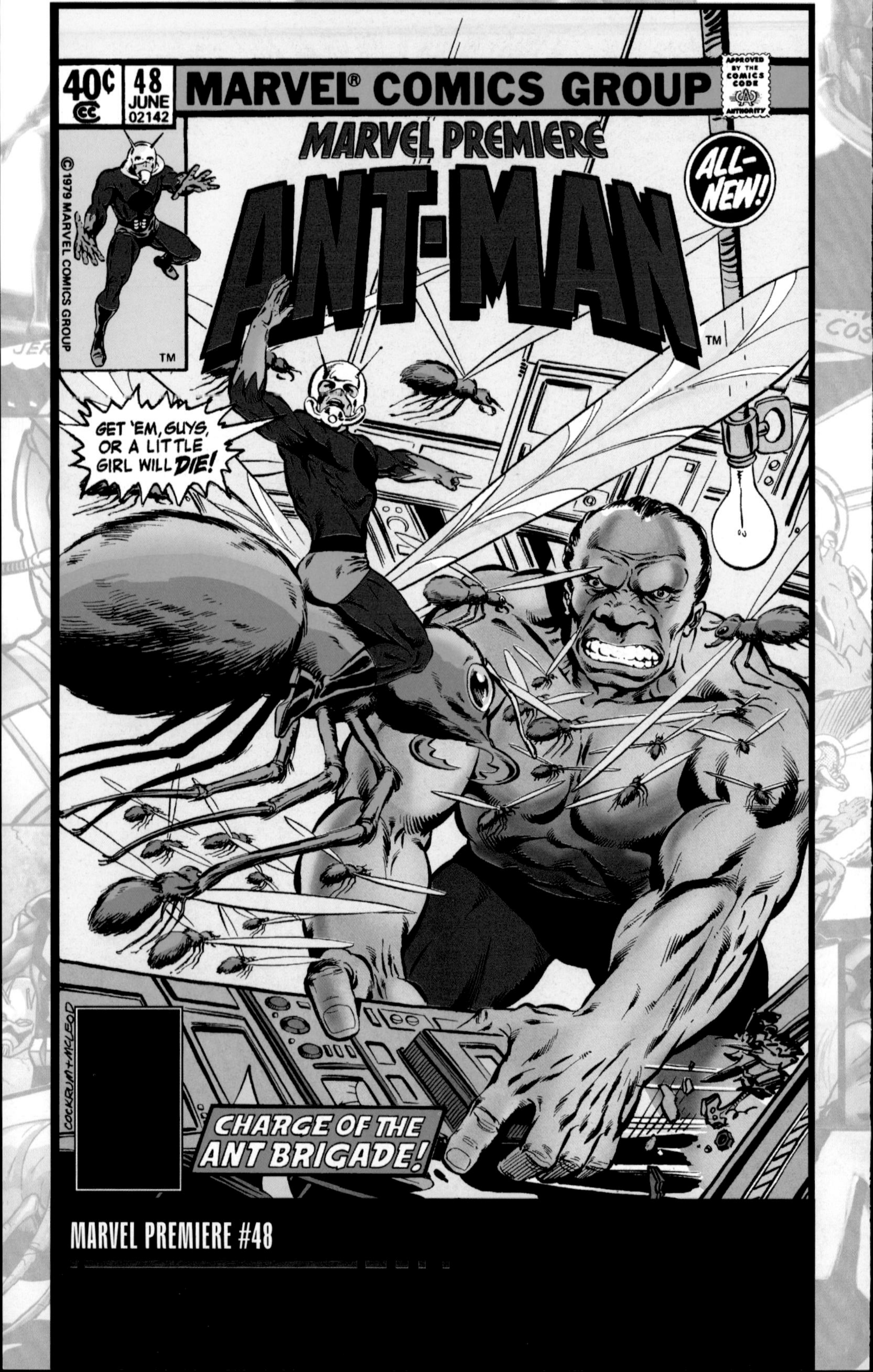
40¢
48
JUNE
02142
MARVEL® COMICS GROUP
APPROVED BY THE COMICS CODE AUTHORITY
MARVEL PREMIERE
ANT-MAN
ALL-NEW!
© 1979 MARVEL COMICS GROUP
GET 'EM, GUYS, OR A LITTLE GIRL WILL DIE!
COCKRUM+McLEOD
CHARGE OF THE ANT BRIGADE!

MARVEL PREMIERE #48

SCOTT LANG. . .electronics wizard, former cat-burglar, ex-convict, and doting father. Then fate took a hand, and Scott suddenly found himself in possession of the shrinking gas and cybernetic helmet of the most astonishing superhero of them all!

STAN LEE PRESENTS: **THE ALL-NEW ANT-MAN** ™

DAVID MICHELINIE WRITER / JOHN BYRNE & BOB LAYTON ARTISTS / DIANA ALBERS LETTERER / MARIO SEN COLORIST / ROGER STERN EDITOR / JIM SHOOTER EDITOR-IN-CHIEF

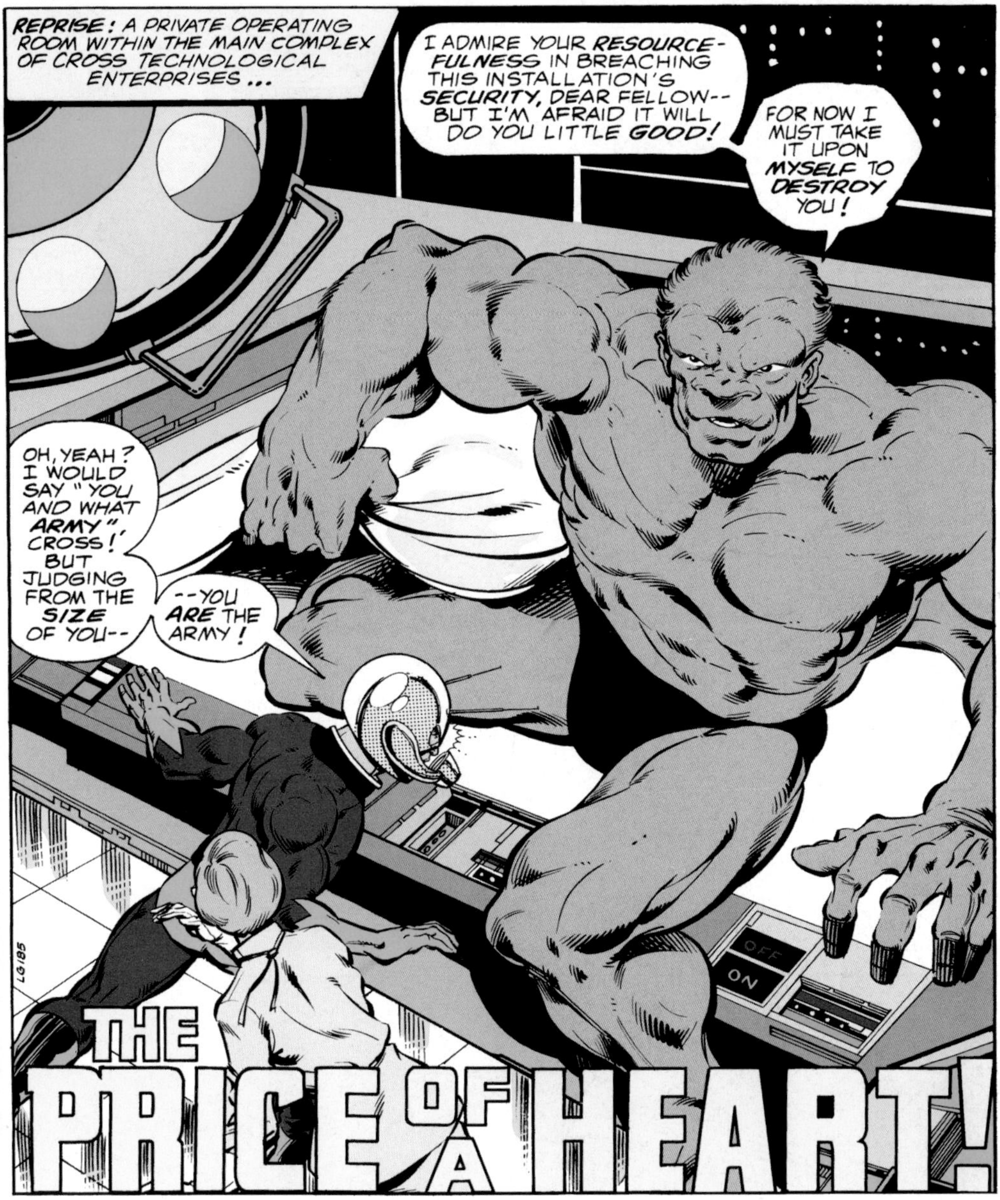

REPRISE: A PRIVATE OPERATING ROOM WITHIN THE MAIN COMPLEX OF CROSS TECHNOLOGICAL ENTERPRISES...
I ADMIRE YOUR RESOURCEFULNESS IN BREACHING THIS INSTALLATION'S SECURITY, DEAR FELLOW-- BUT I'M AFRAID IT WILL DO YOU LITTLE GOOD!
FOR NOW I MUST TAKE IT UPON MYSELF TO DESTROY YOU!
OH, YEAH? I WOULD SAY "YOU AND WHAT ARMY", CROSS! BUT JUDGING FROM THE SIZE OF YOU--
--YOU ARE THE ARMY!
OFF
ON
THE PRICE OF A HEART!

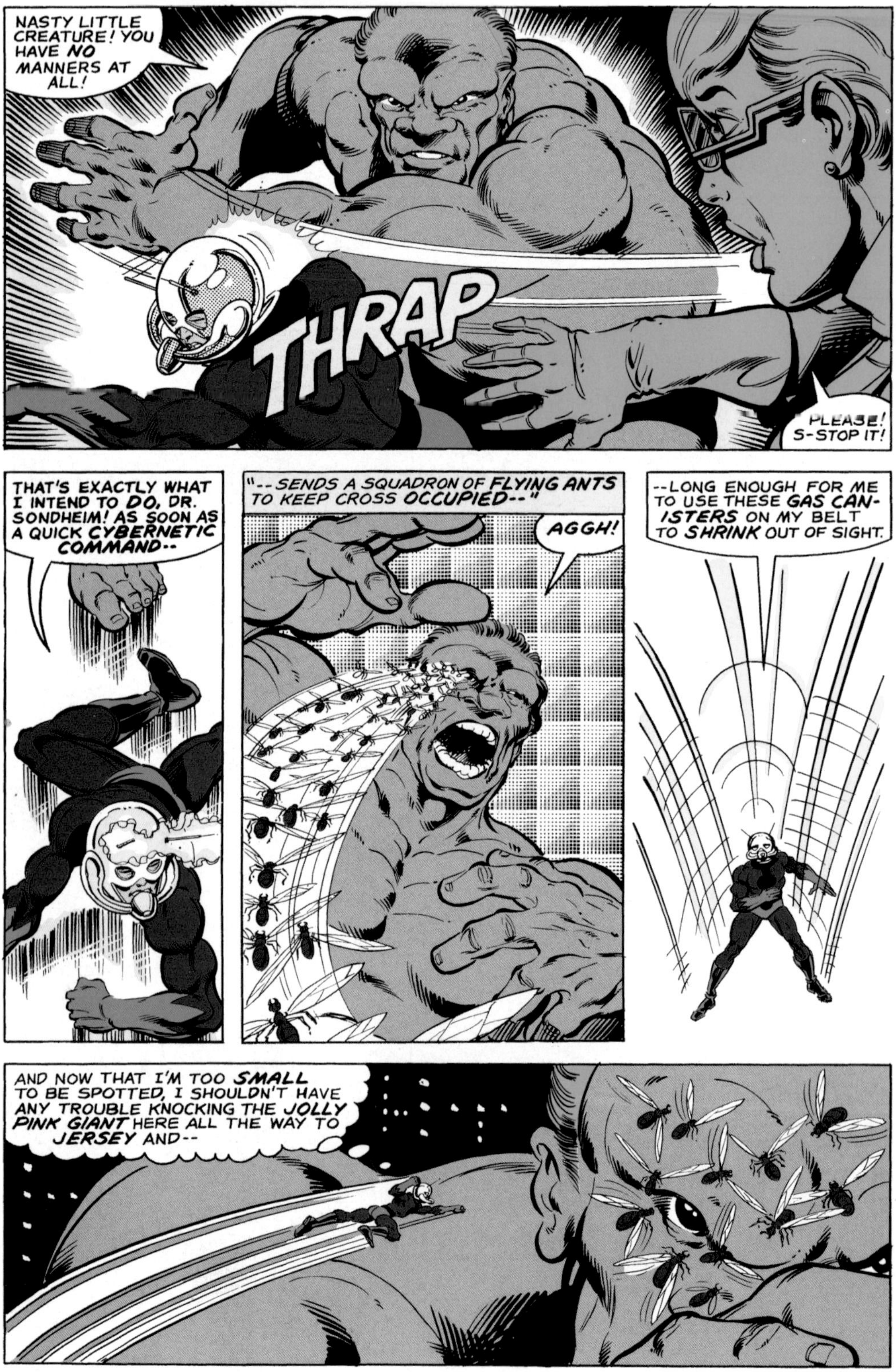
NASTY LITTLE CREATURE! YOU HAVE NO MANNERS AT ALL!
THRAP
PLEASE! S-STOP IT!
THAT'S EXACTLY WHAT I INTEND TO DO, DR. SONDHEIM! AS SOON AS A QUICK CYBERNETIC COMMAND--
"--SENDS A SQUADRON OF FLYING ANTS TO KEEP CROSS OCCUPIED--"
AGGH!
--LONG ENOUGH FOR ME TO USE THESE GAS CANISTERS ON MY BELT TO SHRINK OUT OF SIGHT.
AND NOW THAT I'M TOO SMALL TO BE SPOTTED, I SHOULDN'T HAVE ANY TROUBLE KNOCKING THE JOLLY PINK GIANT HERE ALL THE WAY TO JERSEY AND--

DEAR ME! THE POOR BOY WAS OBVIOUSLY UNAWARE THAT MY, ER, CONDITION HAS VASTLY INCREASED MY SENSORY PERCEPTION.

I COULD SEE HIM EASILY!

W-WHAT ARE YOU DOING?

OH, NOTHING DIABOLICAL, DOCTOR, I ASSURE YOU.

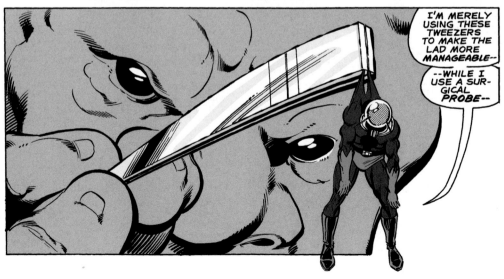

I'M MERELY USING THESE TWEEZERS TO MAKE THE LAD MORE MANAGEABLE--

--WHILE I USE A SURGICAL PROBE--

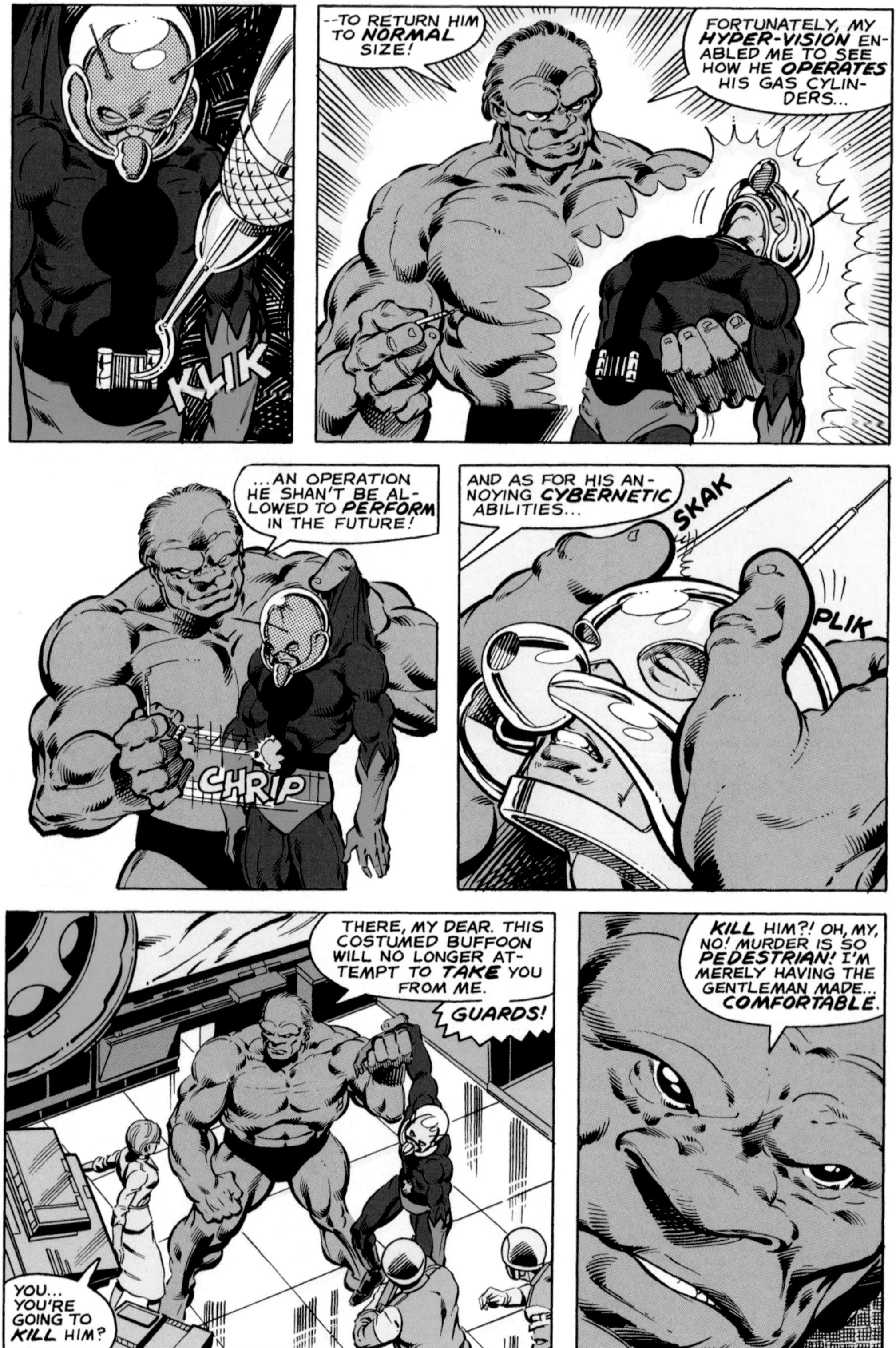
KLIK
--TO RETURN HIM TO NORMAL SIZE!
FORTUNATELY, MY HYPER-VISION ENABLED ME TO SEE HOW HE OPERATES HIS GAS CYLINDERS...
...AN OPERATION HE SHAN'T BE ALLOWED TO PERFORM IN THE FUTURE!
CHRIP
AND AS FOR HIS ANNOYING CYBERNETIC ABILITIES...
SKAK
PLIK
THERE, MY DEAR. THIS COSTUMED BUFFOON WILL NO LONGER ATTEMPT TO TAKE YOU FROM ME.
GUARDS!
YOU... YOU'RE GOING TO KILL HIM?
KILL HIM?! OH, MY, NO! MURDER IS SO PEDESTRIAN! I'M MERELY HAVING THE GENTLEMAN MADE... COMFORTABLE.

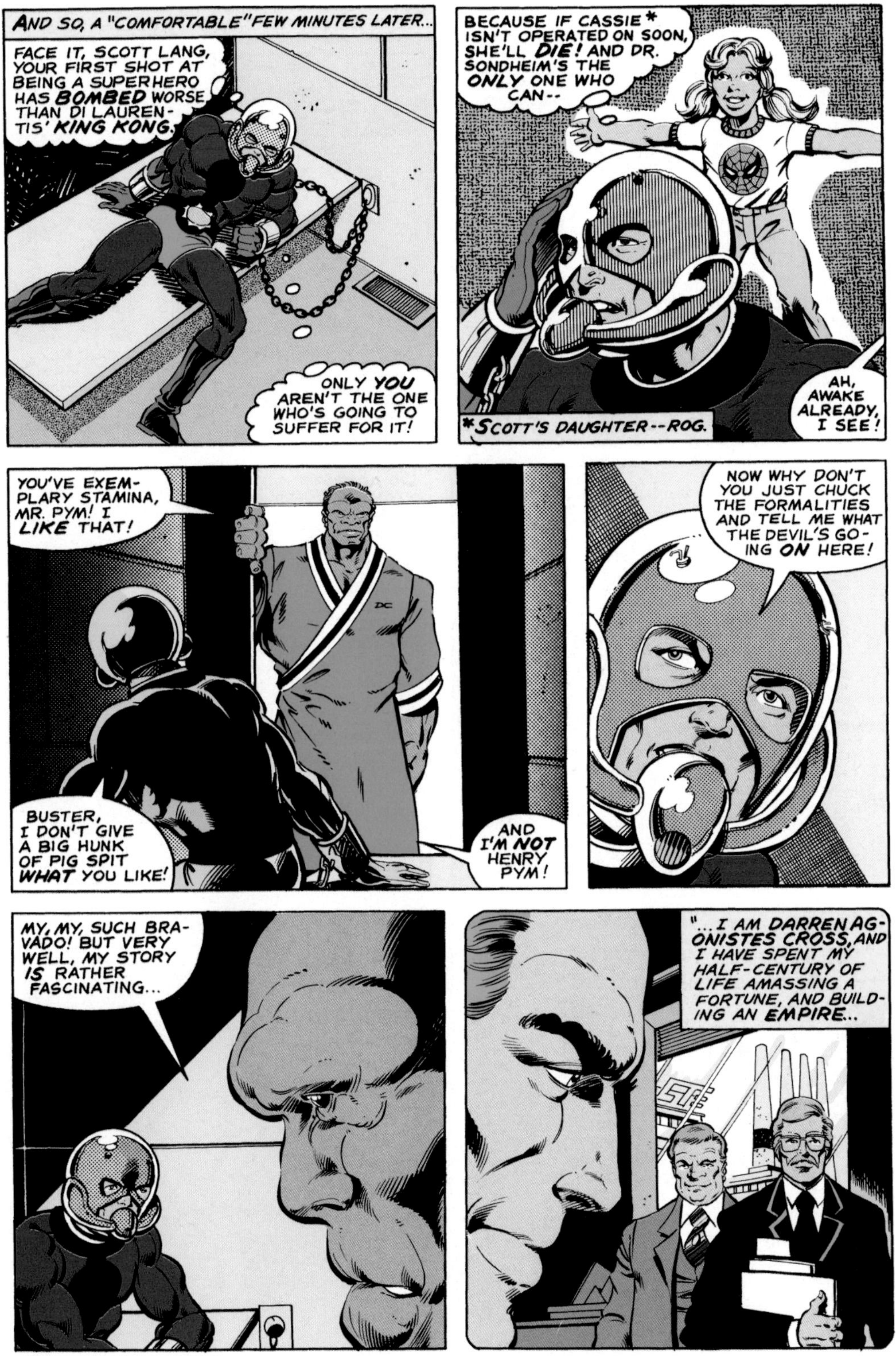
AND SO, A "COMFORTABLE" FEW MINUTES LATER...
FACE IT, SCOTT LANG, YOUR FIRST SHOT AT BEING A SUPERHERO HAS BOMBED WORSE THAN DI LAURENTIS' KING KONG.
ONLY YOU AREN'T THE ONE WHO'S GOING TO SUFFER FOR IT!
BECAUSE IF CASSIE* ISN'T OPERATED ON SOON, SHE'LL DIE! AND DR. SONDHEIM'S THE ONLY ONE WHO CAN--
*SCOTT'S DAUGHTER--ROG.
AH, AWAKE ALREADY, I SEE!
YOU'VE EXEMPLARY STAMINA, MR. PYM! I LIKE THAT!
BUSTER, I DON'T GIVE A BIG HUNK OF PIG SPIT WHAT YOU LIKE!
AND I'M NOT HENRY PYM!
NOW WHY DON'T YOU JUST CHUCK THE FORMALITIES AND TELL ME WHAT THE DEVIL'S GOING ON HERE!
MY, MY, SUCH BRAVADO! BUT VERY WELL, MY STORY IS RATHER FASCINATING...
"...I AM DARREN AGONISTES CROSS, AND I HAVE SPENT MY HALF-CENTURY OF LIFE AMASSING A FORTUNE, AND BUILDING AN EMPIRE...

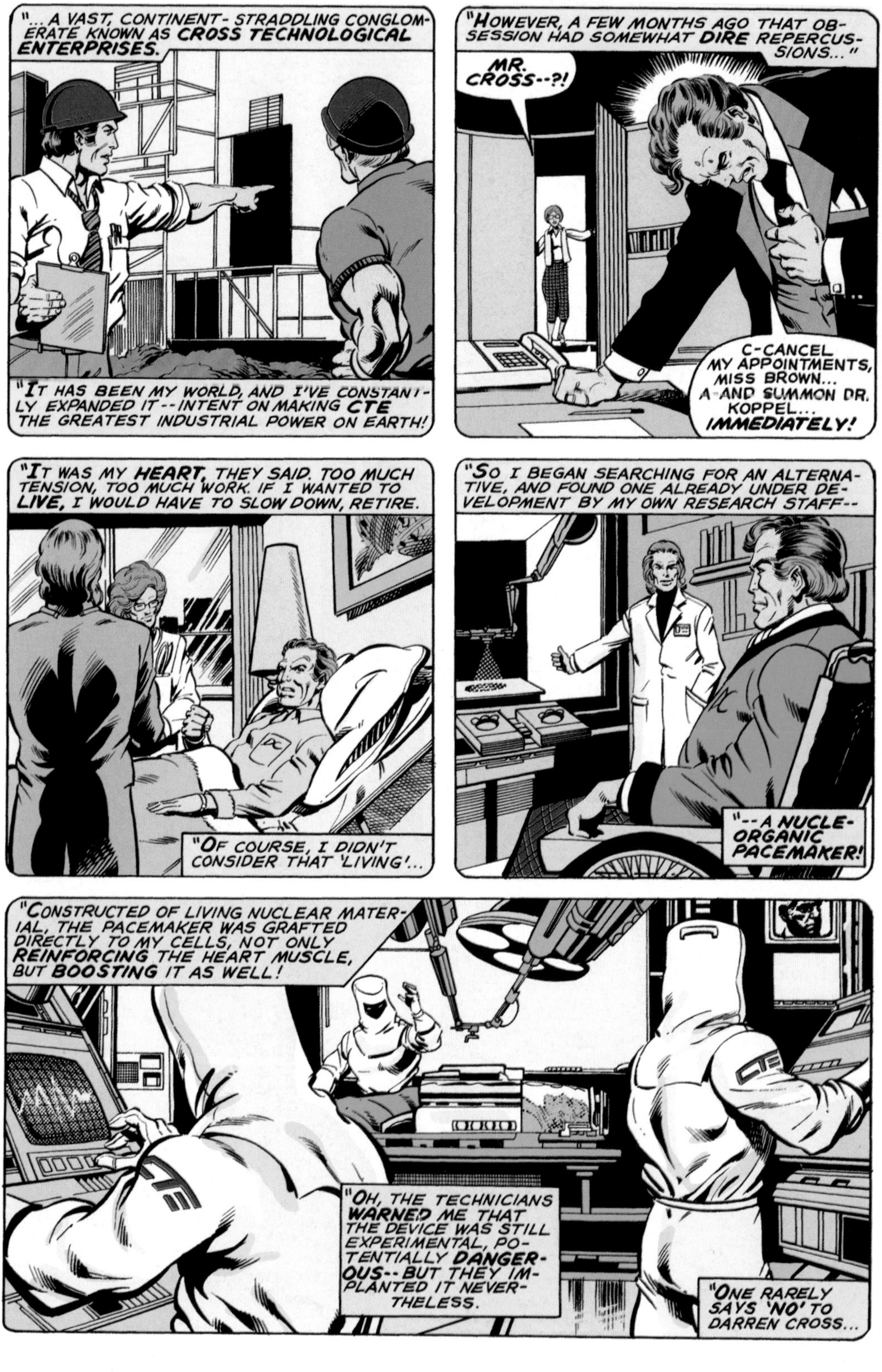
"... A VAST, CONTINENT- STRADDLING CONGLOM-ERATE KNOWN AS CROSS TECHNOLOGICAL ENTERPRISES.
"IT HAS BEEN MY WORLD, AND I'VE CONSTANTLY EXPANDED IT -- INTENT ON MAKING CTE THE GREATEST INDUSTRIAL POWER ON EARTH!
"HOWEVER, A FEW MONTHS AGO THAT OBSESSION HAD SOMEWHAT DIRE REPERCUSSIONS..."
MR. CROSS--?!
C-CANCEL MY APPOINTMENTS, MISS BROWN... A-AND SUMMON DR. KOPPEL... IMMEDIATELY!
"IT WAS MY HEART, THEY SAID. TOO MUCH TENSION, TOO MUCH WORK. IF I WANTED TO LIVE, I WOULD HAVE TO SLOW DOWN, RETIRE.
"OF COURSE, I DIDN'T CONSIDER THAT 'LIVING'...
"SO I BEGAN SEARCHING FOR AN ALTERNATIVE, AND FOUND ONE ALREADY UNDER DEVELOPMENT BY MY OWN RESEARCH STAFF--
"--A NUCLE-ORGANIC PACEMAKER!
"CONSTRUCTED OF LIVING NUCLEAR MATERIAL, THE PACEMAKER WAS GRAFTED DIRECTLY TO MY CELLS, NOT ONLY REINFORCING THE HEART MUSCLE, BUT BOOSTING IT AS WELL!
"OH, THE TECHNICIANS WARNED ME THAT THE DEVICE WAS STILL EXPERIMENTAL, POTENTIALLY DANGEROUS-- BUT THEY IMPLANTED IT NEVERTHELESS.
"ONE RARELY SAYS 'NO' TO DARREN CROSS...
CTE
CTE

"FOR A WHILE, THINGS WENT WELL, BUT THEN I BEGAN FEELING AN ODD... *PRESSURE* IN MY CHEST.

"IT WAS MOST UPSETTING--

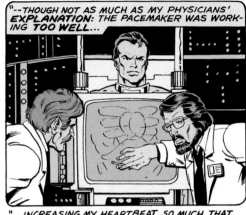

"--THOUGH NOT AS MUCH AS MY PHYSICIANS' *EXPLANATION:* THE PACEMAKER WAS WORKING *TOO WELL*...

"...INCREASING MY *HEARTBEAT* SO MUCH THAT MY ENTIRE CIRCULATORY SYSTEM WAS EN-*LARGING!* AND THE NATURE OF THE BOOSTER MADE ITS REMOVAL CERTAIN *DEATH!*

"AT FIRST, I ALMOST *ENJOYED* THE INCREASED PERCEPTION AND STRENGTH MY ALTERED METABOLISM ENGENDERED. BUT THEN--

"--CAME THE RATHER UN-FORTUNATE *COSMETIC* SIDE EFFECTS!

"SO IT WAS THAT I HAD GONE INTO *SECLUSION* BY THE TIME THE LEARNED MEN OF MEDICINE REVEALED THEIR *FINAL* DISCOVERY--

"--THAT THE ADDED STRAIN WAS *ERODING* MY HEART! NATURALLY, I HAD ANOTHER HEART *TRANSPLANTED*--ONLY THE PACEMAKER EX-HAUSTED *THAT* ONE, TOO... AS WELL AS THE NEXT...

"...AND THE *NEXT*...

"THUS WAS IT DURING THE PERIOD OF DARK BROODING WHICH FOLLOWED THAT I LEARNED OF DR. SONDHEIM, AND HER ADVANCED TECHNIQUES IN CRITICAL FOCUS *LASER* SURGERY..."

BUT EVEN IF DR. SONDHEIM WAS ABLE TO *REMOVE* THE PACEMAKER, WOULDN'T THAT STILL *KILL* YOU?

OBTUSE LAD, YOU MISS THE *POINT!*

PERHAPS *THIS* WILL MAKE THINGS CLEARER...!

CLIK

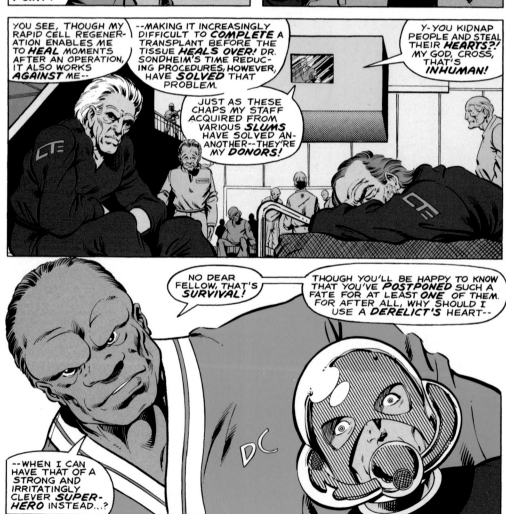

YOU SEE, THOUGH MY RAPID CELL REGENERATION ENABLES ME TO *HEAL* MOMENTS AFTER AN OPERATION, IT ALSO WORKS *AGAINST* ME--

--MAKING IT INCREASINGLY DIFFICULT TO *COMPLETE* A TRANSPLANT BEFORE THE TISSUE *HEALS OVER!* DR. SONDHEIM'S TIME REDUCING PROCEDURES, HOWEVER, HAVE *SOLVED* THAT PROBLEM.

JUST AS THESE CHAPS MY STAFF ACQUIRED FROM VARIOUS *SLUMS* HAVE SOLVED AN-ANOTHER--THEY'RE MY *DONORS!*

Y-YOU KIDNAP PEOPLE AND STEAL THEIR *HEARTS?!* MY GOD, CROSS, THAT'S *INHUMAN!*

NO DEAR FELLOW, THAT'S *SURVIVAL!*

THOUGH YOU'LL BE HAPPY TO KNOW THAT YOU'VE *POSTPONED* SUCH A FATE FOR AT LEAST *ONE* OF THEM. FOR AFTER ALL, WHY SHOULD I USE A *DERELICT'S* HEART--

--WHEN I CAN HAVE THAT OF A STRONG AND IRRITATINGLY CLEVER *SUPER-HERO* INSTEAD...?

DC

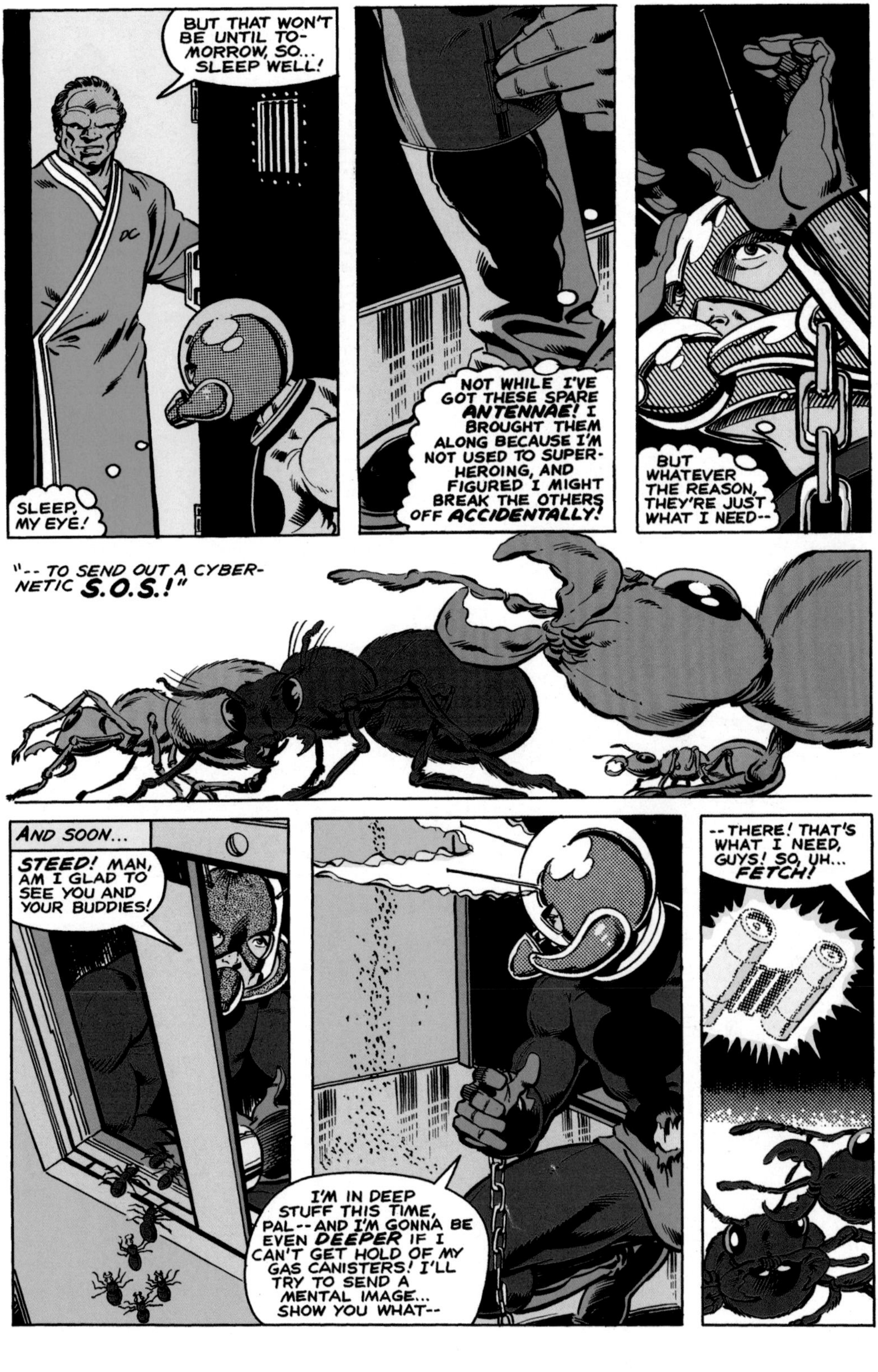
BUT THAT WON'T BE UNTIL TO-MORROW, SO... SLEEP WELL!
SLEEP, MY EYE!
NOT WHILE I'VE GOT THESE SPARE ANTENNAE! I BROUGHT THEM ALONG BECAUSE I'M NOT USED TO SUPER-HEROING, AND FIGURED I MIGHT BREAK THE OTHERS OFF ACCIDENTALLY!
BUT WHATEVER THE REASON, THEY'RE JUST WHAT I NEED--
"-- TO SEND OUT A CYBER-NETIC S.O.S.!"
AND SOON...
STEED! MAN, AM I GLAD TO SEE YOU AND YOUR BUDDIES!
I'M IN DEEP STUFF THIS TIME, PAL--AND I'M GONNA BE EVEN DEEPER IF I CAN'T GET HOLD OF MY GAS CANISTERS! I'LL TRY TO SEND A MENTAL IMAGE... SHOW YOU WHAT--
--THERE! THAT'S WHAT I NEED, GUYS! SO, UH... FETCH!

BUT TO FETCH, ONE FIRST MUST *FIND*--

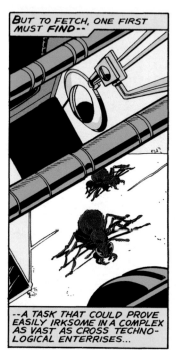

--A TASK THAT COULD PROVE EASILY IRKSOME IN A COMPLEX AS VAST AS CROSS TECHNOLOGICAL ENTERPRISES...

THOUGH THE SIX-LEGGED SEARCHERS EVIDENCE NO SUCH FRUSTRATION--

--GOING ABOUT THEIR SCRUTINY WITH A STOLID PRECISION THAT WOULD MAKE EX-CAT-BURGLAR SCOTT LANG PROUD--

--ESPECIALLY WHEN THEIR HOURS-CONSUMING EXPLORATION PROVES *SUCCESSFUL!*

BUT BY THEN THE NIGHT IS NEARLY *OVER*, AND AS THE OBEDIENT ANTS STRUGGLE TO RETURN THE MASSIVE CANISTERS TO THEIR MASTER, THE QUESTION REMAINS: HAS THEIR SUCCESS COME IN--

--*TIME* SURE GOES FAST WHEN YOU'RE SHAKING IN YOUR BOOTS! I CAN'T BELIEVE IT'S ALMOST DAWN--AND I'VE GOT MY *LIFE* STAKED ON A BUNCH OF *BUGS!*

SOMETIMES I--

--EH? WHAT'S THAT?

Y'KNOW, ERNIE, I'M REALLY GLAD MR. CROSS DECIDED TO PUT THE *SNUFFS* ON THAT ANT-MAN.

EVER SINCE THE LITTLE TWERP *DECKED* ME, I BEEN WANTIN' TO *STEP* ON 'IM MYSELF!

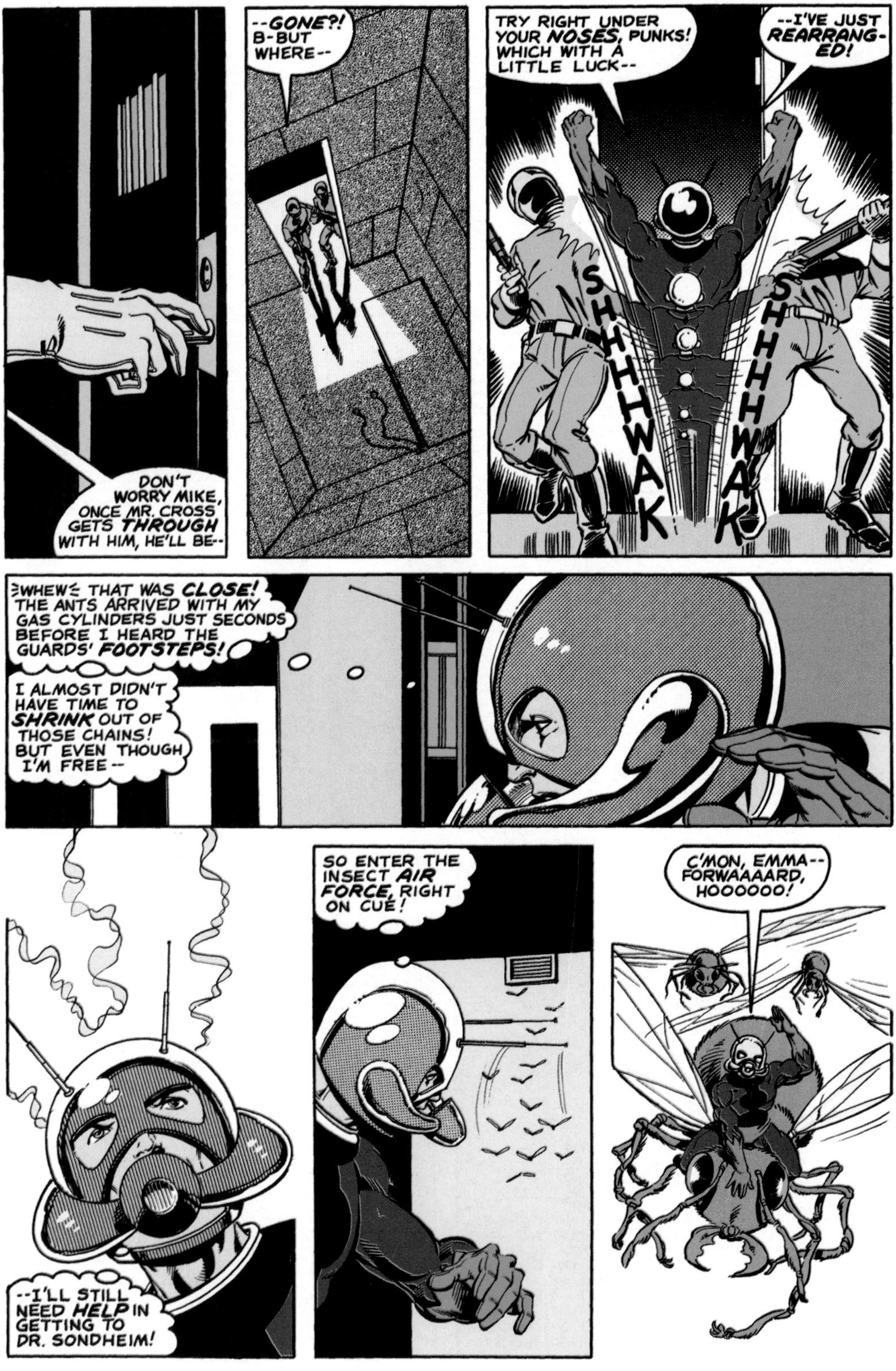
DON'T WORRY MIKE, ONCE MR. CROSS GETS THROUGH WITH HIM, HE'LL BE--
--GONE?! B-BUT WHERE--
TRY RIGHT UNDER YOUR NOSES, PUNKS! WHICH WITH A LITTLE LUCK--
--I'VE JUST REARRANG-ED!
SHHHHWAK
SHHHHWAK
WHEW! THAT WAS CLOSE! THE ANTS ARRIVED WITH MY GAS CYLINDERS JUST SECONDS BEFORE I HEARD THE GUARDS' FOOTSTEPS!
I ALMOST DIDN'T HAVE TIME TO SHRINK OUT OF THOSE CHAINS! BUT EVEN THOUGH I'M FREE--
--I'LL STILL NEED HELP IN GETTING TO DR. SONDHEIM!
SO ENTER THE INSECT AIR FORCE, RIGHT ON CUE!
C'MON, EMMA-- FORWAAAARD, HOOOOOO!

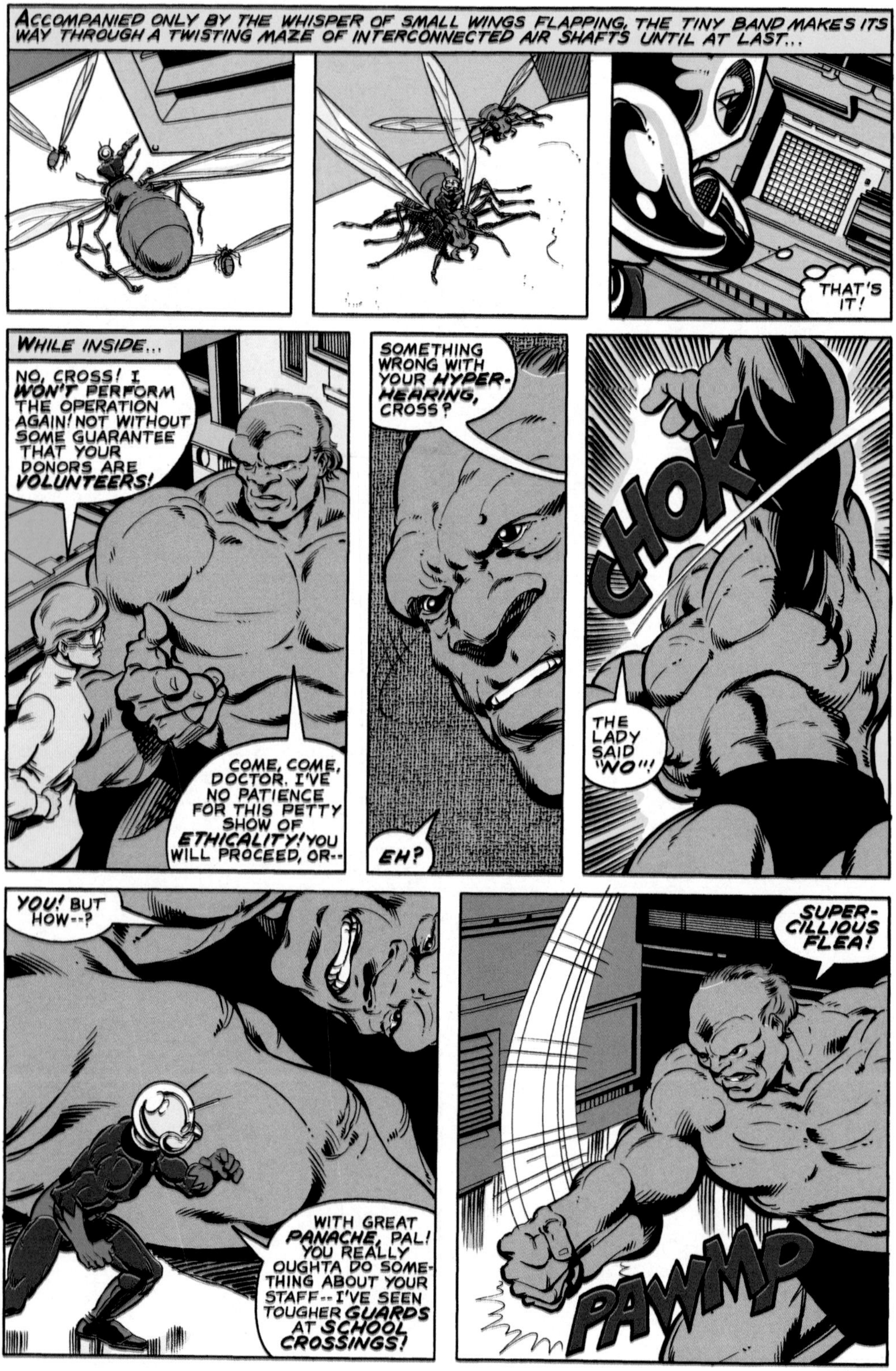
ACCOMPANIED ONLY BY THE WHISPER OF SMALL WINGS FLAPPING, THE TINY BAND MAKES ITS WAY THROUGH A TWISTING MAZE OF INTERCONNECTED AIR SHAFTS UNTIL AT LAST...
THAT'S IT!
WHILE INSIDE...
NO, CROSS! I WON'T PERFORM THE OPERATION AGAIN! NOT WITHOUT SOME GUARANTEE THAT YOUR DONORS ARE VOLUNTEERS!
COME, COME, DOCTOR. I'VE NO PATIENCE FOR THIS PETTY SHOW OF ETHICALITY! YOU WILL PROCEED, OR--
SOMETHING WRONG WITH YOUR HYPER-HEARING, CROSS?
EH?
CHOK
THE LADY SAID "NO"!
YOU! BUT HOW--?
WITH GREAT PANACHE, PAL! YOU REALLY OUGHTA DO SOMETHING ABOUT YOUR STAFF--I'VE SEEN TOUGHER GUARDS AT SCHOOL CROSSINGS!
SUPER-CILLIOUS FLEA!
PAWMP

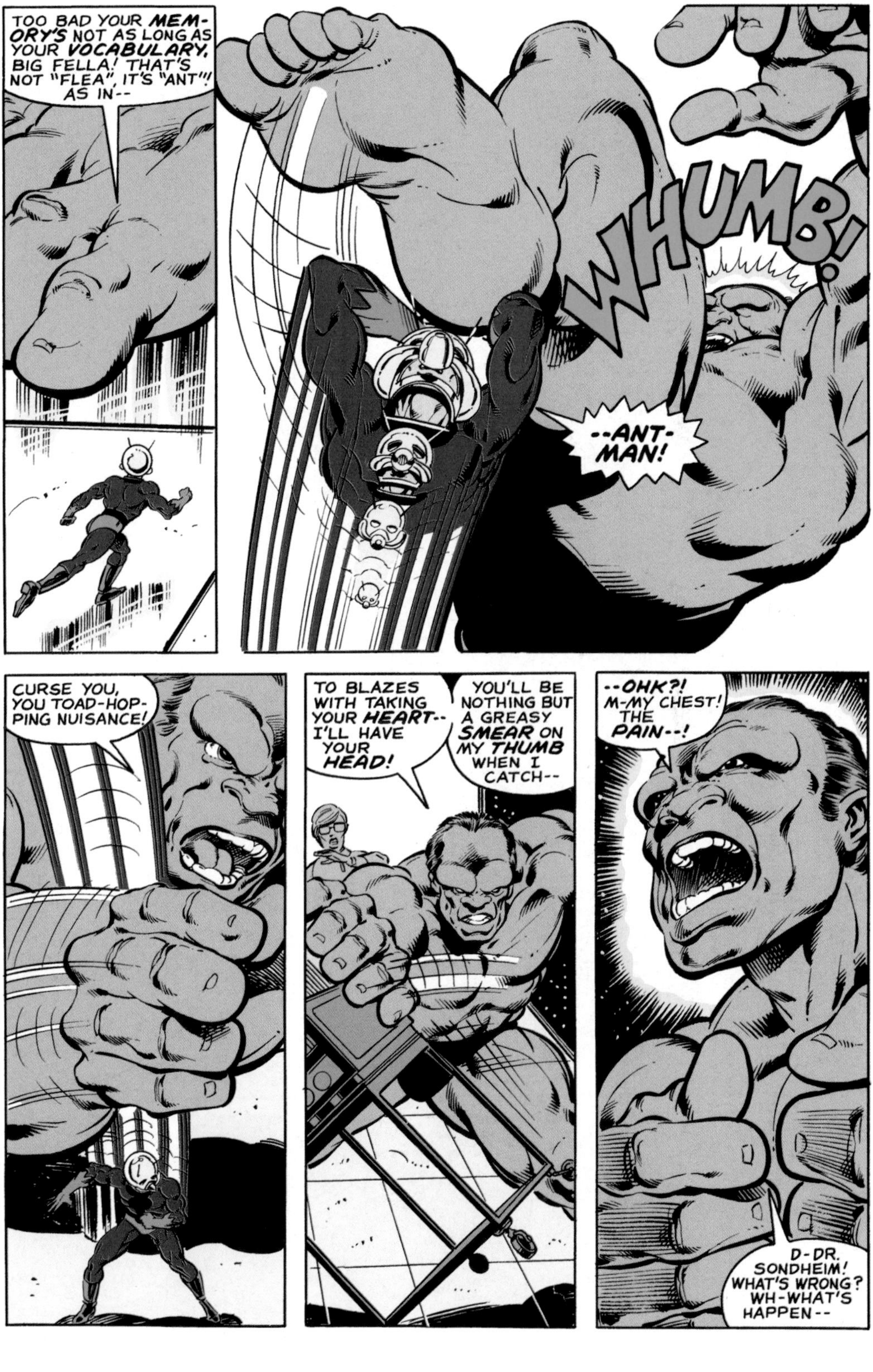
TOO BAD YOUR MEMORY'S NOT AS LONG AS YOUR VOCABULARY, BIG FELLA! THAT'S NOT "FLEA", IT'S "ANT"! AS IN--
WHUMB!
--ANT-MAN!
CURSE YOU, YOU TOAD-HOPPING NUISANCE!
TO BLAZES WITH TAKING YOUR HEART-- I'LL HAVE YOUR HEAD!
YOU'LL BE NOTHING BUT A GREASY SMEAR ON MY THUMB WHEN I CATCH--
--OHK?! M-MY CHEST! THE PAIN--!
D-DR. SONDHEIM! WHAT'S WRONG? WH-WHAT'S HAPPEN--

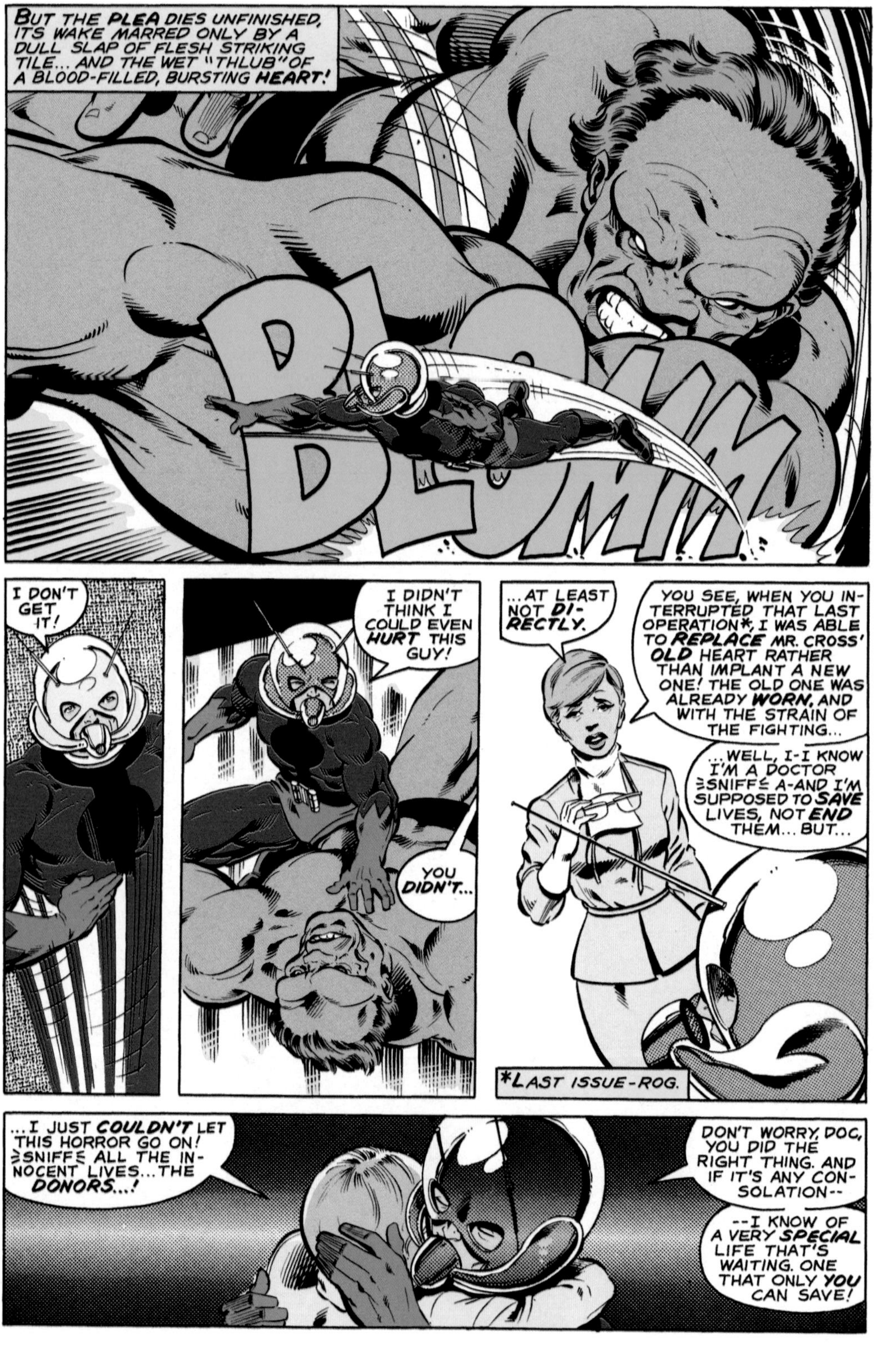
BUT THE PLEA DIES UNFINISHED, ITS WAKE MARRED ONLY BY A DULL SLAP OF FLESH STRIKING TILE... AND THE WET "THLUB" OF A BLOOD-FILLED, BURSTING HEART!
BLOMM
I DON'T GET IT!
I DIDN'T THINK I COULD EVEN HURT THIS GUY!
YOU DIDN'T...
...AT LEAST NOT DI-RECTLY.
YOU SEE, WHEN YOU IN-TERRUPTED THAT LAST OPERATION*, I WAS ABLE TO REPLACE MR. CROSS' OLD HEART RATHER THAN IMPLANT A NEW ONE! THE OLD ONE WAS ALREADY WORN, AND WITH THE STRAIN OF THE FIGHTING...
...WELL, I-I KNOW I'M A DOCTOR ≥SNIFF≤ A-AND I'M SUPPOSED TO SAVE LIVES, NOT END THEM... BUT...
*LAST ISSUE-ROG.
...I JUST COULDN'T LET THIS HORROR GO ON! ≥SNIFF≤ ALL THE IN-NOCENT LIVES... THE DONORS...!
DON'T WORRY, DOC, YOU DID THE RIGHT THING. AND IF IT'S ANY CON-SOLATION--
--I KNOW OF A VERY SPECIAL LIFE THAT'S WAITING. ONE THAT ONLY YOU CAN SAVE!

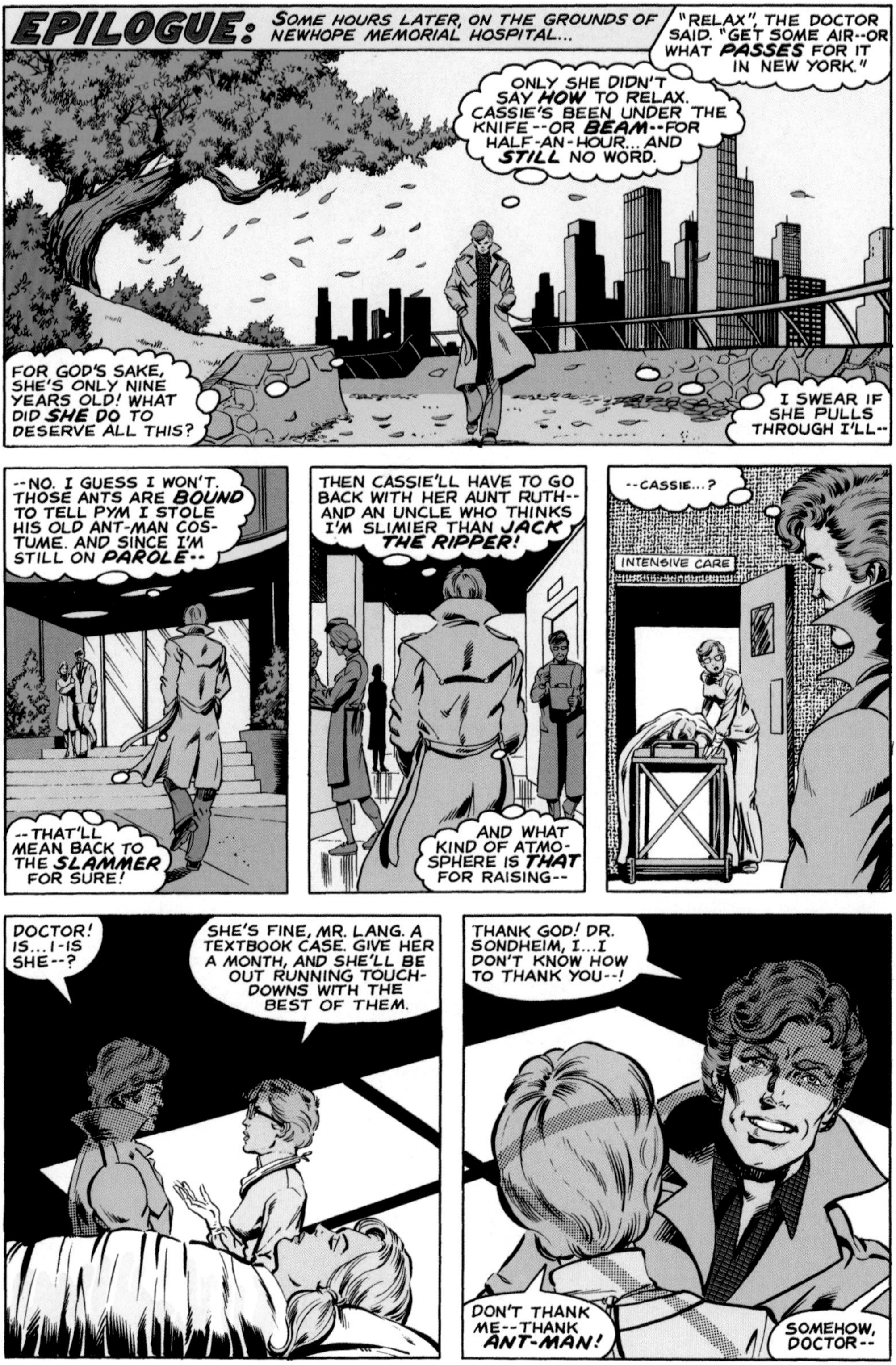
EPILOGUE: SOME HOURS LATER, ON THE GROUNDS OF NEWHOPE MEMORIAL HOSPITAL...
"RELAX", THE DOCTOR SAID. "GET SOME AIR--OR WHAT PASSES FOR IT IN NEW YORK."
ONLY SHE DIDN'T SAY HOW TO RELAX. CASSIE'S BEEN UNDER THE KNIFE--OR BEAM--FOR HALF-AN-HOUR... AND STILL NO WORD.
FOR GOD'S SAKE, SHE'S ONLY NINE YEARS OLD! WHAT DID SHE DO TO DESERVE ALL THIS?
I SWEAR IF SHE PULLS THROUGH I'LL--
--NO. I GUESS I WON'T. THOSE ANTS ARE BOUND TO TELL PYM I STOLE HIS OLD ANT-MAN COSTUME. AND SINCE I'M STILL ON PAROLE--
--THAT'LL MEAN BACK TO THE SLAMMER FOR SURE!
THEN CASSIE'LL HAVE TO GO BACK WITH HER AUNT RUTH--AND AN UNCLE WHO THINKS I'M SLIMIER THAN JACK THE RIPPER!
AND WHAT KIND OF ATMOSPHERE IS THAT FOR RAISING--
--CASSIE...?
INTENSIVE CARE
DOCTOR! IS...I-IS SHE--?
SHE'S FINE, MR. LANG. A TEXTBOOK CASE. GIVE HER A MONTH, AND SHE'LL BE OUT RUNNING TOUCHDOWNS WITH THE BEST OF THEM.
THANK GOD! DR. SONDHEIM, I...I DON'T KNOW HOW TO THANK YOU--!
DON'T THANK ME--THANK ANT-MAN!
SOMEHOW, DOCTOR--

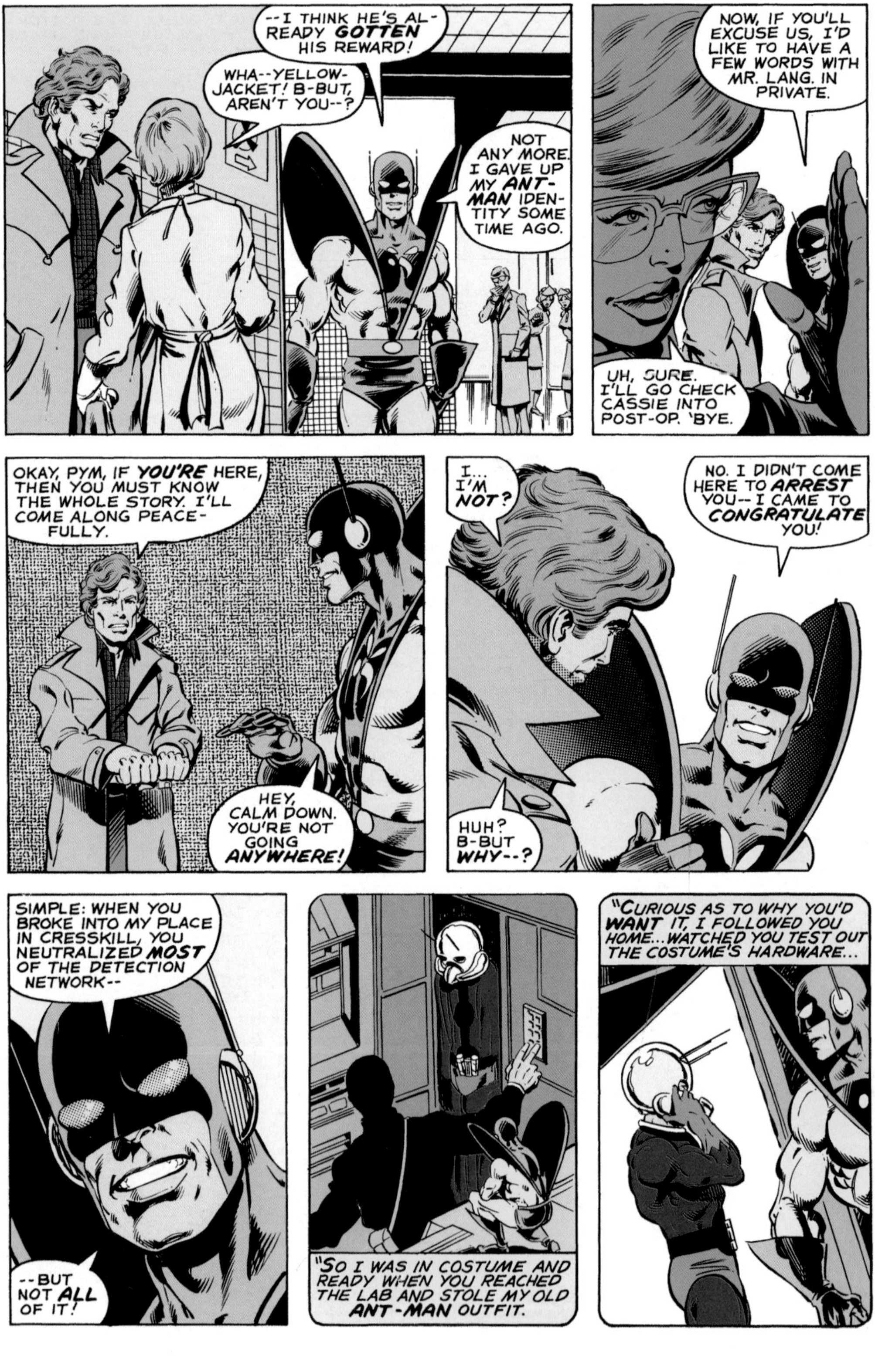
--I THINK HE'S AL-READY GOTTEN HIS REWARD!
WHA--YELLOW-JACKET! B-BUT, AREN'T YOU--?
NOT ANY MORE. I GAVE UP MY ANT-MAN IDENTITY SOME TIME AGO.
NOW, IF YOU'LL EXCUSE US, I'D LIKE TO HAVE A FEW WORDS WITH MR. LANG. IN PRIVATE.
UH, SURE. I'LL GO CHECK CASSIE INTO POST-OP. 'BYE.
OKAY, PYM, IF YOU'RE HERE, THEN YOU MUST KNOW THE WHOLE STORY. I'LL COME ALONG PEACE-FULLY.
HEY, CALM DOWN. YOU'RE NOT GOING ANYWHERE!
I... I'M NOT?
NO. I DIDN'T COME HERE TO ARREST YOU--I CAME TO CONGRATULATE YOU!
HUH? B-BUT WHY--?
SIMPLE: WHEN YOU BROKE INTO MY PLACE IN CRESSKILL, YOU NEUTRALIZED MOST OF THE DETECTION NETWORK--
--BUT NOT ALL OF IT!
"SO I WAS IN COSTUME AND READY WHEN YOU REACHED THE LAB AND STOLE MY OLD ANT-MAN OUTFIT.
"CURIOUS AS TO WHY YOU'D WANT IT, I FOLLOWED YOU HOME...WATCHED YOU TEST OUT THE COSTUME'S HARDWARE...

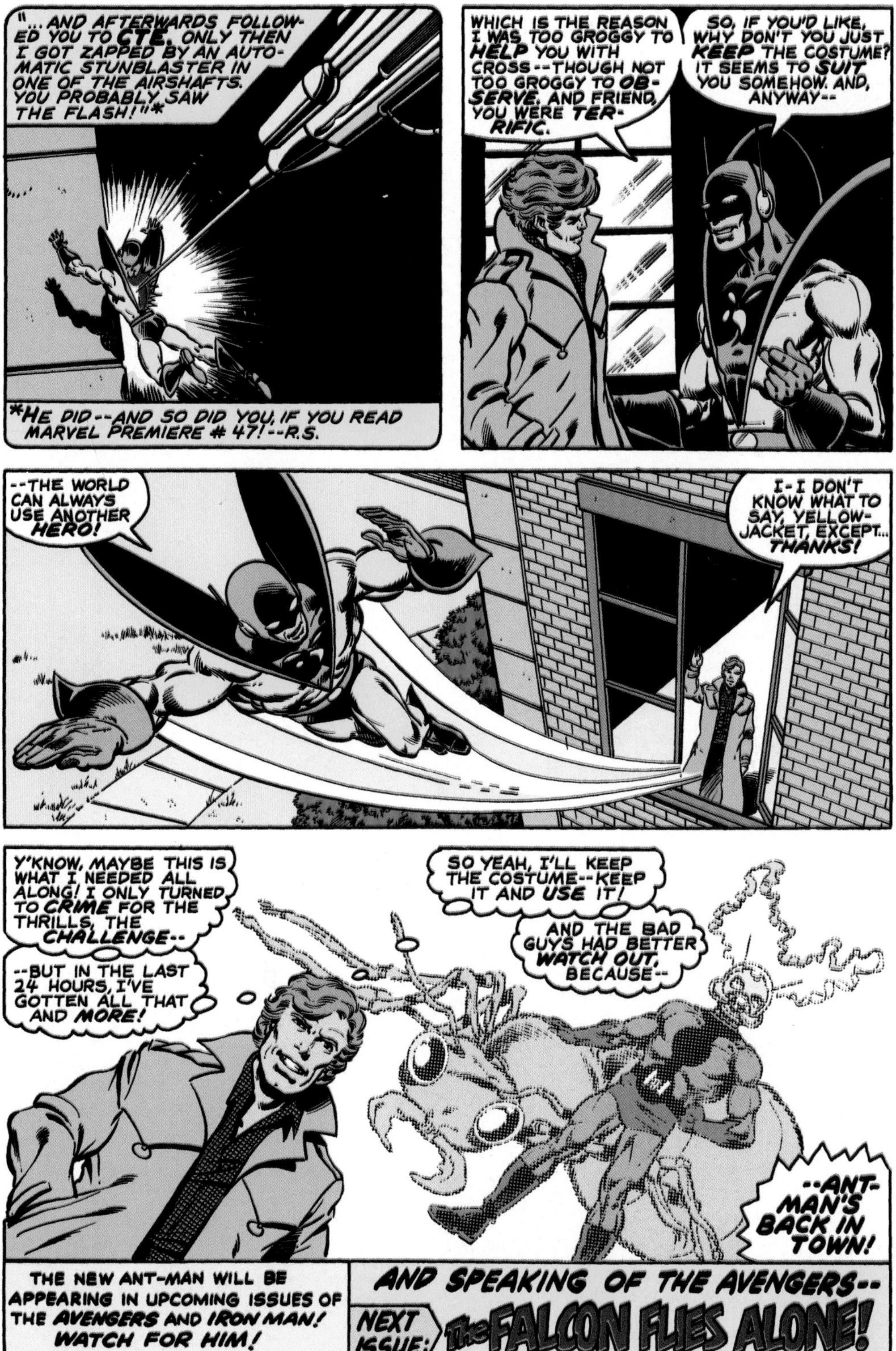
"...AND AFTERWARDS FOLLOWED YOU TO CTE. ONLY THEN I GOT ZAPPED BY AN AUTOMATIC STUNBLASTER IN ONE OF THE AIRSHAFTS. YOU PROBABLY SAW THE FLASH!"*
*HE DID--AND SO DID YOU, IF YOU READ MARVEL PREMIERE #47!--R.S.
WHICH IS THE REASON I WAS TOO GROGGY TO HELP YOU WITH CROSS--THOUGH NOT TOO GROGGY TO OBSERVE. AND FRIEND, YOU WERE TERRIFIC.
SO, IF YOU'D LIKE, WHY DON'T YOU JUST KEEP THE COSTUME? IT SEEMS TO SUIT YOU SOMEHOW. AND, ANYWAY--
--THE WORLD CAN ALWAYS USE ANOTHER HERO!
I-I DON'T KNOW WHAT TO SAY, YELLOWJACKET, EXCEPT... THANKS!
Y'KNOW, MAYBE THIS IS WHAT I NEEDED ALL ALONG! I ONLY TURNED TO CRIME FOR THE THRILLS, THE CHALLENGE--
--BUT IN THE LAST 24 HOURS, I'VE GOTTEN ALL THAT AND MORE!
SO YEAH, I'LL KEEP THE COSTUME--KEEP IT AND USE IT!
AND THE BAD GUYS HAD BETTER WATCH OUT, BECAUSE--
--ANT-MAN'S BACK IN TOWN!
THE NEW ANT-MAN WILL BE APPEARING IN UPCOMING ISSUES OF THE AVENGERS AND IRON MAN! WATCH FOR HIM!
AND SPEAKING OF THE AVENGERS--
NEXT ISSUE: The FALCON FLIES ALONE!

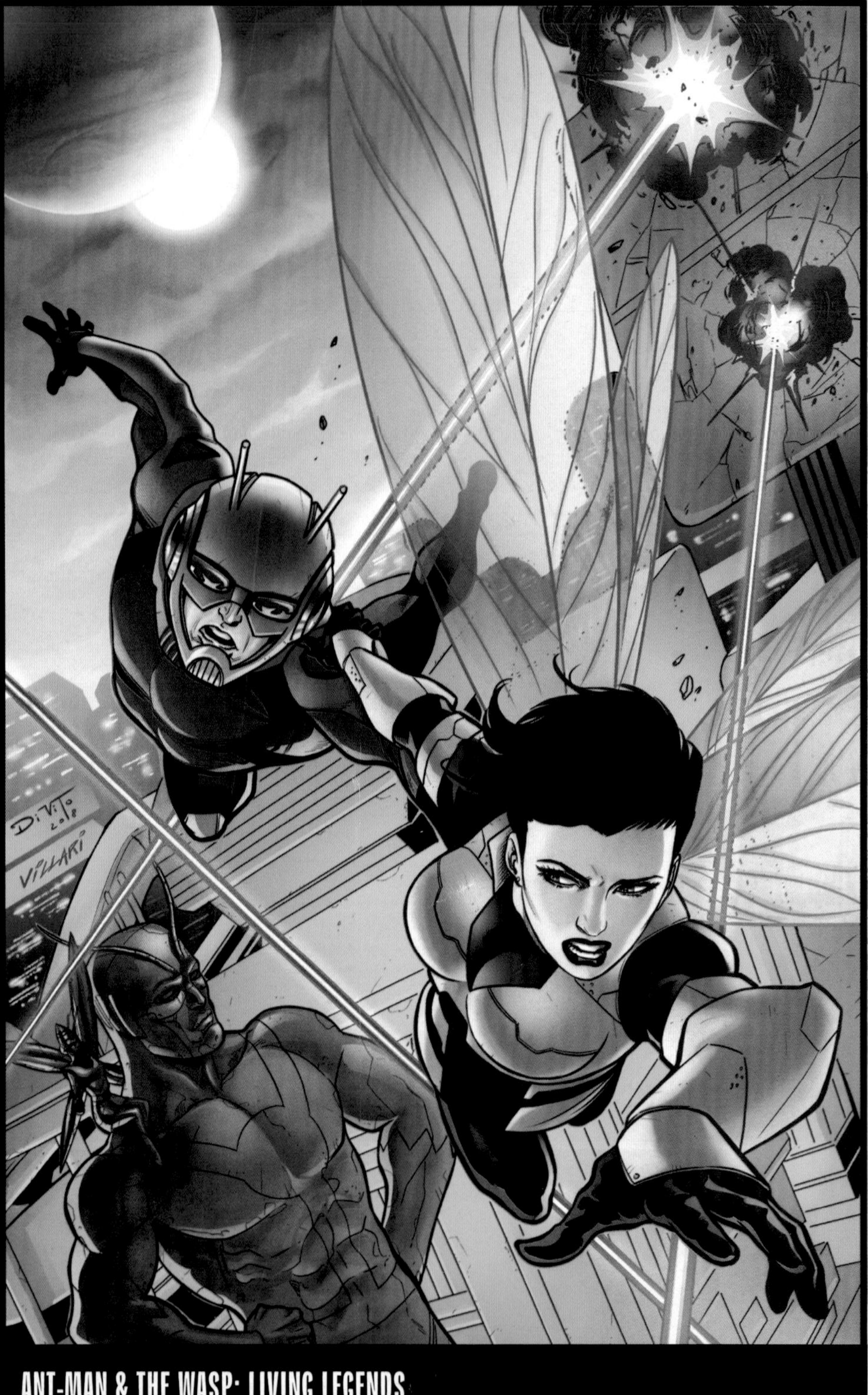

ANT-MAN & THE WASP: LIVING LEGENDS

WHEN THE LEADER OF AN INTERDIMENSIONAL FORCE IS CAPTURED, THEY REACH OUT TO THEIR OLD FRIENDS ANT-MAN AND THE WASP!

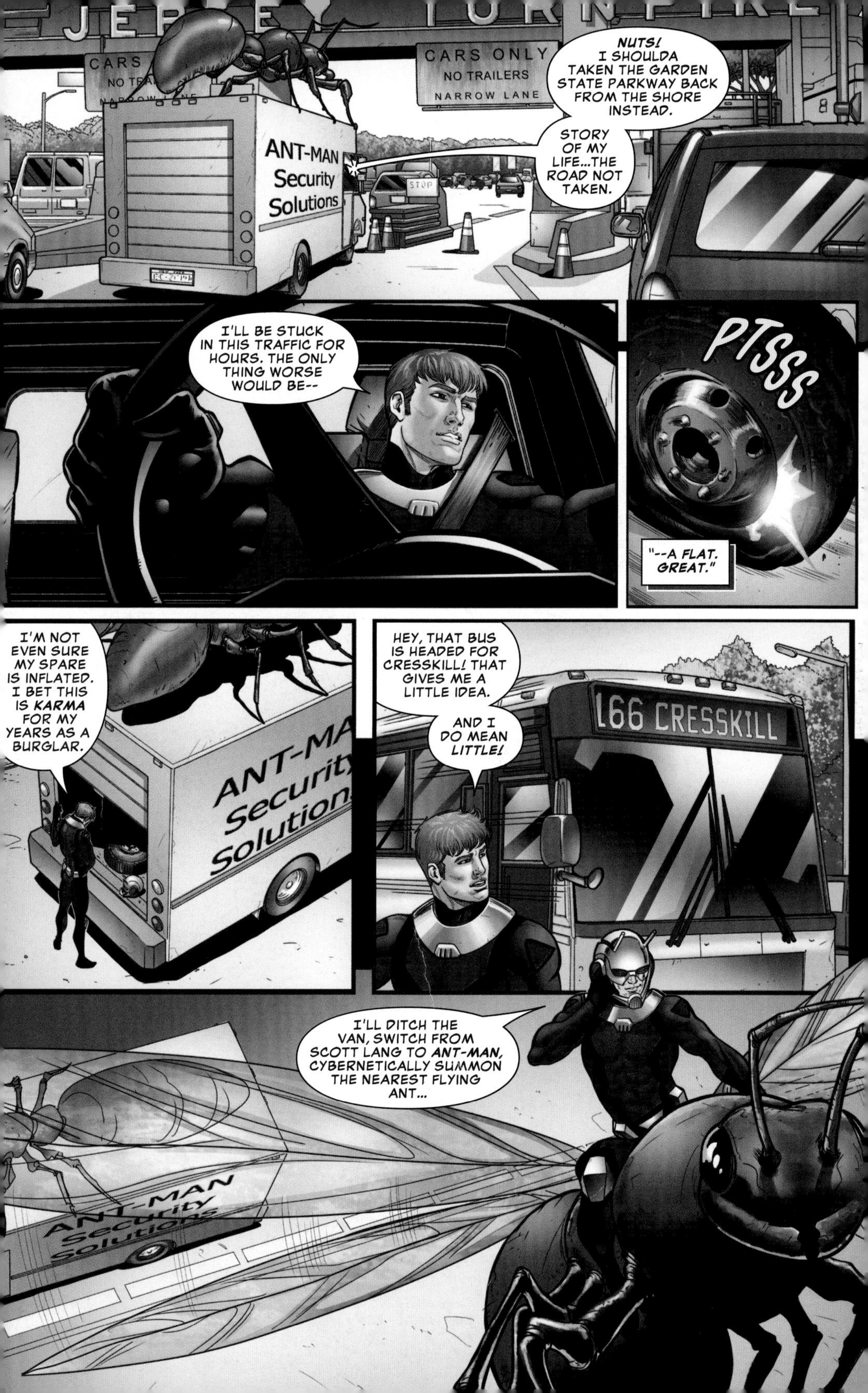

JERSEY TURNPIKE
CARS NO TRAILERS NARROW LANE
CARS ONLY NO TRAILERS NARROW LANE
ANT-MAN Security Solutions
STOP
NUTS! I SHOULDA TAKEN THE GARDEN STATE PARKWAY BACK FROM THE SHORE INSTEAD.
STORY OF MY LIFE...THE ROAD NOT TAKEN.
I'LL BE STUCK IN THIS TRAFFIC FOR HOURS. THE ONLY THING WORSE WOULD BE--
PTSSS
"--A FLAT. GREAT."
I'M NOT EVEN SURE MY SPARE IS INFLATED. I BET THIS IS KARMA FOR MY YEARS AS A BURGLAR.
HEY, THAT BUS IS HEADED FOR CRESSKILL! THAT GIVES ME A LITTLE IDEA.
AND I DO MEAN LITTLE!
166 CRESSKILL
I'LL DITCH THE VAN, SWITCH FROM SCOTT LANG TO ANT-MAN, CYBERNETICALLY SUMMON THE NEAREST FLYING ANT...
ANT-MAN Security Solutions

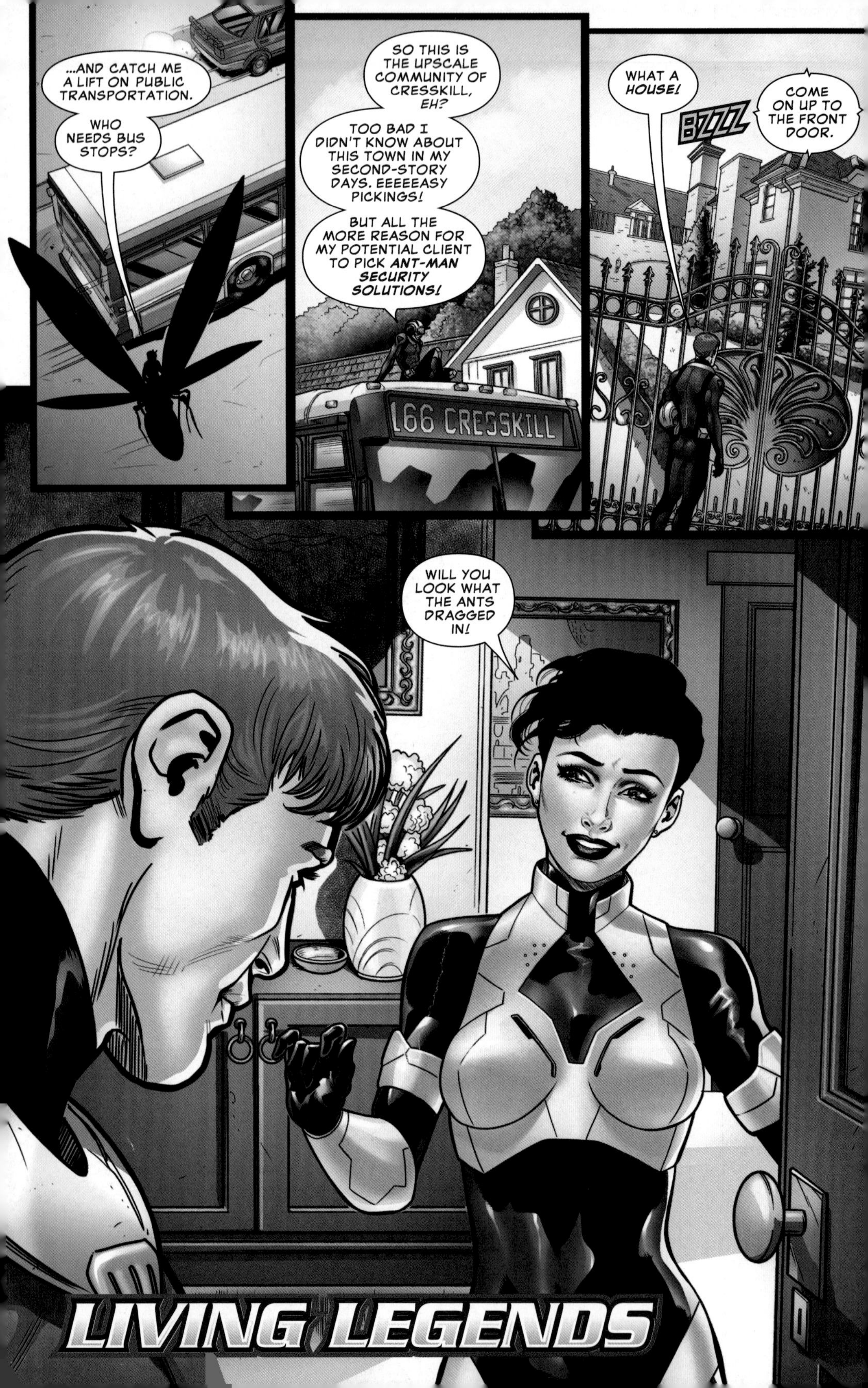
...AND CATCH ME A LIFT ON PUBLIC TRANSPORTATION.
WHO NEEDS BUS STOPS?
SO THIS IS THE UPSCALE COMMUNITY OF CRESSKILL, EH?
TOO BAD I DIDN'T KNOW ABOUT THIS TOWN IN MY SECOND-STORY DAYS. EEEEEASY PICKINGS!
BUT ALL THE MORE REASON FOR MY POTENTIAL CLIENT TO PICK ANT-MAN SECURITY SOLUTIONS!
166 CRESSKILL
WHAT A HOUSE!
BZZZ
COME ON UP TO THE FRONT DOOR.
WILL YOU LOOK WHAT THE ANTS DRAGGED IN!
LIVING LEGENDS

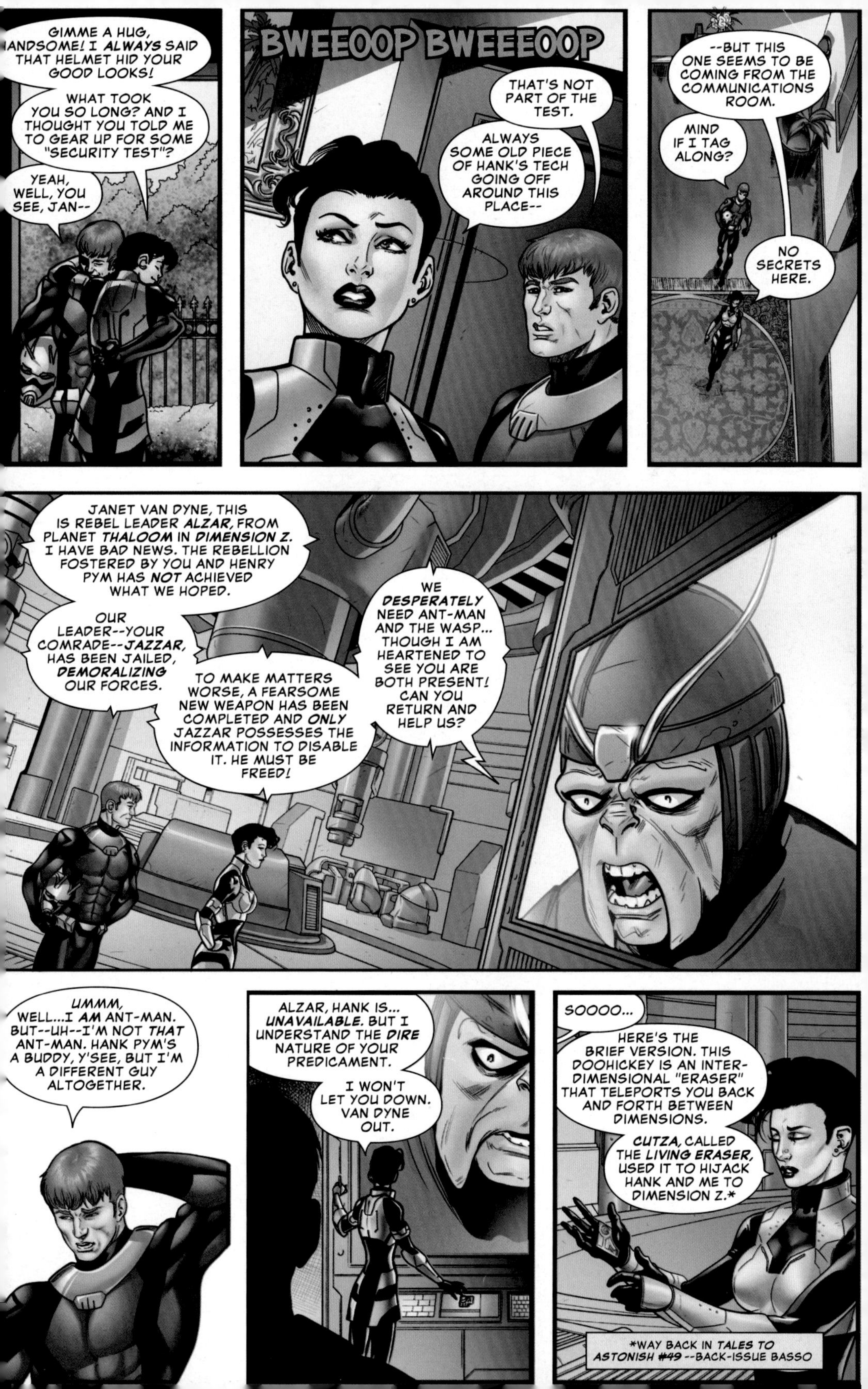

GIMME A HUG, HANDSOME! I ALWAYS SAID THAT HELMET HID YOUR GOOD LOOKS!
WHAT TOOK YOU SO LONG? AND I THOUGHT YOU TOLD ME TO GEAR UP FOR SOME "SECURITY TEST"?
YEAH, WELL, YOU SEE, JAN--
BWEEOOP BWEEEOOP
THAT'S NOT PART OF THE TEST.
ALWAYS SOME OLD PIECE OF HANK'S TECH GOING OFF AROUND THIS PLACE--
--BUT THIS ONE SEEMS TO BE COMING FROM THE COMMUNICATIONS ROOM.
MIND IF I TAG ALONG?
NO SECRETS HERE.
JANET VAN DYNE, THIS IS REBEL LEADER ALZAR, FROM PLANET THALOOM IN DIMENSION Z. I HAVE BAD NEWS. THE REBELLION FOSTERED BY YOU AND HENRY PYM HAS NOT ACHIEVED WHAT WE HOPED.
OUR LEADER--YOUR COMRADE--JAZZAR, HAS BEEN JAILED, DEMORALIZING OUR FORCES.
TO MAKE MATTERS WORSE, A FEARSOME NEW WEAPON HAS BEEN COMPLETED AND ONLY JAZZAR POSSESSES THE INFORMATION TO DISABLE IT. HE MUST BE FREED!
WE DESPERATELY NEED ANT-MAN AND THE WASP... THOUGH I AM HEARTENED TO SEE YOU ARE BOTH PRESENT! CAN YOU RETURN AND HELP US?
UMMM, WELL...I AM ANT-MAN. BUT--UH--I'M NOT THAT ANT-MAN. HANK PYM'S A BUDDY, Y'SEE, BUT I'M A DIFFERENT GUY ALTOGETHER.
ALZAR, HANK IS... UNAVAILABLE. BUT I UNDERSTAND THE DIRE NATURE OF YOUR PREDICAMENT.
I WON'T LET YOU DOWN. VAN DYNE OUT.
SOOOO...
HERE'S THE BRIEF VERSION. THIS DOOHICKEY IS AN INTER-DIMENSIONAL "ERASER" THAT TELEPORTS YOU BACK AND FORTH BETWEEN DIMENSIONS.
CUTZA, CALLED THE LIVING ERASER, USED IT TO HIJACK HANK AND ME TO DIMENSION Z.*
*WAY BACK IN TALES TO ASTONISH #49 --BACK-ISSUE BASSO

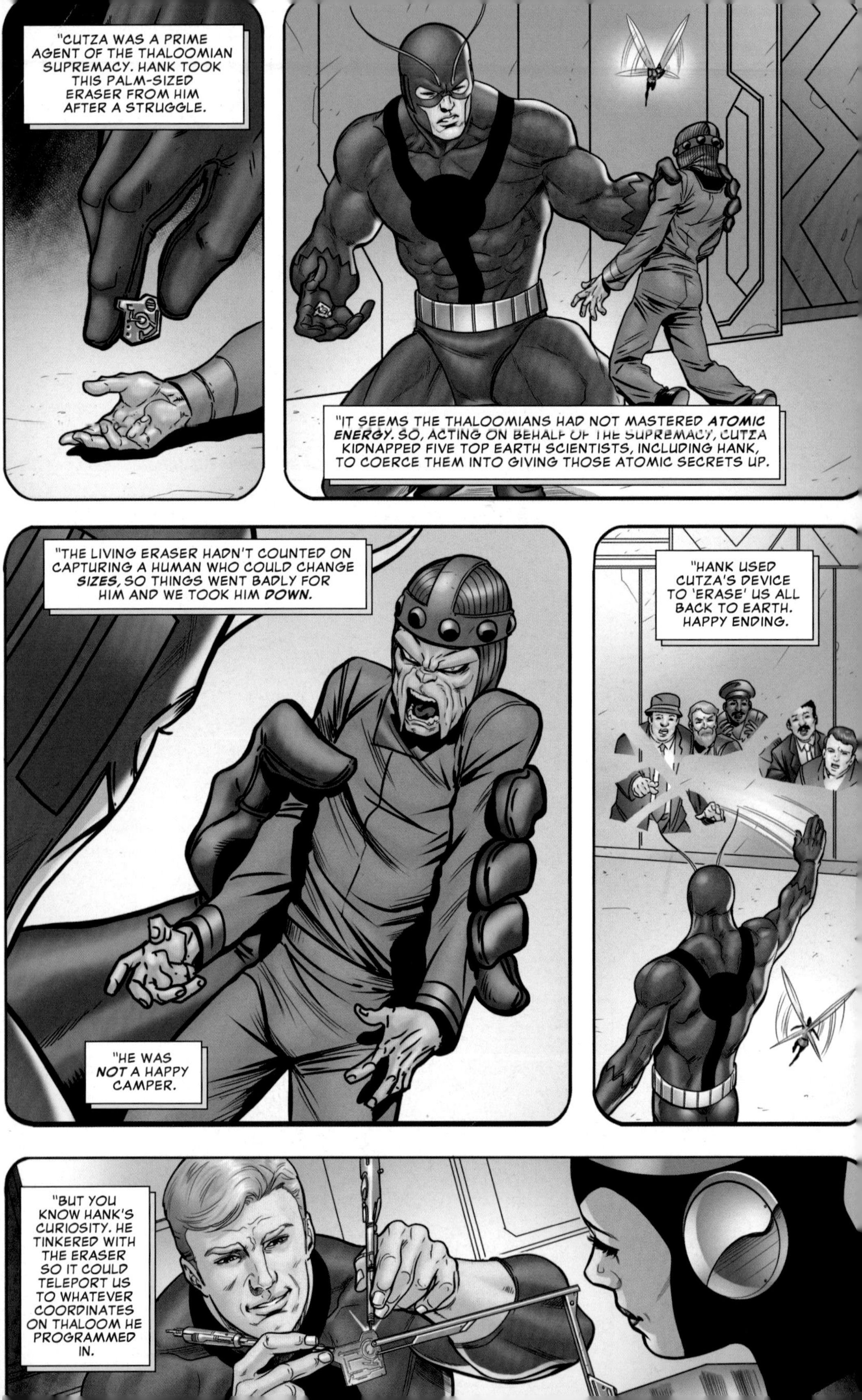
"CUTZA WAS A PRIME AGENT OF THE THALOOMIAN SUPREMACY. HANK TOOK THIS PALM-SIZED ERASER FROM HIM AFTER A STRUGGLE.
"IT SEEMS THE THALOOMIANS HAD NOT MASTERED *ATOMIC ENERGY.* SO, ACTING ON BEHALF OF THE SUPREMACY, CUTZA KIDNAPPED FIVE TOP EARTH SCIENTISTS, INCLUDING HANK, TO COERCE THEM INTO GIVING THOSE ATOMIC SECRETS UP.
"THE LIVING ERASER HADN'T COUNTED ON CAPTURING A HUMAN WHO COULD CHANGE *SIZES,* SO THINGS WENT BADLY FOR HIM AND WE TOOK HIM *DOWN.*
"HE WAS *NOT* A HAPPY CAMPER.
"HANK USED CUTZA'S DEVICE TO 'ERASE' US ALL BACK TO EARTH. HAPPY ENDING.
"BUT YOU KNOW HANK'S CURIOSITY. HE TINKERED WITH THE ERASER SO IT COULD TELEPORT US TO WHATEVER COORDINATES ON THALOOM HE PROGRAMMED IN.

"SOON AFTER, WE ERASED OURSELVES INTO THE MIDST OF A HUGE *BATTLE* ON THALOOM."

"APPARENTLY, IN DEFEATING THE LIVING ERASER, WE'D *INSPIRED* A POWERFUL REBELLION AGAINST THE RULING DICTATORS."

"JAZZAR SAID THIS WAS A *CRUCIAL* BATTLE TO STOP THE COMPLETION OF A WEAPON FOR INVADING OTHER DIMENSIONS TO EXPAND THEIR EMPIRE... STARTING WITH OURS!"

"THE ESSENTIAL COMPONENT WAS IN A WAREHOUSE, BUT IT *COULDN'T* BE TAKEN BECAUSE THE REBEL FORCES WERE PINNED DOWN."

"BUT A LITTLE LASER FIRE WASN'T GOING TO STOP ANT-MAN AND THE WASP."

"WE SLIPPED PAST THE SOLDIERS."

ZRPT

ZRPT

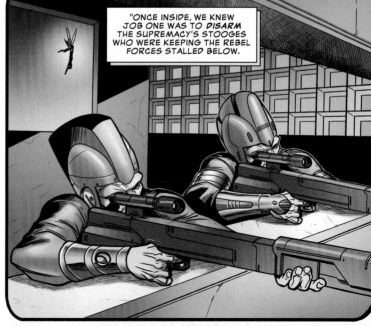

"ONCE INSIDE, WE KNEW JOB ONE WAS TO *DISARM* THE SUPREMACY'S STOOGES WHO WERE KEEPING THE REBEL FORCES STALLED BELOW."

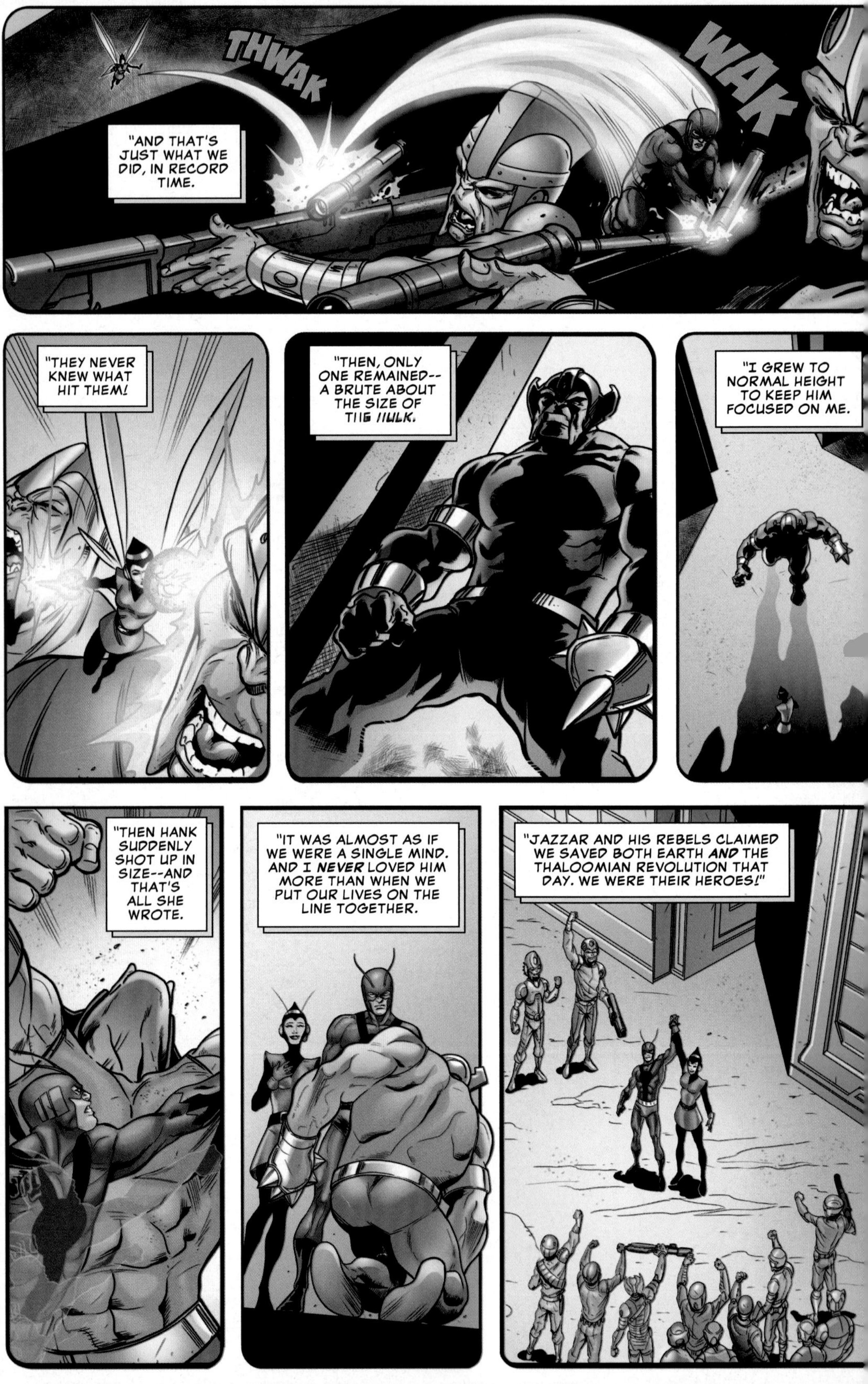
THWAK
WAK
"AND THAT'S JUST WHAT WE DID, IN RECORD TIME.
"THEY NEVER KNEW WHAT HIT THEM!
"THEN, ONLY ONE REMAINED--A BRUTE ABOUT THE SIZE OF THE HULK.
"I GREW TO NORMAL HEIGHT TO KEEP HIM FOCUSED ON ME.
"THEN HANK SUDDENLY SHOT UP IN SIZE--AND THAT'S ALL SHE WROTE.
"IT WAS ALMOST AS IF WE WERE A SINGLE MIND. AND I NEVER LOVED HIM MORE THAN WHEN WE PUT OUR LIVES ON THE LINE TOGETHER.
"JAZZAR AND HIS REBELS CLAIMED WE SAVED BOTH EARTH AND THE THALOOMIAN REVOLUTION THAT DAY. WE WERE THEIR HEROES!"

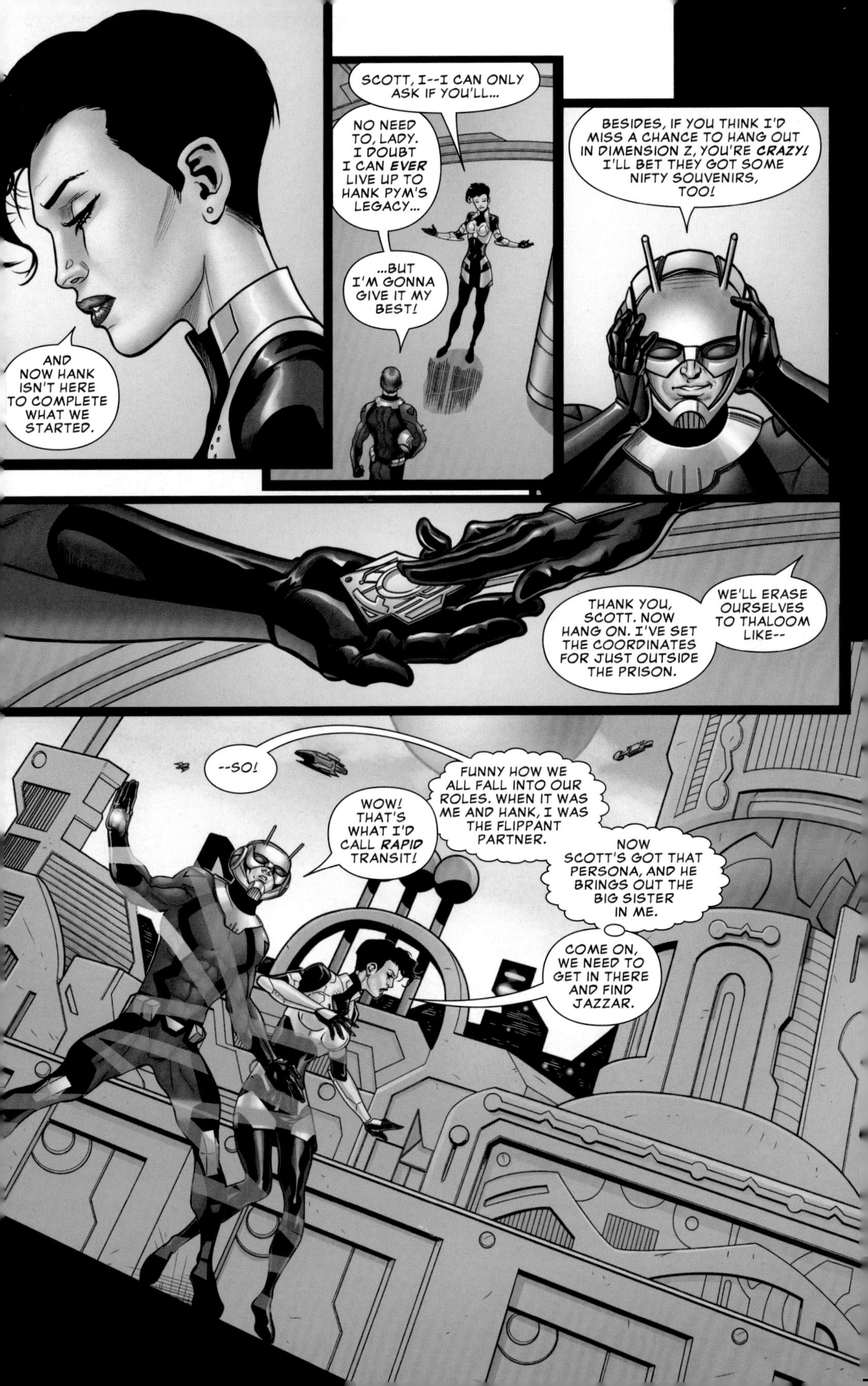
AND NOW HANK ISN'T HERE TO COMPLETE WHAT WE STARTED.
SCOTT, I--I CAN ONLY ASK IF YOU'LL...
NO NEED TO, LADY. I DOUBT I CAN EVER LIVE UP TO HANK PYM'S LEGACY...
...BUT I'M GONNA GIVE IT MY BEST!
BESIDES, IF YOU THINK I'D MISS A CHANCE TO HANG OUT IN DIMENSION Z, YOU'RE CRAZY! I'LL BET THEY GOT SOME NIFTY SOUVENIRS, TOO!
THANK YOU, SCOTT. NOW HANG ON. I'VE SET THE COORDINATES FOR JUST OUTSIDE THE PRISON.
WE'LL ERASE OURSELVES TO THALOOM LIKE--
--SO!
WOW! THAT'S WHAT I'D CALL RAPID TRANSIT!
FUNNY HOW WE ALL FALL INTO OUR ROLES. WHEN IT WAS ME AND HANK, I WAS THE FLIPPANT PARTNER.
NOW SCOTT'S GOT THAT PERSONA, AND HE BRINGS OUT THE BIG SISTER IN ME.
COME ON, WE NEED TO GET IN THERE AND FIND JAZZAR.

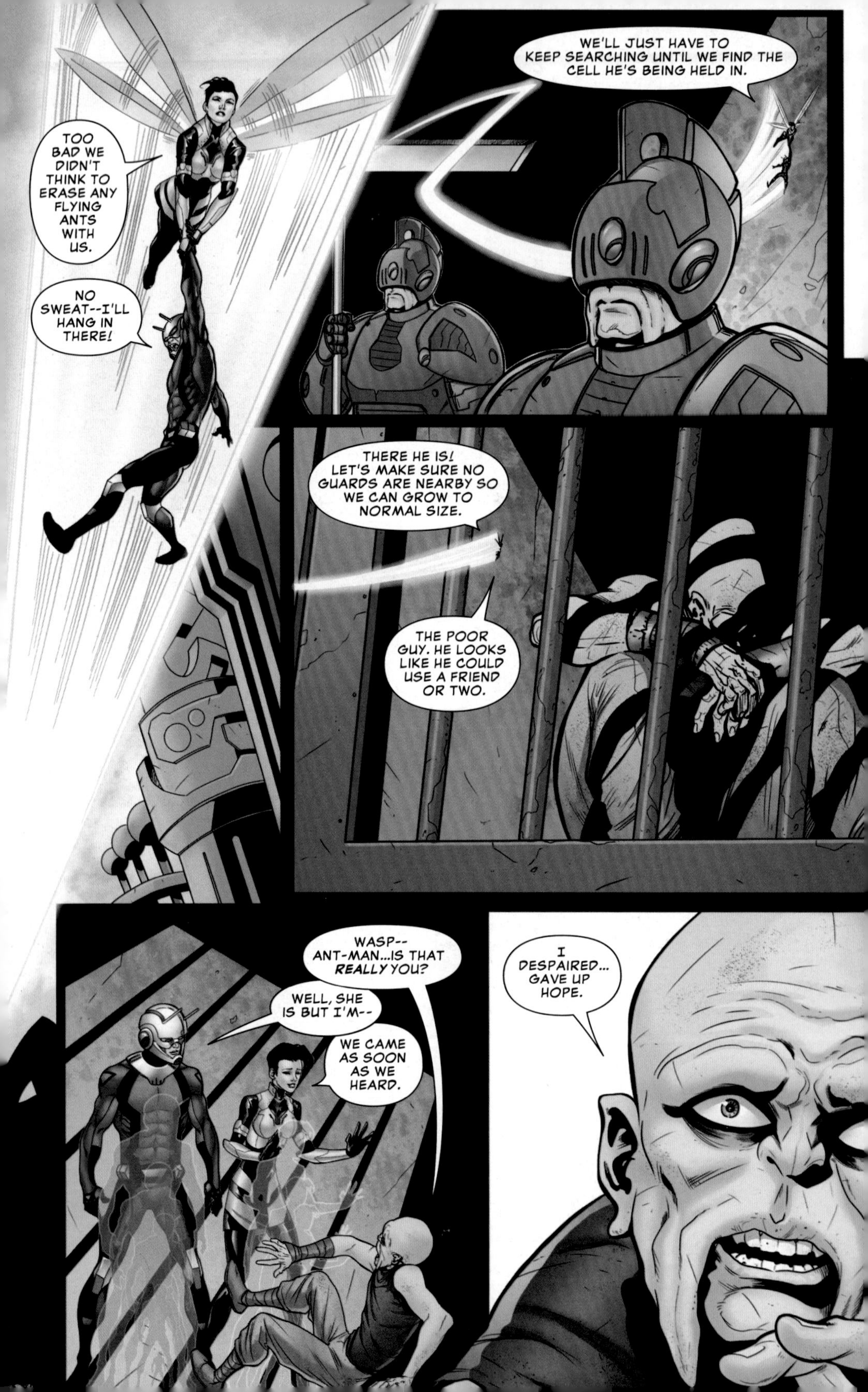
TOO BAD WE DIDN'T THINK TO ERASE ANY FLYING ANTS WITH US.
NO SWEAT--I'LL HANG IN THERE!
WE'LL JUST HAVE TO KEEP SEARCHING UNTIL WE FIND THE CELL HE'S BEING HELD IN.
THERE HE IS! LET'S MAKE SURE NO GUARDS ARE NEARBY SO WE CAN GROW TO NORMAL SIZE.
THE POOR GUY. HE LOOKS LIKE HE COULD USE A FRIEND OR TWO.
WASP-- ANT-MAN...IS THAT REALLY YOU?
WELL, SHE IS BUT I'M--
WE CAME AS SOON AS WE HEARD.
I DESPAIRED... GAVE UP HOPE.

IT'S GOING TO BE ALL RIGHT, JAZZAR. ALZAR EXPLAINED THE SITUATION.

WE GOT THIS COVERED.

AND WE'VE GOT THIS HANDY-DANDY ERASER THINGY TO SAY BYE-BYE TO THE CELL BARS.

"WASP IS GOING TO CUT THE POWER SO NO ONE SEES US SLIPPING OUT IN THE CONFUSION."

"VOILA! INSTANT DARKNESS!"

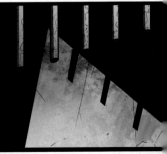

THANK YOU, MY FRIENDS. BUT TIME IS OF THE ESSENCE...

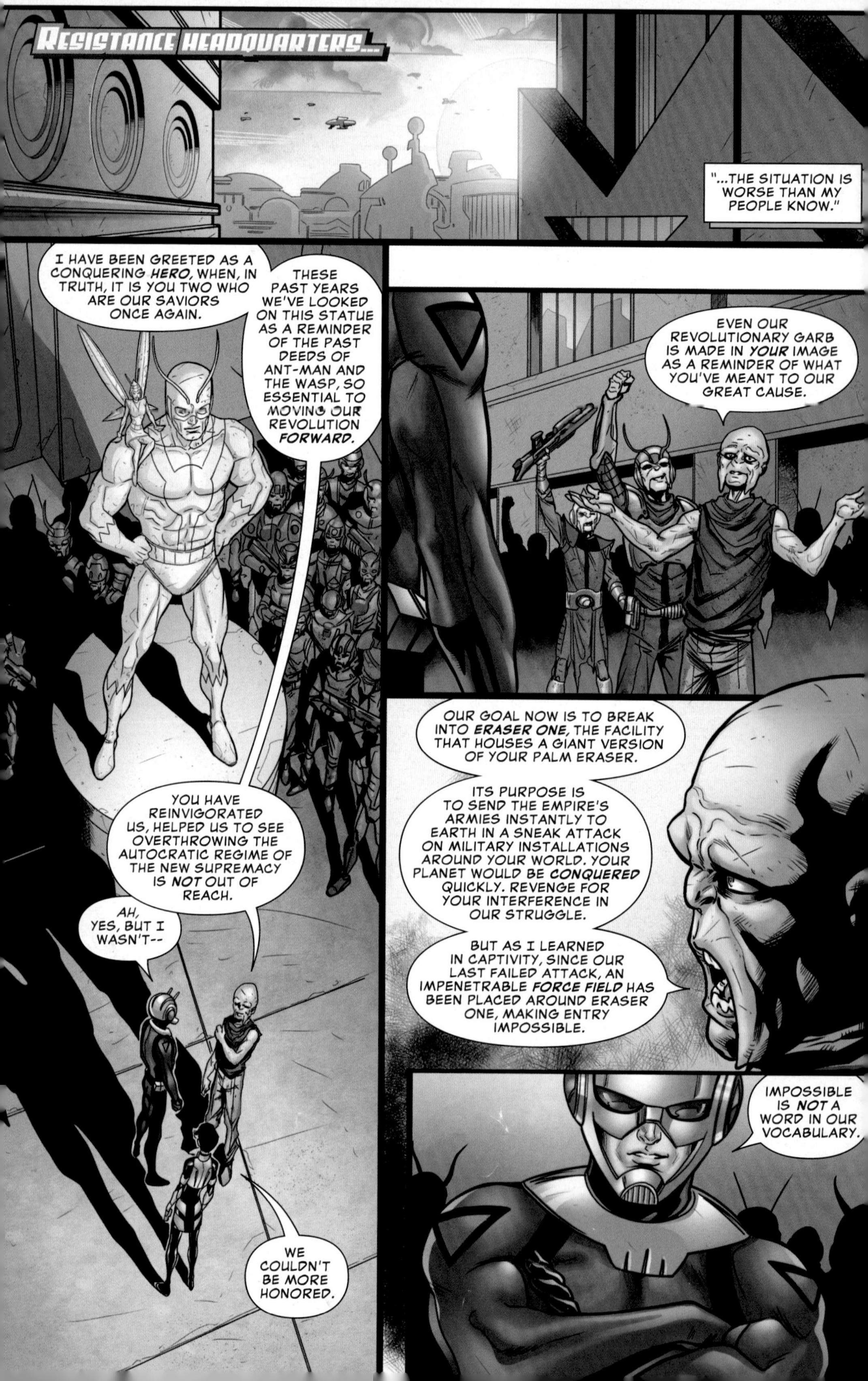
RESISTANCE HEADQUARTERS...
"...THE SITUATION IS WORSE THAN MY PEOPLE KNOW."
I HAVE BEEN GREETED AS A CONQUERING HERO, WHEN, IN TRUTH, IT IS YOU TWO WHO ARE OUR SAVIORS ONCE AGAIN.
THESE PAST YEARS WE'VE LOOKED ON THIS STATUE AS A REMINDER OF THE PAST DEEDS OF ANT-MAN AND THE WASP, SO ESSENTIAL TO MOVING OUR REVOLUTION FORWARD.
YOU HAVE REINVIGORATED US, HELPED US TO SEE OVERTHROWING THE AUTOCRATIC REGIME OF THE NEW SUPREMACY IS NOT OUT OF REACH.
AH, YES, BUT I WASN'T--
WE COULDN'T BE MORE HONORED.
EVEN OUR REVOLUTIONARY GARB IS MADE IN YOUR IMAGE AS A REMINDER OF WHAT YOU'VE MEANT TO OUR GREAT CAUSE.
OUR GOAL NOW IS TO BREAK INTO ERASER ONE, THE FACILITY THAT HOUSES A GIANT VERSION OF YOUR PALM ERASER.
ITS PURPOSE IS TO SEND THE EMPIRE'S ARMIES INSTANTLY TO EARTH IN A SNEAK ATTACK ON MILITARY INSTALLATIONS AROUND YOUR WORLD. YOUR PLANET WOULD BE CONQUERED QUICKLY. REVENGE FOR YOUR INTERFERENCE IN OUR STRUGGLE.
BUT AS I LEARNED IN CAPTIVITY, SINCE OUR LAST FAILED ATTACK, AN IMPENETRABLE FORCE FIELD HAS BEEN PLACED AROUND ERASER ONE, MAKING ENTRY IMPOSSIBLE.
IMPOSSIBLE IS NOT A WORD IN OUR VOCABULARY.

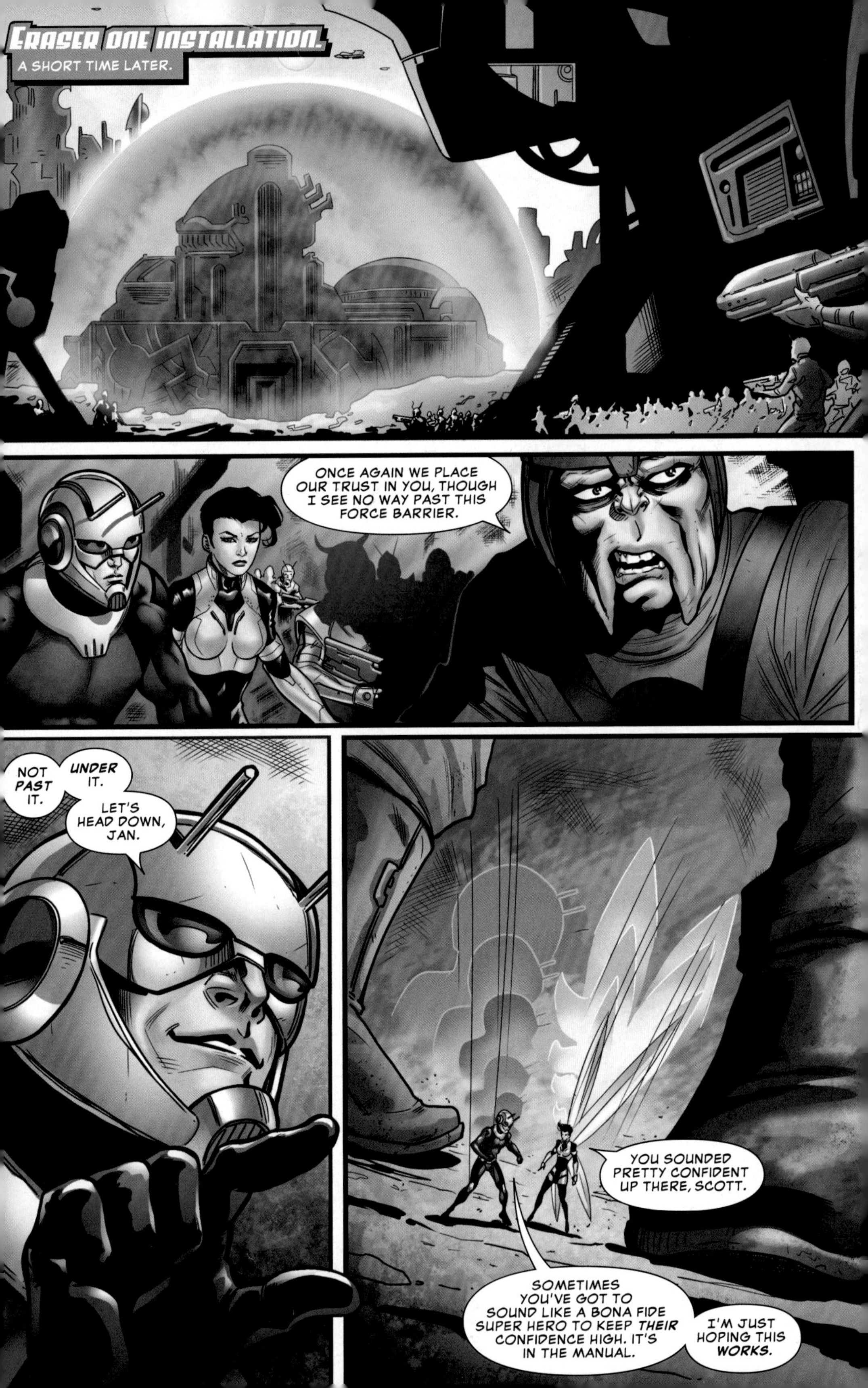
ERASER ONE INSTALLATION.
A SHORT TIME LATER.
ONCE AGAIN WE PLACE OUR TRUST IN YOU, THOUGH I SEE NO WAY PAST THIS FORCE BARRIER.
NOT PAST IT.
UNDER IT.
LET'S HEAD DOWN, JAN.
YOU SOUNDED PRETTY CONFIDENT UP THERE, SCOTT.
SOMETIMES YOU'VE GOT TO SOUND LIKE A BONA FIDE SUPER HERO TO KEEP THEIR CONFIDENCE HIGH. IT'S IN THE MANUAL.
I'M JUST HOPING THIS WORKS.

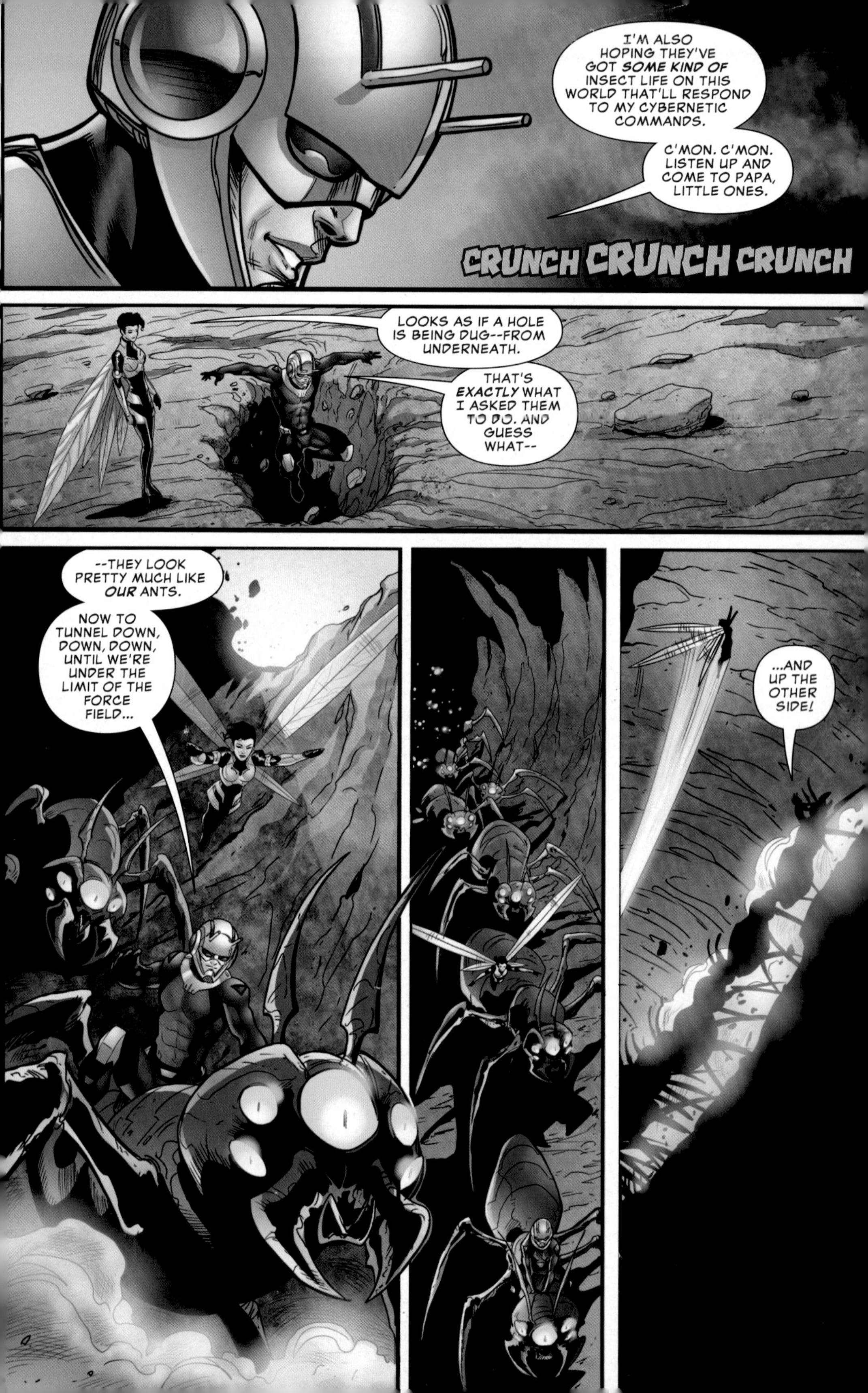
I'M ALSO HOPING THEY'VE GOT SOME KIND OF INSECT LIFE ON THIS WORLD THAT'LL RESPOND TO MY CYBERNETIC COMMANDS.
C'MON. C'MON. LISTEN UP AND COME TO PAPA, LITTLE ONES.
CRUNCH CRUNCH CRUNCH
LOOKS AS IF A HOLE IS BEING DUG--FROM UNDERNEATH.
THAT'S EXACTLY WHAT I ASKED THEM TO DO. AND GUESS WHAT--
--THEY LOOK PRETTY MUCH LIKE OUR ANTS.
NOW TO TUNNEL DOWN, DOWN, DOWN, UNTIL WE'RE UNDER THE LIMIT OF THE FORCE FIELD...
...AND UP THE OTHER SIDE!

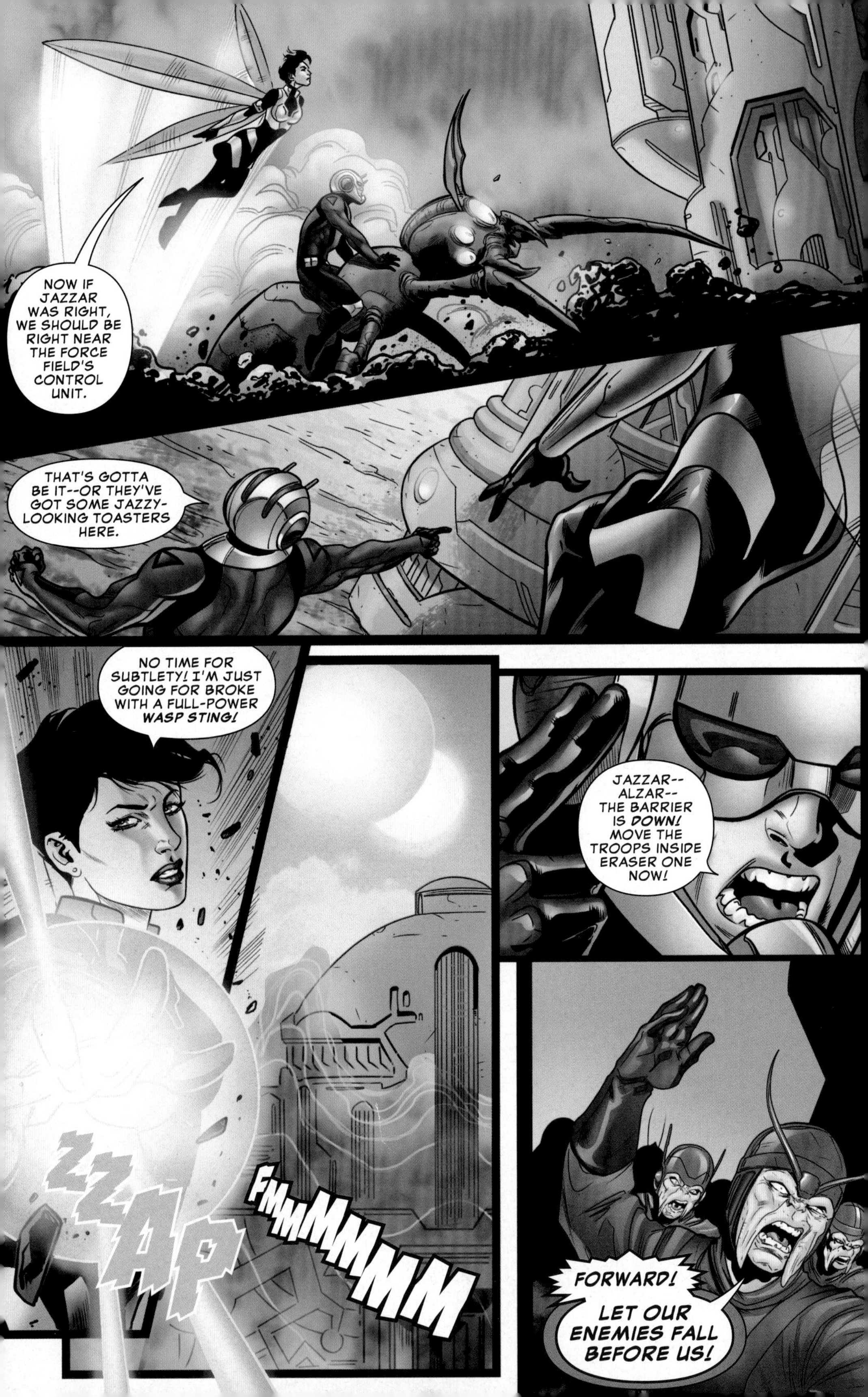
NOW IF JAZZAR WAS RIGHT, WE SHOULD BE RIGHT NEAR THE FORCE FIELD'S CONTROL UNIT.
THAT'S GOTTA BE IT--OR THEY'VE GOT SOME JAZZY-LOOKING TOASTERS HERE.
NO TIME FOR SUBTLETY! I'M JUST GOING FOR BROKE WITH A FULL-POWER WASP STING!
ZZAP
FMMMMMMMM
JAZZAR-- ALZAR-- THE BARRIER IS DOWN! MOVE THE TROOPS INSIDE ERASER ONE NOW!
FORWARD!
LET OUR ENEMIES FALL BEFORE US!

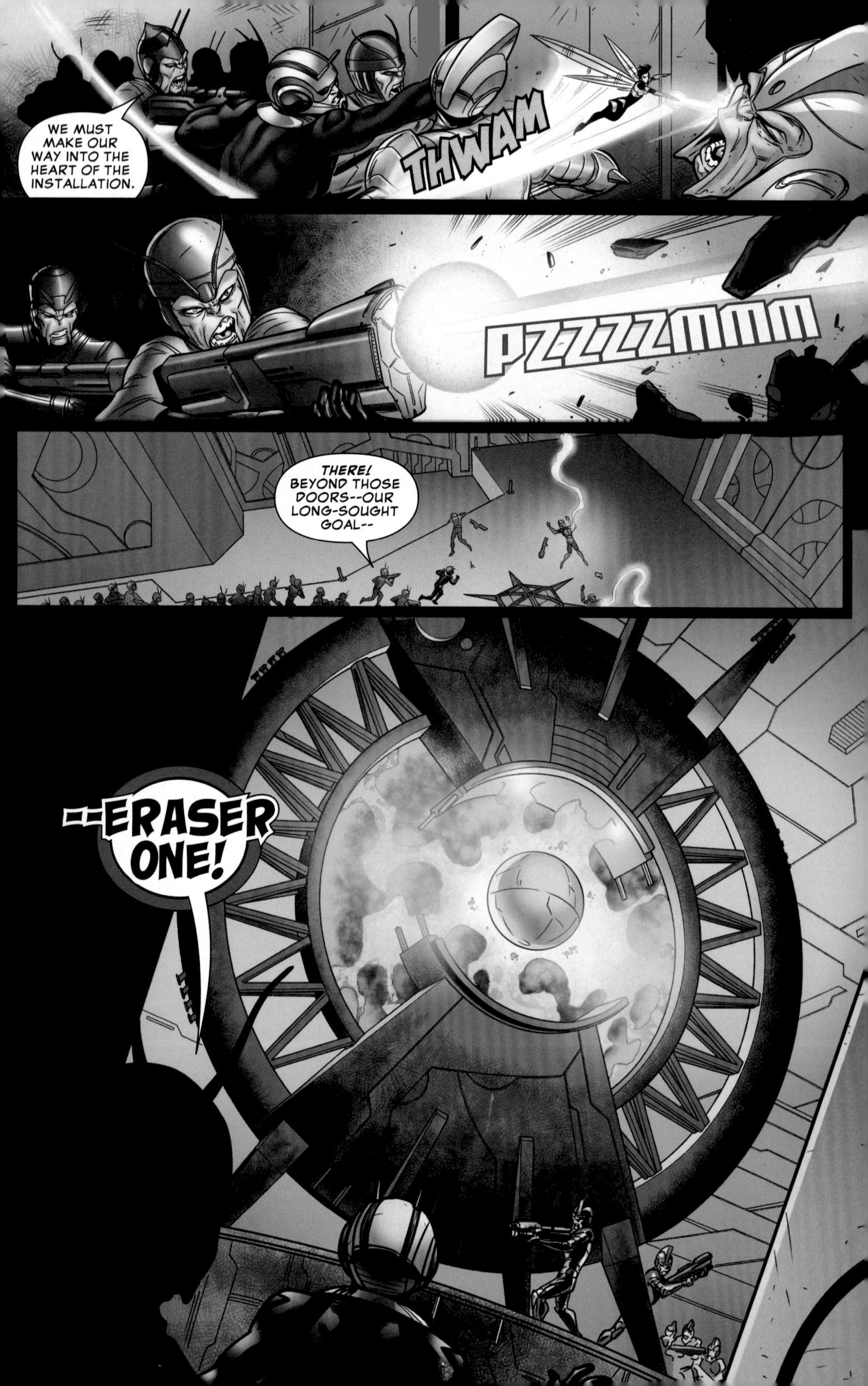
WE MUST MAKE OUR WAY INTO THE HEART OF THE INSTALLATION.
THWAM
PZZZZMMM
THERE! BEYOND THOSE DOORS--OUR LONG-SOUGHT GOAL--
--ERASER ONE!

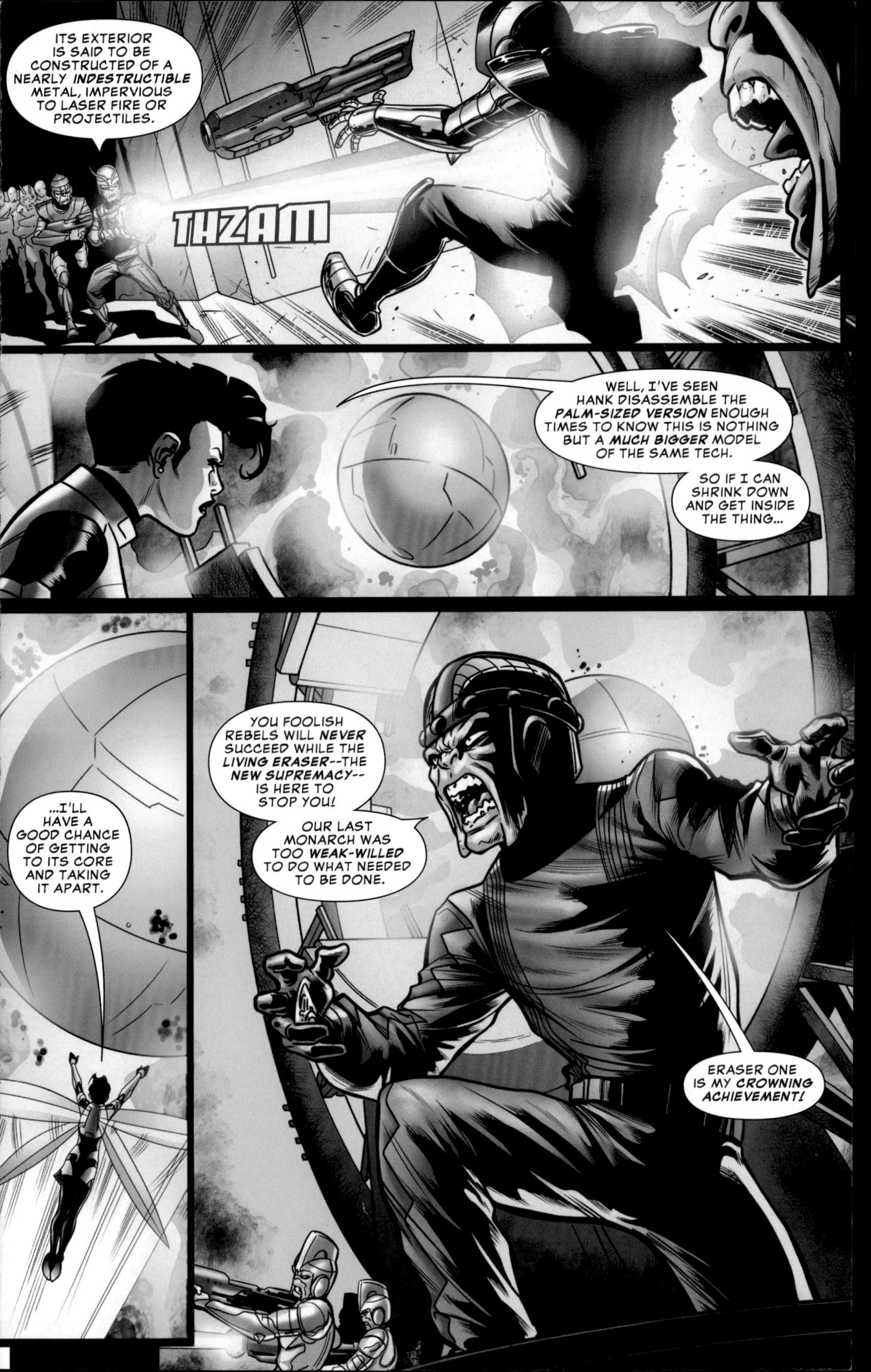
ITS EXTERIOR IS SAID TO BE CONSTRUCTED OF A NEARLY INDESTRUCTIBLE METAL, IMPERVIOUS TO LASER FIRE OR PROJECTILES.
THZAM
WELL, I'VE SEEN HANK DISASSEMBLE THE PALM-SIZED VERSION ENOUGH TIMES TO KNOW THIS IS NOTHING BUT A MUCH BIGGER MODEL OF THE SAME TECH.
SO IF I CAN SHRINK DOWN AND GET INSIDE THE THING...
...I'LL HAVE A GOOD CHANCE OF GETTING TO ITS CORE AND TAKING IT APART.
YOU FOOLISH REBELS WILL NEVER SUCCEED WHILE THE LIVING ERASER--THE NEW SUPREMACY--IS HERE TO STOP YOU!
OUR LAST MONARCH WAS TOO WEAK-WILLED TO DO WHAT NEEDED TO BE DONE.
ERASER ONE IS MY CROWNING ACHIEVEMENT!

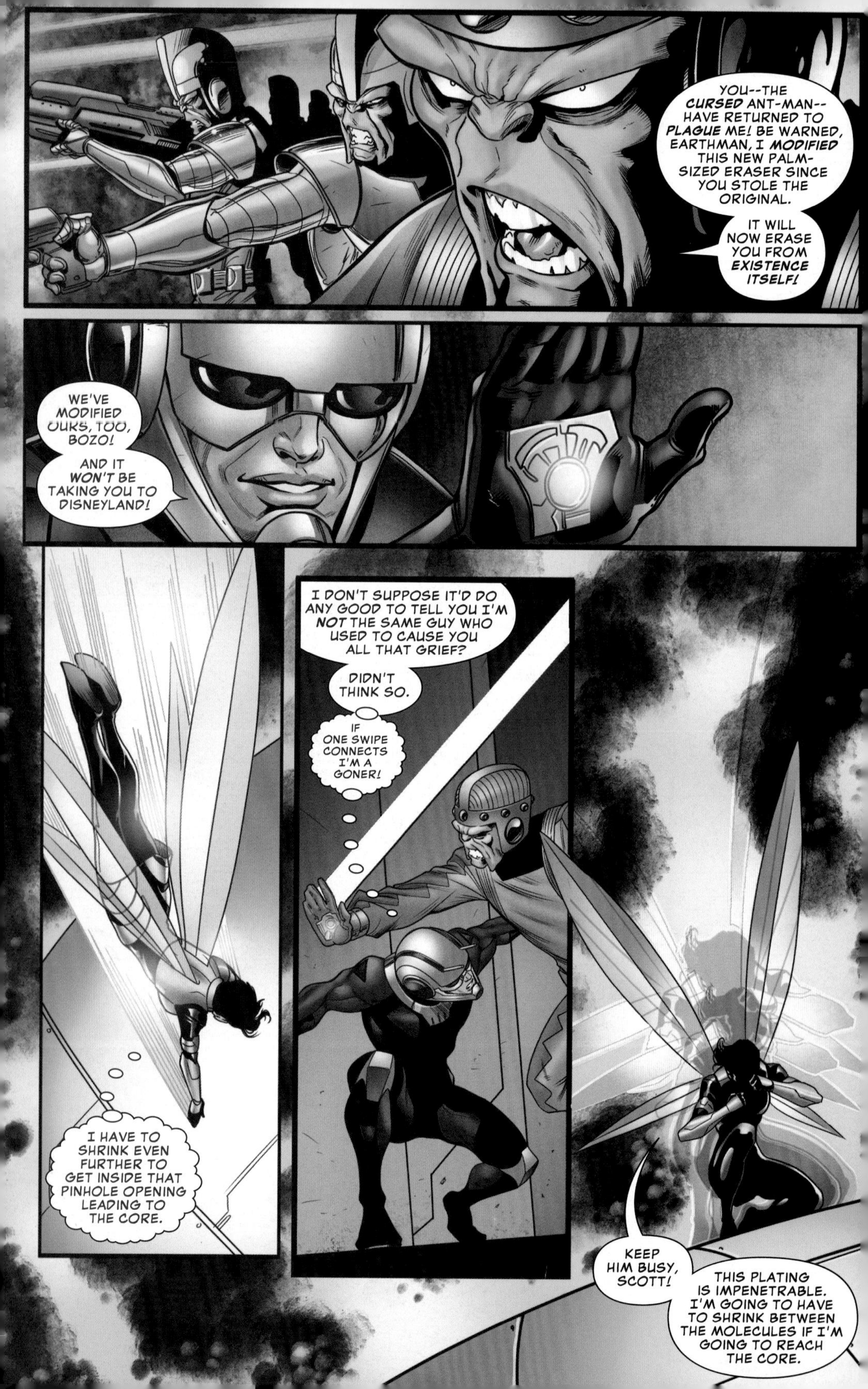
YOU--THE CURSED ANT-MAN--HAVE RETURNED TO PLAGUE ME! BE WARNED, EARTHMAN, I MODIFIED THIS NEW PALM-SIZED ERASER SINCE YOU STOLE THE ORIGINAL.
IT WILL NOW ERASE YOU FROM EXISTENCE ITSELF!
WE'VE MODIFIED OURS, TOO, BOZO!
AND IT WON'T BE TAKING YOU TO DISNEYLAND!
I HAVE TO SHRINK EVEN FURTHER TO GET INSIDE THAT PINHOLE OPENING LEADING TO THE CORE.
I DON'T SUPPOSE IT'D DO ANY GOOD TO TELL YOU I'M NOT THE SAME GUY WHO USED TO CAUSE YOU ALL THAT GRIEF?
DIDN'T THINK SO.
IF ONE SWIPE CONNECTS I'M A GONER!
KEEP HIM BUSY, SCOTT!
THIS PLATING IS IMPENETRABLE. I'M GOING TO HAVE TO SHRINK BETWEEN THE MOLECULES IF I'M GOING TO REACH THE CORE.

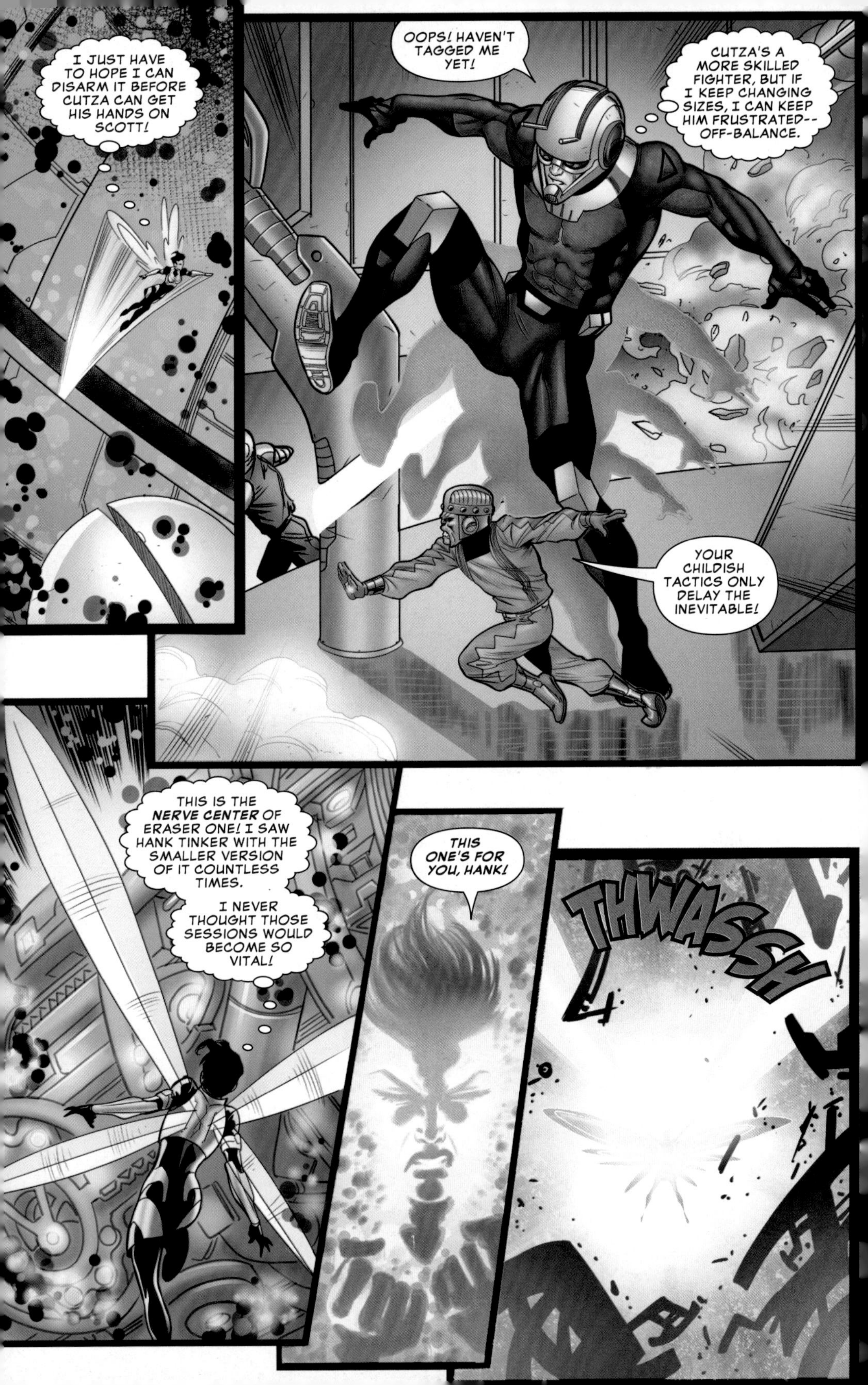
I JUST HAVE TO HOPE I CAN DISARM IT BEFORE CUTZA CAN GET HIS HANDS ON SCOTT!
OOPS! HAVEN'T TAGGED ME YET!
CUTZA'S A MORE SKILLED FIGHTER, BUT IF I KEEP CHANGING SIZES, I CAN KEEP HIM FRUSTRATED--OFF-BALANCE.
YOUR CHILDISH TACTICS ONLY DELAY THE INEVITABLE!
THIS IS THE *NERVE CENTER* OF ERASER ONE! I SAW HANK TINKER WITH THE SMALLER VERSION OF IT COUNTLESS TIMES.
I NEVER THOUGHT THOSE SESSIONS WOULD BECOME SO VITAL!
THIS ONE'S FOR YOU, HANK!
THWASSH

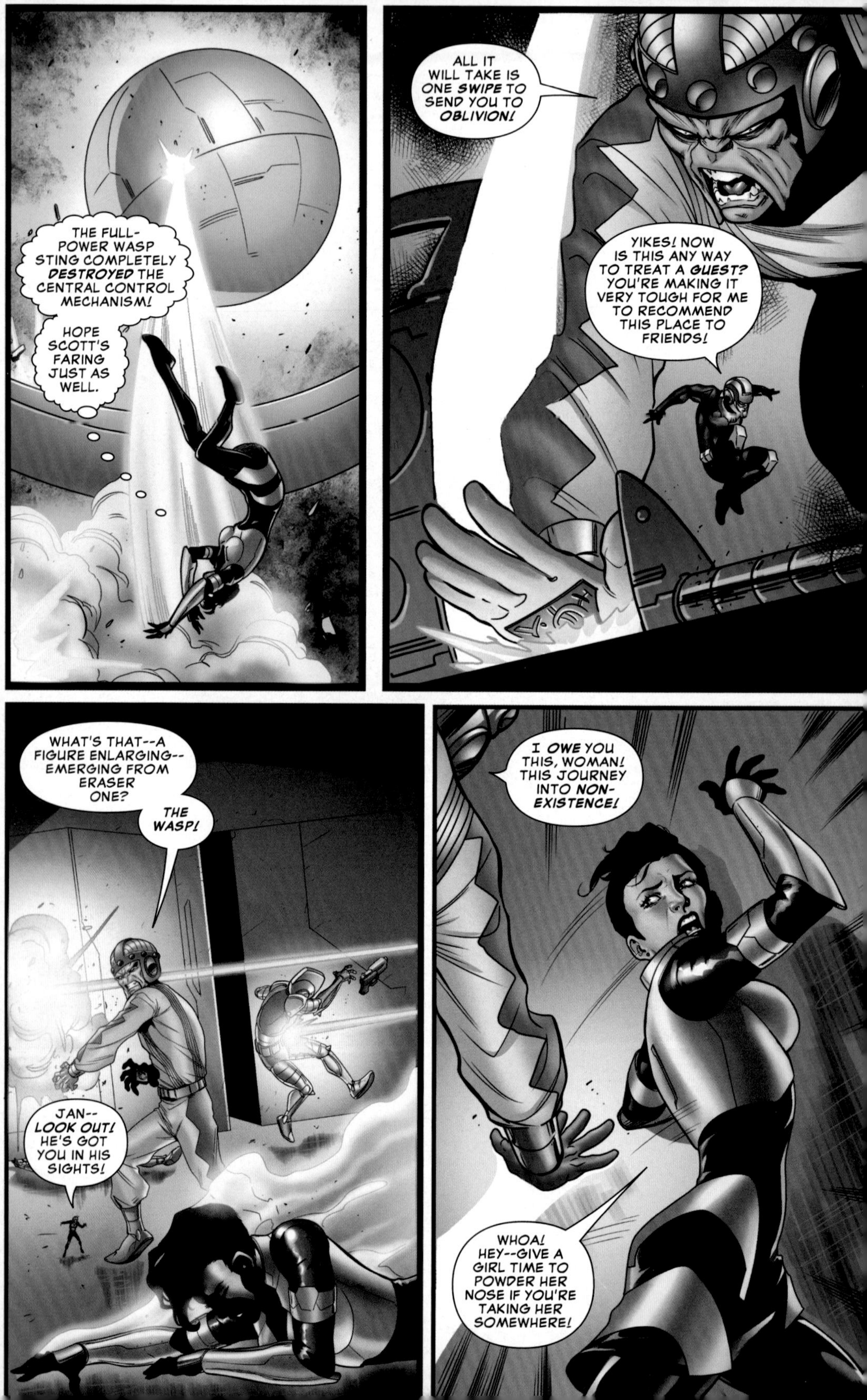
THE FULL-POWER WASP STING COMPLETELY DESTROYED THE CENTRAL CONTROL MECHANISM!
HOPE SCOTT'S FARING JUST AS WELL.
ALL IT WILL TAKE IS ONE SWIPE TO SEND YOU TO OBLIVION!
YIKES! NOW IS THIS ANY WAY TO TREAT A GUEST? YOU'RE MAKING IT VERY TOUGH FOR ME TO RECOMMEND THIS PLACE TO FRIENDS!
WHAT'S THAT--A FIGURE ENLARGING--EMERGING FROM ERASER ONE?
THE WASP!
JAN--LOOK OUT! HE'S GOT YOU IN HIS SIGHTS!
I OWE YOU THIS, WOMAN! THIS JOURNEY INTO NON-EXISTENCE!
WHOA! HEY--GIVE A GIRL TIME TO POWDER HER NOSE IF YOU'RE TAKING HER SOMEWHERE!

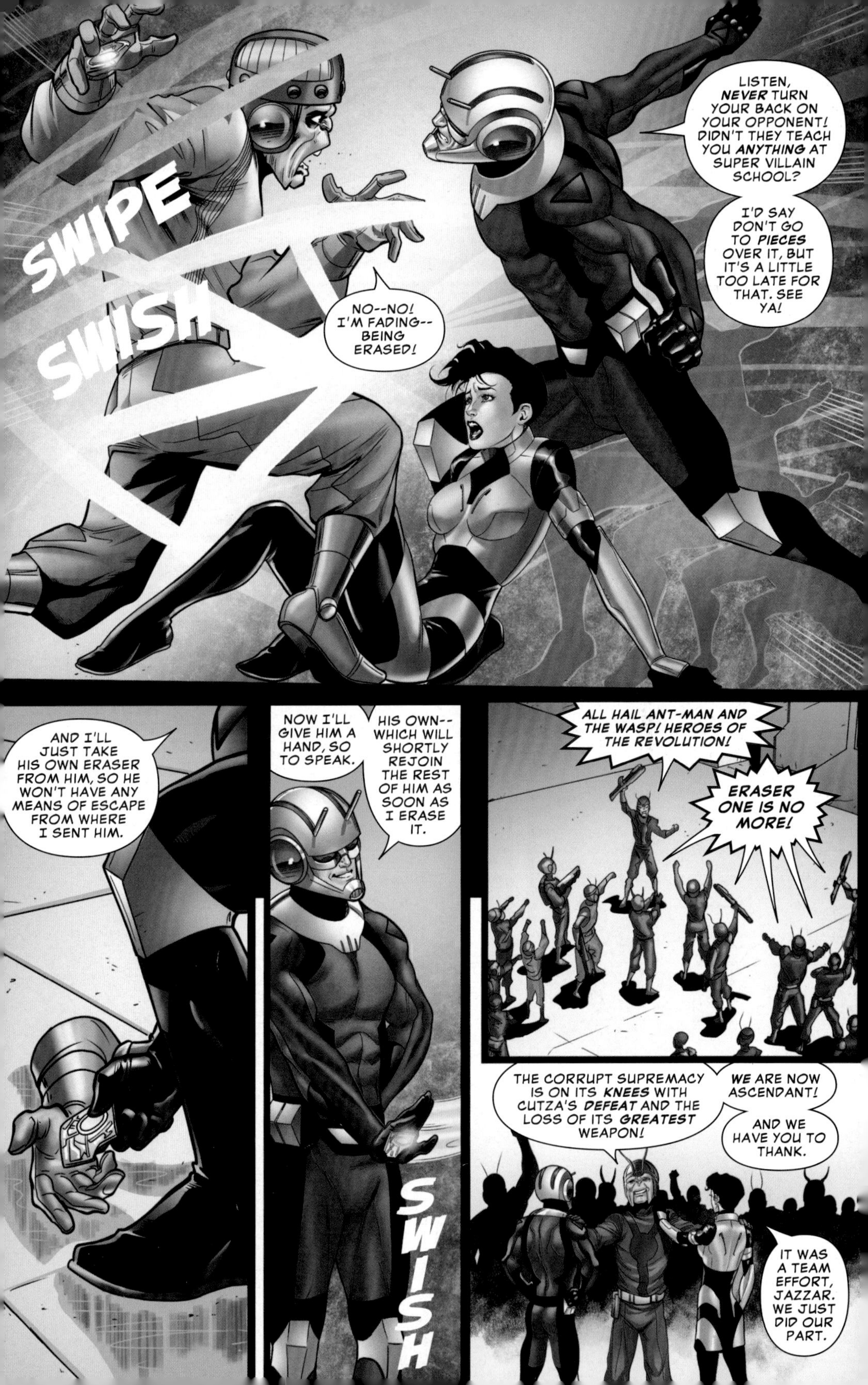
LISTEN, NEVER TURN YOUR BACK ON YOUR OPPONENT! DIDN'T THEY TEACH YOU ANYTHING AT SUPER VILLAIN SCHOOL?
I'D SAY DON'T GO TO PIECES OVER IT, BUT IT'S A LITTLE TOO LATE FOR THAT. SEE YA!
SWIPE
SWISH
NO--NO! I'M FADING--BEING ERASED!
AND I'LL JUST TAKE HIS OWN ERASER FROM HIM, SO HE WON'T HAVE ANY MEANS OF ESCAPE FROM WHERE I SENT HIM.
NOW I'LL GIVE HIM A HAND, SO TO SPEAK.
HIS OWN--WHICH WILL SHORTLY REJOIN THE REST OF HIM AS SOON AS I ERASE IT.
SWISH
ALL HAIL ANT-MAN AND THE WASP! HEROES OF THE REVOLUTION!
ERASER ONE IS NO MORE!
THE CORRUPT SUPREMACY IS ON ITS KNEES WITH CUTZA'S DEFEAT AND THE LOSS OF ITS GREATEST WEAPON!
WE ARE NOW ASCENDANT!
AND WE HAVE YOU TO THANK.
IT WAS A TEAM EFFORT, JAZZAR. WE JUST DID OUR PART.

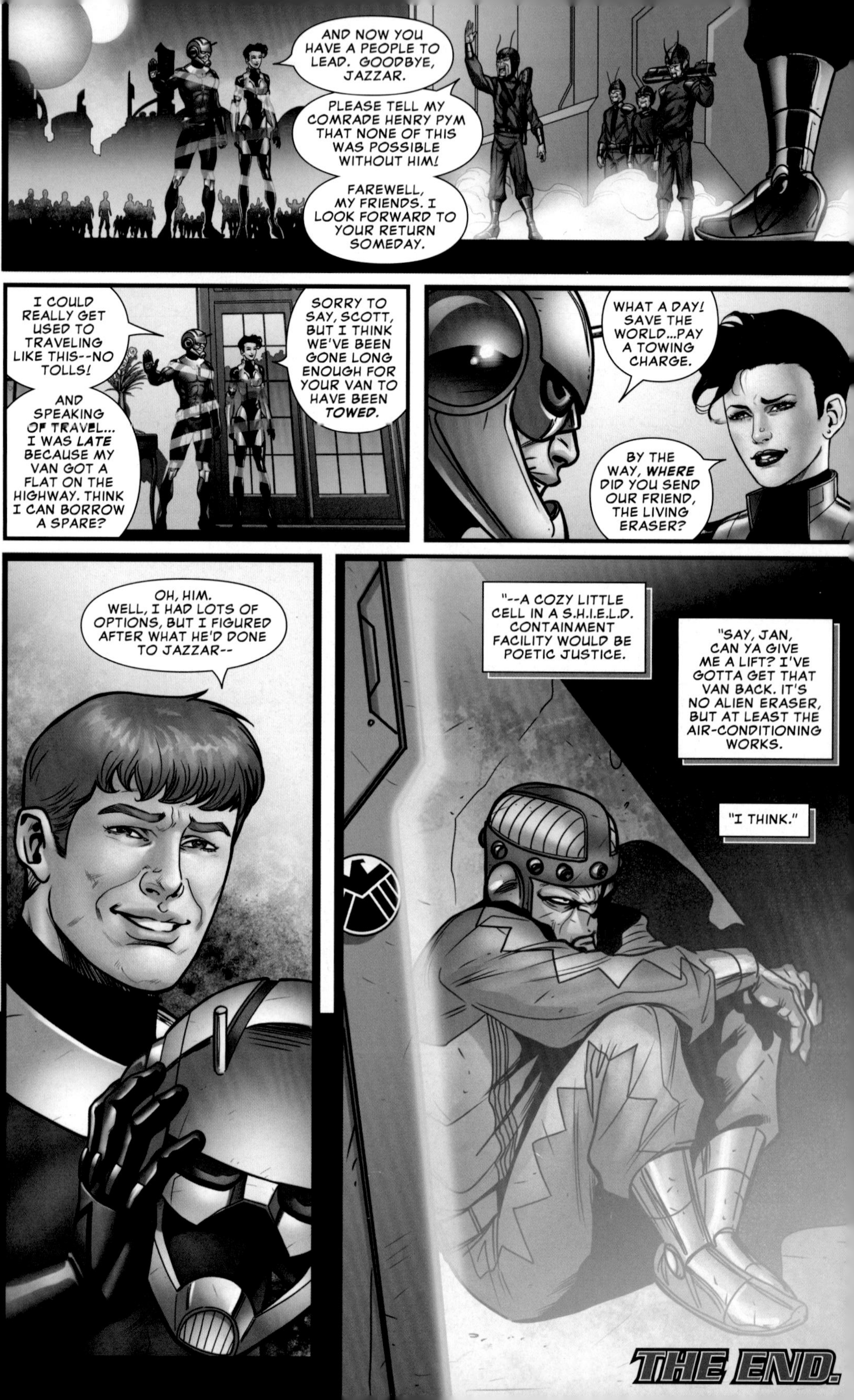
AND NOW YOU HAVE A PEOPLE TO LEAD. GOODBYE, JAZZAR.
PLEASE TELL MY COMRADE HENRY PYM THAT NONE OF THIS WAS POSSIBLE WITHOUT HIM!
FAREWELL, MY FRIENDS. I LOOK FORWARD TO YOUR RETURN SOMEDAY.
I COULD REALLY GET USED TO TRAVELING LIKE THIS--NO TOLLS!
AND SPEAKING OF TRAVEL... I WAS LATE BECAUSE MY VAN GOT A FLAT ON THE HIGHWAY. THINK I CAN BORROW A SPARE?
SORRY TO SAY, SCOTT, BUT I THINK WE'VE BEEN GONE LONG ENOUGH FOR YOUR VAN TO HAVE BEEN TOWED.
WHAT A DAY! SAVE THE WORLD...PAY A TOWING CHARGE.
BY THE WAY, WHERE DID YOU SEND OUR FRIEND, THE LIVING ERASER?
OH, HIM. WELL, I HAD LOTS OF OPTIONS, BUT I FIGURED AFTER WHAT HE'D DONE TO JAZZAR--
"--A COZY LITTLE CELL IN A S.H.I.E.L.D. CONTAINMENT FACILITY WOULD BE POETIC JUSTICE.
"SAY, JAN, CAN YA GIVE ME A LIFT? I'VE GOTTA GET THAT VAN BACK. IT'S NO ALIEN ERASER, BUT AT LEAST THE AIR-CONDITIONING WORKS.
"I THINK."
THE END.

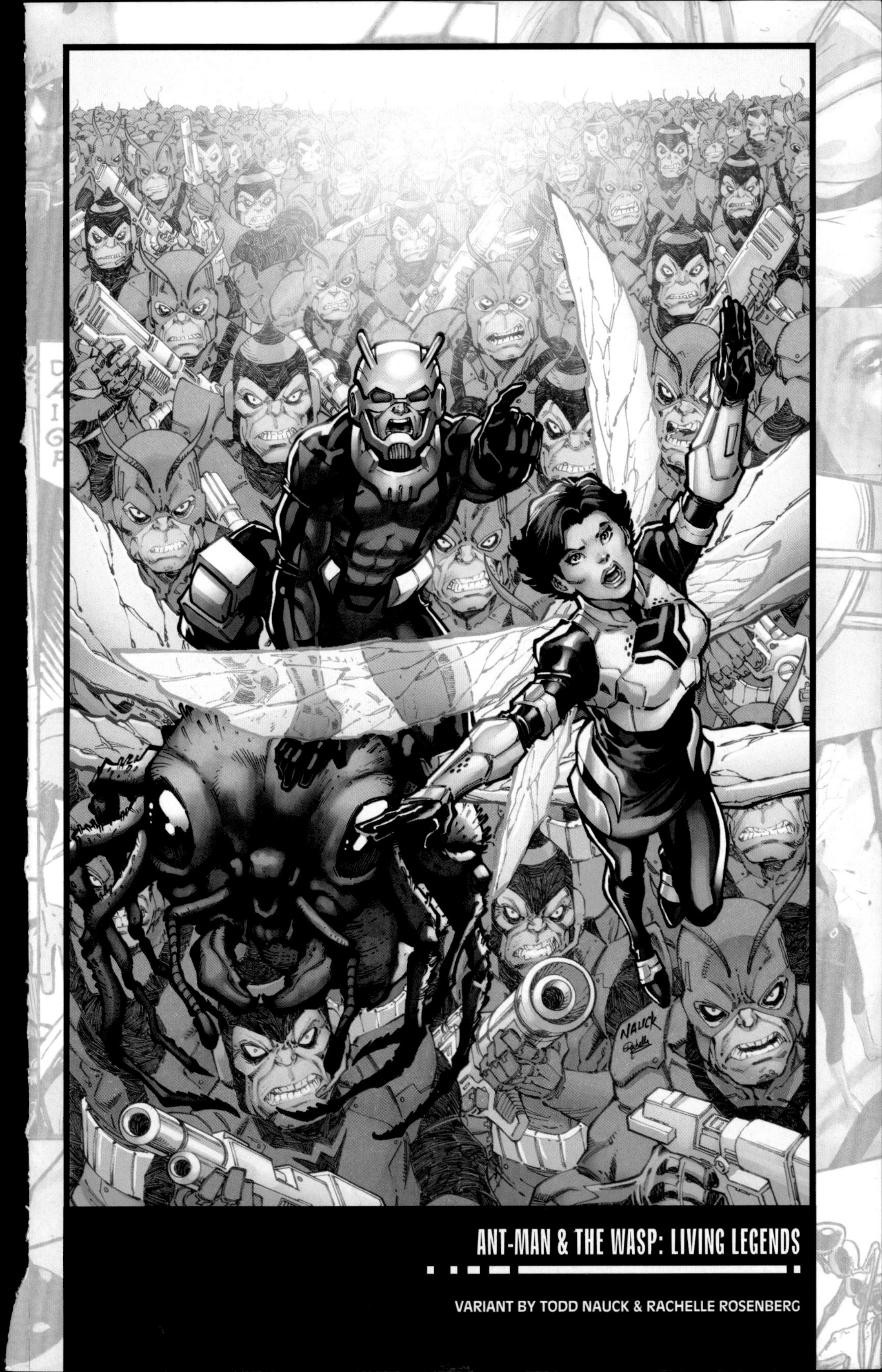
NAUCK

ANT-MAN & THE WASP: LIVING LEGENDS

VARIANT BY TODD NAUCK & RACHELLE ROSENBERG

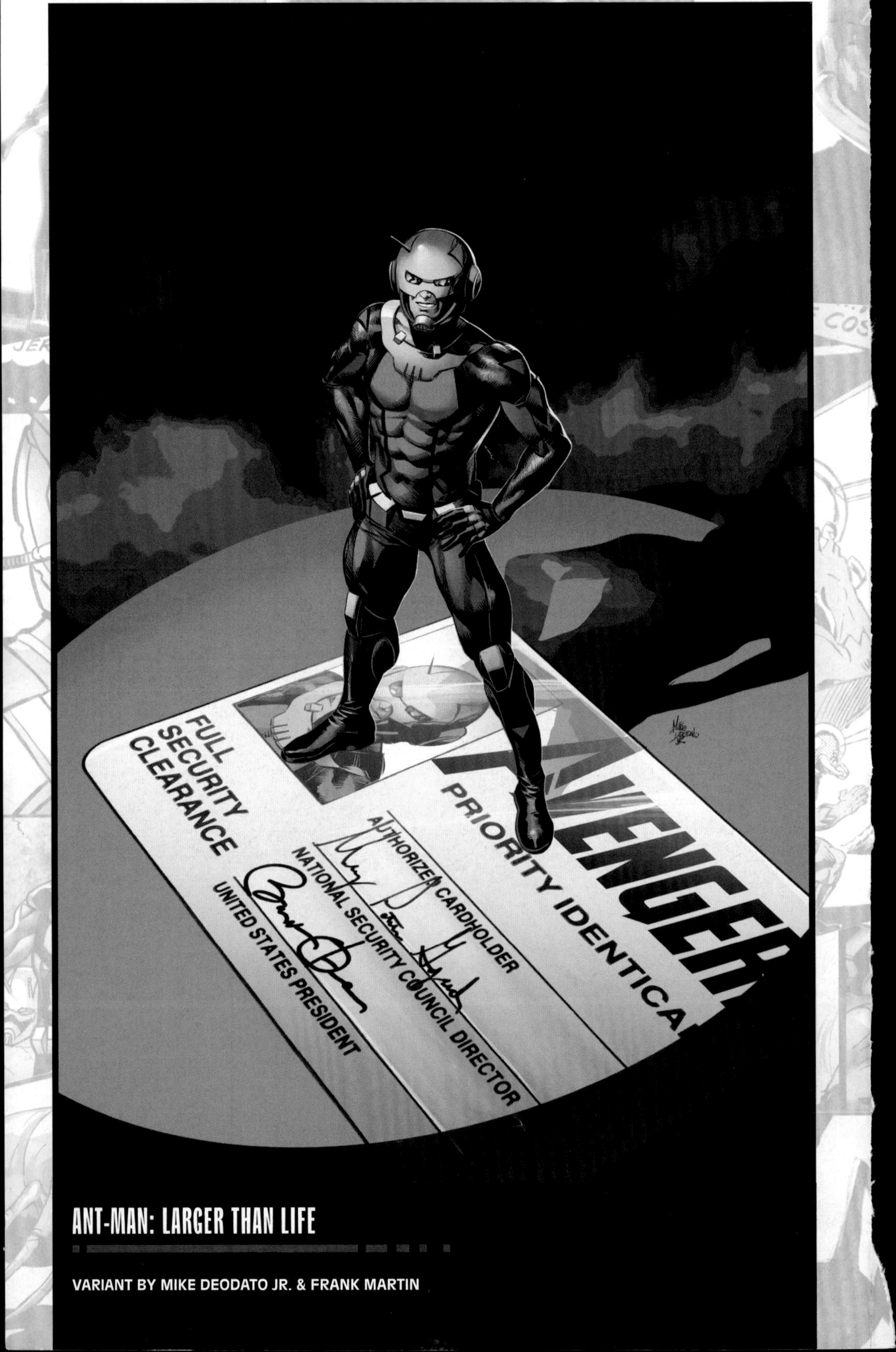
FULL
SECURITY
CLEARANCE
AVENGER
PRIORITY IDENTICA
AUTHORIZED CARDHOLDER
NATIONAL SECURITY COUNCIL DIRECTOR
UNITED STATES PRESIDENT

ANT-MAN: LARGER THAN LIFE

VARIANT BY MIKE DEODATO JR. & FRANK MARTIN

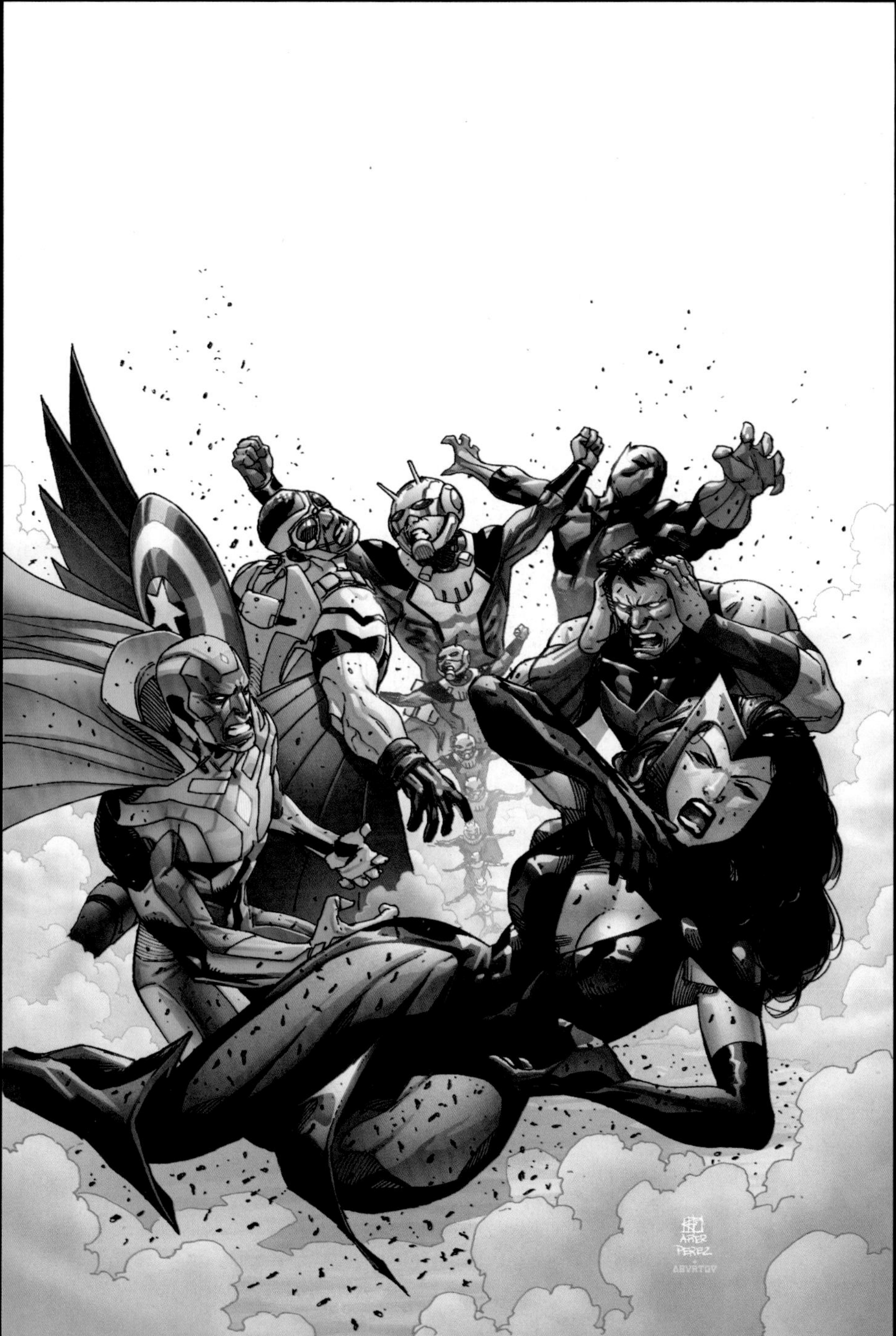

ANT-MAN: LARGER THAN LIFE

VARIANT BY KHOI PHAM & JESUS ABURTOV

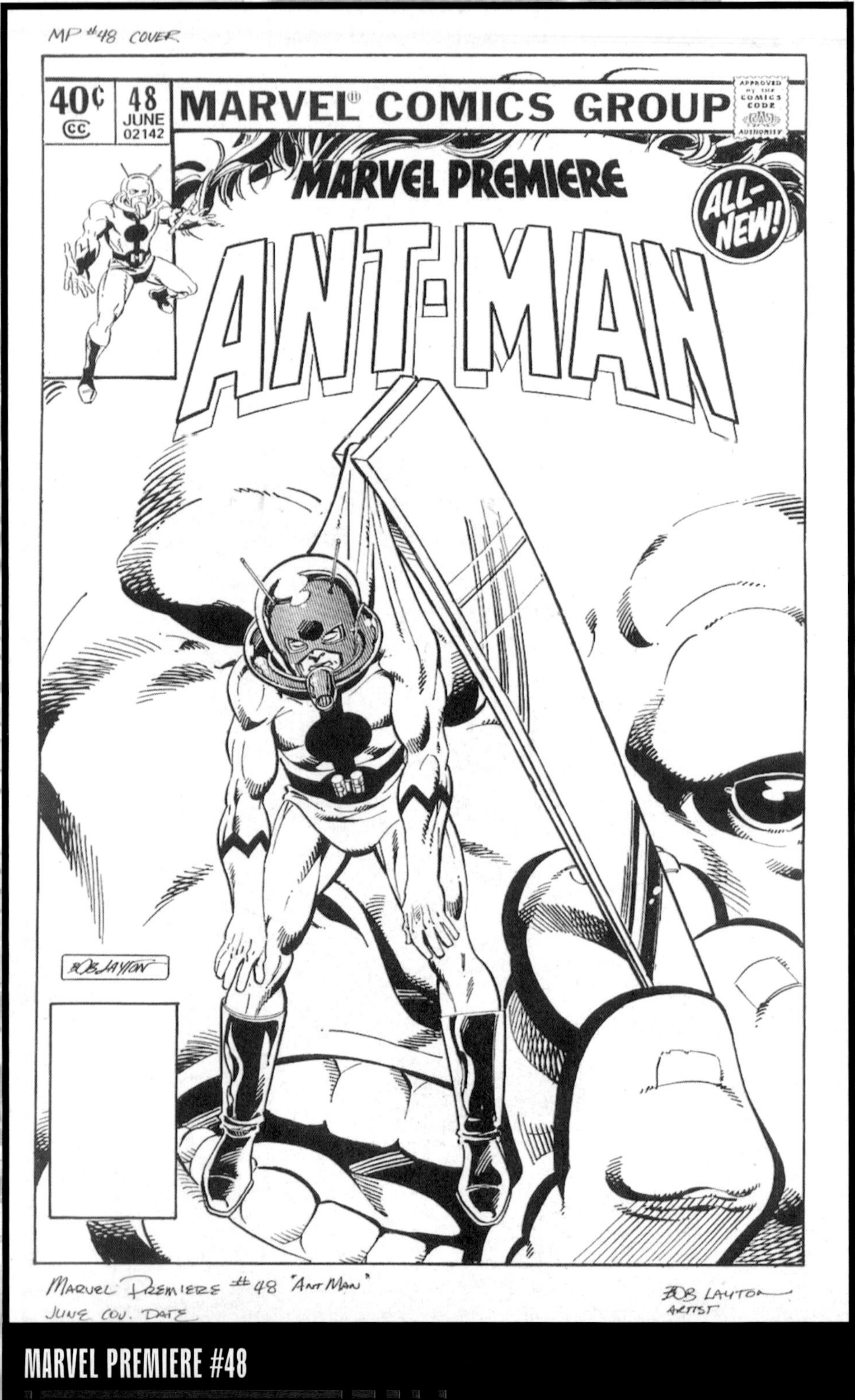
MP #48 COVER
40¢
CC
48
JUNE
02142
MARVEL COMICS GROUP
APPROVED BY THE COMICS CODE AUTHORITY
MARVEL PREMIERE
ALL-NEW!
ANT-MAN
BOB LAYTON
Marvel Premiere #48 "Ant Man"
June Cov. Date
BOB LAYTON
ARTIST

MARVEL PREMIERE #48

UNUSED COVERS BY BOB LAYTON

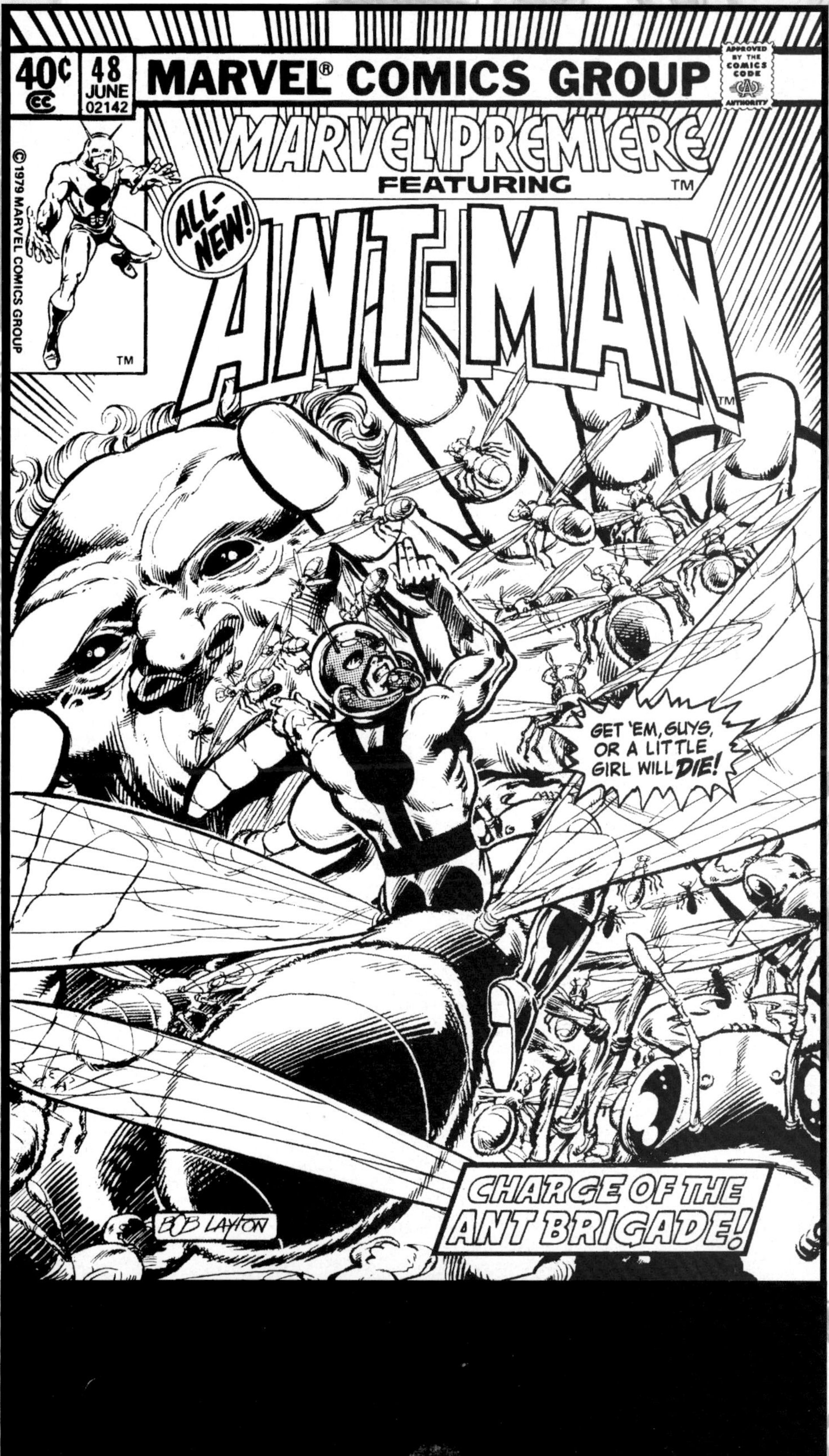
40¢
CC
48
JUNE
02142
MARVEL® COMICS GROUP
APPROVED BY THE COMICS CODE AUTHORITY
MARVEL PREMIERE
FEATURING
ALL-NEW!
ANT-MAN
© 1979 MARVEL COMICS GROUP
GET 'EM, GUYS, OR A LITTLE GIRL WILL DIE!
CHARGE OF THE ANT BRIGADE!
BOB LAYTON

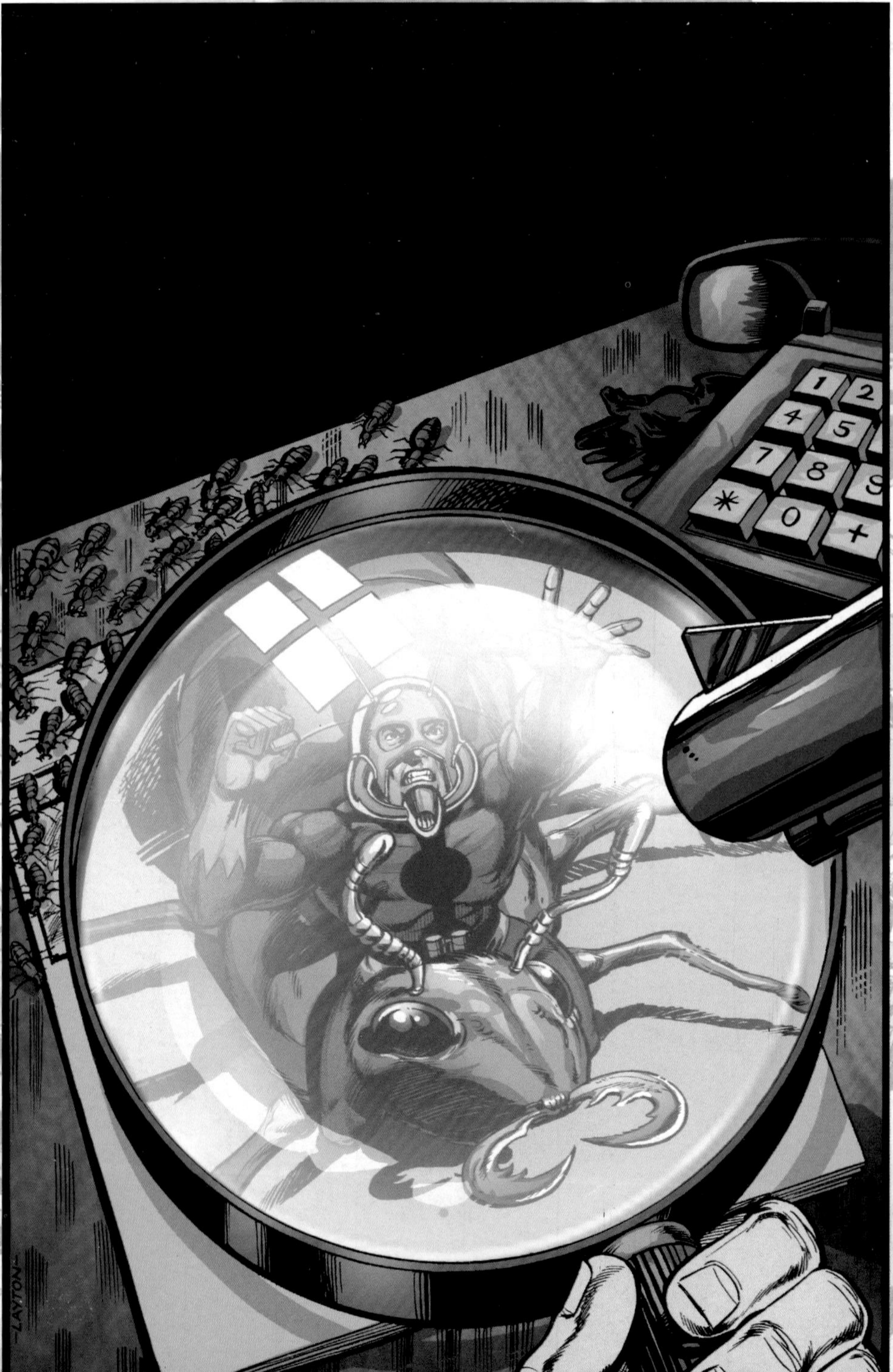

LAYTON

ANT-MAN: SCOTT LANG TPB

COVER BY BOB LAYTON & VERONICA GANDINI